SHADE

SHADE

Charles O'Donnell

Moon Lit. Publishing
Westerville, Ohio
www.moonlitpub.com

SHADE

4-16-2019

Author's website: www.charlesodonnellauthor.com

ISBN: 1-970041-00-5
ISBN-13: 978-1-970041-00-2

*To my mother, who passed away while I was writing this book.
Mom, you filled me full of crazy ideas.*

Also by Charles O'Donnell

The Girlfriend Experience (Matt Bugatti #1)
Moment of Conception (Matt Bugatti #2)
Shredded: A Dystopian Novel (Shredded #1)

Contents

Part Three—Madeleine

Epilogue

PART ONE

DYLAN

1

SCAR CRAWLER

LITTLE KIDS RUNNING in crazy circles, playing a game Dylan didn't know—one boy chasing the others, who froze in place when he touched them. A scattering of chairs. Adults sitting and standing, drinking and chatting. Two tables, one covered in food, another piled with boxes wrapped in bright paper. And by the gift table, a flat, human-shaped void, utterly black, outlined in a narrow rainbow, shimmering as it moved.

"This is so lo-res," Wayne said. He and Dylan had jacked into an outdoor venue. They slouched against a home with a lawn, the kind of property only the well-off could afford. "It's not even your house."

"It's not *supposed* to be *my* house, frobnitz. I don't live in a house. It's supposed to be my *mom's* house."

"*Is* it your mom's house?"

Dylan went to the gift table, Wayne in tow. The tags on the presents all said the same thing: "*Happy Birthday Leeza.*"

"I thought your mom's name is Grace," Wayne said.

"Yeah," Dylan replied. "This isn't her place." He looked at the void, which now appeared to be picking up boxes and shaking them, wrapping paper disappearing under a hand-shaped hole wherever the void held it. "That's not her."

"Then we can go, right?"

Dylan turned away from the table. "Connor, next venue."

The party scene dissolved into a virtual classroom, with desks in rows and columns. Students sat at all but three of the desks; those three were occupied by featureless child-sized silhouettes, the same bottomless black as the birthday girl's, their rainbow outlines noticeably broader.

"They look different," Wayne said. "Why are the edges so fuzzy? The last one we saw was a lot sharper."

"The last one was newer. The older they are, the fuzzier they get. Connor, time and place."

"Time: twenty-two years before present day," a pleasant voice like that of a young man sounded in the boys' headsets. "Place: Public School Venue 1138, age twelve, second quartile."

"Was your mom second quartile?"

"*No,*" Dylan snorted, "first quartile. My mom is *smart.*"

"Hey, asshole, *I'm* second quartile."

The professor took roll, each student in turn raising a hand and responding "Present" when his name was called, until one black image raised a hand, the rainbow blur barely recognizable as an arm. There was no response, only silence.

"Can we get out of here?" Wayne complained. "I found a new lifestream I wanna show you—guys kick-boxing. It's ultra-hi-res."

"Not yet."

"You said it's not even your mom's school!"

"Not yet," Dylan repeated.

The professor continued down the roll. When she called the name *Ellis*, the second void raised its hand without a sound.

"So what *is* this thing? A *scar-crawler* you called it?"

The prof went down the roster. She hadn't yet called on the third void.

"Yeah. It crawls the blockchain for broken links. Then it collects residual data and reconstructs the venue."

"And these black blobs—they're dead people?"

"They're called *scars.* Spots where there was data before, and now there's nothing. They're not dead, they're *shredded.*"

"Oh, yeah. Like your mom. All her data ripped out of the Worldstream. Freaky."

The prof called the final name—*Roxanne*. The last of the three scars raised its hand silently.

"Connor…" Dylan said.

"Hey, tell your guy Conner to take you to Blood Sport Arena Preview. They let you ride five minutes for free. It's awesome."

"Go by yourself. My aunt doesn't let me go to those things."

Dylan's avatar wore sunglasses and a brimless cap over his short-cropped red hair. Dylan liked his hair to be *"low maintenance,"* as he'd told Wayne. *"My life's simpler if I don't have to mess with my hair."* Wayne wasn't sure if Dylan's hair was really that short however—it had been more than two years since they'd met IRL. But it couldn't have been too much longer. The Worldstream didn't permit drastic differences between a user and his avatar.

"You're using my Happy Face, aren't you?"

"Yeah."

"Then Aunt Donna won't know. She'll think you're off on some cultural exchange, or touring some creepy ancient museum."

Dylan took off his sunglasses. His brown eyes made him look older than his sixteen years.

"Hike in the woods," he offered.

"There, see? When she checks your log, she'll see you running around in the forest when you're actually watching some massively hi-res ass-kicking."

"What if *your* Happy Face doesn't work?"

"Jah, bro, if you don't wanna go kick-boxing, just say so. Do whatever you want; I don't give a shit."

"Dylan, do you have a command for me?" Connor's voice asked in Dylan's headphones.

"In a second, Connor." Dylan put his sunglasses back on. "I'll keep at this for a little longer."

"Fine. But there's nothing wrong with Happy Face. I coded it myself."

"Jah, *that* puts my mind at ease."

"Frobnitz. Happy Face is the best protection money can buy."

"I didn't buy it. You gave it to me."

"With a money-back guarantee." Wayne slapped Dylan on the shoulder. "Jacking out, bro. Good luck finding your mom. Batman, Blood Sport."

Wayne's avatar flattened, then broke into horizontal lines, like a raster scan, before winking out. Dylan lingered in the classroom a few more minutes.

These students are grown now, he thought, *in their thirties.*

Some of them might even be dead. Exactly three of them had shredded their lives.

"Connor, next venue."

Dylan skipped from one venue to the next—an office, where coders built elaborate virtual worlds; a concert of old-fashioned music—*Classical* Dylan thought, but he wasn't sure if that was the right term, perhaps *Baroque* was more like it. On to men playing baseball, a game Dylan had played in VR venues as a boy, though he didn't enjoy it much and hadn't seen a game since. In each venue, he saw at least one human-shaped black hole with a rainbow border, some sharp, just a fringe of color, the outlines of very recently shredded people; others so broad and indistinct as to look like little more than a smear of color, the shredded remains of someone who checked out decades ago. *None* of them were Grace.

"Connor, next venue."

The image in Dylan's visor came into focus. It wasn't a baseball game, classroom, birthday party, or any other recognizable human activity. He wasn't sure if he was inside or outside—the sky overhead was purple, changing to blood red as it approached the horizon. Except, he couldn't *see* the horizon—his view was blocked by hundreds of ink-black phantoms, fringed in rainbows, from broad and blurred to razor-sharp.

The crowd moved aimlessly, brushing past one another, sometimes touching, their prismatic outlines merging, two or more human forms melting into one another, forming grotesque shapes with two heads or four arms. The scene was not merely silent, but completely devoid of sound, like a super-anechoic chamber sucking up every last decibel. Dylan felt as if the chamber could absorb his breath, drawing the life out of him. A scene came to mind, a passage from an ancient poem he'd once read, of Odysseus in the realm of the dead:

The souls of the perished came up out of Erebos: young men and long-suffering elders; brides and maidens, and fighting men killed in battle at the points of bronze spears, their bloody armor still upon them. They came swarming from all directions, and terror took hold of me. Then there came to me the soul of my dead mother, still alive when I left for sacred Ilium. I broke into tears at the sight of her and my heart pitied her, but for all my sorrow, I would not let her draw near.

The phantoms moved closer. Dylan tried to get out of their way, but he was surrounded. His chest tightened as they closed in; his breath came faster, until he went light-headed and his vision clouded. He pulled his arms close, crossing them over his chest. A shadow reached out, the hand of a shredded soul, taking hold of him. His arm vanished where the phantom held him, a black band around his wrist, edged in shimmering color. It felt painfully cold.

"Connor, suspend the venue!"

Dylan's wrist reappeared, the shades of the shredded melting together into blackness, the purple-red dome brightening to the featureless white of his staging venue.

Dylan yanked off his headgear and gloves. He fell forward, elbows on knees, panting hard.

Then he groaned.

"Dylan, are you all right in there?" his aunt Donna asked through the door.

Dylan held his wrist where the scar had gripped him. His arm was shaking.

"Dylan?"

"I'm okay, Aunt Donna. I'm fine. Can I have some water?"

"Of course. I'll get it. I'm sure hiking all day in the forest can make you thirsty."

Donna brought Dylan a water bottle and he drained it in

seconds. He closed his eyes until his pulse slowed and his hands stopped trembling. He took a deep breath as he slipped on his gear.

"Connor."

"Yes, Dylan?"

"Scar crawler—next venue."

2

FUNCTION—RENDER

DYLAN FLOATED AMONG a tangle of shining satin threads, dense mats of hair-thin tendrils sprouting like frayed fibers from coarse strings—which were in turn connected to thick silk ropes, each attached to a sphere—one in an endless chain strung like monstrous beads on a massive cable, like that on a suspension bridge. He hovered at the head of the cable, where a new sphere materialized every few minutes, beginning as a tiny ball, its surface dotted with luminous spots. It expanded until it reached full size and attached itself to the end of the chain. Smaller cords floated out of the blackness toward the newly strung sphere, attaching themselves to its glowing spots and leaving a thin ring of light at the base. He might have been inside a living cell, magnified a million times, watching the synthesis of a protein or the replication of the cell's DNA. And in a way, it *was* DNA: it was the blockchain—the genetic code of the Worldstream.

Dylan's scar-crawler, rendered as an insect the size of a freight car, walked the blockchain, poking at it with its antennae and testing the connections of branching chains, looking for the mismatches that would indicate a loss of data. After a year of experiments, trial and error, and close calls with the Worldstream's compliance engine, Dylan had learned to distinguish different types of data losses: a system failure without backup, a hack resulting in data theft, the rare checksum error of a corrupted object, and the *real* target of

9

his interest—data destroyed by the shredding of a life. In this 3D representation of the blockchain and its near-infinite network of connections, Dylan had programmed his crawler to find scars from shredded lives and highlight them in blue.

The tangle of filaments, branches, and connections glowed with innumerable blue points, like lights on an unimaginably dense Christmas tree. An earlier version of Dylan's crawler walked the blockchain at random, hoping to stumble onto Grace's now-eradicated lifestream. Later versions rendered the Worldstream data structure as a network of nodes and connections, with broken links visually enhanced. With further refinement, Dylan could distinguish among various kinds of breaks, highlighting them selectively. Today he was testing new features: functions to light up links from his own life, and those of his Aunt Donna and grandmother Joan. He hoped to spot clusters of related links, clumps of data which might hide Grace's scars.

Dylan rendered the venues surrounding a few of the scars as a test to verify the changes he'd made to this revision had not broken his safeguards against the compliance engine. So far, no problems, and he'd been at it for nearly an hour, while Aunt Donna in an adjacent room was secure in the knowledge that Dylan was skiing in the Andes.

"Connor: function—display nodes; arguments: subject—Dylan, color—red."

A new set of twinkling lights appeared in red, the data nodes associated with Dylan's Worldstream history. Although the blue shredding scars vastly outnumbered Dylan's presence, he was still astonished by the number of red lights —a life, even a young life like his, leaves a large footprint.

"Connor: function—proximity."

"Default arguments, Dylan?"

Dylan looked over the landscape of links and lights. The clumps of blue lights surrounding red were numerous and dense.

"No, Connor. Arguments: space—Lebesgue, p-norm—six, distance—twelve."

"Complete. Return 2.937 exponent eight."

The intensity of blue light dimmed slightly, yet the complex was still choked with scars, nearly 300 million of them in the vicinity of his own life data points.

"Connor: function—proximity; distance—three."

"Complete. Return 4.884 exponent six."

Millions of blue points winked out, leaving a scattering of blue clusters near the head end of the blockchain extending back in time no further than the day of Dylan's birth. "A little under five million," Dylan muttered. "Connor, distance—one."

"Complete. Return 9.320 exponent three."

All but twelve clusters vanished, and those that remained were tightly grouped on the blockchain.

"Conner: function—timestamp; argument: time—present minus 740 days."

"Complete. Return true."

One of the giant spheres in the chain pulsed blue and white. All twelve remaining blue clusters were attached to the chain before that moment—the day of Grace's shredding.

With a gesture, Dylan zoomed in on one cluster, a red node hanging near the end of a filament, surrounded by a half-dozen blue points. He reached out and grasped it, as if he were plucking a grape from a vine.

"Connor: function—render."

The blockchain and its data links pixelated to a uniform gray. Another scene resolved, sharpening to clarity: a medium-sized room, walls lined with screens, and at the center an ornate table between two seated figures—Dylan, age ten, and a black outline in the shape of a woman trimmed in color.

"Do you recognize this place?" Connor asked.

"Yes," Dylan answered. "I think I do. This is the day the authorities forced me to live with Aunt Donna."

The boy at the table kept his head down and arms crossed; his eyes were wet and his cheeks flushed. The black scar reached out and touched the boy's hand but if it was speaking, Dylan couldn't hear what it said. Dylan watched for five minutes, when there was a knock at the door. Aunt

Donna entered.

"It's time, Dylan," she said. *"Let's go home."*

"Connor, suspend this venue." Dylan once again hovered among the fractal complex of the blockchain, red and blue points marking the intersections between his life and Grace's.

"Connor: function—nametag; arguments: venue—last viewed, name—Custody."

"Complete. Return true." A bubble appeared, labeled *Custody*, tethered to the red node.

"Connor: function—personas; arguments: venue—Custody."

"Complete. Return false."

"Huh? What's the problem?"

"Unresolved persona. The venue *Custody* includes links to nonexistent data."

"Shit," Dylan muttered. "I wanted to link Mom's data points to mine."

"Dylan, I don't understand," Connor said.

"Nothing, Connor. Forget it. Cancel. I guess I'll have to do this the hard way."

Dylan enlarged the cluster around the *Custody* venue, until he was surrounded by blue points—scars from Grace's shredded life, all untraceable due to their broken links.

"Conner: function—display nodes; arguments: subject— Donna, color—green." A new set of scattered points appeared in green, three of them in the vicinity of *Custody*. Dylan reached for a green dot.

"Connor: function—render."

Dylan was transported to a room like the one he'd just seen, but instead of seeing himself and Grace's scar at the table, there sat his Aunt Donna and his grandmother, Nana Joan.

Dylan watched from the corner of the room.

"This isn't the way I planned my life," Donna said.

"Oh, and what was *your plan?"* Joan asked, looking at the wall, arms crossed. *"Settle down and raise a brood of your own?"*

"Something like that."

"Children are a burden. The return on investment is sub-par."

"Thanks for the financial advice, Mother."

"We both know what a disaster Grace is," Joan said, placing her hands on the table. *"Dylan will never thrive if he stays with her."*

"It's about Dylan, then?"

"If you have something to say, say it."

"I don't have anything to say." Donna hadn't looked at Joan once throughout the conversation and she still didn't. *"Maybe Grace does."*

Joan sighed and turned away. *"We don't always get to choose our responsibilities."*

"Oh, I'll take care of Dylan, Mother, just like you taught me."

The action in the venue stopped, frozen in time.

"Connor, resume the venue."

"I'm sorry, Dylan, I didn't pause the venue."

"Then what…"

The two figures at the table vibrated; lines flashed horizontally in random colors and widths. Words scrolled across Dylan's field of view: *EXCEPTION THROWN— FUNCTION COMPLIANCE MONITOR—SUSPENDING VENUE.* The scene vanished, leaving Dylan in the staging venue, surrounded in white, the flashing red block letters of the *EXCEPTION* warning scrolling through his field of view.

"Connor: function—stealth compliance!"

"Default arguments, Dylan?"

"Level 10, Connor! *Now!*"

A panel appeared in the venue. A series of messages scrolled by, inquiries issued by the Worldstream compliance engine, each followed by a response from Dylan's *stealth compliance* function, designed to spoof the Worldstream. The messages scrolled faster than Dylan could read them, until he heard a noise, a klaxon so loud it penetrated his headphones.

Dylan tore off his VR gear and tossed it on the floor. The wall screen in his room emitted the ear-splitting sound as it flashed a warning: *DATA BREACH—CEASE ALL ATTEMPTS TO ACCESS THE BLOCKCHAIN— REMAIN AT YOUR LOCATION AND AWAIT CIVIL AUTHORITIES.*

"Connor, *mute!*" Dylan shouted, but the piercing noise persisted, almost but not quite drowning out the pounding on the door and the voice of Aunt Donna.

"Dylan, what's going on in there?"

"Oh, fuck me," Dylan said, slapping his head with both hands. "Fuck, fuck, *fuck!*"

"Dylan, *answer* me! What does this warning mean? What have you been doing?"

The siren stopped, replaced by the door chime. The message disappeared from the wall screen, replaced by an image from the door camera—two agents, dressed in black.

"Citizen, we've detected a violation of the Worldstream data structure. Admit us immediately or we *will* enter forcibly."

❖ ❖ ❖

"Nila, what's that blip?"

"Raúl, the Worldstream has issued a breach fault."

"Jah, the All-Seeing Eye throws a thousand of those a day. What's so special about this one?"

"The parameters of this fault conform to a query you wrote."

"A new one?"

"No, Raúl. You wrote this query two years ago."

"Really? Two years? Put it up on the screen."

"Complete."

"Oh *ho*, my boy Dylan, playing around where he shouldn't! Nila, what's the severity of the fault?"

"Blue—level six."

"Ouch. Not enough for confinement, but his ass is definitely in a sling. Nila, let me see Dylan's activity for the past three months."

"Complete."

"Jah. Prolific lad. Showing some fine potential. Nila, update the query. Whenever Dylan's in a VR venue, set up a tunnel to the venue server, then display parameters, and then alert me. I'll let you know if I want to go in."

"Complete."

"Thanks, Nila. Our little boy is growing up. He'll need a

guiding hand."

3

LIKE MOTHER, LIKE SON

DYLAN SAT MAROONED in Real Life. He stared at the dull room with a bed, chair, dresser with three drawers, closet, and a window into a dim, damp shaft in the building's center. No VR gear nor console; even the wall screen was disabled.

The agents of the civil authorities, a.k.a. the "civils," were not cheerful people. Two of them had entered the apartment with taser pistols drawn, one holding Donna at bay, the other sweeping the space for threats. They found a sixteen-year-old boy in the back bedroom, his cheeks shining with tears, punching his VR console. The agent had ordered Dylan to the floor, hands behind his head, immobilizing him with a knee and strapping his wrists behind his back. Once the apartment had been secured from deadly threats, the agents entered administrative locks into all VR consoles over Donna's objections, which the civils ignored.

The prosecutor had arrived within an hour, in bad temper for having been called to an RL proceeding at a location cut off from the Worldstream. The judgment and sanctions had been swift—judgments were *always* swift. All wrongdoings were recorded in the Worldstream in perfect detail and with unimpeachable accuracy, making time-consuming judicial proceedings obsolete. Due to the nature of the transgression and the age of the transgressor, no confinement was indicated; instead, all of Dylan's illegal apps—the scar-crawler, blockchain explorer, and Happy Face—were confiscated and permanently disabled. The authorities would monitor all of his online activities going forward. Dylan had centered himself in the unflinching gaze of the All-Seeing Eye.

That was hours ago. The prosecutor had gone, VR access was restored, and Dylan was restricted to his room, as isolated as if he'd been committed to a confinement facility. Donna had dispatched a v-gram to her mother Joan, but she already knew. Notification of the immediate family was standard procedure for juvenile offenders.

Dylan went to his dresser and opened the top drawer. He rummaged through its contents, the sorts of things teens hoard—admission tokens and souvenirs from rare RL outings, data drives left behind after the civils had scanned them, confiscating the ones with suspect apps. He pulled out a book with a worn cover and a barely legible title: *Anthology of Victorian Poetry*. He opened to a favorite stanza and read:

> *We are not now that strength which in old days*
> *Moved earth and heaven, that which we are, we are;*
> *One equal temper of heroic hearts,*
> *Made weak by time and fate, but strong in will*
> *To strive, to seek, to find, and not to yield.*

"Dylan, it's time to talk," Donna said through the door. She tried the latch. "Undo the lock."

Dylan closed the book and put it back in the drawer. He turned the latch and went to his chair, sitting with arms crossed and head down.

Donna stood glaring, hands on hips. "Do you know how much trouble you're in?"

"Yeah."

"I don't think you do."

"I *do*, Aunt Donna. I was face-down on the floor with my hands strapped, remember?"

"That was nothing! That was just to get your attention, which I don't think *I* have right now."

Dylan shifted in his chair, turning away.

"*Look at me*," Donna said sternly, grabbing his chin and

turning his head. Dylan swung his arm, knocking Donna's hand away and spinning her around, nearly toppling her. He jumped to his feet, hands clenched, lip curled, almost touching her. Standing straight, Dylan was a good ten centimeters taller than his aunt; with Donna cowering, he seemed even bigger.

"What are you going to do?" Donna asked, one shoulder lifted toward him, her arm crooked over her face. "Hit me?"

Dylan's chest heaved. His curled lip straightened, then trembled. He stepped back, dropping into his chair, turning his tear-streaked face away from his aunt.

"Go away!" he snapped.

"We're going to talk."

"Go *away!*"

"I'm not going anywhere, Dylan—not until we come to an understanding."

"What's to understand?" he muttered.

"What did you say?"

"I said, *what's to understand?*" Dylan faced Donna. "You already have it figured out. If you don't, there's nothing I can say that *you* care about."

"That's not true."

"It *is* true. That's the way it's always been. You didn't want me here and I didn't want to be here."

"That's…" She pressed a fist to her mouth, shutting her eyes tight, taking three short breaths. She sat down on Dylan's bed. "That's not fair."

"But it's true."

Donna held her hands folded in front of her face; her eyes were moist. "When you were ten, your mother was killing herself. And she would have killed you, too, if I hadn't taken you in."

"So you *had* to take me."

She nodded. "I won't lie to you. I wasn't thrilled. I wished there was another way. But I knew it was the right thing, for you. And I'll tell you something: I was scared."

"You're never scared."

Donna smiled and barked a short laugh. "Oh, I'm scared."

She nodded. "All the time. Every day."

Dylan looked into Donna's eyes. He thought he *could* see fear in them, where he'd never before seen anything but anger and resolve. "What are *you* scared of?"

"That I'll hurt you. That I'll do something stupid that'll send you off in a bad direction." She wiped her eye. "And I have. Somewhere, I went wrong."

"It's not your fault. It's mine."

"Oh, it's your fault, all right. And there'll be some changes until I can trust you again. But we're in this together. And I need to figure out what *I* should be doing differently."

He looked down. "So, what's my punishment?"

She stood. "The civil authorities have already taken care of that. No hacker apps, obviously, no blocking apps. No VR venues that I haven't approved. And I'll be monitoring your activity even more closely."

"Okay. Are we done?"

"Jah, you are so much like Grace."

"That's got to drive you crazy."

Donna chuckled. "Yes, sometimes. Jah knows *she* drove me crazy, and your Nana Joan, too. But you need to know: I loved your mother."

"Sure you did."

"You're too young to understand."

"I'm not *that* young."

"You are *so* young. I'm glad I'm not that young anymore."

"Yeah, it sucks."

"Yeah. Sucks bad."

Donna touched Dylan's shoulder. It startled him—Donna *never* touched. He looked up at her. "Anything else?"

"Yes. Then I'll let you get to bed."

"Okay, what?"

"The prosecutor told me what you were doing. I want to hear it from you."

"Why? The All-Seeing Eye already filled you in."

"What did you say?"

"Nothing."

Donna took her hand away from his shoulder. "You said,

'the All-Seeing Eye.' Where did you hear that?"

"That's what everybody calls Jahbulon."

Donna crossed her arms. She looked up and away, sighing. "No, everybody *doesn't*. The Cloak and the Shade—they're the ones who say that."

"Like mother, like son."

Donna gripped Dylan's shoulder and spun him around. "You will *not* have anything to do with those people, do you hear me? They're dangerous. Your mother got mixed up with them and now…"

"And now she's shredded. She's *dead*."

Donna loosened her grip. "Yeah. Dead. Pretty much. I know you miss her."

Dylan kept silent.

"But you're right—she's gone. And you won't find her again by crawling around in the blockchain. They told me that's what you were doing, looking for Grace, even if you won't tell me yourself."

"Okay, so I was. Do you blame me? Mom was the only one who understood me. She's the only one who talked to me like a *person*."

Donna turned, taking two steps to the door before she looked back. "Dylan, I try. I'm not your mother, I'm only your aunt, but Jah, I *try*. And I don't think I've done too bad a job. But now…this…" She raised her arms and dropped them to her sides. "First you turn into a recluse, then your grades go to hell, and now this." She pointed. "You've got a long road back, mister, so get started. And I've got a long road, too. Okay, now we're done. Get to bed."

4

Non-Transferable

The drugged and unconscious patients were oblivious to the shelling; the rest flinched with every burst. Impacts came at irregular intervals, four to ten per minute, some so close together that the force of the blast visibly shook the tunnel walls. Dust sifted down from the ceiling, toppling bottles from shelves to crash on the concrete floor. A single flickering lamp at the near-end lit the passage, a half-pipe three meters high at its peak and not as wide, the cots in a row stretching into infinite darkness. A Filipino orderly went from bed to bed, checking bandages, offering water, doling out morphine from dwindling stocks to the soldiers in the most severe pain. He covered the noses and mouths of the wounded with wet gauze to filter out the dust and fumes, pulling covers over the faces of the dead.

"The ferocious attack on the fortified island of Corregidor continued unabated from December 29, 1941, through May 5, 1942," the narrator droned in Dylan's headset. *"By the final days of the bombardment, the Philippine government had continued within the tunnels of Malinta Hill for four months. General Douglas McArthur, commander of the United States Army Forces in the Far East, had departed the Philippines with his family and staff nearly two months before."*

Dylan shifted in his chair, adjusting his headset and visor, annoyed with the feel of the VR gear on his face. The headgear wasn't uncomfortable, but in venues which failed to keep his interest, it was noticeable.

"On May 5th, Japanese forces began their final assault on Corr…" the narrator paused mid-sentence; the bombardment ceased as the visual froze.

"Connor, resume the venue," Dylan said. The action remained frozen.

"Connor…*Connor?*"

Dylan reached for his visor.

"Jah, where the hell *are* we?"

Dylan didn't know the voice. He left his visor in place, his hand still gripping its sides. The image shimmered, then skewed. The tunnel, the soldiers, and the orderly were distorted, as if printed on a rubber sheet, stretched from corner to corner.

"Who said that?" Dylan whispered.

"This looks like a war zone. Early 20th century?"

"World War II," Dylan replied.

The colors in the image faded to monochrome. The contrast sharpened, until the renderings appeared as line drawings, the black ink strokes shrinking, until everything vanished, leaving Dylan alone in a pure white expanse.

"Connor, suspend the venue." The white surroundings remained unchanged.

"Ancient history," the voice continued. "That's even before *my* time."

"Who *are* you?"

A figure rastered into view, a tall man with a narrow face and bronze-colored skin. His hair was silver, parted in the middle and tied back. His eyes were narrowly set under a generous brow; they seemed to bore into Dylan. He was dressed like people Dylan had seen in venues reconstructed from the 1970s—jeans, a loose red shirt with buttons, and a black vest. The man smiled.

"My, how you've grown."

"Connor, exit the venue!"

"Nila, chair," the man said.

A chair materialized by his side.

"Connor's not in at the moment," the man continued as he sat. He crossed his legs, lacing his fingers across his knee.

"He's taking a break."

Dylan looked behind and to either side of him; he was alone with the stranger.

"I have to stop this venue."

The man raised his hand. "Don't worry about Aunt Donna."

Dylan's head jerked forward. "What do you mean?"

"She still thinks you're in a war zone. What was that, anyway?"

"What?"

"That venue. What was it?"

"The Japanese attack on Corregidor."

"Corregidor. And that's…where?"

"In the Philippines. In the Pacific Ocean."

"Huh." The man kept staring at Dylan without blinking.

"Look, whoever you are, I have to go. My aunt watches my VR venues every minute."

The man laughed. "Dylan, I *told* you, as far as Aunt Donna knows, you're still getting nuked in the Pacific." He leaned forward, opening his hands and uncrossing his legs. "Will you *relax?* I've got this under control. I'm *in* control."

"*Who are you?*"

"My name's Raúl. I'm a friend of your mom's."

Dylan gasped. He leaned closer to Raúl, trying to find some clue in the man's avatar as to whether he was lying or telling the truth.

"You don't know my mom."

Raúl closed his eyes and nodded. "Well, yes, I kind of *do* know your mom. I shredded her."

Dylan's mouth dropped open. "You shredded…"

"…your mom. Yeah."

Dylan's eyes watered, noticeably—if imperfectly—rendered in his avatar. "I don't believe you."

"Nila, let's go to the delivery room."

"Yes, Raúl," a disembodied female voice replied.

Dylan and Raúl were instantly transported to a room filled with people in green gowns and masks. One of them held a squalling newborn. She handed it to the woman on the table, her face damp and flushed, red hair matted. The young woman cradled the baby boy, stroking his head.

Dylan stood up from his chair. "What *is* this?"

"Happy birthday, Dylan. Recognize Mom?"

Dylan moved closer. The new mother was a teen, younger than Dylan, but he knew her face.

"Mom," he whispered. The image distorted as he forced his fingers under the visor to wipe his eyes. He adjusted his headgear until it was clear again, then turned to Raúl.

"This is impossible. *All* of Mom's life data was shredded. Where did this come from?"

"I saved a few snippets. Just a few—my favorites." Raúl stood to get a better look at the mother and child. "This is number one on my list."

Dylan moved around the table, searching from all angles. He bent low to see Grace's face, glowing with sweat, eyes wide, alternately sobbing and laughing as she touched the baby's nose, mouth, and chin.

"What else?"

"Have I got? Some childhood scenes, birthday parties, things like that. Some workday material. I have one of you and Grace in the park. She's in her cloak and hood."

"I don't want to see that one," said Dylan. "I want to see her face."

❖ ❖ ❖

Dylan sat with head bowed and hands between his knees after an hour of clips from Grace's life—the first time Dylan had seen his mother in two years. He watched her thirteenth birthday party, a **Real Life** party, with a cake and presents. Dylan asked Raúl to pause the venue when Grace, grinning, held up her favorite present, a book of Victorian poetry. The custody hearing that he'd seen before, the one with a black void where Grace had been, he watched again with Grace in the venue—the ten-year-old boy who couldn't understand why his mother was abandoning him, and the young mother trying to be strong, deep sadness coming out in her face and in her voice. He also watched for almost ten minutes as Grace, the State Live Services caseworker, tended to the needs of the indigent with patience and understanding.

"Can I have them?"

"The clips? Sorry, kid," Raúl replied, "they're non-transferable."

"How did it happen?"

"How did what happen?"

"The shredding."

"The usual way. Crawl the blockchain, find the links, hack the storage sites, and wipe 'em."

"No. I mean how did it *happen?* Between you and Mom."

"Oh. Okay. Well…" Raúl stood and paced in the all-white venue. "I got a message to meet at the Cloakroom. Someone needed my services."

"What's the 'Cloakroom?'"

"It's a clubhouse for crooks and creeps."

"You mean the Cloak?"

"Yeah, them."

"I thought they just wanted privacy."

Raúl stopped pacing, a skeptical smile on his face. "They'll tell you that. But they're either doing shady stuff or…"

"Or what?"

"Nothing, kid. Whatever they don't want permanently recorded in the Worldstream. Let's just say they go there to get out of sight of the All-Seeing Eye."

"My aunt doesn't like me using that term."

"The All-Seeing Eye? I get that. It's a catchphrase. The Cloak and the Shade use it a lot."

"Mom is Shade."

Raúl walked up to Dylan, stopping to stand in front of him.

"To get back to my story, I met Grace when she was Cloak. She was desperate to shred her life. I knew I wouldn't be able to stop her. Your mom is one stubborn lady."

"You could have *tried* to stop her."

"Oh, I *tried.* I told her exactly what to expect in the land of the Shade. She wouldn't be persuaded. If I hadn't done it, someone else would've, probably some hack. It was my duty to see that it got done right."

"Is that why you did it? A sense of duty?"

Raúl looked startled, then a smile grew on his face. "Jah, you and Grace. You're both the same."

Dylan cracked a smile of his own. "You're not the only one who thinks so."

"To answer your question, kid, no, I'm not a humanitarian. I'm in it for the money—*and* the challenge. A good shredding is damn difficult to pull off without getting caught. And I'm *very* good at it."

"And Mom paid you."

"I'll tell you something," Raúl said, jabbing his finger in the air. "Grace came up short—200,000 credits—and I shredded her anyway. Not only that, I staked her to another 50,000 to get her started. And that I *did* do out of the goodness of my heart. Because I liked her."

"You *liked* her?" Dylan asked accusingly.

Raúl grimaced. "Not like *that*. Jah, I'm forty years older than Grace. I'm not *that* depraved. She was tough—*that's* what I liked."

Dylan looked up into Raúl's eyes. "Is my mom okay?"

"I don't know what she's up to these days, but she's making out."

"How do you know?"

"She paid me back—the 200,000 she owed me and the 50,000 I gave her, plus interest. The money showed up in my crypto account. Anonymous donor, but I knew who it was from. And it didn't take her long—less than a year. Whatever she's into, it pays."

Dylan leaned back in his chair and crossed his arms. "Why are you here? I mean, why *now?*"

"Nila, follow me." Raúl's chair vanished, reappearing next to Dylan. He sat down. "Grace was worried about you—you were the only thing holding her back from shredding. She didn't ask me to, but after she was gone, I kept tabs on you."

"Thanks—I guess."

"Good thing I did." Raúl put his hand on Dylan's shoulder. "This thing you're doing, messing around with the blockchain—it's dangerous. You don't know how close you came to getting your young ass slapped into confinement. What would your mom think of *that?*"

"I was just trying to find her."

"I know what you were trying to do, kid, but you're in way over your head."

Dylan stared at Raúl, clenching his jaw. "I know what I'm doing."

"Then why are you grounded?"

Dylan crossed his arms and looked down. "I slipped up."

"*Yeah,* you slipped up. Because you're an amateur." Raúl gripped Dylan's shoulder. "This ain't no high school VR coding you're into. You are fucking with the molecular structure of the *world.*" He loosened his grip. "When it comes to mastering the Worldstream and all its moving parts, you don't *dabble.*"

"Will you teach me?"

"Sorry, kid, my days are full enough without taking on a protégé. Besides, as much as I thought of your mom, I have no idea if *you* have what it takes to dedicate *your* life to the ways of the Worldstream."

"I've got what it takes."

Raúl nodded. "You show promise, no question. But you're not in it for the challenge. It's a means to an end for you."

"That's my motivation."

"It's not enough."

"You don't know that. Let me try."

Raúl stood up. "Sorry. Not going to happen. I just dropped in to tell you to keep clean. No more wilding around in the Worldstream gears."

"Am I going to see you again?"

"Why would I want to see you again?"

"I don't know. Why'd you see me *now?* Why've you kept tabs on me for the last two years?"

Raúl hooked his thumbs in his belt, shifting his weight to one foot. "You're a smart kid, you know that?"

"Thanks—I guess."

"Tell you what. Next time you wanna talk, bring up another one of these war venues. Something with a lot of noise. If I'm not in the middle of something, I'll drop in. If I'm not there in ten minutes, call a truce."

Dylan nodded.

"Nila, chair." Raúl's chair vanished.

"Wait." Dylan stood up. "Can you find my mom?"

"No. I'm good, but I'm not *that* good. The Shade keep to themselves, and they don't leave footprints. And I wouldn't try, even if I could. She doesn't *want* to be found."

5

ANIMAL GIRL

"HOW'D YOU GET away from Aunt Donna?" Wayne shouted over the music.

It was a frenetic variation on a rock classic from the forties, played on amplified acoustic instruments—a genre popular with teens. Four facsimiles of the band hovered above the crowd, slowly orbiting the dance floor. Wayne and Dylan stood by the wall, Wayne in a jacket glowing mercury blue trimmed in neon orange, Dylan wearing plain clothes in muted colors.

"It's my reward," Dylan replied. "She says I've been good. Like I have a choice. Every move in every venue goes into the log. She set her voice responder on high alert. He warns her whenever I go out of bounds."

"Jah, that is lo-res."

"Yeah. One little level-six alert and I'm in lockdown."

Wayne laughed. "So sorry, bro. You do know Happy Face had nothing to do with that, right?"

"Relax. No one's blaming you."

"Hey, check that." Wayne tipped his head toward two girls their age. One, a blonde, wore a sleeveless dress that hung to mid-calf. Cartoon animals pranced on her skirt: hippos, zebras, and giraffes chasing each other around her legs. The other was a redhead in a loose top with oversized sleeves and tight-fitting pants. Her blouse displayed geometric shapes, circles and polygons in primary colors, moving at random, colliding and caroming in all directions. Their eyes darted in

Wayne and Dylan's direction, then turned away as they whispered behind their hands.

"I think that animal girl likes you," Wayne said.

Dylan lowered his head, looking at the girls from under his eyebrows, with a faint suggestion of a smile. Geometry Girl smiled back. Animal Girl turned away, watching the boys from the corner of her eye.

"So, you like the Geometry Girl," Dylan said.

"I like 'em both. Hey, Batman."

"Yes, Wayne?" said the voice responder in Wayne's headphones.

"Message those girls. Ask them if they know the name of the band."

The girls' heads jerked up, as if reacting to a noise. They stared straight ahead, then smiled and giggled, glancing at the boys before retreating behind their hands for another conference.

Wayne and Dylan saw the response simultaneously, a white scrolling text window floating at near focus, narrated by a young female voice—whether it came from Geometry Girl or Animal Girl they didn't know: *Sock Monkey, Sock Monkey, Sock Monkey! But why are you asking me? Have your headless talker call up the banner! What's its name, anyway?*

The message ended with a floating cartoon head of a teen girl, sticking out her tongue.

"Cheeky!" Wayne commented. He narrated a response: *His name is Batman, but I gave him the night off. Thanks for filling in. Oh, by the way, I'm Wayne, and this loser is Dylan.*

The response was almost instantaneous: *Hi, Wayne. Why don't you get rid of your loser friend in the neon jacket?*

Wayne groaned. Dylan stifled a laugh.

"Batman, turn off the lights," Wayne ordered. His jacket went dark, then transparent, before vanishing altogether, uncovering a solid red shirt.

Thanks, Dylan, the message scrolled, punctuated by the cartoon girl smiling and batting her lashes. *Your jacket was hurting my eyes.*

We toned it down. C'mon over, Wayne replied.

We like it here. The cartoon stuck out her tongue.

Don't be like that.

The girls' response was a string of tongue-sticking emojis.

"Screw 'em," Wayne said out loud. "They look like they're no fun anyway."

Dylan looked annoyed as his eyes darted toward Wayne. He looked at the girls.

"Connor," Dylan said, "message."

You got us wrong, Dylan sent.

Like we don't know what you're after?

No, like he's Wayne and I'm Dylan. You got us wrong.

So, Wayne is the one in the glowing jacket? An emoji, laughing hysterically.

I'm working with him. He's making progress.

More laughing emojis.

I think Sock Monkey tries too hard.

Confused emojis, question marks.

Like, Gavin, the bass player. He knows about three riffs. He tries to improvise, and it fucks up the whole piece.

There was a gap in the exchange. The girls talked behind their hands.

What bands do you like? the reply came.

Dylan's head lowered, his gaze from under his eyebrows slightly more intense, his tight smile a bit wider.

Cadaver Dog.

That retro metal band? Jah, they're terrible. Tongue sticking emoji.

They're just not accessible, by most people, I mean.

Accessible? Question marks.

Yeah. They have raw energy that'll reach you, right down to your core, if you let it. If you're not afraid of it.

Afraid of Cadaver Dog?

Dylan's smile twitched. *Afraid of yourself.*

The girls lifted their hands. They vanished, teleporting next to Dylan and Wayne. Geometry Girl stayed back as Animal Girl, the blonde, got close to Dylan. "Do you think I'm afraid of myself…*Dylan?*"

"Everyone is; it's just that some people get past it."

"I'm Wayne," Wayne interjected.

Animal Girl smiled faintly. "Hello…*Wayne.*" She turned back to Dylan. "Are *you* past it, being afraid of yourself?"

"I'm working on it."

"Hi, I'm Keira," Geometry Girl said. "This is Mia."

"Hi, Keira," Wayne replied.

Mia leaned almost imperceptibly toward Dylan. "You've got your hands full, working on Wayne *and* your fears."

Dylan rubbed a knuckle on his lip. "Working on my fear is full-time. Wayne's more like a hobby."

Mia snorted, covering a laugh with her hand.

"Man, I'm standing right here!" Wayne protested.

Kiera waved her fingers, as if timidly raising her hand in class. "I like Cadaver Dog."

Dylan looked past Mia. "How do they get to you?" he asked Kiera.

"Get to me?"

Dylan went to Kiera, passing by Mia as if she were a lamppost in his way. Mia shot Kiera a stern look.

"Yeah, how do they get to you?" Dylan repeated. He tapped his chest. "In here."

"I just like the way they sound. I like loud."

"Next time you listen, don't think," Dylan instructed. "Focus on what you're *feeling*, what the music's *doing* to you. Close your eyes if you want to. See if it doesn't resonate."

❖ ❖ ❖

A few meters away a dark-skinned man of Indian ancestry stood, a bag hanging from his shoulder. He eavesdropped on the conversation from a distance, using an extension to his venue connection, a mechanism that would have been detected and disabled by the venue if it'd had the latest security upgrades.

The girl named Mia put her hand on Dylan's shoulder. "I know a venue where they're playing."

Dylan turned slowly away from Kiera. He narrowed his eyes. "You won't be afraid?"

"Of myself?" Mia replied.

"Of me."

"Why would I be afraid of *you?*"

"I'm not afraid," Kiera offered.

Dylan turned back to Kiera. "Maybe you should be."

Mia let out a short, nervous laugh. "Oh, you are *so scary.*"

Wayne leaned in. "Look out, he's a dangerous man."

Dylan closed the distance between himself and Mia, until only a centimeter separated them. Mia stood her ground. "I'm not, you know, dangerous."

Mia stood nose to nose with Dylan, hovering, then moving slightly closer.

The dark-skinned man closed the distance between himself and the teens in two steps. He grabbed Mia by the arm and pulled her away.

"What the fuck?" Mia snapped, her avatar staggering backward.

Dylan got in the man's face. "What's this about, asshole?"

The man stepped back but Dylan stayed close, pressing a finger into his chest. Dylan's face filled his field of view—an angry face with fair skin and rusty hair, his features more angular than the last time the man had seen him, more than two years ago.

The man opened his mouth, but he could make no sound. Wayne and the girls stepped back. Others in the venue gathered around the commotion.

"*Say something!*" Dylan shouted.

The man staggered backward, turning slightly before falling to his knees. He pressed a finger into the floor and began to scrawl, leaving a glowing trail. The crowd closed in, some of them mouthing the words as he wrote. Dylan watched as well, tilting his head, furrowing his brow, until his eyebrows rose and his mouth dropped open.

The man finished one line, then started on another until, as he finished the sentence, his avatar shimmered and faded, then vanished.

Dylan knelt beside the inscription. The words flickered like a flame. He ran his fingers over them. The writing flared where he touched it.

"What's it mean?" Mia asked.

Dylan said nothing as the writing faded away like dying embers.

Wayne worked his way to the front of the crowd. "Bro," he began, "is that…?"

"Uh-huh," Dylan muttered. "Famous last words."

I AM THE MASTER OF MY FATE
I AM THE CAPTAIN OF MY SOUL

6

Some Rendering Trick

"I'm impressed, kid."

Dylan and Raúl hovered among cables, cords, and threads in Dylan's rendering of the Worldstream's data structure. Dylan had been jacked into a recreation of the 1916 Battle of the Somme when Raúl barged into the venue. Now safely behind Raúl's firewall, with Aunt Donna satisfied that Dylan was re-experiencing the horrors of World War I, Dylan took Raúl into his Worldstream crawler venue.

"I thought the civils wiped all your apps," Raúl said.

"I hid a copy in a hacker venue," Dylan explained.

Raúl nodded. "Smart move. And you coded this yourself?"

"Yeah. The data visualization was the easy part."

"I'm sure. But it's still a hell of an app. What blows me away is how you managed to tunnel into the blockchain links without setting off about a million alarms."

"I set off *one*, remember?"

"And I've been looking into that. Your stealth code is pretty good, but it's not airtight. Did you write it yourself?"

"Some I did. I borrowed most of it from a hacker venue."

Raúl zoomed in on one sphere in the blockchain. He nodded as he inspected the tangle of cords sprouting from its surface.

"Your stealth code is the heart of your crawler. It *must* be *seamless*. You push it too far, cracks open up, and Jahbulon knows about it. It's *way* too important to trust some hacked

35

code without knowing every line." Raúl poked the block. His finger disappeared into it. "What were you doing when the bells rang?"

"When the what?"

Raúl half-smiled at Dylan. "When the alarm went off, you know, the one that got you grounded."

"Oh. I was rendering an event. My Nana Joan and Aunt Donna, just before I went to live with her."

"Uh-huh. You poked a tender spot." Raúl ran his fingers through a bundle of cords, as if trying to untangle them. "Come here. Look close. All these links, the ones you've rendered as cords off the blockchain. Can you see any difference?"

Dylan peered at the tangle, scratching his cheek. "They're the same."

"They *look* the same, but they're *not* the same. Some of them have tighter security. You stumbled onto one with a hair trigger."

"Um…okay. How do you tell the difference?"

Raúl snorted. "It ain't easy, kid. Took me years to catalog all the security protocols and their signatures. Takes most of my time keeping them current. It's the secret of my success."

Dylan scrutinized the blockchain sphere, its surface covered with tiny rings of light at the base of every cord. He thought the effect looked hi-res, a bit of VR eye candy, but his code made no distinction among the trillions of data sources linked to the blockchain. In this view, data was data, no matter where it came from or where it was stored.

"Can you show me?"

"The protocols?"

"Yeah."

Raúl laughed. "You mean my life's work?"

"Well…"

"Short answer—no." Raúl put his hand on Dylan's shoulder. "Kid, they wouldn't do you any good if I gave them to you. They're useless if you don't know what you're doing."

"You could teach me."

"I thought we covered this. I'm not your sensei, Dylan-san."

Dylan looked past Raúl, biting his lip.

"Look," Raúl said, "I give you my stuff and you think you have the keys to the kingdom, and you start sticking them in locks where they don't fit. Think you got busted the last time? Wait'll you see what happens when you try to access a swordfish-encrypted block with an AEP key. Jahbulon will *flip out*. He'll ban you from the Worldstream for life. Is that what you want? Live the rest of your days IRL reading fucking books?"

"I just want to find my mom."

"Let her rest in peace. She doesn't want to be found."

"I think she does. I think *she's* trying to find *me*."

Raúl's head jerked up. "Huh?"

Dylan crossed his arms, rubbing his shoulders as if trying to get warm. "The other night I'm in this venue for teens, you know, music, dancing. I'm talking with this girl. Then this guy comes running at me from nowhere and pulls her away. I get in his face, but he doesn't say anything."

"And?"

"I think that was my mom."

Raúl blinked hard. "And that's based on…what?"

"It's a feeling I have. He was this short Indian guy. He didn't even talk. But he did something. He got on his knees and he wrote on the floor."

"Wrote?"

"Yeah, glowing letters, with his finger. Some rendering trick."

Raúl scratched his chin. "What'd he write?"

"*I am the master of my fate. I am the captain of my soul.*"

Raúl shrugged. "That obviously means more to you than it does to me."

"Uh-huh. They're lines from a poem, the last thing my mom sent me after…you know…"

"A message from beyond."

"It's her." Dylan put his hands to his head. He turned, hiding his face. Raúl heard sniffling.

"Hey, kid…Dylan," Raúl said kindly, patting Dylan's back. "It could've been anyone."

"No one knows about the poem."

"Are you sure about that? There's *nothing* secret in the Worldstream."

Dylan looked up, his avatar's face wet with tears. "She sent me a book, by drone."

"A *real* book?"

"Uh-huh. I'd never seen one before. I keep it in a dresser drawer and I've never taken it outside of my room. I've never even read it out loud. Mom wrote a message inside, telling me to read that poem. Nobody else knows that."

"Nobody?"

"Well…I did tell my friend, Wayne."

"And Wayne was with you in the venue." Raúl nodded. "There's your leak. He's trying to gaff you—that's *my* theory."

"What's that mean?"

"Playing a joke. Or he's trying to hook you into something. Con you."

"Wayne wouldn't do that."

"Whatever. Better to ignore it."

Dylan looked off into the distance, away from Raúl. The blockchain seemed to extend to infinity, the rippling tendrils reminding him of some fantastic ocean creature, a sea-centipede, its stinging tentacles floating in the current, waiting to capture whatever prey was unfortunate enough to chance into them.

"Connor, suspend the venue."

The blockchain and all its connections vanished. Raúl and Dylan were alone inside Raúl's pure-white staging venue.

"If it *was* Mom, why would she look like some skinny Indian guy?" Dylan asked.

"Nila, can we get a couple of chairs in here?"

Two wooden chairs materialized in the venue. Raúl sat and put his hands on his knees.

"Just on the *extremely* unlikely assumption that Grace is now injecting herself into venues from outside the

Worldstream, I'd guess that she can't use her own avatar. She's got to piece one together from scratch."

"Why can't she use her own?"

"Remember, kid? I shredded *every last trace* of Grace. The venue server renders an avatar from a person's valid data in the Worldstream. No data, no avatar."

"Then it *could* be her."

"This is pure speculation, kid," Raúl replied, slapping his knees. "If that's what she's doing, her technology is a couple levels above *anything* I can do, and I'm damn skilled. And another thing—if that *was* her at the dance, she's just asking for trouble."

"Why?"

"Faking an avatar—it's what the whole mechanism was set up to *prevent*. If someone can masquerade in VR, be someone they're not, then the integrity of the Worldstream collapses. You couldn't trust *any* interaction." Raúl leaned back in his chair, scratching the corner of his mouth. "She'd have to be…"

"Be what?"

Raúl stared into space, then pressed his knuckles against his cheek. "If she were…"

"If she were what?"

Raúl stood up. "Listen. If you see this Indian guy again, give him a message. Tell him to see me in the Cloakroom. Be sure to mention my name. Pick a time and date—doesn't matter when. Then get in touch with me."

"What are you thinking?" Dylan pressed.

"Can you do it?"

"Yeah, yeah, I'll do it, but *what are you thinking?*"

"Can't talk now kid. Gotta go. Have a great day. Nila, suspend the venue."

Raúl vanished. The silent staging venue faded, dissolving into a battlefield strewn with barbed wire, the sound of machine guns and rifle fire coming from all directions, punctuated every few seconds by the ear-splitting explosions of British artillery shells.

Dylan flinched with each burst, but was otherwise

oblivious to the mayhem.
    What's he thinking?

7

THE MISTAKES OF OTHERS

"TWO HOURS," DONNA said firmly. "Then I want you back in your study venue."

Two hours was a bump up—Donna didn't think much of teen music venues, considering them a waste of time. An hour was her usual limit; over the last week she had only allowed Dylan two nights at ninety minutes each. But Dylan's marks had improved, and he'd stopped his hacking (according to his activity log, which Donna checked every fifteen minutes). Dylan had kept his VR time to school and other educational venues, though he seemed to be spending a lot of time in battles—the World Wars, Korea, Vietnam, and the Baltic Conflict for the most part. What boys found so fascinating about war she didn't get, but figured it was harmless—or at least *normal*.

Dylan nodded like an obedient servant. "Thanks, Aunt Donna."

"What's the band?"

"They're called Cadaver Dog," Dylan replied, already heading for his room.

"That metal band you like." Donna winced. "*Cadaver Dog.* What a name!"

Within seconds, Dylan was jacked in, materializing in a vacant vestibule to the venue. The crowd was light, a hundred or so teen avatars, their clothing running together in a chaotic band of animated decorations, blending into a mural of color and motion. A few wore hats, also lit up and animated, which hovered over them like UFOs. Above the scene, as if on an invisible revolving platform, four replicas of the power trio Cadaver Dog played, their distinctive style of retro metal pounding in Dylan's ears.

Dylan stepped out of the vestibule, keeping close to the walls, lined with immersive gaming booths where teen avatars could pay fifty credits for ten minutes in a private venue, all wholesome themes—air combat, martial arts, zombie hordes—the kind of fun parents felt comfortable with, the games that they'd grown up with themselves.

Dylan circled the dance floor, scanning the crowd as he went. He needed to concentrate—the visual jumble of shapes and colors made it nearly impossible to pick out a face from the crowd. But he assumed that the person he was looking for, a short, slim, dark-skinned man, wouldn't be in the crowd anyway. Keeping close to the wall was his best bet.

A message popped up, floating in space directly in front of his eyes: *Are you feeling it?* Dylan looked for some clue as to who had sent it and found none.

"Connor, reply."

Feeling?

The response came almost instantly.

Feeling. Reaching. In your core.

Dylan scanned the crowd again, finding her near the wall, ten meters away, barely visible through the mob of dancers—a blonde, not dressed as Dylan remembered, with animals galloping across her skirt, but wearing dark clothes, almost invisible in the dim light. He dictated his reply.

Always, Mia. Are they reaching you?

Mia's avatar dissolved, reappearing a meter from Dylan, leaning against the wall.

"I'm not sure I'm getting it. I need a guide."

"Like don Juan."

Mia wrinkled her brow. "Don Juan? Like that lover guy? You going to sweep me away to your love chamber?"

Dylan stayed impassive. He looked past Mia, still searching for the Indian man.

"No, don Juan, like that Yaqui guy," Dylan replied without

inflection, as if he were discussing the weather. He looked at Mia, who seemed confused. Then he took a step toward her, looking deep into her eyes. "A spirit guide. Someone to help you find all the threads of your existence, to show you where they come together."

Mia's face went blank. "What does that mean?"

"It means your ties to the universe are all knotted together in here." Dylan tapped his forehead. "The knot keeps you stuck in one place. When you learn to move the knot, move it outside your body, a hundred new worlds open up."

Mia turned away. Then she turned back, eyes wide, mouth open. "Ah-ha. Ha." She shook her head slowly, lowering her eyes. "You are *so* weird."

"If you think that's weird, then I'm probably not your guide."

"Well, maybe you're not." Mia put her hands on her hips, looking at everything and everyone except Dylan. "So, all that universe and knots and stuff, you get all that from listening to Cadaver Dog?"

Dylan lowered his head, glancing at Mia sideways. "No. That's totally different. That's about feeling *something* instead of *nothing*, when living your whole life in a fake world has taken your feeling away."

Mia dropped her arms to her sides, letting them dangle like loose ropes. "Is that how you are, like you don't have any feeling?"

"Oh, yes."

Mia crossed her arms, nodding slowly. "Me, too."

The band reached a crescendo, the frontman playing a blistering guitar riff, the drummer beating out a rhythm line, his sinewed arms—covered in fluorescent tattoo serpents—a blur of motion.

"Do you feel that?" Dylan shouted. He took Mia's hand and pressed it against his chest. His heart was pounding. "That's the only time I feel my heart beating, when they play like that, when they're so loud and raw they make my body vibrate." He put his hand on Mia's chest. "How about it, Mia? Are you feeling something?"

She looked down, putting her hand over his. She locked eyes with him, leaning closer. Dylan leaned in to meet her, glancing away for an instant. He stopped, dropping his hand from her chest.

Next to a booth with a scrolling marquis—*ARMY MARKSMAN…ENEMY COMBATANTS…KILL OR BE KILLED*—stood the Indian man. The man shook his head —*No.*

Dylan put his hand on Mia's shoulder and pushed her aside.

"*What?*" she shouted. "What are you doing?"

"Not now," Dylan answered, walking past her.

"Jah! What? Where are you going?" Mia called after him.

The man's eyes followed Dylan as he approached. He raised his hands, palms out. Dylan stopped.

"Who are you?"

"Dylan," the man said in a high, thin voice with a mild accent, "are you well?"

"Am I what? Who *are* you?"

The man kept his hands raised, as if to hold Dylan at a distance. "I just want to know if you're doing well. I want to know if you're happy."

"Oh, *this* guy again," Mia sneered, coming to Dylan's side and taking his arm. Dylan kept his eyes on the man.

"Tell me who you are," Dylan repeated, "because I think I know."

The man glanced at Mia. "Girl," he said, "for your own good, please leave."

Mia tightened her grip. "No, *you* leave." She tugged Dylan's arm. "C'mon, Dylan."

Dylan stayed put. "Mia, later. I need to talk to my…to this guy."

Mia let go of Dylan's arm, pushing him away with both hands. "Jah, be an asshole, then." She got in the man's face, tilting her head toward Dylan. "You should know, he's a lo-res weirdo."

Mia gave Dylan one last stony look before blending into the crowd.

Dylan watched her leave, then turned back to the Indian man. "Are you…?"

The man shook his head. "Don't ask, Dylan. I'm only here to see if you're doing well."

"You said that. What's that to you?"

The man lowered his hands. "I want to tell you not to repeat the mistakes of others."

"Others? What others? What mistakes? *Who are you?*"

"I can't tell you. But I know someone who's made a lot of mistakes. Her whole life was a mistake, except for one thing —just one. *You*, Dylan. You're the only thing she did right. And she wants to know that you won't go the same way she did."

Dylan's mouth went dry. "What way is that?"

"She used people; she preyed on them, for her own pleasure."

"I'm not doing that."

The man nodded. "Good. That's good, Dylan. And Mia, she'd back you up on that?"

"She's nothing to me."

"Nothing—and yet you went after her."

Dylan's face burned. "I don't know why I did that."

"An addict never knows why."

"An *addict?* Addicted to what?"

"That feeling of power—power over another person. It's like a drug."

Dylan was breathing hard, heart still pounding. He lunged at the man, grabbing his shoulders. "That's not me! That's *not me!*"

The man's avatar wavered, sheared and flickered.

"Wait!" Dylan shouted. "Raúl wants to meet with you."

The man's face skewed. Static-filled color flashed in diagonal bands. His mouth moved in slow motion, his face rippling as if seen through waves on water.

"Raúl? Where? When?"

"The Cloakroom. Soon—tomorrow…nine o'clock. At night."

The man's avatar rastered out, leaving Dylan grasping

empty air.

"Mom," he said, spinning around. A few teens turned his way. One caught his eye, a girl with black hair, who gazed at him with a mixture of sympathy and longing.

Dylan stared back. She turned her head slightly, keeping her eyes on him. The image of the Indian man, and his cryptic warning, fled from his mind. He lowered his head, looking from under his eyebrows, smiling a thin smile.

"Connor…"

"Yes, Dylan?"

The Indian man's words sounded in his head: *An addict never knows why.*

"Dylan?"

He gulped. "Connor, exit the venue."

8

Transformed Alert Cherubs

Dylan and Wayne stood apart from other avatars, jacked into a hacker venue outside the Worldstream. The boys' features were rendered in low resolution—large, uniform voxels flashing artifacts when they moved. The other avatars looked no better, some strobing with eye-fatiguing intensity, others rastering in and out. Avatars close together bled into each other. The crappy rendering was a telltale sign that the server was loaded beyond its capacity, throttling back its resolution, coherence, and deconfliction to keep up with demand. *A low-end server*, Dylan figured, the kind that jobless guys low on credits might set up. Tonight, with forty or fifty avatars online, the venue was particularly glitchy. Thinner crowds always looked better.

"Didn't your Aunt Donna take away your Happy Face?" Wayne asked.

"The civils did," Dylan answered.

"Then how are you hiding? Aunt Donna's got you under a microscope."

"I coded my own shroud."

"*You* coded it?"

"Yeah, frobnitz, *I* coded it. What, surprised?"

"Kinda."

"Don't be. It's pretty simple, but it's reliable. The only drawback is that it won't cloak Worldstream venues. But it'll block this hacker hideout."

"Where does she think you are?"

"First moon landing, 1969."

"Nice choice."

"C'mon. I need to talk to that guy."

Dylan and Wayne moved toward a group of avatars gathered under a floating apparition, a section of cable with large spheres strung on it, sprouting hundreds of tentacles. It looked almost exactly like Dylan's blockchain rendering. One avatar towered over the others, a young man with a long beard and stubble for hair, his vertical dimension exaggerated, rendering him as if he'd been stretched to twice his normal height. The stretched man lectured the group, highlighting features of the blockchain as he spoke.

"You bind this graphical primitive to the data structure using the render_node function," the beanpole said with a twang that reminded Dylan of an Old West venue. "That'll return a handle you can plug into the bind_link function, and that's a recursive routine that'll hunt down every last link to the block. Give it a try, but don't let on to nobody it was me told ya."

He scanned the crowd, his cartoonish eyes coming to rest on Dylan, then gave a wink.

A few avatars blurted out questions. The speaker held up a hand as he shrank to normal size, as if he were an image on a rubber balloon, once stretched, now relaxed.

"Love to talk more, friends, but I need to catch up with my boy Dylan over here."

The hovering sphere and its attached tendrils pixelated and vanished. The knot of avatars dispersed, some rastering out, the rest teleporting to other groups.

"Hey, partner," the now normal-sized avatar greeted Dylan. "Sprung y'self from the penalty box, I see."

"Yeah. Micah, this is Wayne."

Micah stuck out a voxelated hand. "Hey, Wayne, how you doin'?" He slapped Dylan on the back. "So what'd you do? Redirect?"

"Shroud," Dylan replied. "It only works on off-stream venues."

"Yeah, that's the problem with them invisibility cloaks.

Gotta be jacked into a legit Worldstream venue. Where's yours?"

""The Eagle has landed.'"

"One giant step!" Micah shouted, pointing skyward, his arm skewing crazily.

"'One *small* step,'" Dylan corrected. "'One giant *leap*.'"

"Huh?"

"Never mind," Dylan replied. "Anyway, Micah, I have a question."

"Lay it on me, partner."

"Suppose someone was shredded, but they wanted to get back into the Worldstream. How would they do that?"

Micah scratched his chin. His fingers left livid marks behind, which ran like watercolors. "Hmm. That's a poser. I s'pose you could spoof the 'stream with a stolen key. That'd only last until the owner jacked in."

"I don't think that's happening."

"Happening? You sayin' this ain't a hypothetical situation?"

"Maybe, maybe not. If it can't happen, then it can't be happening, right? I'm just trying to figure out what's possible."

"Okay." Micah stared off into space. His avatar sharpened for a moment, then pixelated and blurred, before going monochrome. "Don't see a way without stealing a key. And then, like I said, only temporary."

"What happens to keys when people die IRL?"

"Keys is like property. Goes to the next o' kin. But only for memorial purposes. Can't use 'em in a venue."

"Why not?"

"The Consortium. It's *their* rule. Once the guy's dead, the Powers That Be lock down his key. Retire it. That'll propagate through the blockchain before the fella's cold."

"What if the death doesn't get reported?"

Micah laughed, his avatar going solid for a moment, gray-green like bread mold, before his color returned. "Th' All-Seein' Eye, remember?"

"Jah, can't a person even *die* in private?" Dylan muttered.

Micah pointed his finger at Dylan as if aiming a taser. "Brother, you can't even *shit* in private."

"What if you're shredded, what happens to your key?"

"Worse'n death. Key gets shredded same as you. Like you was never born."

"Okay," Dylan said, "stealing a key's not the answer. Can you enter a venue *without* a key?"

"Nope. That's where it all starts. You can jack into some hacker or pirate venues without a legit key, or with a stolen key, but we're talking about Worldstream venues, correct?"

"That's right."

Micah's lips appeared to melt together, running down his chin in a red streak. An indistinct hole opened as he spoke. "Then you gotta have a key."

"What if I forged one?"

"Can't be done."

"What if I could?"

"Y'can't."

"I said, *what if I could?*"

"Okay. Just for the sake of fuckin' argument—you forge a valid key, then you jack into the venue. Jahbulon blesses your credentials. Then what? The Worldstream starts looking for your data so it can render your avatar. And what does it find? Nada. 'Cause the key don't belong to *nobody*." Micah scratched his head, fingers digging furrows in his scalp.

"You said the Worldstream renders the avatars?"

"Damn, partner, that ain't what I meant. The Worldstream don't render *nothin'*. The *venue server* does that work, but it gets its raw material from the blockchain."

"From the Worldstream," Dylan pressed.

"Same damn thing," Micah replied dismissively. "Anyway, since we're still in hypothetical territory, I *suppose* if you could feed the venue server fake data, get between it and the Worldstream, you could pull it off, but they's all kinds of checks on *that* shit. I don't know *nobody* knows 'em all."

"I might."

Micah tilted his head. "Might what?"

Dylan put his hand to his mouth, fingers melting into his

face. "Nothing. I might have to look into it. That's what I meant."

"Uh-huh. Well, if you figure that out, let me know. That'd be highly marketable knowledge."

"Yeah, I'll do that. Thanks for the background."

"Sure thing. What else can I help ya with?"

"What do you know about security protocols for linked data?"

Micah winced. "Y'all trying to keep from setting off bells and whistles again. I follow. You just got sprung and you don't wanna go back in stir."

"Yeah. So, what do you know?"

"Partner, *that* is a complicated subject. I gave ya everything I got."

Dylan nodded. "I figured. Thanks, Micah."

Dylan and Wayne turned to leave. Micah's avatar popped up in front of them.

"Before you go, I have a little thingy here you might wanna see." Micah held out his hand. A disc appeared, a smooth, flat, glossy white cylinder the size of a saucer.

Wayne touched the surface of the disk. "What is it?" he asked.

"It's your key grabber, isn't it?" Dylan said.

"Yessir," Micah replied. "Rev seven."

"What's it do?" Wayne asked.

Micah flipped the disc like an oversized coin. It hovered in space, spinning end over end. "Find a person you wanna pose as. This extension'll copy his key. You can use the key y'self, or sell it on the stealth stream. Could be a nice little moneymaker, or you can find out what it's like being a star for a day."

"How much?" Wayne asked.

"Fifty thousand."

Wayne slapped his forehead, leaving a deep palm print behind. "Jah. Who has that many credits?"

Dylan plucked the disc from the air. "Interesting, but Wayne's right. We don't have that kind of scratch."

Micah watched as Dylan turned the disc over in his hand.

"A hot key can fetch a thousand cred. The hottest ones—more than five thousand. I can let ya have it on a profit-sharing basis."

Dylan handed the disc back to Micah. "No, thanks. Connor, exit…"

"No, wait," Micah interjected. "I'll let ya have it on approval—no charge, no obligation. If you're not satisfied, return it, no questions asked. If you like it, we'll come to an agreement. Deal?"

Dylan looked at the disc, then back at Micah. His features sharpened briefly, then his face broke out in artifacts.

"How do you know it works?"

"Jah, partner, who're you talking to? This is *Micah*."

"I know who you *are*. You're the guy who wrote the stealth code I was counting on to cover my tracks."

"Oh yeah. Can't say what happened there. Did you mess with the code?"

"I made some tweaks."

"There you go. Coulda been either one of us fucked up." He held out the disc. "What d'ya say?"

"Uh-uh. No. Connor…"

"Wait, wait, *wait*." Micah's avatar flattened and skewed. "Y'all are up into digging through the blockchain, right? Mining the data, right?"

"I guess."

"You never did swipe a key before, did ya?"

Dylan shrugged. "No, I haven't."

"If you're digging for data, a key's like a shovel."

"What's that mean?"

"You can find out anything you want about the owner if you got his key."

Dylan took the disc. *"Anything?"*

Micah's face morphed, zombie-like, his mouth widening into a bloody grin. "Yeah, man. Who his friends are, what venues he likes, all his nasty little habits."

"Can you find out where they are? Where they're located, physically?"

"Hell, yeah! I can show ya how to do that, too."

Dylan waved the disc. "What's the passphrase?"

"*Transformed—Alert—Cherubs*. Good for one key."

"All right. I'll let you know."

"Do that, partner." Micah pointed a finger at Wayne. "Nice to meet *you*, Wayne. See ya again real soon. Clint, exit the venue."

Micah's avatar oscillated for a few seconds before exploding into a cloud of confetti with a sound like a popped balloon.

"Nice effect," Wayne commented. He pointed to the disc. "What're you going to do with that thing?"

"Like Micah said, frobnitz: I'm going to steal a key."

9

Target Acquired

THE CALIBRATION GRID converged as Dylan adjusted his visor and pulled on his tactile gloves.

"Connor, staging venue."

Dylan's bedroom faded into an expanse of white.

"Connor, install an app for me."

"Yes, Dylan. Passphrase, please."

Dylan took a deep breath and pressed a finger to his throat. His heart was beating at twice its resting rate.

"Transformed…Alert…Cherubs."

"Accessing." A soft chime repeated at one-second intervals. Dylan tried to swallow, but he was too dry. He opened his mouth to speak, but Connor beat him to it.

"Dylan, this is not a registered application. It could be dangerous. Do you want to proceed?"

Dylan rubbed his gloved hands together.

"Dylan?"

"Proceed."

"Yes, Dylan. Please stand by."

The chimes continued. Dylan drew another deep breath.

"I'm sorry, Dylan. This application can only be installed from a valid venue."

Dylan gripped the arms of his chair until his hands stopped shaking, then he tugged the fingers of a glove, half-removing it. He stopped mid-tug, one finger stretched tight, and put it back on.

"Connor, dance venue."

The staging venue dissolved to the music club. It was a light crowd, no more than fifty teen avatars. The band was a quartet playing the type of insipid atonal crap that Dylan despised. He looked for the Indian avatar, but didn't see him, or anyone else who resembled him.

A message scrolled through his field of view.

Dylan, what are you doing in that venue? I didn't give you permission!

Dylan searched for the Indian man. He was nowhere in the venue.

Dylan, answer me!

"Connor, reply."

Sorry, Aunt Donna. Wayne messaged me about a school assignment.

Dylan kept looking.

And you thought that was a good place to talk about school? Get out of there and get back to work!

Dylan walked around the dance floor, staying close to the walls. He passed one staging vestibule after another, all of them vacant.

In a minute, Aunt Donna.

He was halfway around the floor.

Now!

"Connor…"

Dylan saw a glow in a vestibule ten meters away. The Indian man rastered in.

"Yes, Dylan?" Connor replied.

Dylan, are you reading me?

"Connor, reply."

Wayne's here. We're almost done.

Dylan hurried toward the vestibule. The man stepped out, holding up his hands as his eyes met Dylan's.

"I saw Raúl," the man said. "He told me what you're up to."

Get out this second!

"Mom," Dylan pleaded, "I…"

"Don't talk, just listen. Do *not* try to find me. *I'll* find *you.* Do you understand?"

Dylan, get out of there or I'm coming in your room.

Dylan looked first at the text scrolling in his visor, then at the Indian man.

"Connor," Dylan said, "*Transformed…*"

I'm coming in there, young man.

"Dylan?" asked the man.

"Yes, Dylan?" asked Connor.

"Transformed…Alert…Cherubs."

Crosshairs appeared in Dylan's visor.

"Dylan," the man said, "listen to me!"

The crosshairs centered themselves on the face of the Indian.

"What's that?" the man asked. "What's happening?"

A message appeared: *Confirm Target.*

"Confirm!"

The man's avatar went flat, going pure white, as if lit up by a strobe. Another message appeared: *Target Acquired.*

Dylan felt a hand gripping his shoulder. He turned to see who it was, then realized that the hand was from outside the venue. The image in his visor skewed and pulled away. He was sitting in his room, Aunt Donna standing in front of him, holding his visor.

"Do you want to explain?" she asked.

"Connor, exit the venue."

"Talk to me!"

Dylan stood up, taking the visor from her hands.

"I told you, Wayne and I were talking about school. About a project."

Donna looked up at the boy's face. "Don't lie to me."

"I'm not."

Donna eyed him. "What project?"

"Are you gonna interrogate me?"

"Fine. I'll message Wayne's parents. Right now."

She took two steps toward the door.

"Wait."

Donna turned around. She crossed her arms, putting her weight on one foot.

"I went there to meet a girl."

Her face softened. She dropped her eyes for a moment.

"What's her name?"

"Mia. I met her there a couple weeks ago."

"Just you and Mia."

Dylan passed the visor from one hand to the other, then dropped it on his chair. "No, Wayne was there, too. Mia has a friend. Kiera."

"So. You and Mia, Kiera and Wayne."

"Yes, Aunt Donna. Wayne messaged me and said he needed a break. He said Kiera messaged him and asked if we could meet them." Dylan put his hands in his pockets. "Look, message Wayne if you don't believe me. Or his parents. Go ahead."

Donna looked at the floor. "No. I won't do that." She looked up again, dropping her arms to her sides. "Dylan, if you wanted to go to the venue, why didn't you ask me?"

"We were only going for a little while. I didn't think you'd mind."

"I don't mind that you went," Donna sighed. "I mind that you went without telling me."

Dylan picked up the visor and tossed it onto his bed. "Do I have to ask permission for *everything?* Jah, I was only going for a few minutes!"

"Do I have to remind you that you're on probation? That you violated Worldstream prohibitions? Do I have to remind you of what you already *know?*"

"No, Aunt Donna, I…"

Dylan and Donna covered their ears reflexively when the klaxon sounded. The wall screen flashed a message in yellow block letters on a red background: *LEVEL NINE TRANSGRESSION DETECTED—WORLDSTREAM ACCESS SUSPENDED—REMAIN AT YOUR LOCATION AND AWAIT CIVIL AUTHORITIES.*

Donna took a handful of Dylan's shirt in her hand, backing him into a corner.

"Oh, Jah," she choked. "What did you *do? Dylan…*" She turned back to the screen, the message flashing in time with the alarm. The sound stopped; the screen flashed. An image from the door cam popped up, of three agents with a battering ram.

"Citizen, we've detected a violation of Worldstream protocols and an illegal act. Admit us immediately, or we will enter forcibly."

Donna let go of Dylan's shirt and dropped her hands to her sides. She turned away, shoulders rounded, head hanging, looking deflated.

"Dylan. Jah, what did you *do?*"

10

THE GUIDELINE IS TWENTY

DYLAN WAS SEATED in a chair without VR gear, in a room with no wall screen. Furnishings were sparse: the chair, a bed, a nightstand, and a few pieces of art hung throughout. The door was locked from the outside, a fact Dylan had verified personally. A side door led to a windowless bathroom. There was no closet, not that one was needed. The only clothes Dylan had were the pajamas he'd been issued: red flannel with a pattern of blue fish.

A day and a night had passed since Dylan's induction into the intervention facility. The three agents who had taken him the previous day both looked and sounded threatening, but Dylan did not put up a fight and the agents used no unnecessary force, once his hands were strapped. The ride to the facility took less than an hour. The intake procedure and room assignment, all handled professionally and courteously by middle-aged ladies in polka-dot dresses and frilly aprons, were a dream-like memory from an age ago.

Dylan had lain awake well past midnight, unable to turn, his hands secured to the bed frame by Kevlar straps. Exhaustion drove him eventually to sleep for a few hours. At daybreak, a woman named Prudence brought breakfast and fresh pajamas. She released his restraints, then sat by, smiling sweetly, as Dylan ate. She remained in the room while he showered and dressed. That was two hours ago. Since then Dylan had sat inert, slumped in the comfortable chair, alternately dozing and gazing at the bland paintings.

The door latch turned. Prudence stood in the open doorway, still smiling, and light from the hallway streamed into the dimly-lit room.

"Dylan, how are you feeling?" she asked.

Dylan raised his head, face slack and eyes red. He simply nodded without speaking.

"You have visitors." Prudence stood aside, and Donna entered, followed by Dylan's grandmother, Joan.

He grimaced at the sight of them. Donna gasped.

"Dylan, you look…Oh Jah, are you all right?"

Dylan's lip trembled and his eyes teared up. His head fell to one side, then forward; his body heaved with sobs.

Donna went to him and knelt at his side, putting her arm around him and pulling him to her.

"He had a rough night, I'm afraid," Prudence said.

Donna glared at the woman as if her eyes could shoot tasers. "What did you *do* to him?"

Prudence stepped back with a start. "*Nothing!* We just… restrained him."

Donna looked at the bed. The arm straps—dull black woven strips with steel buckles—hung from the bed frame like fixtures on a torture device.

"Why'd you do that?" Donna growled.

Prudence put up her hands. "It's standard protocol for level-nine transgressors."

Donna snorted. She lifted Dylan's head and stroked his hair.

Joan stepped forward, until she stood looking down on Dylan.

"Listen to me: you're in a lot of trouble," she snapped. "You used an illegal app to steal the key of another citizen's avatar. That's a level eight transgression. But you were on probation, remember? So you get a bonus—*level nine.* Do you know what that means, young man? *Level nine?*"

Dylan shook his head.

"There are only ten levels. Physical transgressions are level ten. You're one step below a *rapist.*"

Dylan began crying again.

"Mother!" Donna rasped, as she cradled Dylan's head in her arms.

"It's important that he understands the consequences of his actions," Joan said coldly.

"I *get* it, Nana," Dylan said. "I get it. I'm fucked."

"That sums it up," Joan agreed. "But I've seen to it that you're not as fucked as you might have otherwise been."

Donna turned to Joan with a puzzled look. Dylan wiped his eyes.

"What?" he asked.

"I called in a favor from the community magistrate. You're getting a hearing."

❖ ❖ ❖

The hearing venue was a chamber of ornate decorations—paneled walls with carved wainscots; a long, low, heavy table and padded chairs, where the transgressor and his advocate sat; and the magistrate's bench, a high wooden desk rendered in the style of an old-time superior court. Dylan sat at the table with his advocate, the sleek, impeccably rendered avatar of a man of fifty, awaiting the magistrate's arrival. His advocate looked straight ahead, as if he didn't know that there was a frightened teenage boy sitting next to him.

"What's going to happen?" Dylan asked.

"I'll make your case," the advocate replied, still facing forward. "The magistrate will decide your punishment."

"Then I'm going to be punished?"

The advocate finally looked at his client.

"Listen, Dylan, I'm not going to lie to you. I *might* be able to get a reduction in your term of confinement." He turned away again. "You know, I took this case only as a favor to your grandmother Joan. She's got some kind of pull."

"Doesn't everyone get a hearing?"

"No. Don't they teach you this in school? Every circumstance of your transgression is permanently and perfectly recorded in the Worldstream. The only ambiguity comes from what you were able to conceal. But the facts can't be contested. What's there is there. And the law is the law."

"What's the point, then? Why are we here?"

"The magistrate has some leeway in sentencing, if circumstances warrant." The advocate put his hand on Dylan's. "I'll do my best for you."

The magistrate rastered into the venue and took his seat at the bench. He wore a black robe and a horsehair wig, like an old English barrister. He peered down his nose at Dylan and his advocate.

"I have the facts before me," the magistrate said, his eyes moving as he read the charges scrolling through his visual field. "Acquisition of a personal key, a level eight transgression. As a violation of probation, this transgression is elevated to level nine. The facts have been registered and validated by the requisite number of nodes." His eyes stopped moving and focused on the advocate. "You may begin."

The advocate stood. "Magistrate, the transgressor is a young man with no prior offenses…"

"He was on probation for illegal attempts to access the blockchain structure."

"Yes, magistrate, forgive me, I should have said no prior confinement."

"I don't understand why that distinction is relevant."

The advocate paused. Dylan felt nauseous.

"Perhaps not, magistrate, but the circumstances of both transgressions suggest that lenience is called for."

"*Circumstances?* Did you hear me say that the facts have been recorded and validated? The circumstances are known and are *not* in dispute."

"But the boy's motive, magistrate…"

"His motive? Also irrelevant."

"What I'm saying, magistrate, is that the boy wasn't trying to profit from this act."

"Advocate, if you're going to continue to make statements unrelated to the facts or the law, we can end this…"

"I was trying to find my mother," Dylan interjected. The advocate scowled at him.

"Your mother?" The magistrate's eyes scanned the scroll

in his visor. He raised his eyebrows. "I have no records. Who is your mother?"

"Magistrate, Dylan's mother, Grace, shredded her life," the advocate replied. "The boy has been separated from her for more than two years."

The magistrate put a hand to his mouth. "It's tragic, I know." His eyes kept scanning. A look of surprise came over him, then anger. "But the citizen whose key you stole—his identity was verified as Ashok Nanda, a slightly built male of Indian ancestry. Clearly *not* your mother." He looked at Dylan, jaw clenched. "I won't tolerate false testimony in my venue."

"I thought…" Dylan stopped when the advocate put his hand on Dylan's shoulder.

"Magistrate, Dylan is convinced that his mother was masquerading as citizen Nanda."

"A spoof? There's no evidence of that in the record."

"No, magistrate."

The advocate gestured, as if beckoning someone to approach. A series of miniature venues rastered into view on the magistrate's bench: a room in a courthouse with young Dylan sitting across from the rainbow-rimmed black silhouette of a woman; a rendering of a lander on the surface of Mars, next to Dylan and a black void where Grace's avatar once stood; a desert landscape amid a saguaro forest, Dylan and the void hovering near the nest of a pygmy owl.

"The venues you see in front of you are all from Dylan's recent VR history," the advocated continued. "They're all scenes from his mother's lifestream, all exhibiting the same scar where Grace's life data was shredded." He gestured. The dance venue appeared, packed with partiers aged twelve to nineteen, plus one older Indian man. "Magistrate, this citizen, who's been identified as Ashok Nanda, repeatedly visited this venue for teens, and *only* when Dylan was already in the venue."

"What's your point, advocate?"

"Magistrate, my client believes that Grace has forged a key and synthesized an avatar."

The magistrate rose from his seat. "What you're claiming is physically impossible."

"Magistrate…"

"Not another word!"

"…you must hear me out."

The magistrate leaned over his bench. "You're in dangerous territory, advocate."

The advocate rastered out and teleported to the magistrate's bench.

"Whether it's possible or impossible, my client *believed* it. He didn't commit this transgression for profit, or extortion, or any motive other than to *reunite with his mother.*"

The magistrate stood stony-faced, then sat again. He pointed at Dylan. "Citizen, what do you have to say about this?"

Dylan looked at the advocate, who nodded.

"My mom is trying to find me. She told me so."

"She told you?"

"She…he…the man, I mean, told me to stop looking for her…for him. He said he'd find me."

"That's true, magistrate," the advocate confirmed. With a gesture, he replayed the final scene in the dance venue.

The magistrate's expression abruptly softened. "As I'm sure your advocate has told you, the outcome of this hearing was never in doubt. The facts are in the blockchain. They're irrevocable. And the law is clear. But I *do* have some discretion." He stood and adjusted his wig. "I will override the sentencing guidelines and order you to be confined for a period of not less than five years, deprived of access to *all* VR venues. Your confinement will continue *indefinitely* pending the successful completion of reintegration therapy."

The magistrate rastered out.

"Five years!" Dylan rasped breathlessly.

"You're blessed," the advocate said softly. "The guideline is *twenty.*"

11

Nice Gear

Of the fifteen confinees in a windowless transport, Dylan was the youngest; the oldest was over fifty. The trip to the confinement facility via hypertube took less than thirty minutes. The PA system informed the passengers every sixty seconds that they were under continuous surveillance, and that they must remain in their seats at all times; most of them did not even move a muscle for the duration.

At the facility, a steel tunnel sealed itself seamlessly to the transport before the doors opened. The confinees formed a line inside the tunnel, which was narrow enough so that no one could push past the person ahead or behind. The passage emptied into a room with a high-vaulted glass ceiling. The walls were lined with windows, looking out onto a landscape of green hills and trees, and the sun streamed in, filling the space with light. After a half-hour in the transport and the long walk through the steel tunnel, the confinees gasped and squinted, rubbing their eyes at the brightness.

Throughout the room there were rows of benches fixed to the floor, facing a raised platform. The confinees stood scattered at the rear, uncertain of what to do next. They all turned in unison when a tall woman entered from the back. She wore a uniform of black trousers and a tunic; her hair was tied up under a black brimless cap. Walking to the center of the platform, the woman stood straight, arms at her sides, and smiled.

"Greetings," she said in a clear and loud, yet unthreatening voice. "Please be seated, five to a bench, front row to rear." She waited until all the confinees were seated before continuing: "Welcome to the Nodaway District Confinement Facility, where you will remain for the duration of your confinement. My name is Isabel. I will be your orientation officer."

Isabel clasped her hands behind her back and paced the platform. "I know you have many questions, so let me begin with this: We are not a prison. We do not exist to punish you. We have two purposes: with regard to those of you in permanent confinement, our purpose is to isolate you from society, so that your deviant behavior will no longer disrupt the lives of our citizens." Her smile never wavered, even when she said *permanent confinement* and *deviant behavior*, calmly and evenly, as if she were describing a flower. "For those of you in temporary confinement, we have an additional purpose: to understand and correct your deviance and reintegrate you with society." She gestured toward the windows. "Your surroundings are pleasant. Your time here need not be disagreeable. I could warn you to follow the rules, but that won't be necessary. You are under constant surveillance. Any transgression within the boundaries of this facility will be detected and suppressed instantly." Isabel paused, her smile unchanged.

"Your orientation and room assignment will begin immediately," she went on, pointing in turn at two doors on either side of the platform. "Those in permanent confinement, line up at the door to your right. Those of you in temporary confinement, line up on the left."

The confinees hesitated, until Dylan stood and took the first position at the left door. The rest of them lined up as directed, twelve to the left and three to the right.

The doors opened to another steel tunnel, and closed once they were inside.

❖ ❖ ❖

Dylan's cell measured two meters by four meters, with a cot, desk and chair, and a screen bolted to the wall, flashing a slide show of landscapes and animal photos. There was a window too small to crawl through set high into the concrete wall opposite the door. The only other fixtures were the steel sink and toilet in the corner.

The orientation lecture was short—the facility had few regulations. The confinees were to remain in their rooms at all times with the exception of meals, hygiene, Common Time, and reintegration therapy. Confinees were allowed in the outdoor courtyard—weather permitting—or the commissary in bad weather during Common Time, scheduled daily at two p.m. The commissary served meals at seven a.m., noon, and six p.m. Therapy took place daily at ten a.m. Schedules, Dylan learned, were *rigidly* enforced—there was no such thing as a grace period in confinement.

The confinees could choose from a range of entertainment, news, or instructive content on their wall screens. Dylan checked the listing and saw nothing that interested him—he was far too accustomed to daily VR sessions in an infinite variety of venues, and a 2D, non-interactive experience struck him as artificial. As he paged through the options however, one item eventually caught his eye: on request, he could access the collection of print books in the facility library.

❖ ❖ ❖

Dylan's first therapy session came on day two, in a windowless room containing two steel chairs facing each other and a table piled with VR gear. The therapist, a paunchy unkempt fifty-year-old man named Adolf, directed Dylan with one- and two-word commands: *Sit there! Belt! Gear!* Adolf watched with tiny eyes under enormous eyebrows as Dylan outfitted himself.

"*No!*" Adolf barked as Dylan put on the Belt. "Like this!" Adolf rearranged the Belt, opening and reattaching the closures, tugging it lower on Dylan's hips. He sat back and pointed. "See?"

"Sorry," Dylan mumbled. "I've never used one of these before."

"Hmmph," Adolf grunted.

Dylan slipped on the gear. The headset was well-used, with

deflated padding, and straps which held the visor loosely. As the reticle came up, Dylan recognized it as an older gen visor, lower-res than he was used to, with a sprinkling of bad pixels showing up as random black dots, or thin, black lines across the field of view.

"Nice gear," Dylan commented.

Adolf scowled. "Gear!"

Dylan pulled on the unarticulated headphones, which pressed his ears uncomfortably flat against his head. The gloves were frayed at the cuffs and too big for his hands.

The reticle converged. The room faded, transporting Dylan to a hacker venue, not unlike the one where the hacker Micah had given him the key-grabber. It had the same imperfect rendering—artifacts, pixelation, and bad deconfliction, with blurry avatars making contact and melting into grotesque multi-limbed monsters.

"What's this?" Dylan asked.

"Pay attention!" Adolf growled through the headphones.

Dylan stood alone in the center of the venue, one of twenty avatars scattered in small groups. He could hear the conversations, typical of hackers: *I can get you twenty keys, five hundred credits each—This shroud will work even in Worldstream venues—I need two coders to help with an app for a share of the take.*

"What am I supposed to do?" Dylan asked.

"Pay attention!"

Dylan moved toward a pair of avatars. He overheard them talking. One phrase got his attention: *Key-grabber.*

Dylan got closer. The two avatars looked at him.

"What's *your* malfunction, frobnitz?" asked one of them, a short, round avatar with two chins, wearing a sweater with broad zig-zags.

Dylan stopped short. "I heard…"

"Heard *what?*"

The avatar was shorter than Dylan, but heavier. Dylan wondered if he could take him, then realized it was a meaningless comparison, especially in a hacker venue outside the Worldstream.

"Nothing," Dylan replied, turning away.

"Are you looking for *this?*" The fat avatar held up a smooth, white, glossy disk, exactly like the one Micah had given him.

Dylan gaped. "Yes. Where did you get it?"

The fat man flipped the disk behind his back, grabbing it in mid-air. "This is contraband, you know. Get you in deep shit." He tossed the disk again and it hovered, spinning in a wobbly orbit around the avatar's head. Dylan reached for it.

Jagged blue streaks, like lightning, shot from the disk to Dylan's hand with a sizzling sound, followed by a loud *crack.*

"Jah damn!" Dylan shrieked as a pain like fire tore through his arm and into his chest. He jerked his hand away, cradling it with the other hand. The pain subsided, leaving his arm numb. He let go, and his arm fell limp to his side.

Dylan tore off the headset with his good hand.

"Gear!" Adolf shouted.

"Fuck you!" Dylan snapped.

Two agents in black entered. One of them pulled Dylan's arms behind him. The back of the steel chair dug into his biceps. The second agent jammed the gear onto Dylan's face.

"You won't like the consequences if you do that again," Adolf said menacingly, his first full sentence of the session.

The agent released Dylan, who massaged his arm. The numbness subsided, replaced by a dull ache.

Then the session resumed. Dylan transported from one venue to another, spanning a range of themes: more hacker venues, some social venues, and venues with abstract renderings, like Dylan's own blockchain crawler. In each venue, he faced a scenario in which he acted instinctively, reaching or touching or speaking, sometimes with no ill effects, and sometimes with another painful shock. After the first half-hour, Dylan was exhausted. At the end of an hour and a half, Dylan was incoherent. His entire body ached, and he was nauseous. An agent escorted him to his room, where he collapsed on his cot.

"Midday meal in twenty," the agent said before closing the door.

Dylan slept, waking just before noon. He jogged, arriving

at the commissary at three past twelve, where he was turned away for being late.

12

NOBLE TRAGEDIES

IF NOT FOR Common Time, Dylan would have cracked.

In good weather, confinees went outdoors, in a well-tended area quite unlike the dilapidated public parks in the cities: a grassy courtyard surrounded by trees, perfect for an impromptu soccer game; patio areas with tables and chairs, where they played cribbage and bridge with well-worn playing cards, and basketball and tennis courts available by reservation. Only the sound of drones patrolling the perimeter—bounded by a fence topped with razor wire—reminded the residents that they lived in a confinement facility.

Today was good weather.

Dylan sat alone at a table by a massive oak tree. Afternoon sun filtered through the leaves, dappling the ground. His memory of the past two weeks—daily therapy sessions, the times he'd refused and was manhandled into submission, missed meals and long, hunger-filled afternoons—had faded, temporarily purged from his mind by a passage in a book.

When these things unite in a man of superior natural force, with a globular brain and a ponderous heart; who has also by the stillness and seclusion of many long night-watches in the remotest waters, been led to think untraditionally and independently; receiving all nature's sweet or savage impressions fresh from her own virgin voluntary and confiding breast, and thereby to learn a bold and nervous lofty language—that man makes one in a whole nation's census—a mighty pageant creature, formed for noble tragedies.

"What's that you've got?"

Dylan looked up, shielding his eyes. The boy asking the question stood with the sun at his back, his face in shadow.

"It's a book."

As the boy sat down Dylan realized that he was about his age, with coffee-colored skin and curly, light-brown hair. He had dark eyes over high cheeks and full lips. His neck was slender and his body slim. He smiled, his face betraying the weariness shared by all the confinees who'd been in confinement more than a day.

The boy tilted his head. "What book?"

Dylan lifted the cover to show the title—*Moby Dick.*

"Is it good?"

Dylan nodded. "Yeah. Really good."

"What's it about?"

Dylan stared at the words. "It's about being obsessed."

The boy pressed his lips together, saying nothing.

"How long have you been here?" Dylan asked.

The boy looked off in the distance. "Three years. You?"

"Two weeks—wow—three *years?* What's your term?"

"I'm here for key theft."

"Key theft. Me, too. What's that—ten years?"

"Fifteen."

"*Fifteen?* Oh, Jah."

"Yeah. Second offense, so I got bumped. Level nine," Muhammad explained.

"Me, too. I was on probation."

"What's *your* term?"

Dylan looked down as he closed his book. "Five."

"Five years? Someone must've been looking out for you."

"My nana. She flipped some switches. She's a very important lady."

The boy shook his head. "She must be." He put out his hand. "I'm Muhammad."

"Dylan."

"Hey, Dylan."

"Hey."

The two boys glanced in all directions without making eye contact.

"Three years," Dylan repeated after a pause.

"Yeah."

"You've been in therapy all that time?"

Muhammad grinned. "Every fucking day."

"Oh, Jah," Dylan groaned. "I've been in it for two weeks and I'm already wiped out. Three *years!*"

"Then you haven't found the trick."

"The trick?"

Muhammad leaned closer. "Yeah, the *trick*. You gotta mung with the Belt."

"What? The Belt?"

"Sure. All that hand-zapping and ball-kicking and stomach-churning that makes therapy such a party? All that comes from the Belt."

"I get that, but *mung* with it? How?" Dylan asked.

"Real simple." Muhammad pulled the book toward him and turned it around, opening it to the first page. "*Call me Ishmael.*" He looked up. "Ishmael—the father of my people."

"That might have been a different Ishmael." Dylan pushed the book aside. "What about the Belt?"

"Oh. Well, you've probably noticed that the VR gear in the therapy chamber isn't exactly latest gen, right?"

"It's pretty shabby."

"Yeah. That goes for the Belt, too. If it's like mine, it's gen two, gen three at the latest."

"I don't know. Is that important?" Dylan asked.

"*Yeah* it's important. Early gen Belts have a little flaw in them that I hear they fixed in gen four."

"What flaw?"

"When you put on the Belt," Muhammad said, gesturing around his waist, "you attach closures on one side, right? Well, those closures aren't just to hold the Belt closed."

"They're not?"

"No. They make electrical contact. If the circuit's not

closed, the Belt doesn't function."

Dylan scratched his ear. "How does that help me?"

"You just misalign the closures. Offset them by a centimeter. It messes up the circuit—something about impedance. Anyway, all the sensations are massively reduced. You'll hardly feel the lightning."

"That won't work. My torture master Adolf is picky about how the Belt goes on. The first time I tried it on, he fussed all over it."

"Yeah? Has he done that lately?"

Dylan thought. "No. Actually, he hasn't."

"My guy did the same thing for the first few sessions. After I got into the program, he stopped checking. As long as I look shagged by the end of the session, he figures he did his job. And so did the Belt."

Dylan took a deep breath. Muscles in his chest and back that had been tense for weeks suddenly relaxed. He felt some of his energy returning. "Thanks, Muhammad. I'll try it."

"Be careful. One centimeter at least, but no more than two. They need to make *some* contact, or the diagnostic will raise an alarm. Then Adolf will get *really* picky."

A chime sounded from the facility.

"Recess over," Muhammad said. The two boys headed back inside.

"Muhammad, I'm really sorry about your term, especially when I got off so easy. Jah. Fifteen years."

Muhammad clapped Dylan on the back. "Don't sweat it, brother. Everyone gets what they deserve, in the end." He leaned close and lowered his voice. "Besides, I don't plan to spend even *one* more year in this place."

13

THE END OF THE BEGINNING

MUHAMMAD MARKED DYLAN'S first month with a party.

It was raining, so Common Time moved to the commissary. Dylan thought that Common Time held indoors was worse than useless. Outdoors, the confinees could decompress or recover from therapy, move and get their blood pumping, maybe find a small measure of privacy at a remote table or among the trees. But the commissary was only just big enough for every confinee to find a seat at a table. There was no room to move, even for simple exercises. Forget about privacy. For Dylan, indoor Common Time did nothing to relieve stress; instead, it focused and concentrated the stress, as if the pent-up discontent of every confinee in the commissary seeped into this sealed space, rising to suffocating levels. If attendance were not compulsory, Dylan would have passed the time alone in his cell, rather than take part in indoor Common Time.

But this day was different. Muhammad had charmed one of the commissary cooks into baking a cake. It wasn't a party-sized cake—four servings, maybe six—but a cake was such a novelty in confinement that it drew a crowd. Dylan laughed out loud when he saw it.

"Congratulations, my brother," Muhammad said, his wide, toothy grin showing how pleased he was with himself for having pulled it off. "The first year's the hardest."

"I've only been here a month," Dylan replied, with a grin almost as wide.

"So we're here to celebrate one month toward the end of the beginning."

"Wow, when you put it that way, it sounds like I'm practically back in the world!"

Dylan turned the cake around. It was covered with green frosting, with a white *D* on top. "How do we eat it? No utensils allowed outside of meal time.

Muhammad dug his fingers into the cake, tearing off a mouth-sized chunk. He held it to his mouth, pausing, looking at Dylan and tilting his head toward the cake.

"The caveman method," Dylan said, digging into the cake. He and Muhammad shoved it into their mouths, smearing frosting on their chins. They laughed through full mouths, spitting crumbs on the table.

"You just gonna eat that in front of us?" asked one of the confinees, a skinny Asian kid who looked a little older than Dylan.

"Help yourself, Nate," Muhammad replied. "First come, first served."

Nate and two other confinees dug out chunks and wolfed them down, leaving a residue of cake crumbs and frosting on the paper plate. Another confinee snatched the plate away, turning his back to the table to lick it clean. The rest grumbled and went back to their places.

"How did you get a freaking *cake?*" Dylan asked, licking frosting from his fingers and flicking crumbs off his shirt.

"You know that guy from the kitchen, the short, fat guy with man boobs?"

"Owen? He hates everyone."

"I sweet-talked him." Muhammad batted his eyelids.

Dylan laughed out loud. "Watch out, Hammad. He'll want something more than a shameless flirt for that cake."

"I can handle him." Muhammad leaned forward, resting his arms on the table. "So, Dylan. Your first month. Are you holding up?"

Dylan heaved a sigh as his shoulders fell. "I don't know. I'm okay, I guess. I'd have rastered out if you hadn't told me about the Belt trick."

"You are welcome, my brother. How're your acting skills?"

"I'm mastering my craft. Adolf the Dungeon Master is convinced I'm wasted by the end of each session."

"And he hasn't checked your closures?"

"Not once."

Muhammad nodded. The boys kept their eyes on the table without talking. A minute passed.

"What're you reading now?" Muhammad asked.

Dylan pulled a paperback from his pocket. "It's an old book. *A Clockwork Orange.*"

"Good title. What's it about?"

"Free will."

"Bro, what's it *about?*" Muhammad pressed.

Dylan smiled. "It's about this guy, Alex. He's a thug—he steals, rapes—but he's a teenager, younger than us. And he gets apprehended for murder and they put him in this treatment where he has to watch violent videos, and they give him a drug that makes him sick. So he gets conditioned, see? He can't do anything violent or he gets sick."

"Sounds like therapy."

"Yeah. Sounds a *lot* like therapy."

"You think they're taking away our free will?"

Dylan shrugged. "I wonder if we ever had free will to begin with."

"Huh? Sure we do. Free will's what makes us human."

"So, if they take away our free will, does that mean we're not human anymore?"

Muhammad bit his lip. "Not *as* human."

"But still kind of human." Dylan brushed cake crumbs to the edge of the table and onto the floor. "So free will can't be the *only* thing."

"It's the *main* thing."

"I don't know about that."

"What do *you* think? What's the big thing that makes us human?"

Dylan gripped Muhammad's hand. "Feel that?"

"Yeah. Your sweaty palm."

Dylan grinned. "How's it feel?"

"Wet."

"How many times have you touched someone's hand in VR?"

"That would be telling."

"Hammad, I'm serious."

Muhammad rolled his eyes. "I don't know what you're getting at. It feels like your hand."

"Does it feel the same as VR?"

"Yeah. It feels just exactly the same."

"But *is* it the same?"

Muhammad looked at Dylan's pale white hand, and at his own brown hand wrapped around it. He stared, trying to imagine that he was holding Dylan's hand in VR, the visual rendering clean and lifelike, his tactile gloves simulating the smoothness of his skin, the warm sweat, the pressure of Dylan's fingers as he gripped. And he *could* imagine it, even thinking for a moment that he'd lost himself in a VR venue, forgetting that it wasn't real, before remembering that it *was*.

Muhammad gripped tighter. He looked away from Dylan's hand, and into his eyes. "No," he whispered, "not the same."

Dylan let go of Muhammad's hand. "Look, I don't know that we're not part of some giant venue, and that everything we do isn't already programmed, and part of the program is to make us think we have a choice."

"Yeah, but you don't buy that."

"If it's true, then we're not human and we never were. We're code."

"I'm not code."

"How do you know?"

"I just know."

"*How?*"

Muhammad grabbed Dylan's hand. He squeezed it, not so hard that it was painful, but hard enough to make a point. "*This* is how I know."

Dylan squeezed back. "That's what I'm saying, Hammad. That's how I know I'm human. And when I can't tell VR from RL, that's when I stop being human."

Muhammad nodded. "You're a smart guy."

Dylan relaxed his grip and wiped his hand on his shirt. "It's not *that* sweaty. Is it?"

"It's pretty sweaty, bro."

The boys' eyes wandered around the room.

"Oh, hey," Muhammad said, "you know Nate, right?"

"The guy who stole my cake?"

"Yeah," Muhammad laughed. "He told me about what he was doing out in the world, before he got nabbed."

"Yeah, so?"

"He told me some hacks you might be able to use."

Dylan spread his arms. "In here? What am I going to do with a hack in this place?"

"You won't be here forever. Didn't you say you were stealing data when you were hacking the blockchain? You know, when you got on probation?"

"I wasn't *hacking* the blockchain. I was poking around. And I wasn't *stealing* anything. Borrowing, at worst."

"Whatever. Anyway, you told me about your man and how he's been cataloging all the security protocols for the Worldstream."

"Raúl."

"Yeah, him. Well, Nate says *he's* cataloged dozens, maybe a hundred."

"Is that a big number?"

"*I* don't know. But you were poking around when you set off an alarm, right?"

"A 'hair trigger' is what Raúl called it."

"There you go. You didn't know what you were dealing with. Faulty intel."

"And Nate has the answers?"

"He's got this catalog. Says he can provide access."

"Nothing I can do with it. Not in here." Dylan looked away. "You know what Raúl told me? He said even if you know all the protocols, they're useless if you don't know what you're doing."

"Maybe Nate knows."

"I doubt it. Raúl told me he spent his whole life figuring it out."

A chime ended Common Time. Tables and chairs skidded on the floor; four hundred confinees got to their feet. The horde moved toward the exits.

"I told Nate about your transgression," Muhammad said.

"I wish you hadn't done that."

"Sorry. So I should tell Nate you're not interested?"

Dylan looked at Muhammad's expectant face. "Yeah, tell him that. Like I said, they're worthless to me in here."

The boys shuffled along with the crowd.

"You know what else, Hammad?"

"What?"

"Even if I *could* do something with them, I'm not sure I'd want to."

"No?"

"No." Dylan riffled through the pages of his book. "VR just doesn't grab me like it used to."

14

Prisoner's Dilemma

"That's a long shot, Hammad."

Dylan and Muhammad sat at the most remote table in the courtyard, still forty meters away from the perimeter fence. Muhammad leaned closer.

"No, really. Watch."

The boys trained their eyes at one spot on the fence. Two drones approached from opposite directions.

"Wait for it," Muhammad whispered.

The drones passed each other at high speed.

"*Now.*"

Dylan counted, trying to make each count as close to a second as possible.

Eighteen…nineteen…twenty…

Two more drones approached the same spot.

"*Time,*" Muhammad said as the drones passed each other.

"Thirty-two," Dylan replied.

"Yeah. That's about right. More than thirty seconds. That's a long time."

"It's a short time."

Muhammad sat up, dropping his hands to the table. "Bro, we'll be through that fence and forty meters away before those drones come back."

"And then they'll spot us, and then Jahbulon'll tag us and our asses'll be right back in."

"No, no! Those drones are looking *inside*, not outside. They won't know we're gone until Common Time's over."

"Bullshit. You don't know that."

Muhammad grabbed Dylan's arm. "Let's take a walk."

They approached the fence, crossing the ten-meter exclusion limit.

"Here they come," Muhammad said.

The drones approached as they had before, stopping a few meters apart, and pivoting toward the boys. Two cameras and four taser magazines zeroed in on them.

"Confinees," said two perfectly synchronized voices, one from each drone, "you are within the exclusion zone. Step back immediately."

Dylan walked back, pulling Muhammad with him. The drones hovered until the boys had retreated to a distance of thirty meters, then turned and resumed their patrol.

"I've been watching their panning pattern," Muhammad whispered. "Each drone only has one camera. When it wants a closer look at something, it pans away from the fence—but always *inside*, not outside."

"Bro," Dylan said, furrowing his brow, "those are wide-angle cameras. They have a two-seventy field of view. They don't have to *pan* outside to *see* outside."

Muhammad tilted his head, looking at Dylan down his nose. "Yeah?"

"Yeah."

They stood staring at the fence as the drones passed again.

"But…" Dylan trailed off.

"But what?"

Dylan pointed discreetly. "That stand of bushes there. About ten meters out. See?"

Muhammad looked. "Wouldn't take long to reach that cover."

"A couple seconds."

"We hide, wait for the drones to pass. Buys another thirty seconds. We could be two hundred meters away."

The boys looked at each other. Dylan burst out laughing.

"Bro, look at that fence! What are we going to do? Bite through it?"

"We'll get some wire cutters."

Dylan walked a few meters toward the facility, then glanced back. Muhammad hadn't moved.

"Hammad, come on. Common Time's almost over."

Muhammad walked slowly over to Dylan. "I could get the cutters."

"Forget it, Hammad. Even if we make it out, then what? Where could we go that the All-Seeing Eye wouldn't find us?"

Muhammad toed the ground. "I guess."

The chime sounded, marking the end of Common Time.

"It's fun to think about though," Dylan said.

"Yeah," Muhammad mumbled. "More fun than another twelve years on *this* side of the fence."

It was another rainy day, another Common Time in the commissary. Dylan found Muhammad leaning against the wall, hands in his pockets, eyes darting left and right.

"Hammad."

Muhammad faced forward, as if Dylan weren't there. "I'm going out," he whispered.

"Hammad, stop munging around."

"I'm serious, bro. First outdoor CT."

Dylan poked Muhammad's shoulder. Muhammad looked at him through narrowed eyes. "I got some cutters," he whispered.

"You did not."

"I did. From that maintenance guy with the mustache."

"Armand. Why would he give you wire cutters?"

"Not wire cutters. These are big-ass bolt cutters. Go through that fence like a spider web."

Muhammad's eyes were shifting everywhere, as though he was on the lookout for civils.

"Did you sweet-talk him? Like you did Owen for the cake?"

Muhammad dropped his eyes to the floor. "Something like that."

"So, Armand handed you over a big pair of bolt cutters, just like that. What'd you do, stick 'em in your underwear?"

"He's going to hide them. By the fence, right at that spot near the bushes."

Dylan looked at Muhammad as he scanned the commissary, until Muhammad turned toward him and their eyes met. The boy was serious, and Dylan knew it.

"You can't do it," Dylan said.

"Can and will. Are you with me?"

Dylan felt his chest tighten. He gripped Muhammad's arm. "You'll be caught."

"Look, bro, I'm going with you, or without you."

"Where are you gonna go? Hammad, seriously, there's *no place* you can go that Jahbulon can't find you."

Now Muhammad turned his whole body toward Dylan. He pulled at his shirt. "This thing's not connected. Not my shirt, not my pants, not my shoes and socks…not even my underwear."

"You don't know that."

"I *do* know it. Armand told me."

"Armand again."

Muhammad turned away, his back to the wall in a casual pose.

"Armand knows all the maintenance procedures," he said. "Every one of the maintenance staff has to cover for the rest, so they all know each other's routines. And he says there're no RFID readers, no location beacons, nothing like that in the whole facility. They think nobody can get through the perimeter, so they don't bother. If we're out there, and we're not connected, no Jahbulon is gonna find us."

"And you believe him?"

Muhammad's head snapped toward Dylan. "Are you in or out?"

Dylan looked away, scanning the commissary. Confinees sat at the tables, some playing cards, others talking or arguing, but most sitting idly, not even looking around, their blank eyes staring at the walls and ceiling. Some of them he knew, but didn't consider any of them friends—except for Hammad.

The chime sounded. Confinees rose wearily and shuffled

toward the exits.

"Don't do it," Dylan said.

"First outdoor CT. I'll let you know ahead of time."

Muhammad pushed ahead, leaving Dylan standing alone.

❖ ❖ ❖

It rained for three days straight before Common Time moved outdoors. Dylan took his usual spot at a table near the woods, forty meters from the fence, engrossed in a copy of *Slaughterhouse Five*. He looked up when a shadow fell across the pages.

Muhammad stood between him and the sun. "I'm going," he said.

Dylan looked back at the fence, then at his friend. "Now?"

"As soon as the drones pass. Right where we planned it."

"Where *you* planned it."

"Are you coming?"

Dylan's mouth went dry. He stared at the book, but the words didn't register. He forgot to breathe.

"I...Hammad...I can't."

Muhammad nodded as he looked into the distance. "Fine. See you someday."

Dylan heard the high-pitched buzz of the drones approaching. Muhammad moved toward the fence, breaking into a run as the sound of the drones dropped in pitch.

Dylan kept staring at the book. One line seemed to stand out, as if it glowed:

> *Among the things Billy Pilgrim could not change were the past, the present, and the future.*

Dylan looked at the fence. Muhammad was crouched at its base, searching the brush.

Dylan closed his book, stuffed it in his back pocket, and sprinted for the fence.

❖ ❖ ❖

Muhammad looked up for no more than a second as Dylan approached.

"The cutters are here somewhere. Help me look."

Dylan crawled along the fence, searching in the long grass. His hands fell on one steel rod, then another. He picked up the thing—a vicious industrial-grade tool, which looked like it could cut through the bars of a prison cell.

Muhammad grinned. "Give it here," he said, taking the tool from Dylan's hands.

Muhammad positioned the cutters to snip through the wire mesh and squeezed. The blades of the cutter barely moved.

"Harder," Dylan urged in a hoarse whisper.

Muhammad squeezed until the veins popped in his forehead.

"Let me," Dylan said, shoving Muhammad aside. He pressed the handles together and the cutters shook as he put all his strength into them.

"It's not working," Muhammad whispered. "Why isn't it working?"

Dylan let go of the handles, panting with exertion. The fence, an alloy of tungsten and vanadium, showed not even a dent.

"Let's get out of here," Dylan wheezed.

Muhammad grabbed the cutters and tried again, squeezing so hard that Dylan was certain his arms would break.

Dylan's head snapped erect as the drones approached.

"Hammad, let's *go*." Dylan grabbed his friend's arm, but Muhammad pulled free, redoubling his efforts at cutting through the fence.

The drones approached at full speed until one, then the other, pitched backward and came to a full stop, hovering in place. Four taser magazines pivoted toward the boys.

From the facility came a sound that neither Dylan nor Muhammad had heard before, a horn blaring staccato blasts, followed by a voice from three directions: "*Perimeter breach in progress, section 29. All confinees return to the facility immediately.*"

Six agents in black shot toward them at a dead run.

Muhammad dropped the cutters and ran, with Dylan close behind. They only made it ten meters, about as far from the fence as the stand of bushes on the outside, before taser rounds struck them and they went to the ground in shuddering heaps.

❖ ❖ ❖

Dylan didn't know this place. After seven weeks in confinement, he was certain he had seen every part of the facility, but he'd never been in this room. The walls were painted a cheerful yellow, as were the single steel door on the far side of the table and the two chairs in front of him. The only other piece of furniture was the metal chair he was strapped to, bolted to the floor.

His throat was dry, and his head ached. The taser impact points on his back and thigh throbbed. The ten minutes since he'd been roughly escorted to the room and strapped to the chair passed like ten hours before the door finally opened and two women entered.

One was short and the other tall, both dressed in the same black uniform as Isabel, the orientation officer at his arrival. Unlike Isabel, they weren't smiling; also unlike Isabel, they wore opaque augmented reality visors, hiding their eyes, making them look like malevolent cyborgs. The tall one stood while the other sat, her hands folded in front of her.

"Dylan," the sitting one said, "do you understand your transgression?"

Dylan nodded.

"*Speak!*" the tall officer barked.

"Yes, citizen officer, I understand. I attempted to breach the perimeter."

"There are few transgressions more serious than this one."

"I'm sorry," Dylan replied.

"*Silence!*" the tall officer shouted.

The short officer flinched. She paused, her head moving slightly left to right, as if she were reading. "Your record up to this point has been flawless—exemplary, in fact." She paused again. "So this incident is inexplicable." She paused.

Dylan looked from one visored face to the other.

"*Speak!*" snapped the tall one.

"It was an impulse," Dylan replied.

"An impulse." The officer read the text scrolling in her

visor. "We discovered the cutting tool at the spot. We know you didn't have it at the start of Common Time, so it must have been planted beforehand. This shows advance planning, not an impulsive act."

"I don't have an explanation."

"Did your friend, Muhammad, make the arrangements? Did he persuade you to participate? Is that what happened?"

"We were in it together."

The two officers glanced at each other. "Muhammad didn't devise this plan by himself and urge you to join him? And he didn't persuade one of the maintenance staff to hide the tool by the fence?"

Dylan looked at the officers, unable to judge their mood behind their visors.

"Yes, he got the tool. I told him to. It was my plan. He didn't want to do it, but I talked him into it."

The officers exchanged another glance.

"Dylan, Muhammad has already confessed that it was *his* plan, that he'd obtained the tool in exchange for sexual favors, and that *you* were the reluctant one."

"Sexual favors?"

"Yes, Dylan—the same way he persuaded one of our kitchen staff to bake you a cake."

Dylan's head fell back. He closed his eyes and exhaled in a breathy sigh. His throat closed up as his head fell forward again.

"He's trying to protect me," Dylan choked. "It was my idea, all mine."

"I see," the sitting officer said. She kept reading the scroll. "Dylan, your term was five years at the time of your admission. Because of this transgression, your status has changed. Your term has been extended by ten years. You will continue in therapy for the duration of your term, after which you will be reintegrated into society."

The officer stood. "The orderly will be here shortly to escort you to your cell."

They turned to leave.

"Wait," Dylan said, "what about Hammad?"

The officers turned back. "Muhammad's status has also changed. His confinement is now permanent."

"*Permanent?* But…why didn't…why aren't…"

"Why aren't *you* permanent?"

Dylan nodded.

"Under normal circumstances, we *would* have confined you permanently for this transgression. But we were given alternative directions. Someone on the outside likes you."

15

Hang in There, Kid

"There will be some changes today."

Adolf stood with his thumbs in his belt, hands snug under the belly spilling over the top of his pants. Dylan's escorts removed his restraints and left, closing the steel door with a clang.

Adolf rummaged in the pile of VR gear on the table. He held up the Belt. It looked different—shinier, cleaner, its edges unfrayed. Adolf grinned, small eyes peering out between woolly eyebrows and fleshy cheeks.

"Looky, looky. A nice, new, gen four Belt. You're only the second confinee to use it."

Dylan dropped wearily into the chair. He took the Belt from Adolf and put it around his waist. As he felt for the closures, he took a sharp breath. The hair on his head rose.

"These closures…" he began.

"They're different." Adolf lifted Dylan's shirt. The closures were two perfectly mated, molded parts, impossible to misalign.

"Low impedance," Adolf said close to Dylan's ear in a breathy, obscene voice. "Maximum fidelity. The last guy said it was the most intense he'd ever felt. They had to carry him out." Adolf connected the closures, drawing them snug. He checked the fit, then pulled Dylan's shirt down and sat back in his chair, lacing his fingers over his belly. "Yes. *Very* intense. *Very* therapeutic."

Dylan put on the rest of the gear. His headphones chimed

as the reticle converged.

"Two hours today," Adolf's voice said in the headphones.

"Ninety minutes!" Dylan protested.

Adolf chuckled. It was the first time Dylan had ever heard him laugh.

"What's so funny?"

"Your recent transgression, my young friend. Did you think life would go on? No changes? No *consequences*?"

"You added ten years to my term."

"*And* we've upped your therapy session. It'll be longer—two hours."

"I'll miss lunch."

"Today you will. Tomorrow we'll start a half-hour earlier. Should leave you plenty of time to get to the commissary."

"Wonderful."

Dylan was transported to a dance venue, crowded with teens under four orbiting platforms where a retro metal band played. Dylan thought it looked familiar—the same layout, same colorfully dressed teens, and same entertainment booths, including one with a scrolling marquis—*ARMY MARKSMAN…ENEMY COMBATANTS…KILL OR BE KILLED*. Dylan's mouth went dry. It wasn't *like* his dance venue; it was the *same* dance venue.

"I've been here," Dylan said.

"Pay attention!" Adolf shouted.

Dylan wandered around the periphery. As he passed each staging vestibule, he peered in, expecting, perhaps hoping, to see the Indian man. He'd made it almost all the way around when a message appeared in front of him.

Lo-res weirdo makes the venue. Where've you been, weirdo?

Dylan looked in all directions for the sender. He spotted her at the edge of the crowd, ten meters away, in an illuminated outfit glowing in primary colors, shifting from red to yellow, and green to blue.

"Reply."

Mia, what are you doing here? How did you get here?

The girl put a hand on her hip, rolling her eyes.

How do you think? Jah, you are weird.

Dylan teleported to a spot directly in front of her, so close that she stepped back.

"Are you really here?" he asked, putting his hand on her arm.

Mia pulled away, turning sideways and looking at him over her shoulder. "Like you care," she said.

Dylan studied her face. She was exactly as he remembered her.

"Sorry, Mia, I didn't…wait—how long do you think I've been gone?"

"You ought to know."

"C'mon, Mia, how long?"

"Weeks—ever since you ditched me for that little brown guy." She crossed her arms and lifted her chin. "You could've told me you're gay."

"Gay…no, nothing like that. I've been out of commission, that's all," Dylan replied.

Mia shrugged. "Not serious, I hope."

He checked out the venue again, noticing every detail. If this wasn't the same dance venue, it was an exact duplicate. He turned back to Mia, lowering his head and looking at her from under his eyebrows. "I'm past it."

Mia's eyes wandered. "Were you sick?"

"No, not sick. My body is fine."

She looked at him with narrowed eyes. "Your head, then."

"I think, yeah, maybe."

"Maybe your head?"

"My head, my heart."

"Oh, your *heart*."

"Mm-hmm. My heart. It wants something. My head doesn't know what my heart wants."

Mia's expression went blank, then she sneered. "Jah, you are *so* weird."

Dylan stepped closer. "I won't say I'm normal. If you want to call me *weird*, I won't tell you different."

"You throw me away for some guy, disappear for weeks, then raster in talking like a crazy person. What do *you* call it?"

"All greatness is but disease."

"Oh, now you're *great.*"

Dylan closed the gap between them, his lips almost on hers.

"Yes," he whispered.

Mia flinched as Dylan approached, then stood her ground. She closed her eyes as their lips touched.

It felt to Dylan like getting hit in the mouth with a steel pipe. His head jerked backwards, mouth flying open, soundless at first, followed by a shriek. His muscles lost control, as if he'd been tasered. He hovered on the brink of consciousness, thoughts scrambled, until the pain subsided and his vision returned. He found himself alone in the white staging venue.

"How do you like the new gear?" Adolf asked, his voice barely penetrating the ringing in Dylan's ears.

Dylan took short, sharp breaths. The spot on his lips where he'd kissed Mia still ached; pain radiated through his head.

"Just another hour and fifty minutes to go," Adolf added.

❖ ❖ ❖

Dylan slept through lunch, then through Common Time, waking up just in time to make it to the commissary for the evening meal. He sat at a table near the wall, head hanging over his plate, taking just a few bites before the nausea rose up in his belly. He stifled a gag as he pushed the tray away.

"You gonna eat them potatoes?" an older confinee asked. Dylan shook his head.

The old man grinned a toothless grin as he scraped the potatoes onto his plate.

"Bro, you look half dead."

Dylan looked up to see Muhammad silhouetted against the ceiling lights. Muhammad pulled up a chair to the corner of the table.

"I guess you heard about my term," he said.

"I'm sorry," Dylan mumbled.

"Sorry? You can't be apologizing to *me.* *I'm* the mastermind of our little jailbreak." His smile was thin. "Our *stupid* little jailbreak."

"You're permanent."

Muhammad straightened himself. "Yep. Lifetime achievement award. I spent some time with the other permanents this morning. Nice bunch. A little older than me, but they're all right." Muhammad put his hand on Dylan's back. "Word is they're using gen four for therapy now. Is it rough?"

Dylan nodded.

"Now *I'm* sorry." He kneaded Dylan's shoulder. "The one good thing about permanent status is, no therapy. No *hope* of ever getting out of this playpen, but no daily torture."

"They upped my term," Dylan said. "Ten years on top of my five."

"I heard." Muhammad put his hand behind Dylan's head, pulling him close, until their foreheads touched. "My fault. Put the blame on me."

◈ ◈ ◈

Dylan endured a week of daily therapy sessions before he reached an equilibrium between resignation and dread—a dull, persistent, zombie-like state. Each day he sat alone at Common Time, until Muhammad came to sit with him, the two boys exchanging a few words before sitting in silence. Dylan had stopped reading.

◈ ◈ ◈

"Gear!"

Dylan pulled on the Belt, carefully attached the closures, then put on the headset and gloves, going as slowly as possible without antagonizing Adolf, a pace he'd determined from experience. The staging venue came into view.

The venue dissolved to a classroom. The students were younger than Dylan, mere children by comparison. The professor stood at the head of the class, lecturing on the fundamentals of analytical geometry. A three-dimensional figure hovered in space, a cylinder centered on three axes.

"Dylan," the professor called out, "we see here the equation for this surface in Cartesian coordinates. Please restate it in cylindrical coordinates."

Dylan stared at the figure rotating slowly in space, and the equation hovering to one side. He was sure he knew the answer but couldn't recall it.

"I don't know, prof," Dylan mumbled.

"Speak up!"

"I said *I don't know.*"

The professor teleported to Dylan's side. A ruler materialized in his hand. The professor swung it, striking Dylan on the bridge of his nose. The pain was excruciating, far worse than such a blow would hurt IRL. Dylan barely flinched.

"It's a simple problem," the professor shouted close to Dylan's ear. "The equation for a cylinder in cylindrical coordinates."

"I don't know it."

The professor raised his hand again. Dylan closed his eyes and braced for impact.

It never came.

"You'd better yell like you feel it."

The familiar voice wasn't the professor's. Dylan opened his eyes. He was back in the staging venue, sitting across from a tall man with a thin face and silver hair.

"Raúl?"

"Don't talk. Your dungeon master can hear you. This'll have to be a one-sided conversation."

Dylan nodded.

"Okay. I'll make this short. I'm busting you outta here. I can't go into detail, but I'll lay it out for you over the next few days."

Dylan mouthed the word *how.*

"How? Did I get in here? It took some finesse, let me tell you. I've been trying to find you for weeks, ever since the alarms went off and they tubed you to this dude ranch. Then yesterday I got a clue. They started probing your old haunts for therapy material. They left tracks. I followed them here and tunneled through the firewall." Raúl leaned forward, putting a hand on Dylan's knee. "You gotta hang in a little while longer." He stood up. "Jah, kid, you look terrible. Nila, *vamonos!*"

Raúl vanished. The classroom venue rastered into view. The ruler rushed toward Dylan's face in a blur, knocking his head to the side, the pain exploding in his brain with a burst of light.

16

Perimeter Breach

A few tables were reserved for the old-timers—not a formal rule, but everyone knew. The temporaries treated permanent confinees with deference, especially those who had served for decades. As time went on, Muhammad hung more with the perms and less with the temps. *Might as well get used to it,* he thought.

Their game was four-handed cribbage. Muhammad's cards were good—two fives, a ten and a four, with a six turned up. He'd tossed a jack in the crib. His partner Vic, a perm with twenty-two years in the facility, nodded as Muhammad led with the four, the player to his left pegging two with a pair, then Vic scoring six with another four. The opposing player scored two more with a three. Muhammad smiled as he played his five for three more points.

"Hammad."

"Can it wait?" Muhammad asked dismissively. "I'm playing cards, and I'm winning."

"Hammad."

Muhammad glanced over his shoulder. Dylan stood behind him with the sun in his face. The dull, hopeless look was gone from his eyes, replaced by an intense gaze—his slack expression had turned into clenched-jaw determination.

"Vic," Muhammad said, "I gotta go."

Vic's mouth dropped open as he sat up straight. "You can't leave in the middle of a hand! Not when we're fixing to skunk these bastards."

"Sorry." Muhammad handed his cards to the man standing beside him. "Angel can play my cards."

He rose from the table, leaving Vic fuming.

"Come here," Dylan said under his breath. The boys put some distance between themselves and the squabbling cribbage players.

"What?" Muhammad asked.

"I'm getting out of here," Dylan whispered.

"Bro, you can't."

"I want you to come with me."

Muhammad looked back at the table of perms. Vic was waving his arms and cursing.

"Is that your future?" Dylan asked. "Sixty years of card games?"

Muhammad looked at the ground and rubbed his lip. "I listen to them talking, you know? They tell me all the stories of guys who came here, lived their lives. The guys who died here."

"Are they happy stories?"

"No. But they also told me about the perms who tried to get out. They *all* failed."

"You haven't heard my plan yet."

Muhammad took hold of Dylan's arm. "I want you to think about something. We got caught, and they bumped your term ten years. They made me *permanent*. If we try again, and we're caught, where do they go from there? What more can they do to us?"

"They'll make *me* permanent," Dylan replied.

"Yeah, they'll do that, but what about me? I'm already a perm."

"They can't do anything more to you."

"That's where your wrong. There's a *lot* more they can do. That's what the old-timers told me. Remember how I said that the only good thing about being permanent is no therapy?"

Dylan looked back at the table. Four confinees laid down cards in turn, each pegging their score. A dozen more confinees stood in a circle, watching.

"They'll put you back in therapy?"

"There was a perm—his name was Lucas—who tried to bust out. He was young, like us. He got caught. Then he did two hours of therapy a day for ten years. Ten years, almost exactly, before they found Lucas in his cell with his wrists slashed. He used a knife he stole from the commissary— sharpened it on the concrete wall for a week. Lucas wasn't the only one to check out, but he has the record—ten years. All the rest of them found a way to off themselves *way* sooner than that."

Dylan pointed to a low building, away from the main facility. "You know what that is?"

"Offices, I heard," Muhammad replied.

Dylan nodded. "Yeah, they've got some offices there. But they also have a crematorium. Whether you kill yourself or die naturally, *that's* where you'll end up."

Muhammad pushed his face a few centimeters from Dylan's. "I don't...I don't know."

"Hammad, I think you *do* know."

Muhammad got closer, rounding his shoulders, as if to make a private space with his body. "When?"

"Soon."

Muhammad looked back at the table. Vic was standing now, shouting across the table at Angel. The other two players studied their cards. Onlookers stood motionless, showing neither interest nor amusement.

Muhammad turned back to Dylan.

"What's the plan?"

❖ ❖ ❖

"Will you get your head in the fucking game?" Vic shouted.

"What?" Muhammad said.

Vic pointed to the last four plays, reaching across the table to stab the cards with his finger. "Three. Five. Two. Four. That's a run. Four points. Peg 'em."

Muhammad stared at the cards for a long moment before making the connection. "Oh, yeah," he said as he moved the peg.

"What's wrong with you?"

Muhammad glanced around as discreetly as possible. Dylan was nowhere to be seen. "Something on my mind is all."

"Get your mind on the *cards*. Jah, we're getting our tails waxed."

"Four for eighteen and a pair," said the perm to Muhammad's left.

"Nine for twenty-seven," Vic replied.

"Two for twenty-nine."

"Go," said Muhammad.

"Two for thirty-one and a pair for four."

"Jah!" Vic slapped his head. He glared at Muhammad, who merely shrugged. Then he looked past Vic toward Dylan, now thirty meters' distant. Dylan nodded.

"Vic, I'm not feeling it today," Muhammad said, laying down his cards.

"Obviously."

Muhammad pushed away from the table. "Angel, take my spot, okay?"

"No way," the player to Muhammad's left objected. "The hand's not over and that little sneak's seen *all* our cards."

"Muhammad, finish the hand," Vic ordered.

But Muhammad was already twenty meters away.

❖ ❖ ❖

Dylan and Muhammad walked to the spot near the fence where drones had tasered them before. They kept well away from the ten-meter limit.

"What happens now?" Muhammad asked.

"Wait for it."

Drones approached on their surveillance route, passed each other at high speed and buzzed away.

Muhammad looked at Dylan, who was impassive.

"Now what?"

"Wait for it."

The Doppler-shifted sound of drones approaching suddenly dropped in pitch. The drones halted, hovering in place, panning their cameras toward the boys. Green lights flashed in a steady pattern.

"Now?" Muhammad asked.

Dylan held out his arm to hold him back and shook his head *no*.

Muhammad turned, startled by the sound of a klaxon, followed by the announcement, *"Perimeter breach in progress, section 61. All confinees return to the facility immediately."*

"Jah!" Muhammad shouted. He made for the facility when Dylan grabbed his arm with both hands.

"Stop," Dylan said firmly. *"Look."*

Confinees moved toward the facility in a mass, while six agents in black ran toward the point of the perimeter breach —at the *opposite* side of the compound.

"This way," Dylan said, pulling Muhammad toward the fence.

The drones' cameras panned to follow their movements as the boys approached the fence. Muhammad got to his knees, looking for a tool to cut through the fence, until he felt Dylan's hand on his shoulder.

"Hammad, out there."

A figure dressed in camo from head to foot broke from the stand of bushes and sprinted to the fence, kneeling on the other side. Two eyes looked through a narrow slot in the camo balaclava, a pair of black goggles perched above.

"Get back," a muffled voice ordered from under the head covering.

"Who are..." Muhammad began.

"No time for Q & A. *Get back.*"

Camo reached a gloved hand into a side pack and pulled out a device like a small-bore pistol, with a pointed end, surrounded by rings of metal. It was tinged yellow and blue, as if it had been subjected to intense heat. A tube ran from the handle into the pack. With a twist of a knob on the butt end, the pistol made a sound like steam escaping from a broken pipe.

"Plasma torch," the muffled voice explained. "Only way to cut through this fucking alien alloy." The opaque goggles came down as a white flame ten centimeters long burst from the muzzle of the pistol with the intensity of the sun. Dylan and Muhammad slammed their eyes shut, the image of the flame fading slowly from their retinas. The torch made a sound like sizzling bacon, with a brief *zap* as it cut through each wire of the fence. Ten seconds later the sound stopped. Dylan and Muhammad opened their eyes.

Camo pulled away a section of fence, leaving a hole barely big enough for one boy at a time. "C'mon. Those drones'll wake up any second. And keep clear of the edges—the wires are still damn hot."

Muhammad scrambled through the opening and Dylan followed. The three of them ran, diving into the bushes just as the drones resumed their surveillance.

"Wait," Camo ordered. Two drones approached. "Ready…" The drones converged and flew on. *"Now!"*

They sprinted down a hill and into the woods, ducking low-hanging branches, splashing through a shallow creek to a clearing, where they found a vehicle unlike anything Dylan or Muhammad had seen IRL, although it resembled something Dylan had once experienced in a venue from ages past, when it was legal to drive vehicles like this on sand hills: an open-frame, fossil-fueled buggy.

Camo hopped in the driver's seat. The vehicle roared to life with the push of a button, emitting a low, rumbling sound.

"One of you will have to crouch in stowage," Camo yelled. "I was only expecting one passenger."

"Sorry about that," Dylan shouted. He took the shotgun spot as Muhammad crammed himself into the space behind the seats. "I couldn't leave Hammad behind."

The vehicle lurched forward, speeding away from the confinement facility into open country. Dylan leaned out, letting the air hit him full in the face, hair fluttering, eyes blinking against the wind. The air smelled clean, like grass and rain.

"If that's Hammad in the back, then you must be Dylan," the driver said.

"Yeah," Dylan confirmed. "And who are you?"

The driver pulled off the goggles and balaclava, to reveal a striking woman with bronze skin, long, black hair, sharp features, and eyes of chocolate brown. In her camo gear, Dylan thought she looked like a warrior.

"I'm Naia," she replied.

"Where are we going?" Muhammad shouted.

Naia looked over her shoulder at the boy in the cargo area and smiled.

"I'm taking you to your new home, Hammad."

17

ORWELL

THEY DROVE FOR seven hours. The rush of air and the rising and falling rumble of the engine pounding Dylan's and Muhammad's ears made conversation impossible. After a few shouted questions to Naia, her answers lost in the wind, the boys were silent, mesmerized by the passing landscape.

The route took them along highways once paved, now cracked and pitted. Road signs stood in disrepair; names, distances, and directions now unreadable—*Des M—n-s 1-4—Mi—e-pol-s 3-6—H-stor-c Si-e—Fo-d Gas L-dg-ng*. They passed fields and farmland, row on row of cloned crops stretching to the horizon, robot harvesters looming in the distance like Brobdingnagian alien crafts emerging from the afternoon haze. Where roads became impassable, they drove across open pastures, forded streams, and skirted woods overgrown with impenetrable foliage, the sights, smells, sounds, and sensations as real as the most sophisticated VR venue rendered in highest res, using the latest gen gear.

As the sun set, Naia turned onto a gravel-covered road, in surprisingly good repair. The headlamps of the buggy lit the way. Animals crossed in front of them, eyes shining in the lights—a rabbit, a raccoon, a squirrel. Night fell more deeply as the buggy sped down the road, trailing a cloud of dust.

Naia slowed down and smiled at Dylan.

"What?" he asked.

"There."

Two spots appeared in the distance, then four, then four

more. Naia crept forward until the owners of the glowing eyes fell entirely within the beam.

Naia stopped a few meters from the deer, a buck with antlers. The animal stood his ground, rack rising from his head like a crown. At the highest point of his antlers, the buck was more than two meters tall. A smaller buck trailed him, and two does.

Naia turned off the engine. They heard country sounds— chirping crickets, thrumming bullfrogs, calling owls. The deer herd stood motionless for a few seconds before the big buck moved on, followed by his entourage. More deer crossed. The boys counted twelve in all.

"Jah, they're beautiful," Dylan whispered.

"You've seen deer before, haven't you?" Naia asked.

"Not IRL," Dylan replied.

"But in VR?"

"Yes."

"So, what's the difference? They look the same, in VR or IRL."

"It's not the same," Muhammad chimed in.

"Oh," Naia said with a smile, as she started the buggy and eased it forward.

❖ ❖ ❖

They topped a hill, then descended into a shallow valley. A grid of lights appeared in the distance.

"Is that it?" Dylan asked.

"That's it," Naia confirmed. "Orwell."

The buggy approached the outskirts of the village, passing single-story houses with windows glowing yellow. Some homes had porches, where people sat, waving to the buggy as it passed. The houses got closer together as they went further into town, until the buggy turned onto a street lined with vehicles of all description, from hacked bicycles with engines mounted on welded platforms, to long, low machines with fat black tires, to monstrosities which looked like rolling houses.

Naia parked the buggy in front of a brick building; above its door the words *Community Savings & Loan* were chiseled in stone. The door—made of wooden slats—was propped open, allowing the light from inside to spill onto the sidewalk. When Naia shut off the engine, Dylan and Muhammad heard a commotion, like the sound of machinery mixed with the voices of people shouting over the noise.

Naia and the boys got out of the buggy. Naia stretched, working out the kinks from seven hours in one position. She twisted her neck with an audible *pop*.

"C'mon boys," she said with a wave. "There's someone here who wants to meet you." Dylan and Muhammad followed her into the building.

The entire first floor was open space, with a grid of load-bearing brick columns. It was crammed with all manner of machinery, motorcycles and other vehicles in pieces, wood projects in various stages of completion, and plants in glass cases under glowing panels. To the back were glass-walled rooms housing robotic mechanisms two meters tall, their arms moving in chaotic patterns as three-dimensional objects took shape on their platforms, one thin layer at a time. A screen blocked one corner from view, the walls behind it lit up with blue-white flashes, synchronized with the crackling of an arc welder. A high-pitched whine persisted under the cacophony, the sound of rotating machinery, rising in volume and dropping in pitch as their blades bit into planks of wood. The air smelled of sawdust, ozone, and machine oil.

"What's going on?" Dylan shouted to Naia.

"Thursday night, that's what," Naia shouted back. She pointed. "That guy, there."

He was a short man, with sleek, short black hair, dressed in a t-shirt and well-worn jeans, patched on the knees and seat. The man fed a long piece of wood through a growling machine, walked around and held the plank as it came out. He set the board on end and ran his hand over its surface, then sighted along its edge, as if to search for any deviation from a perfect plane.

Finally he noticed Naia, pulling out his earplugs as she approached. Naia pointed at the boys; a brief look of confusion came over the man's face, followed by recognition and a nod. He set the plank aside and walked toward them.

"Dylan," the man said as he approached, looking from Dylan to Muhammad and back, settling finally on Dylan and pointing. "I'm guessing that's you."

The man had a day's growth of beard on a deeply tanned face, well-muscled arms, shoulders bulging under the sleeves of his tee, and his forearm bore an artful tattoo of a globe of the Earth, made of glass, the words *Vitreous Orb* in elaborate script overlaying it.

"Yes," Dylan answered.

"Then who the hell is this?"

"This is Muhammad," Dylan replied. "I brought him with me."

The man scowled. "*That* wasn't part of the plan."

"I was torching the fence while drones were ticking away over our heads," Naia explained. "It wasn't a good time to argue over the passenger list."

"Shit."

Naia grinned. "Relax, Jackson. They'll be good."

"That's your name?" Dylan asked. "Jackson?"

Jackson pulled his lips back as he regarded Dylan. "Yeah." He ran fingers through his hair and looked at Naia. "They'll have to share quarters," he said simply, then turned and walked away.

"Wait!" Dylan called. Jackson stopped and looked back. "What is this place? What do you do here?"

Jackson sneered. "You can't tell? We're making stuff."

❖ ❖ ❖

Dylan and Muhammad sat at a table in a kitchen, lit by an overhead panel which glowed the color of a candle's flame. Naia stood at the stove, tending a pot of boiling water and a slab of meat on a grill. The smell of the meat mixed with the aroma of bread baking in the oven was intoxicating.

Naia dropped four ears of corn in the pot, then turned the meat one final time.

"Get yourself some plates," she said, with a tilt of her head toward the cupboard. "They're up there. And butter in the refrigerator."

Dylan set the table, while Muhammad fetched a large brown crock filled with pale yellow butter. Naia served each boy a thick slice of meat, then pulled two ears of corn dripping from the pot and laid them on the plates.

Dylan and Muhammad stared at the ears of corn. Muhammad looked up first. "What do we do with it?"

"It's corn, still on the cob," Dylan replied. "I think we eat it."

Muhammad picked up his ear of corn and quickly dropped it.

"It's hot."

"Well, *yeah*." Naia scooped butter from the crock and spread it over Dylan's corn. The melted butter ran down the sides and settled in a glistening pool on the plate. "Go ahead."

Dylan gingerly took one bite, then another.

"Oh, Jah," he said, mouth full. He attacked the ear.

"Hey, Muhammad," Naia said, "I think he likes it."

Naia sliced and served bread as the boys ate like hyenas. After ten minutes with no sound other than chewing, slurping, and swallowing, the boys sat back, satiated.

"Didn't they feed you in that place?" Naia asked.

"Not like this," Muhammad replied. "That was…" The sentence was interrupted by a long, liquid burp.

"It was good," Dylan finished for him, laughing. "Like, *incredibly* good."

"Glad you enjoyed it." Naia cleared the dishes from the table. "Now get over here and clean up. My dishwasher's busted. *You're* my dishwashers now."

❖ ❖ ❖

"This was all Jackson's idea."

Naia walked a step ahead of Dylan and Muhammad down the main street of Orwell. Though it was past eleven at night, most buildings were lit, occupied, and bustling.

"You saw our maker space," Naia said. "That's where we make our furniture, repair parts, new machinery, whatever we need. Or we create, just for fun."

They came to a cross street where a building stood, its wide doors open; men and women emptied tractor-pulled wagons heaped with snow-white bales.

"That's the cotton mill. Most of our textiles are cotton, but we also harvest wool and flax."

"Do you make *everything* you need?" Dylan asked.

"Almost everything. And it's sustainable." She pointed at another building fifty meters away, where more wagons dumped mounds of yellow grain. "We'll process that corn into the plastic we use to print almost anything."

Dylan saw activity everywhere he looked—tractors hauling loads of food crops, wood, and ore to processing plants; other wagons sat filled with finished goods. No one he saw was idle.

"What do you do for entertainment?" Dylan asked.

Naia made a sweeping gesture as she answered, "We *live*."

"You boys must be wiped out," Naia remarked when they reached the end of the street. "Let's head back to the house, get some sleep. We'll set you up tomorrow." She put a hand on each boy's shoulder. "You're going to like it here."

On the way back they passed a building with windows glowing, but unlike every other building in Orwell, it was quiet. The door was open; Dylan went in.

The walls inside were lined with shelves, and more free-standing shelves stood in rows. There were a few tables, and some overstuffed chairs. People sat silently, engrossed in the books pulled from the thousands filling the shelves. Dylan stared, mouth open.

"Do you like to read?" Naia whispered behind him.

Dylan nodded. "Is this a library?"

"You've never been in a library, have you?"

"Not IRL."

Naia squeezed his shoulder. "You'll be IRL from now on —mostly. This place, the library—*this* is *our* Virtual Reality."

18

AN IMMERSIVE EXPERIENCE

"WHEN THE WORLD moved to VR, these little towns emptied out."

Jackson stood at the stove in Naia's kitchen, turning slices of bacon in between flipping pancakes. Naia sat at the table with Dylan and Muhammad, the boys still wearing the clothes they had slept in.

"Everything went to the cities. Farming's almost a hundred percent automated, so the number of farmers has gone to squat. No point living in the country—you want an outdoor experience, have it in VR. You want to visit somebody, jack into a venue—no tedious traveling. Better'n a damn starship transporter. No wonder infrastructure's gone to hell. More pancakes?"

Dylan and Muhammad held up their plates.

"Yeah, the roads were terrible," Dylan said.

"No travel, no cars—no cars, no roads," Jackson went on. "Private companies keep up local networks, enough to move freight to the hypertube terminals. Maintenance workers and confinees—that's the only human cargo anymore, and they all go by tube."

"How'd it happen?" Muhammad asked.

"You youngsters—you missed all the fun." Jackson turned the bacon again. "Well, the remote towns were the first to die. They had coast-to-coast coverage back then, but the little rural towns just didn't have the bandwidth to support a... how do you put it, Naia?"

"An *immersive experience*."

"Yeah. So they all went to the population centers, the kids did, while the old folks died out—literally." Jackson inspected the plates. He forked slices of bacon onto each. "Then the service providers spent their money adding bandwidth where the people were, and the rural areas went dark." Jackson fixed himself a plate and took a seat at the table. "Which is *okay by me*."

"We couldn't jack into a venue from here even if we wanted to," Naia said. "No bandwidth. I mean *none*." She nibbled on a bacon strip. "Notice anything else about Orwell?"

Dylan and Muhammad exchanged puzzled looks.

"No drones?" Dylan offered.

"No drones, no cameras, no Jahbulon," Jackson confirmed. "No All-seeing Eye. The Worldstream ends about five hundred klicks from here, except for little bubbles around the population centers—Lincoln, Sioux Falls, like that."

Jackson forked a slice of pancake into his mouth. The tattoo on his forearm caught Dylan's eye.

"What's *'Vitreous Orb?'*"

Jackson grinned, bits of pancake stuck between his teeth. "Us. We're *Vitreous Orb*. Everyone here in Orwell, and others. Six towns in all. Over ten thousand at last count."

"What does it mean?"

Jackson leaned forward, wiping his mouth on the back of his hand. "Have you ever heard of *Vita Occulta?* The V.O., some call it?"

"Yes, I think so. They're the Cloak, right?"

"Yeah, more or less. *Vita Occulta* means *hidden life*. They escape the All-seeing Eye by covering up. *Our* V.O.—*Vitreous Orb*—we take a different approach. We live outside Jahbulon's reach, out in the open, in a glass globe, so to speak —a *Vitreous Orb*."

Jackson scraped remnants of pancake from his plate and sucked them off his fork. He pushed back from the table, looking first at Dylan, then at Muhammad, and scratched the back of his neck. "I don't suppose you two have any skills, do you?"

"We can code," Muhammad replied.

Jackson snorted. "Not much call for that here." He turned to Naia. "Where are we short?"

"It's harvest season. We have more tractors than drivers."

"You two ever drive a tractor in any of your exciting VR venues?"

The boys shook their heads.

"No worries," Jackson said. "It's a useful skill which is also easily mastered." He stood. "Naia, take 'em down to the cornfield. Have Benny teach 'em to drive. Don't let 'em into town until they can back up a hitch."

The tractors were old, their green and yellow paint scratched and faded. They idled with a rough, low grumble, the seats vibrating pleasantly under their drivers. The biodiesel exhaust wafted past their noses. The smell reminded Dylan and Muhammad of their pancake breakfast.

The boys figured out the controls quickly. They practiced in a fallow field, racing in circles, getting a feel for the machine's physics, learning how fast and how tight to take a turn without tipping. By nine a.m., they could drive like pros.

Then Benny, a lean, weathered man who towered over the boys, hitched a wagon to each tractor and challenged them to back up.

"Turn the bottom of the wheel in the direction you want the wagon to go," Benny told them.

What seemed like a simple problem the boys found maddeningly complex. It took until noon before Benny certified their tractor skills as "barely adequate" and they picked up their first load: 15 tonnes of corn, poured into the wagons like a golden fountain from the chute of the harvester.

By three p.m. they'd made five trips, maneuvering the tractors and their hitches, positioning the wagons over the grain bins with precision, as if they'd been farmhands since boyhood.

Dylan leapt from his tractor to open the wagon door. The yellow grain flowed with a satisfying rustle, like the sound of rain on a metal roof, as fine chaff rose in a cloud smelling dry and sweet.

"You're getting the hang, I see."

Jackson stood by the grate, hands on hips. Dylan grinned, his face flushed, dripping with sweat.

"Damn, boy, are you staying hydrated?" Jackson disappeared into the building and returned with two metal containers, both wet with condensation. Dylan took a long drink, the icy water almost painful on his throat.

"Take this one, too. I'm sure your buddy's just as negligent."

"Sure, thanks," Dylan said.

Jackson shook his head. "Newbies."

◆ ◆ ◆

The sun was low when Benny called it a day. "You did good, tyros," he said. "I guess all your time in the fake universe didn't turn you into a couple of limp dicks."

Dylan laughed as he wiped his face on his shirt. Muhammad's brown face was streaked with dirt, chaff and sweat. Though he looked exhausted, the red rays of the sun glinted off his eyes and imparted a glow to his face, as if he radiated from the inside.

"You look like you're having too much fun, Hammad."

"I'm working my ass off," he said, grinning. "Who knew it could feel good?"

"Hmm," Benny snorted. "See how ya feel in a week. Now go get cleaned up. Community meal in an hour at town hall."

◆ ◆ ◆

The hall hummed with conversation and the sound of utensils on dinner plates. A long table against the wall was piled with food—grilled pork chops, salad greens, potatoes in many preparations—baked, mashed and fried—and steaming ears of corn, Dylan's new favorite vegetable. People standing in line to the buffet chatted, argued, and laughed, bumping and patting shoulders. Dylan and Muhammad joined the line, having just come from Naia's house and a steaming shower.

"Who're you?" the man standing in front of them asked, a husky young man with sparse hair and round cheeks. "New kids?"

"I'm Dylan. This is Muhammad."

"Oh, I remember. You hauled grain. First time on a tractor?"

Dylan grinned. "Did it show?"

The man laughed. "You got better." He stuck out his hand. "I'm Max. I run the grain elevator. Sorry I didn't recognize you at first. Without the dirt, you look like *people*."

The boys filled their plates as the line moved along, aromas filling their noses, stirring already huge appetites.

"Join us over here," Max said. He led the boys to a table in the middle of the room. Three others were already seated, two men and a woman, dressed as many others were—in undyed cotton shirts and pants, like medieval peasants.

"Eddie, Frank, and Jenny," Max said, pointing to each in turn. "Meet Muhammad and Dylan. They drive tractors."

"Pleasure," Eddie said. "Keeping busy, I'm sure. Yield's insane this season. Ten tonnes a hectare, they're saying."

"No way," Jenny countered. "Nine, tops. Never had more than nine."

"Dylan, Muhammad, where you from?" Frank asked.

The boys looked sideways at each other. "It's kind of complicated," Dylan replied.

"Oh," Jenny said, nodding. "Jackson busted you from confinement, I bet."

"How'd you know?"

Jenny ate a forkful of mashed potatoes, washing it down with a drink of milk. "Wouldn't be the first time. I'm surprised the facility hasn't caught on. Damn lax security, it seems to me."

"I had some help," Dylan replied, "from a friend of my mom's."

"Good friend to have," Frank said. He lifted a glass of iced tea. "Welcome to Orwell."

The boys cleaned their plates and went back for seconds. Jenny, Eddie, Frank, and Max gave them a brief orientation, explaining government, economics, discipline, trade with other *Vitreous Orb* communities, and relations with the outside world, the foundational principle being no more contact than absolutely necessary. The hall began to empty after an hour, as the Orwellians went back to their homes, jobs, or recreation.

Frank reached into a pack hanging from the back of his chair. He pulled out a bottle filled with clear liquid.

"Just so you know that not *all* that corn you hauled gets processed into corn meal and plastic." He poured a generous shot into Dylan's and Muhammad's glasses. "And not all the alcohol gets burned up in the buggies."

Dylan lifted the glass to his nose. The smell caused him to wince and turn his head.

"Thanks, but I think I'll head for the library," he said.

"That's a gift, boy," Frank warned, lowering his eyebrows. "Don't insult me by turning it down."

Dylan looked from face to face, seeing a mix of sympathy and expectation. He sipped the corn liquor, feeling it burn all the way down.

"Good," Dylan wheezed. "Good stuff."

Frank beamed. "Now you," he said to Muhammad.

Muhammad held an open palm toward the moonshine. "My faith prohibits alcohol."

"Oh," Frank said. "Well, *my* faith prohibits *wasting* alcohol." He drained Muhammad's glass, then his own.

Dylan and Muhammad left the table, feeling refreshed and full.

"Your *faith?*" Dylan prodded. "Since when?"

"Since Frank stuck that buggy fuel in my nose," Muhammad replied with a grin. "Just the *smell* of it got me right with Allah."

The boys had made it almost to the door when Jackson came in, followed by another man, older, tall and thin, with a narrow face and bronze-colored complexion. Dylan stopped short and stared.

"You all know each other, don't you?" Jackson asked.

Muhammad shrugged. "I don't think so."

"I've only met your avatar, but I know you," Dylan replied. "*Raúl.*"

19

THE MEAT GRINDER

RAÚL LEANED ON the bar in the taproom (as Jackson called it), a clapboard shack with a few castoff tables and chairs. To one side a plank straddled two sawhorses, behind it a pump mounted on the wall. Jackson pulled on the ponderous pump handle, squirting beer into a tall mug, raising a paltry head. He gave it to Raúl, who took a long drink.

"Hacking the drones was the easy part," Raúl began. He set the mug on the makeshift bar and wiped foam from the corners of his mouth with a fingertip. "What did you change? It's different. Better. I hardly noticed how warm and flat it is."

"If you don't like it, you can go back to that canned crap y'all drink in the world," Jackson shot back. He filled two more mugs and set them in front of Dylan and Muhammad

"I like it. I *said* I like it."

"Raúl," Dylan prompted.

"Oh. Yeah." Raúl took another swallow. "The drones. I hacked 'em. Tunneled in through an old protocol. They don't keep current in the facility."

"We noticed," Dylan replied. "Everything seems a gen or two behind. Except the Belt."

"Yeah? They have gen five Belts?"

"No, gen four. There's a gen *five?*"

"Oh, that's right, you've been out of commission for a while. The new gen fives are kickass. When they released them, they put all the gen fours on clearance. The confinement facility probably got a bargain."

"You were saying? About the drones?"

"Ancient technology. I implanted a command to halt their surveillance pattern, and another one to sound the perimeter alarm. That was my part, the hacking and planning. Naia did the heavy lifting, driving seven hours there and back. And cutting through the fence."

"Someone in the hall told me you've done this before."

"Me? Twice, maybe three times. Jackson?"

Jackson lowered his mug, foam flitting from his lip. "Twice. Last one more than a year back. But we've busted out maybe eight, total."

"And they don't catch on?" Muhammad asked.

Jackson and Raúl laughed.

"*No*," Raúl replied. "They don't care. One less mouth to feed."

"They busted us hard the first time we tried," Dylan said. "They made Hammad permanent, and they added ten years to my term. Doesn't that mean they care?"

"They care that you fucked it up."

"You're not saying that they *wanted* us to break out, are you?"

"Of *course* they did."

Dylan and Muhammad looked at each other in disbelief.

"I can tell you're skeptical," Raúl said. "Let me explain. Jackson, give me a refill." Jackson pumped another draft for Raúl, and one for himself. "What'd they run you two hooligans in for?"

"Do you mean what was our transgression?"

"Yeah—*transgression*."

"Key theft," Muhammad answered. "Both of us."

"Right. A little harmless hacking. Someone's a little inconvenienced because you have his key and you can pose as him. What a tragedy. And what was your term?"

"Fifteen," Muhammad replied.

"Five," Dylan added, "but they bumped it to fifteen."

"Fifteen years, just for filching a key. A little harsh, don't you think?"

"Well, *yeah.*"

"Why do you suppose you got hammered like that?"

"It's the Worldstream, right?" Dylan said. "That's what they told us in orientation—how important it is to protect the integrity of the Worldstream."

"And if they'd given you just a year? Or two or three? And an hour or two in the torture seat every day? Wouldn't *that* be incentive enough not to sink back into your wicked ways?" Raúl asked.

The boys nodded.

"Of course it would. And a one-to-three year term you could probably stick out, even with the daily mind fuck."

"Get to the point, Raúl," Jackson said.

"Let me tell it my way," Raúl countered. He passed his empty tankard to Jackson. "Make yourself useful." Then he turned back to the boys. "So, what's up with the double-digit terms?"

"Like you said—they *want* us to break out," Dylan replied.

Raúl looked at Jackson with a grin. "See? I told you he was smart."

"But why?" Dylan pressed. "Why drag us into confinement in the first place if they want us out?"

"Now that you're out, what're your options?"

"I don't know. Stay here in Orwell, I suppose. If we get anywhere near Jahbulon, he'll know it."

"Of course he will. Unless…"

Dylan stared at the table. "Unless we're cloaked."

"Cloaked?"

Dylan looked up, eyes wide. "Or shredded."

"Jackson, I think he's got it."

"They *want* us to shred our lives. Go off-Worldstream." Dylan turned in his chair, pressing his fingers to his forehead. "So we're out of commission. No longer a threat."

"Keep going, Dylan," Raúl prompted.

"No…they don't just want us out of the way. We were out of the way in confinement. They want more Shade."

"And why?"

"Slave labor," Muhammad replied.

"*Bingo*, my young friends. The Worldstream needs coders. There's a bottomless demand. The Shade are 99% coders who got caught and shredded out. They don't have many options, so they work for next to nothing. Why should Jahbulon pay retail when he can shop from the bargain bin?"

"Then the confinement facility…"

"Part of the pipeline." Raúl drained his mug. "I've lost count of the number of hackers I've busted out of confinement and shredded."

"Like Mom?"

"Grace." Raúl sat down and leaned back, a distant look on his face. "Grace had her own reasons. She was facing a different kind of hell." He lifted his mug, as if to drink, then handed it back to Jackson. "Anyway, that's the meat grinder they threw you in. Hack, get caught, go to jail, bust out, shred, go to work for the man."

"But we're not shredded," Muhammad said.

"Yeah, that's what made your case a challenge. Like I said, I've only done a couple of breakouts for the Orb. I had to hack into your therapy stream—that was the tricky part, tunneling in without the screws getting wise—then jigger the drones and cause a diversion. All from the outside. A ton of moving parts there. It's a lot easier when I have a buyer."

"Why's that?" Dylan asked.

Raúl smiled. "When it's someone for the Shade, I can schedule it."

"You mean…"

"The confinement super is in on it. Hell, he gets a kickback for every new Shade we shred."

Dylan and Muhammad looked down at the table, both realizing that they hadn't touched their beers. They drained the mugs and pushed them across the bar for a refill.

❖ ❖ ❖

The corn harvest went on for another week. Dylan's and Muhammad's tractor skills improved so much that Benny gave them nicknames: *Kubota* and *John Deere*.

The whole town of Orwell gathered for a celebration on the last day of the harvest. The cooking, eating, and drinking started mid-morning and continued late into the night. Dylan and Muhammad were pressed into service as outfielders in a game of softball.

"You two are the worst ball players I've ever seen," Benny said in the dugout. "Good thing you can drive a tractor."

"I played baseball when I was a boy," Dylan replied. "I don't remember sucking this bad."

"You played VR baseball, right?"

"Yeah, so?"

Benny closed his eyes and shook his head, a look of pity on his face. "You don't know, do you?"

"What?"

"Those VR little leagues handicapped you poor, unsuspecting ball players."

"Handicapped?"

"Made the game harder for the good players and easier for the crappy players. It's supposed to be good for your *self-esteem*."

"Oh, Jah. That is messed up."

"Welcome to Real Life."

Dylan grinned. "What's next? You won't need us to drive tractors full-time, now that the corn is in."

"That's up to Jackson. He'll figure something out. He always does." Benny picked up a bat and gave a few chops with it. "You picked up the tractor pretty quick. Maybe you can figure out how a hammer works—maybe. It's only a little like a softball bat."

Ultimately, Benny's team lost in a lopsided score.

"Sorry," Dylan apologized.

"Don't worry about it," Benny replied.

As they left the field they caught sight of Raúl's tall figure walking into the lights on the ball field. Behind him walked three more figures, shorter than he was, their faces hidden in the shadows.

"Raúl, you left days ago," Dylan said. "Didn't you?"

"I did," Raúl answered. "Something came up and I had to come back. Something pretty important."

"Okay." Dylan waited for Raúl to continue, but he only

smiled. Dylan looked past him, at one of the people behind Raúl—the shortest one—as she came into the light.

She had brown eyes and red hair, the same color as Dylan's, but with thin streaks of gray that Dylan didn't remember. Her face was fuller, older, than the last time Dylan had seen her.

Dylan took a step forward but stumbled, dropping to one knee. The woman ran forward and knelt by him, taking his face in her hands, turning him toward the light. She wiped away his tears, then wiped her own.

"Dylan," she whispered, "it's Mom."

PART TWO

GRACE

20

OUR ZEN THING

KALAHARI GRASS, ADRIAN called it—sharp-edged, dry, and nearly as tall as he was. Grace and Adrian waded eyes-deep in an endless, undulating sea of grass. Though it blocked their view beyond a few meters, the grass hid them from their quarry. They walked with the breeze in their faces—a white rhino's eyesight is not keen, but the big bull would surely smell two humans upwind.

Grace kept a death grip on the rifle, her right hand curled around the stock, finger on the trigger guard, her left hand clutching the forestock, ready to level the gun, aim, and fire in an instant.

"Ease off," Adrian whispered. "Your fingers are turning white."

Grace looked up at him. The brim of his bush hat cast a shadow on his face, hiding the friendly brown eyes she'd seen for the first time less than a month ago, though she'd known him for nearly a year. The rest of his face was lit by a savage sun hanging in a cloudless Namibian sky. His mouth, so easy to smile, was grim.

She relaxed her grip. "I want to be ready," she whispered back.

Adrian nodded, his smile coming at last. "You'll be ready."

They pushed the grass aside with their guns as they moved, until it gave way to a sandy clearing, surrounding an acacia tree by a wide spot in a stream. A lone waterbuck drinking at the stream's edge looked up with a start. Adrian and Grace froze in place. The big animal stood motionless, staring, its menacing horns a warning to keep their distance. It looked aside before bending down again to drink. A second waterbuck approached, another male, not as big, and then another.

Grace lowered the rifle to her side, holding it with one hand. "Jah," she murmured, "how gorgeous."

"Look—here comes one more. Another male. It's a bachelor herd."

She grinned. "A bachelor herd! I'll bet they're up to no good, the troublemakers."

He snorted. The waterbucks looked up and braced to run. "Don't make me laugh. You'll give us away."

"Not me. *You're* laughing."

"Fine. You know what I mean."

Adrian's face was now in full sun. Grace thought he was handsome—not terribly so, but nice looking, with soft curves in his face, and full lips—a kind face with a trace of sadness which intrigued her, and made her want to keep looking at him.

The waterbucks calmed down and went back to drinking.

"How many times have you been to Africa?" Grace asked.

"I've lost count. Four or five times to this place. I don't know how many times in all. What do you think?"

"It's stunning. I had no idea. Thanks for bringing me here."

Adrian glanced down at Grace's rifle, hanging casually from her hand. He looked back at the waterbuck herd. "I'm glad you like it."

The waterbucks reacted before Grace heard it, or rather, felt it—a sub-sonic rumble, like a minor earthquake. The herd scattered, bounding off in three directions. She tightened her grip on the rifle.

"Do you feel that?"

Adrian grabbed Grace's arm and pulled her toward him as the grass beside them parted, like water before the prow of a ship. The bull rhino emerged into the clearing in a gallop, a gray blur of wrinkled hide and churning legs, its long head held low, a horn like a scimitar on its nose.

Grace struggled to regain her footing as she raised the rifle to firing position. She placed the stock against her shoulder, sighting for the fold in the hide above the rhino's forelegs—the location of its vital organs. She pulled the trigger.

The recoil forced the muzzle of the rifle upward. The stock slipped off Grace's shoulder onto her arm, whipping her around. She went to one knee, keeping a tenuous hold on the gun. She looked up, first at Adrian, then at the rhino. The bull was kneeling on four legs, struggling to stand. Adrian stood still and silent.

The rhino stood, then stumbled forward, barely staying on its feet. It wagged its head as if trying to clear it, then lifted its snout and cried out. Grace blanched and her stomach tensed at the sound, a high-pitched cry, like a child screaming.

"It's a shoulder hit," Adrian noted, "not fatal. That animal is suffering."

"I know that," Grace growled. She stayed kneeling, squaring her body to the line of fire and raising the rifle, taking care to shoulder the stock firmly. As she took aim at the rhino's vitals, it turned to face her. The animal began its charge.

"That's a head shot, Grace," Adrian said calmly as the rhino came at them in a run. "You'll be lucky to bring him down."

"Shut up. I'm busy here."

Grace inhaled deeply and exhaled slowly. She pulled back the bolt, chambering another round. The African grassland faded away as she focused on the charging rhino, its head bobbing as it ran, alternately exposing, then concealing, its vulnerable spot. At five meters the rhino raised its head, ready to thrust its horn forward at the precise instant to do the most damage. Its chest was exposed. Grace squeezed the trigger.

The rhino's front legs buckled. The massive body pitched forward, hindquarters rising, then falling with a force that shook the ground. Grace raised the rifle skyward, using her arm to shield her face from the spray of sand and pebbles.

The big bull lay motionless as a cloud of dust curled around it.

Grace laid down the rifle. She propped herself up on one arm, waiting for her heart to stop pounding. Adrian looked down at her. He hadn't budged since the rhino first appeared. His rifle was pointed down, as if he had never raised it.

"Touch its eye," Adrian said.

Grace stared at him in horror.

"If it blinks, it's still alive. Touch its eye. You need to make sure it's dead."

She chambered another round as she approached the rhino. The animal lay still; it didn't appear to be breathing. Gently, she touched the rhino's eyeball. It didn't blink.

Adrian stood beside her. "How do you feel?" he asked.

"I feel sick," Grace whispered. "Look at it."

The rhino was gigantic, surprisingly bigger up close than it seemed from a distance. Its huge head sported two horns, the larger one nearly three-quarters of a meter long. Its hide was mud-caked and wrinkled, with coarse folds around the neck and joints. It was ugly, primitive-looking, and yet... utterly *awe-inspiring*.

"Did people really shoot these animals for sport?"

"Yep," Adrian replied. "Wiped them out." He touched her arm. "Tell me what went wrong."

"The waterbucks distracted me. I forgot why we were here, and I got careless."

"Yep. Then what?"

"I panicked. I aimed for the mark, but I fired too quickly. I wasn't holding the rifle properly—the recoil spun me around." Grace opened the bolt of the rifle and removed the round. "I failed to master the moment—the moment mastered *me*."

"But you got back up and you finished it, even while I was needling you. When it was clutch time you got outside of yourself and you found your mark." He put his hand on her shoulder. "You did a lot better than I did my first time out. I'm proud of you."

Grace bent low to feel the rhino's skin. It was unlike

anything she'd felt before, in VR or IRL, a sensuous, organic texture.

"The next time we do our zen thing, let's pick another venue," Grace suggested.

"It's the unpredictability, the life-threatening situation, the need to act, especially if the action is unpleasant, that tests your inner calm."

"I get that." Grace straightened up, holding the rifle at her side. "But there must be some way to test my inner calm without slaughtering a magnificent animal."

Adrian nodded. "Yep. I get *that.*"

"Let's get out of here."

"Daystar, suspend the venue."

The dead rhino faded away, the rifles disappeared, and the blistering sun quenched as the African savanna dissolved around them. Their clothing transformed from bush gear to the plain black cloaks of the Shade. They were alone in the center of a large room with a concrete floor, windowless cinder block walls, and a single steel door, secured by two locks. Long tables lined two walls, each heaped with circuit boards, electronics in plastic and aluminum cases, VR headsets and tactile gear in various states of disrepair, from vintage to current art, jumbled together with meters, emulators, and protocol analyzers. The piles overflowed onto chairs and spread out over the floor. The overhead lights glowed white, but everything in the room appeared orange from the light reflected by the copper-covered walls and ceiling. A row of racks stood opposite the door, filled with computers blinking red, green, and white, a haywire mix of serviceable and obsolete hardware, looking as much like a salvage yard as a computing laboratory. The racks emitted a constant rush of pink noise—the sound of air pulled past computers through a duct to the roof, dumping thousands of kilowatts into the atmosphere.

Grace and Adrian removed their VR headgear and gloves. Grace slid her hands under her cloak to remove her neural interface belt. She held the wide black strap—criss-crossed with silver wires—draped over her arm.

"Where did you get these?"

"I borrowed them from the Bast."

Grace's eyebrows arched. "The Bast owe us money."

"Yep. I promised them an extension on the loan. It's the only way they'd give up two of their most expensive pieces of gear."

"You should have discussed that with me first."

"I didn't think you'd mind."

Grace locked eyes with Adrian, her forehead lined and lips pressed together. He stared back, then lowered his eyes, looking contrite. She softened her expression. "It'll be okay, I guess. But in the future…"

"Absolutely. Of course." Adrian took off his Belt. "They're incredible, aren't they?"

"I felt it all—the grass against my skin, the breeze in my face—it was amazing. The recoil from the rifle—the smells, even." She ran her fingers over the Belt's surface, tracing the regular pattern of metal electrodes. "I've used the Belt before, but it was never like this."

Adrian took the Belt from her. "It's the latest version, brand new technology. There's almost no sensation it can't reproduce."

"What about the emotions? The anxiousness—the fear? Was that me, or the program?"

"When the rhino appeared and you freaked out…"

"I didn't *freak out!*"

Adrian shrugged. "Yep, well, in any case, I didn't program that reaction. Those feelings were real. But the serenity you felt at the watering hole, your calm before the rhino showed up—*I* programmed that."

"You *wanted* me to lose focus."

"Part of the exercise."

Grace sighed and walked to a row of hooks by the door, where hoods hung, made of the same black fabric as their cloaks. She took them from their hooks and handed one to Adrian.

"Thank you for the venue," she said. "I learned something."

He touched her cheek. "I'm glad."

The sound of the door handle rattling followed by a knock sent both of them scrambling to pull on their hoods. Adrian opened the door. A cloaked and hooded figure stood in the doorway.

"I'm called Bjorg," the figure said in a mechanical voice, rendered by the synthesizer in the hood. It was inhuman-sounding, impossible to identify. "Nemesio? Chrysalis?"

"I'm called Nemesio," Adrian replied in the same mechanical voice.

Bjorg came in, looking from Nemesio to Chrysalis and back.

"What was it this time?" Bjorg asked.

"Rhino hunting in Namibia," Chrysalis answered.

"Killing wild animals. I don't understand."

"It's an exercise," Nemesio said, "a test of personal mastery."

"Don't try to explain," Bjorg replied. "Are you done with the Sandbox? I'm doing some rendering. I need to run a test."

"Yep," Nemesio said. "It's all yours. But before you get started, I have something to tell you—you and Chrysalis—and Elisha, too."

Chrysalis and Bjorg looked at each other. Chrysalis shrugged. "Okay. What is it?"

"Can you guess?"

Chrysalis paused. "The persona. You finished your proof of concept."

"Yep!"

"Nemesio, that's wonderful," Chrysalis said. "Congratulations!"

"We can test it right away," Nemesio replied. "If it works, it'll be a big step toward putting us in total control."

21

Prophet of Jahbulon

THE SUMMERLAND WAS a complex of chambers, from tiny closets to open spaces the size of banquet halls, connected by a warren of dimly-lit passages. The makeshift structure, built up from scrounged materials over the decades since the advent of Jahbulon, occupied a multi-level underground parking ramp, abandoned in an era of VR dwellers and self-driving transits. No map existed for the Summerland; newcomers relied on long-time residents to learn the layout, if they could find someone willing to teach them. Knowledge was currency among the Shade, and *quid pro quo* was their law. The answer to any question—even how to get from the dormitory to the commissary—came at a price, payable immediately, or kept on account.

Only unaffiliated Shade lived in the Summerland. They survived on scraps shared by the sponsored crews, either as subcontractors on big projects, or jobs too small for the affiliated crews to bother with. The tasks were simple, and pay was meager, sometimes no better than subsistence.

The affiliated Shade crews were a little better off. Their sponsors, Cloak members of the *Vita Occulta* cartel, straddled the divide between the connected world and the Shade underground, giving them an edge in the competition for resources. They bought equipment and supplies above-board from vendors in the Worldstream. And they had the credits to do so—programming, rendering, and other Shade services were in high demand, and sponsors kept the bulk of the fees for themselves. Sponsored Shade enjoyed state-of-the art facilities and a steady income, but their average pay was only slightly higher than the freelance crews.

Grace, known among the Shade as Chrysalis, had beaten the system. After shredding her life, she came to the Summerland, a temporary landing spot until she could find a sponsor. She'd begged for food and a place to sleep, racking up debt, until she checked her cryptocurrency account, expecting it to be empty, but instead finding a balance of 50,000 credits. The gift was anonymous, but she knew who it had come from—her shredder, Raúl. The crusty old bastard had a soft spot for Grace, it seemed. And he'd put Chrysalis in an enviable position among the destitute Shade—50,000 credits was a fortune to the unaffiliated.

The Shade *always* needed credits, and Chrysalis had them. After settling her accounts, she made her first loan at a confiscatory rate, putting the profit toward expanding the business, offering a wide range of services—deposits, money transfers, escrows—lucrative enough to cover her own expenses, and then some. Two years later, her 50,000 credit stake had grown to more than four million.

❖ ❖ ❖

Chrysalis, Nemesio, and Bjorg followed the meandering route from the Sandbox to the Kaleidoscope's cramped dormitory, sidling past hunched figures in black cloaks within narrow passages, some murmuring in mechanical monotones, the rest shuffling in silence. They stopped at the Engine Room to pick up Elisha, the fourth member of the Kaleidoscope. Their dorm, behind a locked door, was the only place on earth where the Kaleidoscope showed their faces. Grace, the Kaleidoscope's leader; Celeste, Shade Bjorg, the manager; Thomas, Shade Elisha, the account collector; and Adrian, Shade Nemesio, the coder, uncloaked as they debated the next step in their plan to reenter the Worldstream.

"We've run all the tests we can in the Sandbox, put the persona into all kinds of venues—public, private, small crowds, big crowds," Adrian said. "The Worldstream simulator never peeped."

"It's a simulation," Celeste countered.

"The live demo should work the same."

"*Should*," Celeste replied, smiling. It was a smile that Adrian knew well—first the smile, then the slam. "When I hear *should work*, I ask *what if it doesn't?*"

Adrian blinked slowly. "I'll monitor the Worldstream. If it acts up, I'll abort."

"Acts up?" Grace asked.

"If it throws an alarm," Adrian answered. "The Worldstream expects every avatar to be connected to a real person. If the All-Seeing Eye spots an unattached avatar, it'll complain."

"It'll do more than complain," Celeste said. "It'll raise *hell*."

"We'll pull out if it gets too hot."

"Grace, you're in charge," Celeste snapped. "Here's where I'm at: We've all gone to a lot of trouble to get out of the Worldstream and to *stay* out. If we raise our heads too high, we'll bring Jahbulon and all his agents down on us."

Grace looked back and forth between Celeste and Adrian. "Celeste, why are you bringing this up now? We all agreed. *You* agreed. You knew this was coming."

"Yes, *Grace*, I knew it was coming. And I'm still on board. But it's risky. That's why we're talking, isn't it?"

Grace bit her lip. "What'll it take to ease your mind?"

"I want my finger on the abort button."

"No!" Adrian blurted. "It's *my* test. I can handle it."

"We're all in on it," Celeste countered.

"No one questions that," Grace said. She looked first at Celeste—one of Grace's longest acquaintances in the Summerland and a founding member of the Kaleidoscope—then at Adrian, only recently admitted to the alliance at Grace's request. "Celeste is right—we're all at risk. I don't think it's too much to ask for her to be involved in the test. Adrian, can you live with that?"

Adrian glared at her for a moment before his eyes darted sideways at Celeste. "Don't abort too soon. Wait for my signal."

Celeste gave him a thin smile. "I'll try."

"Where's the test?" Thomas asked. "And when?"

"Right now," Adrian answered. "In the Engine Room."

"Who's going in?"

"Me," Grace replied. "I'm the leader—my risk."

The Summerland Engine Room was small compared with the engine rooms of the affiliated Shade crews: thirty meters long and fifteen meters wide, with four aisles of high-powered computing hardware connected to the Worldstream through a fat stealth pipe. Glass walls surrounded dozens of workstations in tiny cubicles, each manned by a Shade. A few wore hoods; most wore the colorful masks popular among the Cloak and the Shade, which covered their eyes to the backs of their heads, leaving their mouths and chins uncovered. On a busy day, one could hear their conversations in coarse whispers to disguise their voices—the Shade masks, unlike their hoods, had no built-in voice synthesizers, the devices which gave all hooded Shade the same inhuman voice.

The Engine Room was the Summerland's money-maker, where the Shade provided services for clients, jacked anonymously into the Worldstream. There were a few spaces where teams of four or five Shade could meet, closed off from the common area. The Kaleidoscope gathered in one of these for the test of Nemesio's persona: an avatar with no human counterpart, undetectable by the Worldstream—in theory.

Chrysalis stood in the middle, in full VR gear: a 180-degree visor, which rendered photorealistic 3D scenes; headphones with frequency and dynamic response beyond that of human hearing; tactile stimulus and response gloves that could simulate the substance and texture of any rendered object; and the Belt, capable of inducing whole-body sensations. Thus equipped, a user, when inserted into the virtual world, could not distinguish her surroundings from Real Life.

Nemesio and Bjorg sat at workstations side-by-side, while

Elisha stood facing a row of wall screens, each screen showing the same scene: a massive crowd surrounding a raised platform. A speaker stood on the platform, a circle of ten people behind him. The speaker was a short man with a round face and a mane of thick, black hair which hung to his shoulders. The hair was the first thing Elisha noticed: it shifted and bounced as the man moved, which he did constantly, speaking with whole-body gestures. Other than the hair, the man was unremarkable: a plain face with close-set eyes, large nose and a square mouth, which remained square even when he spoke.

The man started out quietly, gradually increasing in volume and becoming more animated, until he punctuated the oration with closed fists thrust into the air, and spread his arms wide. He bowed his head, crossing his arms over his chest as the crowd went insane. They hushed again when he opened his arms and raised his head to repeat the cycle of crescendo, climax, and pause.

"What's this venue?" Elisha asked. "It looks like a mass meeting of some kind."

"A political rally," Nemesio replied. "I wanted a public venue with a big crowd, something that pushes the Worldstream to its limits. According to the feed, there are almost a half-million avatars around 200 replicated stages."

"Why so big?" Bjorg asked.

"The high body count should make it harder for the Worldstream to detect an unattached avatar."

"Don't we want the exact opposite?" Bjorg challenged. "A venue that would make it *easy* for the All-Seeing Eye to detect the persona? That would be a better test."

"One step at a time. If this works, we can try it out in smaller venues." Nemesio glanced at Bjorg. "Weren't you the one who was worried about risk?"

Bjorg clenched her jaw, visible beneath a saffron-colored mask. "I've got my finger on the button," she pointed out.

"Enough," Chrysalis said. She adjusted her headgear until the reticle in the visual field converged. A test pattern appeared—a gray 3D grid superimposed on the pure white staging venue—indicating that the VR gear was functional, and the rendering engine was running. "Let's go," she said finally.

❖ ❖ ❖

Chrysalis materialized in a staging vestibule at an open spot in the middle of the crowd, equidistant from three stages, just three of two hundred identical stages in a massive public venue. She'd been in such venues before; they were popular for music concerts, where huge numbers of fans could get close to the performers.

This was unlike any concert venue she'd ever seen.

The avatars in the crowd spanned the range of age and appearance. Most wore hats or shirts, or carried signs that flashed one slogan after another, like an electronic billboard cycling through its ads:

VERMIN LIVE IN THE SHADE
JAHBULON IS THE LIGHT
KLIEGL IS THE TORCH
DAX IS THE TORCHBEARER

"Chrysalis, check your avatar," Nemesio's voice sounded in her ears. She took a pocket mirror from the bag hanging by a strap from her shoulder, placed there by Nemesio's persona. Looking at her reflection, she saw that the persona had successfully bypassed the Worldstream's rules engine. Instead of Grace, a red-haired, brown-eyed, fair-skinned woman, Chrysalis saw a dark-skinned man of apparent Indian ancestry. She gave Nemesio a thumbs up.

Her mission was to mingle, but lightly—respond when spoken to, but otherwise keep engagements to a minimum. Every contact triggered the venue server to deconflict avatars, nail up or tear down vicinity connections, and verify credentials; each invocation of the validation algorithm was an opportunity for detection. There would be enough hits on the server for a valid test just by being in the venue without *making* them happen.

Chrysalis moved toward one of the stages, squeezing

between attendees and trying to avoid contact. Each avatar she bumped into reacted normally, as if the Indian man with the shoulder bag were a legitimate avatar with a Real Life counterpart who looked just like it.

"Excuse me," she said to a large man as she brushed past him. The voice in Chrysalis's head wasn't hers, but a man's voice, high and thin, with an Indian accent. She looked up at the stranger's face and stopped short. His forehead had a crawl on it, like the news crawl at the bottom of a wall screen, but instead of the weather report and current events, the glowing text scrolling across his forehead read DAX—PROPHET OF JAHBULON…KLIEGL—LIGHT OF PURITY…SHADE—DARKNESS AND DEATH. Chrysalis stared at the crawl until the man stared back and scowled.

"Something you want from me, guy?"

Chrysalis stepped back, bumping into another avatar, a plump woman with bright yellow hair in a body-hugging leotard, her body stocking displaying full-motion scenes from Dax rallies as if projected on a woman-shaped screen. The woman stepped aside with a grunt.

"Excuse me," she said to the leotard woman, never taking her eyes from the man's glowing headline.

"Are you getting the message?" the man asked, pointing to his forehead.

"What's 'Dax?'" Chrysalis asked in reply, without thinking.

"Steady, Chrysalis," Nemesio's voice urged. "Minimum contact."

The headline man laughed. "*That's* Dax," he said, pointing at the man onstage with long black hair, his arms waving in mid-harangue. "That's the guy who'll find these Shades that are ruining our peaceful society."

"He's our savior," the leotard woman added from behind Chrysalis.

"What are the Shade doing to ruin society?"

"Chrysalis…" Nemesio cautioned.

"Haven't you been paying attention?" the headline man countered. "We're in a crime wave."

"What crime wave?"

"*Chrysalis!*"

"We haven't had a violent crime in this city or any other city since Jahbulon came online," the headline man explained. "That's more than thirty years."

"There were some," the leotard woman objected, "but not many."

The man grunted, narrowing his eyes at the leotard. "And now there've been thirty assaults just in the last two weeks."

"I don't think we've had *thirty* assaults," the woman corrected.

"That don't matter, lady. What matters is, the world is falling apart."

"It's the *Shade*, citizen," the leotard woman concurred, nodding vigorously. "They're outlaws. They hide from Jahbulon."

"*Keep moving,*" Nemesio's voice commanded.

"I'm sorry," Chrysalis said, "but I have to go now."

Leotard grabbed Chrysalis's arm. "Stay and listen. It's Dax and the Kliegls who will rout the Shade. He's like an exterminator. If you had roaches, you'd call an exterminator, right?" She squeezed harder, fingers sinking deep into Chrysalis's arm, as if into raw bread dough. Chrysalis's flesh squeezed out through the woman's fingers, the protruding knobs of flesh surrounded by an aura of color, until almost her entire hand was embedded in the deformed arm.

"What's happening?" the bewildered woman asked, voice quavering. She tried to pull her fingers free but they stuck, melted into Chrysalis's arm, the flesh stretching like taffy.

"*Oh! Oh Jah!*" the leotard woman cried. She jerked her hand away but the flesh remained stuck, a thick swarthy ribbon from the woman's hand to the arm. "Jahbulon, what's happening? *Get away from me!*"

Heads turned toward the commotion, the people around them going silent, a hush expanding in a perfect circle like a shock wave from a bomb blast. The avatars of Chrysalis and the leotard woman flickered between transparent and opaque, their colors bleeding, images shimmering, like a video on a defective wall screen.

"Something's happening," Nemesio said into Chrysalis's headphones. The next voice she heard belonged to Bjorg: "I'm pulling the plug."

"Give it a second," Nemesio commanded. "I need to know what's going on."

The crowd surrounding Chrysalis broke their silence.

"Are you seeing this?" the headline man asked his neighbor.

"Yeah. There's an alarm on my console," the neighbor replied. "It's pointing at that Indian guy. Like a spoof detection, only worse."

"We've got to pull out," Bjorg said.

"One second!" Nemesio pleaded.

"What do we do?" the headline man asked.

"Jahbulon, help us!" the neighbor cried.

"I'm getting her out!" Bjorg shouted.

"Okay, okay, *do it!*" Nemesio shouted back.

The rally flashed and vanished. Chrysalis stood once again in the Engine Room, surrounded by the Kaleidoscope. She pulled off her headgear.

"What happened?" she demanded.

"That's what I'd like to know," Bjorg challenged.

Nemesio squinted at his console. "The venue server seems to have glitched. It'll take me some time to figure this out."

"Yes, please do that," Bjorg growled. "And while you're at it, figure out if the Worldstream found us. I'd really like to know just how *fucked* we are."

"Are you okay?" Nemesio asked Chrysalis.

Chrysalis was just pulling off her gloves. "Yeah, I'm fine. When do you think you'll have an answer?"

"It's my top priority."

Bjorg shook her head as she pulled on her hood. Elisha put on his hood next and followed Bjorg out of the room.

"I'll get to the bottom of this," Nemesio said, staring at the data stream.

"I know you will—Adrian," Chrysalis said softly. "And I've got some research to do, too."

Nemesio looked up from the screen. "What research?"

"I'm going to find out everything there is to know about someone named Dax."

22

POKER PARTY

GRACE AND CELESTE watched from a distance as the scene played out: two men and two women reclining on the floor, a man and a woman wearing only briefs, the others naked, playing poker in a ring of discarded clothing. One woman dealt a hand, the players drew or stood pat, then showed their cards. They roared with laughter as the man with the low hand stood and slowly slid off his briefs. The women applauded, shouting their appreciation for his handsome erection.

"Does this look familiar?" Celeste asked.

"Daystar, pause the venue," Grace commanded. She moved among the motionless players, all in their late teens or early twenties, paying special attention to the quality of the rendering.

In her time at the Summerland, Grace had honed her VR coding chops. She knew quality work when she saw it. Less-than-hi-res rendering, which a casual stream rider might find satisfactory, which she herself might have enjoyed at one time without complaint, now appeared crude and amateurish. A good rendering was lifelike when static and convincing while in motion, with only minor artifacts.

"Daystar, resume the venue." The poker game continued, the last of the clothing tossed aside, the subsequent hands played for different stakes: the low hand had to perform whatever act the high hand demanded. Each new game was a challenge to prove how inventive the winner could be.

Grace knelt down, close to the action.

"Enjoying the view?" Celeste asked.

Grace scowled. "Daystar, pause the venue." She stood up. "The rendering is perfect."

"Some of the best I've seen," Celeste agreed with admiration. "The motion is fluid. I can't spot an artifact anywhere."

"Have you tried this in first person?"

"No," Celeste snorted. "I'm not into group sex. I'm a one-on-one girl."

"Yeah." Grace knelt again among the strip poker players. The rendering didn't break down, no matter how close she got—just centimeters from a player's thigh, the sparse hairs, the pores in his skin—were all indistinguishable from Real Life.

"What's the title?" Grace asked.

"Penelope's Poker Party."

"Which one is Penelope?"

"The one with her ass in the air."

Penelope's avatar was a slightly thick girl with dull brown hair. She was on knees and elbows, her head twisted, looking back at the winner of the last poker hand, who was perched on his knees with his hands on her back.

"I'm going first person," Grace said.

"Do you think that's wise, given…you know?"

Scenes from Grace's past flashed through her mind: men and women in all combinations, night after night, no act out of bounds. It was a time in Grace's life she'd struggled to put behind her, when she was driven by a compulsion out of her control—when *she* was out of control.

"I'm not looking forward to it, believe me. But it's the only way I'll know for sure."

"Look, Grace, I can do it."

"No. I've been in her lifestreams before. I'll know if it's one of hers."

"Okay. Do you mind if I don't watch?"

"I prefer it that way. But stay close by."

"You got it," Celeste said. "Daystar, exit the venue."

Celeste's avatar rastered out. Grace stood up and stepped back.

"Daystar, first person."

Grace's point of view cut to Penelope's. She suffered a moment of disorientation—Penelope's line of sight was parallel to the floor, tilted on its side. The poker players appeared sideways, shouting and clapping. A muscular thigh partially blocked her view. She felt two hands gripping her hips, squeezing too hard for comfort.

"Easy, Spike, not so rough," Penelope pleaded.

"I'm just getting started, Penny," the man replied. The other couple howled.

"Just so you know," Penelope said, *"I'm a back-door virgin."*

Another round of hoots and hollers.

"I'll be gentle."

Grace felt the nausea rising in her throat. She wasn't sure if it was her own stomach that felt sick, or if the sickness was induced by the Belt. But the other emotions—fear, shame— and sensations—the discomfort of rough hands gripping her midsection, pain as the man entered her—came straight from the neural interface strapped to her waist, as intense as if she were bodily in the scene, being sodomized by a man with no sense of restraint.

"Daystar, suspend the venue!"

The image in Grace's headgear cut to a view of the Sandbox. Celeste stood in front of her, wearing the Shade robe, the saffron mask dangling from her hand.

"That didn't sound like much fun."

Grace slipped out of her gear. "No. It wasn't." She stood and walked to the wall hooks slowly, as if she were still in pain. She hung up the gear and took down her hood.

"Well?" Celeste asked.

"Are you able to trace it?"

"Risky from inside the Summerland. That kind of probe can raise an alarm even through a stealth pipe."

"Oh." Grace's lip trembled. "I can't tell for certain, but it looks like the same source."

"The Eye of Providence—your old nemesis."

"Her name is Madeleine."

"Your therapist, so-called."

Grace pulled up a chair and dropped into it. "I'm not feeling too well."

Celeste stood, arms limp at her sides, and studied Grace's face.

"What?"

Celeste frowned, eyes drooping. "You never told me what happened."

"I told you."

Celeste pulled another chair alongside Grace's. "Yeah, you told me *about* what happened. But *what happened?*"

"I had my life taken away. The only way I could get it back was to shred it."

"I know that part."

Grace fiddled with the fabric of her hood. She could feel the round enclosure of the voice synthesizer sewn into it, a self-contained device the size of a hockey puck. She kept her eyes down as she spoke. "The way I found out my life was hacked was a v-gram from an old pervert. I heard it in the morning. By the time I went to bed that night, I had forty more v-grams. The next day—hundreds. By the time I rode my lifestream for myself, it had millions of rides. And the *comments...*"

"From the riders? Brutal?"

"Yeah. It wrecked me, or almost did. I was ready to jump off a building. Seriously. I was on the edge, about to tip myself over. Already recorded my suicide note. Set up a transfer of all my credits to Dylan."

"What changed your mind?"

"I thought I'd lost control." She looked up. "Nothing makes me crazier."

"Yeah, you do like to be in charge."

Grace smiled, then bit her lip. "I hesitated. Looking down the side of a twelve-story building was a new perspective."

"But you didn't..."

"I decided to take one last look at my lifestream. Maybe it would remind me of why I was checking out. Boost my resolve."

"And did it?"

"In a way, yeah. When I jacked into the lifestream, I found out that it'd gotten longer. The weavers were adding on."

"And you couldn't go through with it, knowing that after you were gone, they'd keep stealing your life."

Grace nodded. "They're doing it again, stealing lives. It's been more than two years since I shredded. None of the lifestreams we've seen since then are anything like the one they wove out of *my* life." She tilted her head to one side, toward the center of the Sandbox, where the virtual poker party had played out. "That one is. The same production quality, but that's not the giveaway. We've seen good rendering before. But the whole experience, the sensations and emotions…*that's* what set my lifestream apart." She tilted her head back, looking at the ceiling, letting her hands fall between her knees. "This *Poker Party*, how's it playing?"

"It's viral. Hundreds of thousands per week."

"Yeah. The emotions go straight for the lizard brain, like some VR-induced neurotransmitter. Electronic opium."

"There are others."

"Other lifestreams?"

"Uh-huh. This isn't the only one I pirated. I've got a snippet of another. It's called *A Walk in the Park*."

"How's *that* one doing?"

"Ten times bigger."

"Oh, Jah. What's it like?"

"Ugly. Assault, rape, murder. Hits you like a taser shot."

"Jah, what's *wrong* with people?"

"We're all twisted fucks." Celeste took her hood off the hook. "That's why pandering is so lucrative."

"She's not doing it for the credits."

"Then how come?"

"She has this idea that she can treat people's mental illness with VR. This is a big experiment to her. She weaves these viral lifestreams, then when a rider jacks in, she measures their reactions. The credits are gravy; it's how she funds her development."

"Measures reactions? How?"

"Didn't you know? The Belt is a two-way device."

Celeste's mouth dropped open. "Get *out!* Why didn't I know this?"

"Nobody knows it. It's not a supported feature. But the Eye and her crew have figured it out."

"I need to check into that." Celeste bit her knuckle. "So, she wants to help sick people. That's good, isn't it?"

"Those poker players—they're *real people*. If they're like me, they didn't sign up to star in a viral lifestream. And that other one, the rape, think about *that*. First a woman gets violated in person, then she's violated a *million* times in the Worldstream. I wouldn't be that cruel to a lab rat."

"I think that woman died."

Grace stood up and pulled on her hood. "Then she's one of the lucky ones."

23

The Torchbearer

CHRYSALIS JACKED IN from the Engine Room, the interaction limits set at minimum—no talking. It was a reconnaissance mission—speaking with the other avatars in the venue wasn't necessary. With any luck, she could hang at the edge of the crowd without being noticed.

It had taken almost a week to find the venue. She'd contacted clients, and even rivals, to get whatever she could on Dax and the Kliegls. News was hard to come by in the Shade world, and nearly impossible in the Summerland. Any stealth pipe to the Worldstream was strictly limited to the task at hand—work assignments accepted in encrypted packets; work products returned in the same way. Any unnecessary activity risked exposure. Putting an avatar in the Worldstream from inside the Shade firewall was a serious breach of the unwritten rules.

Despite that, Chrysalis had obtained a token for a Kliegl rally from another alliance doing piece work for *Kanpur Virset*, a designer of VR venues and assets. The Kliegls had contracted with Kanpur for the design of rally venues, everything from neighborhood get-togethers to 200-stage mass rallies. For a small bribe, one of the Shade gave up a token for a precinct rally, and an approximate time when it would be occupied. Sharing client information was another breach of the rules, but the Shade, generally speaking, were not rule-followers—especially where credits were concerned.

"Daystar, enter the venue."

Chrysalis rastered into a staging vestibule at the edge of a circular room thirty meters across. The ten-meter-high wall surrounding the room was alive with floor-to-ceiling, full-motion murals of Dax in action, posturing, lecturing, gesticulating—a 360-degree theater of Dax. The floor was a bowl-shaped hollow, giving everyone in the venue a clear view of the center. Chrysalis estimated there were fifty avatars, dressed as she'd seen them at the mass rally, in clothing with animated decorations, and lurid tattoos crawling across their arms or faces, depicting Dax or other heroic figures—Zeus hurling lightning bolts; Perseus atop winged Pegasus; the risen Christ.

In the center, at the bottom of the bowl, one avatar stood on a central platform, a tall woman with braided flaxen hair, each of her four replicated avatars facing a different direction. She wore a dress with its hem to the floor, like dresses Chrysalis had seen in historical venues from the 19th century. Every avatar was fixated on the speaker.

Chrysalis stepped out of the vestibule unnoticed.

"Citizens," the flaxen-haired woman said, "the council has *one job*, just *one!* It's not controversial. It's not a difficult job. Any of *us* could do it." She held up a finger. "*One job*. Do you know what it is?"

The avatars turned to one another, murmuring, some shrugging.

"Let Jahbulon protect us! That's it! Just get out of Jahbulon's way. And the Citizen's Independence Party and their hack leader Sato couldn't even get *that* right. If they had, we wouldn't be afraid to walk the streets. You know what's happening. You've heard the stories, the *horrible* stories, of these criminal attacks on our citizens."

The crowd turned up the volume. Some clapped, others raised fists. Glowing slogans appeared above them, waving as if on invisible fluttering flags.

"*That's* the legacy Sato and her traitors to Jahbulon have left our children and grandchildren—a return to the dark days before Jahbulon, when gangs of murderers roamed the streets. They weren't even out to rob, just for *sport*. Evil thugs, pure evil, who got their thrills from assaulting peaceable citizens going about their business."

The decorated avatars worked themselves up, jostling one another, shouting at each other face-to-face, centimeters apart. The murals on the walls turned menacing: scenes of dark, ancient streets, figures flitting into lamplight for a moment, then vanishing like shadows.

"The old world, when criminals hid themselves from Jahbulon, that's where we're headed with Sato and the so-called Citizen's Independence Party. Independence from what? From the pleasures of the Worldstream? From its infinite variety and choice? From the security of Jahbulon's watchful eye?"

The murals morphed into an ominous mob of indistinct figures, silhouetted against a dark sky. Flashes of lightning lit up an electric outline of the advancing horde. Chrysalis strained to hear—the crowd was so loud that even the speaker's direct audio feed was hard to follow.

"In our grandparents' time they feared marauding gangs of robbers and assassins, but at least those hoodlums showed their faces. At least they spoke with their own voices. If they went out in public, Jahbulon could find them. If they spoke, Jahbulon could hear them. But there's a new threat from the ones who live outside the Worldstream, who hide themselves, who disguise their voices, who commit their crimes with impunity. Citizens, we are at the mercy of the faceless, voiceless *Shade!*"

In the murals lightning flashes lit up the faces of the mob, but they had no faces. They were all wearing the black cloak of the Shade.

The crowd exploded. Every avatar sported some kind of accessory and they were all activated—flashing slogans, animated t-shirts, glowing faces, the crowd morphing into a multicolored light show.

"No Shade—light!" they chanted, the volume increasing with each repetition: *"No Shade—light!"*

"What's that supposed to mean?" Chrysalis asked, but Nemesio's safeguards muted her voice in the venue. "The

Shade are responsible for a *crime wave?*"

The crowd quieted as the woman continued: "In this moral crisis, in this falling away from Jahbulon, one person understands the threat of the Shade; one person has the vision and the courage to confront it."

"Dax! Dax! Dax!" the crowd chanted. The mural dissolved from the ominous wall of Shade, the black cloaked figures morphing into an army of Dax: fierce, dressed in white, arms wide, long, black hair flowing as if blown by the wind.

"Where do vermin live?" the woman called.

"Shade!" the crowd responded with one voice.

"Who is the light?"

"Jahbulon!"

"Who is the torch?"

"Kliegl!"

"And who is the torchbearer?"

"Dax! Dax! Dax!"

The chant continued without diminishing; the avatars jumped up with each shout, their fists raised overhead, glowing embellishments flashing at peak intensity. The jumping crowd expanded, approaching the walls, the mural now displaying the crowd itself, giving the illusion of avatars extending to infinity.

Two avatars—both women—bounced toward Chrysalis, shouting *"Dax! Dax! Dax!"* as they approached. She backed against the wall, but the women kept coming.

"What's wrong with you?" one shouted, an older woman whose forehead flashed *DAX* in neon red every time she shouted the name. *"Dax! Dax! Dax!* What's the matter? Why aren't you cheering?"

Chrysalis moved along the wall toward the staging vestibule, but the woman grabbed her arm.

The woman's fingers melted into Chrysalis's flesh, a vivid red outline of her hand remaining on Chrysalis's arm as the two limbs merged.

"Oh, Jah! My hand!" the woman screamed. Her companion grabbed both arms and tried to separate them, but her own hands melted into the arms, forming a triangle of flesh.

"Daystar, exit the venue!"

The convergence reticle appeared in Chrysalis's visor. She removed her headgear and pressed a finger to her neck. Her pulse was racing.

❖ ❖ ❖

Back in the dormitory, out of her Shade costume, Grace sat with her head down and a hand pressed to her mouth. She looked up when a Shade entered.

"Bjorg?" Grace asked.

The Shade removed her hood. Celeste narrowed her eyes. "Something's wrong. What's wrong?"

"I've been thinking about the test last week."

"Did Adrian figure out the problem?"

Grace shook her head. "He made changes. But the problem is still a problem."

Celeste glanced sideways at Grace. "Does that mean something?"

"I went back in."

Celeste's head fell back, eyes closed and mouth open. "Oh, no. You didn't." She lowered her head. "You *did*."

Grace nodded. "And the same thing happened. The deconfliction engine lost its mind."

"Bad as last time?"

"Same messages, but not as many. A lot fewer, in fact."

"That's progress, I suppose. Adrian is combing through the logs?"

"Adrian wasn't with me."

"You went in *alone?*"

"I had the safeties engaged. Minimal interaction. No voice. But I didn't go in to test the persona."

"Huh?"

"I went into another Dax rally."

Celeste tilted her head and sat down. "So, what did you learn?"

"This guy Dax—he's a threat. He could win. And if he does…" Grace gripped the front of her chair and leaned forward. "…he'll come for *us*."

24

MOTHER AND CHILD

GRACE SAW THROUGH the eyes of a rapist, his pants at mid-thigh, standing before the body of a woman, her legs splayed.

"Daystar, suspend the venue."

Grace tore off her visor. "Jah, what was *that?*"

"*A Walk in the Park*," Celeste replied. "Fucking brutal, isn't it?"

Grace leaned forward, holding her arms over her stomach. She felt nausea rising. "Yeah. Brutal." Her body convulsed, and she tasted vomit in the back of her throat.

"You gonna be okay?" Celeste asked.

"Water."

Celeste passed a bottle. Grace took a sip.

"I've got a bunch more," Celeste said. "All from the same source. The rendering is distinctive, practically a signature."

"Are they all this bad?"

"Worse. I've got one called *Subterranean Blues*. Puts you right in the head of a psychotic serial killer. Abducts his victims and hides them in his basement, taking little snips off them with a big-ass pair of scissors until they expire. I lasted about five seconds before I bolted for the door."

Grace stood, holding the arm of the chair. She faltered before righting herself.

"The Eye," she said.

"Of Providence. You sure?"

"She's a transgression counselor. She handles all the

extreme cases for her district, physical transgressions, like that. She has access to a lot of perverts."

"I still can't believe that these lifestreams are real people. This one. *Especially* the basement one."

"My lifestream was her first. *That* one was real—I can testify to that." Grace collapsed back into the chair.

Celeste stood. "Grace, you don't look well."

"I'm not."

Celeste put her hand on Grace's cheek. "You're ice cold." She held up the VR headgear. "Let me show you another one."

Grace felt her nausea return and clutched her stomach. "Jah, *no.*"

"Grace." Celeste slowly approached, holding the VR headset. Grace turned away.

"Trust me," Celeste said. Grace stayed still, turning her face up to Celeste as she slid on the headgear.

"Daystar," Celeste commanded, *"Mother and Child."*

Grace was transported to an outdoor venue—a snow-covered mountainside, stands of tall evergreens on either side. The trees sped by in a blur as the avatar Grace inhabited slalomed down the slope. Powder billowed from her skis, leaving a sparkling wake.

"This isn't helping," Grace said, her throat tightening, stomach churning.

"Give it a minute," Celeste replied through the headphones.

The avatar veered into a field of moguls, launching herself expertly off of each one, crashing down with a pole plant, then hitting the next mogul and caroming off in a new direction. Grace felt the stress on her knees, heard the wind in her ears, and tasted the cold air. It was a convincing venue, the rendering competent but not exceptional—in every way an average lifestream, not nearly the level of craftsmanship of the Eye's perverted venues.

"Why am I looking at this?"

"Just a few more seconds."

The action froze. A message flashed in front of Grace's

eyes, in vivid red letters:

*PROLONGED APNEA EVENT—BEGIN
RESUSCITATION*

Grace saw her VR headgear pull away. She put her hands to her face to replace it, then realized that the VR gear was part of the lifestream. She was no longer on a ski slope, but in a small flat, a three-by-four meter room with a single chair and a wall screen. The screen sounded an alarm, like a siren, while flashing the same message—*PROLONGED APNEA EVENT—BEGIN RESUSCITATION*. The rendering quality was superb.

The avatar tossed the gear aside as she stood up, running into the next room, a bedroom with an adult bed and a crib. She bent over the crib to see a tiny baby, hardly bigger than a newborn, lying still.

"Baby!" the avatar shouted. She flicked her finger on the baby's foot. *"Baby, wake up!"*

The infant didn't react. Grace's heart raced and her breathing quickened. She wanted to look around for some way to wake the baby, or simply to pick him up, but she was just a spectator in the lifestream, powerless to move the avatar's head and arms.

The avatar turned to a dresser by the crib, opened the top drawer, and pulled out a tiny mask with an elastic band. She slipped it over the baby's head and pressed a button on the side of the mask. A light flashed, indicating that the mask was forcing air into the baby's lungs. The avatar put her hand under the baby's back and pressed two fingers to his chest. She compressed the baby's chest in time with the flashing light.

"Baby?" the avatar's voice sounded in Grace's head. Grace felt tears coming, seeping down between her visor and her face. The tension in her chest, rapid breathing, pounding heart all intensified, bordering on panic. A minute passed, then another.

"Baby!"

The child twitched, then flailed, bawling into the mask. The avatar picked up the baby, cradling him in her arms, slipping off the mask and dropping it into the crib, the light still flashing, the sound of rushing air continuing as the mask pumped away.

Grace looked down on the squalling infant. His mouth was a wide oval taking up almost half his face, round and red. The avatar touched the baby's wrinkled nose; he pushed the finger aside with a pudgy doll hand. She stroked the baby's forehead, lifting the infant to her face and smelling him. His cry was loud enough to hurt Grace's ears, but Grace laughed as relief washed over her like a warm shower. She stayed in the lifestream until the baby quieted.

"Daystar, suspend the venue," Celeste said.

The bedroom dissolved and the alignment reticle appeared.

Grace took off her headgear, wiping the wetness from the visor and her face.

"What'd you think of that one?" Celeste asked.

"Amazing. *Amazing!* The feelings, the way the panic came, and then it passed. And the little baby..." More tears came. Celeste handed Grace a tissue.

"Yeah, that's some emotional whiplash."

"Is it from the same source as...you know..."

"The sick flicks? You tell me."

"The rendering was perfect. The emotions were...*Jah*... they were overwhelming." Grace dabbed her eyes. "If it's not the same source, then there are *two* weavers out there with phenomenal skills."

"I agree, and not just because of the rendering and the emotional face punch. I've pulled out some metadata—that was a challenge. They're all from the same crew."

"Crew?"

"They're Shade for sure. They used steganography."

"I don't know what that means."

"They buried the metadata in the visual stream. It's a common stealth method. It was a chore to tease it out."

"That's how you know it's a Shade crew?"

"The Shade use it a lot. I don't know anyone else who does. There aren't many legitimate uses for it."

"And they're all the *same* crew?"

"Pretty sure. I just don't know if it's your BFF Madeleine."

"I'm pretty sure about *that*. She's at it again—stealing people's lives." Grace stood up and lifted her cloak high enough to remove the Belt. "First sex and drugs, then violence, and now tender moments. What's she up to?"

Celeste took the Belt from Grace and turned it over in her hands. "*Mother and Child* wasn't *all* tender feelings."

"Right." Grace nodded. "It was a rollercoaster, really."

Celeste held out the Belt. "That's the common feature. The emotional response. The intensity. The mindfuck coupled with the gut punch. Compliments of the Belt."

❖ ❖ ❖

Grace donned her hood and went as Chrysalis to the common restroom on the lowest level of the Summerland, a row of stalls, each barely large enough for its user to turn around, with a shower, sink, and toilet. She found a vacant stall, took off her hood and mask, and splashed water on her face. She looked in the mirror as she toweled off.

Touching her face, studying her eyes, *Mother and Child* still vivid in her mind, Grace reached for more distant memories: a newborn in her arms, wet and red, crying his first cry—a headstrong boy, testing her patience—a teen with the same hair and eyes she saw in her own reflection, bubbling over with questions, challenges, and dreams. She closed her eyes, trying to conjure a vision of his face, imagining what he must look like now, two years since she'd last seen him. It was a fuzzy, faded image, like an avatar rendered by an overloaded server.

"Soon, Dylan," she whispered. "Soon."

25

LUCKY DAY

"HE'S IN THE Engine Room. Yellow and black stripes."

"Okay."

Elisha left Shade Hamish, his slight, shivering informant, cowering in the corner of a dead-end passage on the third level of the Summerland. The Engine Room was on the fifth and lowest level, two flights down and a five-minute walk. Elisha found his man, Shade Cyril, seated in a cubicle in the far corner, in full VR gear, gesturing in his venue, a yellow-and-black-striped mask visible over the top of the cube wall.

Elisha grabbed a handful of Cyril's cloak.

"What the fuck?" Cyril pulled off his headset and looked up at the Shade towering over him.

"I'm called Elisha."

"Shit!"

Cyril twisted in his seat, trying to break free, but Elisha kept a tight grip on Cyril's cloak. Cyril lifted his arms and slid out of the loose garment. He ducked under Elisha's outstretched hand, slipping past him and out through the opening in the cubicle. He was halfway down the aisle when Elisha caught him by the arm.

"Not cool, Cyril," Elisha droned.

"You interrupted my gig," Cyril rasped. "How can I get your credits if you won't let me work?"

"Twelve thousand," Elisha demanded.

"I know how much it is. Jah, I'm trying, but you're messing me up."

158

"When?"

"Tomorrow."

Elisha tightened his grip. "*Not good enough.*"

"Ow! Jah! Five! I got five! That's all. That's all I've got."

"Twelve."

"I don't *have* twelve." Cyril thrashed. Elisha maneuvered him into a corner before letting go, and blocked his escape. Cyril massaged his arm.

"*Anyone* can come up with twelve," Elisha said.

Cyril leaned into the corner, sliding down to the floor. He held his arm over his chest and his head fell to one side.

"I can't," he choked. "Elisha, I *can't*. I can't even pay my fees. The five thousand? That's for my fees. They're due tomorrow. If I pay the Kaleidoscope, they'll kick me out of the Summerland. Then what?"

"Whose problem is that? Yours, or mine?"

"Elisha, think about it. If I pay you, I'm out on the street. You'll never see me again. Then where's Chrysalis's 12K?"

Elisha crowded Cyril further into the corner. "How much are the fees?"

"Four."

Elisha stepped on Cyril's ankle.

"Three-five! Ow, get off!"

Elisha let up. "What does the gig pay?"

"Five hundred."

Elisha's foot hovered over Cyril's ankle.

"Okay, *okay!* A thousand!"

Elisha pulled his foot back. "This is your lucky day, Cyril. I'm about to cut you a humungous break."

Cyril twisted where he sat. The eyes showing through his mask were wet with fear.

"Fifteen hundred today," Elisha said firmly. "Like *now*. Make the transfer while I'm waiting."

Cyril nodded.

"Pay your fees tomorrow. That thousand you're pulling down? That's *ours*. From now on, you work for Chrysalis. We'll cover your fees. We'll give you an allowance for food. We'll get you your gigs. But the pay comes *our* way. Any questions?"

Cyril shook his head.

"And I want to correct you on one thing. If you go out on the street, we *will* see you again. And we *won't* be friendly."

Cyril nodded. A long moment of silence ensued.

"What?" Cyril asked.

"The transfer. Fifteen hundred."

Elisha followed Cyril back to his cubicle. He stood and watched as Cyril transferred fifteen hundred credits out of his account.

"Chrysalis thanks you," Elisha droned. "Welcome to the Kaleidoscope."

❖ ❖ ❖

Thomas lay on his cot in the Kaleidoscope dorm. He kept staring at the bunk above him as the door opened and a cloaked figure walked in. She took off her hood.

"Cyril?" Celeste asked.

"Uh-huh."

"How'd it come out?"

Thomas turned wearily, an arm resting on his forehead. "Fifteen today. A thousand tomorrow. Indentured servitude from here on."

Celeste pulled the cloak over her head and sat down heavily. "You okay?"

"Yeah." Thomas sighed. "I'm good. I'm always good."

Celeste leaned closer, putting her hand on his knee.

"It's your job, Thomas. We count on you."

"Cyril's got nothing," Thomas replied. "Less than nothing. He owes us, and he's working gigs for spare change."

"It's not forever."

"That's what you keep saying."

Celeste moved from her chair to the edge of Thomas's bed. "When the persona's done, we can give up the banking business. Or at least we won't have to put the arm on people to pay what they don't have."

"That'd be nice."

"Even better—this crew we're building up? Cyril and the rest? Once we can bypass the sponsors and go direct to the clients, we'll make it up to them. They'll be first in line for the credits that the sponsors are hogging for themselves."

"Great," Thomas said, rolling on his side. "I'll go tell Cyril he'll be in deep credits once we finish the persona. Maybe he'll forgive me for almost breaking his foot."

"You can't tell him."

"Yeah, I know." Thomas sat up, crouching to avoid the bed above. "Just how big a deal is this?"

"*Big*." She patted his leg. "That time we subbed for a sponsored crew, I asked one of them about the split."

"And?"

"Their sponsor keeps *eighty percent*. Eight credits out of ten."

"But the sponsor covers their expenses, right?"

"Some, but not all. Not even most. Their facility fees are covered, but the crew still pays for room and board out of *their* share—to the *sponsor*."

"Wow. So why are you trying to back out?"

Celeste stood. "I'm not backing out. I just think we're moving too fast. Adrian's a techie—he's in it for the challenge. And he's way too confident in his chops."

"And Grace?"

"Grace." Celeste leaned against the bunk, sighing. "Grace just wants to hug her boy again."

26

Room Occupied

Grace lay propped up on one arm, holding the sheet high enough to cover her breasts.

"Adrian, you need to *tell* me these things."

Adrian sat leaning forward on the edge of the bed with his back to her, elbows on his knees, and a cloak pulled across his lap.

"I hit a plateau after the last test," he replied. "I couldn't find the problem." He looked at Grace. Her red hair, which he'd buried his hands in minutes ago, sprayed out in a wild tangle like a lion's mane. Her face and neck were flushed, her lips pulled tight in a pout. "I needed some help. It's just a few coders."

Grace put her hand on his thigh. "I understand that. But you should have told me. And the others."

"The others? You mean Celeste?"

"And Thomas—the Kaleidoscope. We're a *team*."

"Is Celeste going to make decisions for us?"

"No, Adrian." She sat up, pulling the sheet high. "We agreed that's *my* responsibility. But I involve *all* of you."

"Celeste never would have gone along."

"You don't know that. You never gave her a *chance* to go along."

"I needed resources. I needed skills."

"Adrian, you went outside the Kaleidoscope. You used resources that belong to *all* of us." Grace pulled the sheet higher. "You should have told me."

Adrian put on his cloak as he stood. "I told you just now. Okay?"

Grace turned her head, looking at Adrian from the corner of her eye. "Don't get *angry*."

"I'm not angry." He picked up his briefs and pants, pulling them on under his cloak. "Do you want me to get rid of him?" He pulled off his cloak before putting on his shirt. *"Well?"*

Grace sighed. "Give me some more details."

"His name's Armengol—that's his Shade name."

"You said 'a few' coders."

"Three. I'm using three coders, but Armengol is the key. He knows the Worldstream stack. He knows the blockchain. He *really* knows the security protocols, way better than me."

"What do they think they're working on?"

"Two of the coders, they're just doing units. They don't know the architecture."

"And Armengol?"

Adrian held his cloak with both hands, twisting it like a wet towel. "He knows."

Grace put a hand to her head. "Oh, Adrian."

"He *has* to know. He's working on core processes."

"You went *outside* the group; you revealed our project to an *outsider*. Is he affiliated?"

"No."

"How do you know?"

"He told me."

"Oh, *Jah*. Adrian! He *told* you?"

Adrian dropped his arms to his sides, letting his cloak unfurl, black fabric pooling on the floor in a wrinkled heap. "Yeah, he told me. And I believed him. Why would he lie?"

Grace's hand dropped limply to the bed. She turned her face to the ceiling, eyes closed. "He's *Shade*. *We* are Shade. We *all* lie. We're all hiding *something*."

Adrian turned sideways and pulled on his cloak, trying to smooth the wrinkles. "Grace, I can't finish this without Armengol's help."

Grace pulled on her briefs and pants. "I get that," she

replied, standing, wearing the sheet like a toga. "You just put us in a bad spot, that's what I'm saying."

"I didn't mean to."

Grace dropped the sheet to pull on her top, followed by her cloak. She fussed with the closures, adjusting the fit, arranging the fabric on her shoulders, then went to check her appearance in the mirror. She pushed at her hair, trying to make it less unruly, and pressed her fingers against her cheek, pulling the skin tight, then releasing it. The fine wrinkles returned.

"Grace?"

"How much are you paying them?"

"I promised them a thousand credits a day."

"For all of them?"

"A head."

Grace saw her face tense in her reflection. "Three thousand credits a day?"

"Thirty-five hundred. I promised Armengol fifteen hundred."

"*Oh, Jah,*" she whispered.

The door latch moved. Grace and Adrian went for their hoods at the sound of the lock disengaging, a turn, and the opening of the door.

The Shade who entered closed it, then removed her hood. Celeste looked first at Grace, her face still flushed and hair still untidy, then at Adrian, head down, looking sideways at Grace.

"Oh, lovely," Celeste quipped. She went to her desk and opened the drawer. "Good thing I didn't get here five minutes earlier." She rummaged through the contents, pulling out a memory chip, and held it up. "I just came back for this. I need it. You know, to *work.*"

"Yep, I was just getting back to work, too," Adrian said. He pulled on his hood.

"Oh, yeah," Celeste replied, "coffee break's over, back to work."

Celeste's eyes followed Nemesio as he left the room.

"I'm sorry," Grace said.

"Don't apologize. I'd be fucking *my* boyfriend in the middle of the day if *I* had the time."

Grace sat on the bed, staring at the floor.

"Hey, I have an idea," Celeste said, wearing an impossibly wide smile. "I'll get one of those *Room Occupied* signs, like they used to have, when hotels still existed. You know, *Do Not Disturb*? Then we can avoid these embarrassing moments."

"That's *enough*, Celeste. I said I was sorry. We won't do it again."

"No need to go *that* far. You *are* going to *do it*. Just *do it* someplace else."

"Uh-huh."

Celeste put her hood back on and reached for the door, then stopped and pulled it off again in one smooth motion. "You know, I wasn't going to say anything, because I figured you were in the loop, but can you tell me why Adrian is transferring credits out of our account? Twenty-one thousand in the last week?"

"Yes. I know. He has some freelancers working for him."

Celeste squinted and pulled in her chin. "On what?"

Grace stood up and walked to the mirror. "The persona."

"The *persona?* Why does he need help with that?"

Grace frowned. "The errors from the last test. He's having trouble tracking them down."

Celeste narrowed her eyes, lips forming a straight line. "Nemesio, Ninja coder, can't find the bug?" She snorted. "Not the miracle man he thought he was."

Grace's shoulders drooped. Her head fell to one side, a pleading look on her face.

"That was snarky," Celeste said. "Sorry. We all hit a wall eventually. You understand, right?"

Grace nodded wearily.

"Yeah. What *I* don't understand is how Adrian can spend Kaleidoscope credits without the Kaleidoscope knowing about it."

"Yes. That's a problem."

"And what are you going to do about it?"

"I'll tell Adrian to cut back on his freelancers. Then I'll call a meeting of the Kaleidoscope." Grace looked at herself in the mirror. She really did look older than when she first came to the Summerland. In fact, she thought she looked older than she had earlier that very morning. "Give me a week. We can talk about it then."

◆ ◆ ◆

"Adrian and I have a proposal."

The Kaleidoscope were seated at the table in their dorm, door locked, hoods and cloaks off. Grace stood. Thomas laid his ample arms on the table; Adrian sat straight. Celeste slouched in her chair, arms crossed.

"We've all talked with Armengol. You have an idea of his skills."

"Yeah, I talked to him," Celeste agreed. "He's good."

"Good," Grace replied. She drew a deep breath. "That's good. We think so, too."

"Good, then," Celeste said. "We all think Armengol is good."

"Uh-huh." Grace sat down. "Thomas, what do you think?"

"Ah…yeah," the big man answered, shrugging. "I mean, he seems nice. He knows a lot."

"Good." Grace folded her hands and placed them on the table. "Adrian and I would like to bring him into the Kaleidoscope."

Celeste hung her head. "Jah. You are making a fucking joke, right?"

"We think that Armengol's skills will be valuable to the alliance."

Celeste put her elbow on the table and pointed at Adrian. "You mean valuable to *him* and his science project."

"It's *our* project," Grace corrected.

"It'll change how the Shade interact with the Worldstream," Adrian added, leaning in.

"Or get us all rounded up and thrown in confinement," Celeste countered, dropping back into her slouch.

"So—what?" Adrian asked. "You want to suspend the

project?"

"I want a *say!*" Celeste responded, her voice filling the room.

"You want to kill it," Adrian said, "because you can't understand it."

"Don't start with that!" Celeste snapped, rising from her chair, fists resting on the table. Adrian mirrored her stance.

"Enough!" Grace shouted, loudly enough that both Adrian and Celeste turned to her with a start. "Sit down."

Adrian and Celeste stared at each other for a few seconds before complying.

"Adrian cut his freelancers loose," Grace said softly, "but we're still paying Armengol."

"You said we were going to discuss that," Celeste replied.

"We're discussing it." She looked sideways at Adrian. "Go ahead."

Adrian lowered his eyes. "It was a mistake…"

"A *mistake?*" Celeste questioned.

Adrian gritted his teeth. "*I* made a mistake. I spent credits without consulting the crew."

"You're *still* spending…" Celeste said.

"Only on Armengol."

She turned to Grace. "I'm so glad we're talking about this. You know, working as a *team?*"

"Celeste…"

"Grace, *spare* me. First you spend our credits without telling us. Now you want to bring Wonder Boy into the group."

Grace felt her skin growing hot. She was certain it showed. "It's a proposal. Let's discuss it."

"Yeah, *let's*. I'm having second thoughts about the persona."

"You agreed to it," Adrian said.

"And I'm reconsidering. The thing is dangerous."

"That's why we need Armengol. He knows the protocols."

Celeste pulled her arms tighter and pressed her lips together.

"Doesn't he?" Adrian challenged.

"Yeah," Celeste conceded. "He knows."

"Better than I do," Adrian added.

"That's got to be tough for *you* to say."

"*Celeste!*" Grace admonished.

Celeste turned away, then dropped her arms to her sides. "All right. I'm still with the program." She sat forward. "But I didn't know it was going to cost us 1500 credits a day on top of *your* upkeep."

"I pull my weight," Adrian countered.

"You do just enough piecework to cover your room and board." Celeste stared directly at Grace. "Any other benefits you provide aren't exactly shared equally."

Adrian rose from his chair. "Is *that* what this is about?"

Celeste sat forward. "You want to know what this is about? I'll tell you what this is about. *I'm* the one who keeps this alliance afloat. *I* do more piecework than *all* of you put together."

Grace held up a hand. "And we appreciate that…"

"Don't patronize me."

Grace dropped her hand. "Celeste, you're right, your freelance work brings in a lot of credits. But you know that the majority of our income is from our banking operation."

"Which *I* manage." Celeste nodded. "Mm-hmm. Yeah. *I* get the gigs, *I* run operations. *Thomas* manages the accounts. *You* two blow the money *we* earn without telling us—when you're not canoodling in the dorm room."

"Canoodling?" Thomas asked.

Grace rose up, hands down on the table. "*What about Armengol?*"

"I can't even believe you're bringing it up," Celeste snorted. "The three of us worked together for almost a year before we formed this group." She waved her hand toward Adrian. "Even *him* we knew for nine months before he took off his hood. You've known this *other* guy for how long?"

"Four weeks," Adrian answered.

"Right. Not even a month. And Thomas and I have only talked with him a couple of times. Now you want to bring him in? A little premature in my opinion."

"We don't want to lose his skill set," Grace explained. "He's unaffiliated, but he's been approached by other alliances."

"If he's so good, why isn't he *already* with another alliance?"

"I asked him that," Grace replied. "He likes working freelance, but he also wants in on the persona. And we believe having him inside the Kaleidoscope is the best way to keep the project secure."

"If Armengol's working on the persona, who pays his bills?" Celeste asked.

"He'll do enough freelance work to cover his fees. He understands that."

Celeste shook her head. "It's still early. I'm against it."

"That's one vote no. Adrian and I vote yes."

"*Adrian* and I?"

Grace burned red. "*I* vote yes."

Adrian glared. "So do I."

All eyes turned to Thomas. Celeste stared—not an angry stare, but stern. Adrian lowered his eyebrows menacingly. Thomas looked at Grace. Her eyes were soft. She smiled.

"I vote yes."

"Fine." Celeste stood up. "He can't bunk in here—we're already overcrowded. Makes it damn hard to find any privacy." She locked eyes with Grace. "Right?" She pulled on her hood. "Meeting over. I've got a paying client, and I'm on a deadline."

27

A CRUSH OF BODIES

"It's the same avatar that raised two alarms," Chrysalis said. "Is it safe?"

"We think so," Nemesio answered. "The alarms aren't related to the actual avatar."

"You *think* so? Aren't you sure?"

"Yes," Armengol interjected. "I know what I'm doing."

Chrysalis raised her hands. "I'm not questioning your expertise, Armengol. I'm just thinking, why risk it? Shouldn't we use a different avatar?"

"Not necessary," Armengol objected. "It's the validation stack that's raising the alarms. It thinks the avatar's not associated with a real person. It doesn't care what the avatar looks like."

"I don't want to sound like a stuck stream…"

"Look, Chrysalis," Nemesio interrupted, "it took *months* to stitch together the Indian avatar—a *lot* of coding hours. If you want a different avatar…"

"It's not what I *want*, it's the *risk*…"

"I know, I know. Fact is, I *could* have put together another avatar if *you* hadn't taken away my freelancers."

"Oh, Nemesio, please…"

"Well, it's true."

"It's under control," Armengol said firmly. "Let's move on."

Nemesio glared at him through the holes in his mask.

"I mean…" Armengol muttered, "you know—it's *your*

test."

"Right," Nemesio responded, "*my* test." He turned to Chrysalis. "You said you wanted to pick the venue?"

"Yes," Chrysalis answered, pointing to a desk screen. "This is it."

The screen showed a party scene, young people dancing in pairs and in groups, the musicians duplicated at the four corners of the venue, orbiting above the dance floor. Curtains of light, like an aurora, rippled across the crowd. The dancing avatars wore all manner of dress, from simple outfits one might see on the street IRL, to clothing in fantastic colors, glowing decorations, or moving images.

Nemesio and Armengol sat nearby, scrutinizing their consoles.

"A venue for teens," Nemesio commented. "Let me guess."

"It meets your criteria," Chrysalis said flatly. "It's a crowd, lots of action. If something goes wrong, we won't attract attention. It's perfect."

"You think Dylan will be there."

Chrysalis adjusted her headgear and slipped on her tactile gloves. "Do you want me to use the Belt for this test?"

"That's not necessary," Armengol replied. "The adjustments I made have nothing to do with the peripherals."

"Okay," Chrysalis said, "anything else I should know?"

"Do you *know* that Dylan is there," Nemesio asked, "or do you only think that he *might* be there?"

"I don't know if he's there or not. I only know that I used to go to these things when I was Dylan's age. Maybe he's there, maybe not."

"That seems like a long shot."

The reticle in Chrysalis's visor sharpened; the stereo images converged. She focused her eyes first on the near field, then the far field, verifying that the dynamic depth of field was properly calibrated. She flexed her hands. The gloves were properly fitted.

"I think he's there."

"How could you possibly know that?"

"I don't *know* it. I just have a feeling about it."

Nemesio turned from the console. "Excuse me, *Grace*," he whispered, "but when it comes to facts, you're not the *feeling* type. How do you *know?*"

Chrysalis removed her headgear. "I've been doing some work on my own."

"What *work?*"

Chrysalis kept her eyes down. "Accessing the blockchain."

"Oh, Jah," Nemesio said. "Are you serious?"

Chrysalis tugged at her gloves. "I'm being careful."

"Careful or not," Armengol interjected, "it's *dangerous.*"

"I'm using all the stealth protocols. I'm simply monitoring. No manipulation."

"That doesn't matter. If Jahbulon sees you snooping around, he'll raise an alert that could lead him straight to us," Armengol replied.

Chrysalis fiddled with the headgear in her hands. "I was keeping tabs on Dylan, following his VR activities. I couldn't join the venues, of course—I just knew when he was jacked in and where."

"You could track his venues?" Nemesio asked.

"They weren't even venues, really. It was like he'd bypassed the venue servers entirely. It was so strange—he seemed to be exploring past events at random, no pattern at all. Then he dropped out of sight. I only found him again a few days ago, always in legitimate venues, always through a server."

"And you found him in *this* venue?"

"Yes." She looked up at Nemesio. "I want to see him."

Nemesio looked at Armengol. "What do you think?"

"I don't know. Looks like any other venue to me. Could be risky; I just don't know."

Nemesio shook his head. "I don't know, either."

"Nemesio—*Adrian*—*please*. I don't know when I'll find him again."

Nemesio and Armengol crowded together at one console, checking the parameters of the venue—more than three hundred avatars, server load over eighty percent, the operating system several revisions old.

"This server is slammed," Armengol stated, "and their security protocols are practically obsolete."

"I know," Chrysalis replied. "I checked that, too."

Nemesio winced. "Thought of everything, didn't you?" He put a hand behind his neck, pulling his mask tight, and looked at Armengol.

Chrysalis held her breath. Armengol shrugged.

"All right," Nemesio conceded. "I'll send you in. But I'm locking you down. You can approach an avatar, but you can't speak. You'll hear them; they won't hear you. If you touch any avatar intentionally, I'll end the test. Clear?"

"I'm clear," Chrysalis replied, replacing her headgear. The calibration grid converged. "Let's go."

❖ ❖ ❖

Chrysalis stepped out of the staging vestibule into a crush of bodies, teens in outrageous costumes, most brightly colored, many animated, as if the dancers were competing for attention, like elaborately plumed birds. The avatars closest to her seemed startled when a slight Indian man at least twice their age appeared from the vestibule. Some giggled behind their hands; others sneered.

The music pounded in Chrysalis's head until she tapped her ear as a signal to Nemesio. The volume dropped to a tolerable level.

"You can eavesdrop," Nemesio said. "Zero in on an avatar in your proximity and tap your forehead. I'll throw the switch. You'll hear everything the avatar hears and says."

Chrysalis kept close to the wall as she explored the venue. She scanned the crowd, not sure if she'd recognize Dylan, not even sure if she remembered his face. She kept her hand on the wall as she circled the crowd, past arcade games, vendors selling virtual clothes and accessories, and staging vestibules, nearly colliding with a teen rastering in.

Chrysalis took a step and her heart stopped. She saw a tall boy close to the wall, dressed in muted clothes, with another boy and two girls. She knew him—he was older, but she *knew* who he was. If they'd been apart for twenty years, she'd have known him. She could see the boy's face, the way he held his body, the look he gave to the girl, head lowered, eyes raised, a hint of a smile on his face…a smile she recognized.

The smile of a predator.

"Is that him?" Nemesio asked.

Chrysalis nodded *yes.*

"No contact," Nemesio warned.

She inched closer, centering the boy in her field of view, then tapped her forehead. Their conversation suddenly filled her head, a girl's voice and a boy's voice—a *man's* voice—as if she were standing next to them.

"Do you think I'm afraid of myself…Dylan?"

"Everyone is, just that some people get past it."

Chrysalis gasped. She was transported to a time when she surrendered nightly to a compulsion she'd since learned to control, an indistinct itch that demanded scratching. In those days she had used a repertoire of tricks to win her sexual conquests, appealing to the physical urges of her targets, or playing on their emotions—anxiety, loneliness, ambition, or —most effectively—fear.

"You won't be afraid?"

"Of myself?"

"Of me."

The girl had a look, fascination mixed with uncertainty. Chrysalis knew that look—she'd seen it many times, on the faces of her countless victims. And she knew that Dylan knew the look, too.

Chrysalis took a step.

"No contact!"

"I'm not afraid."

"Maybe you should be."

"Oh, you are so scary."

"Look out, he's a dangerous man."

"I'm not, you know, dangerous."

Dylan bent closer. The girl raised her face, presenting herself.

Chrysalis bounded forward, reaching for the girl's arm. *"Don't!"* she shouted, but they couldn't hear her.

"Chrysalis, what are you doing?" Nemesio yelled. The venue

went silent as Nemesio cut the audio feed.

The boy got between Chrysalis and the girl. She stared into the contorted face of her son, the angriest she'd ever seen him, his mouth forming words she couldn't hear, his finger pressed against her chest. She stepped back, then stumbled.

"Daystar, moving finger!" Chrysalis shouted.

She knelt on the floor and began to write in flaming letters. The venue dissolved around her as she finished the second line: *I AM THE CAPTAIN OF MY SOUL.*

❖ ❖ ❖

Chrysalis pulled off her gear, panting and perspiring. "You pulled me out," she said accusingly.

"You're damn right I did," Nemesio snapped. "I told you not to make contact."

"Did it cause any problems?"

"We're checking."

"I was looking in his *face*, Adrian. He was *this* close." She held her hand a few centimeters in front of her nose. "He's changed—he's a man."

Nemesio and Armengol bent close to the console, studying the data dump. "You could've admired him from a distance," Nemesio replied. "I set up the eavesdrop extension so you wouldn't *have* to get close."

"Nothing," Armengol said. "The Worldstream didn't even peep."

Nemesio nodded. "This is good." He slapped Armengol on the back. "I think you might've plugged the hole." He turned to Chrysalis. "Grabbing that girl—what was *that* about?"

"He was going after her."

"Dylan? They're *kids*. They were talking."

"They were *more* than just talking. Dylan was, anyway. He was hunting."

"Hunting?"

"Uh-huh. Like I used to."

"Yeah, well, you never told me much about your life in the world." Nemesio turned back to the screen. "And what was that thing on the floor?"

"A message. You wouldn't let me talk. I'm surprised you didn't pull the plug before I finished."

"I almost did. But I wanted to see what it said."

Chrysalis closed her eyes. She recalled the image of Dylan, of his enraged face, imagining what it would be like to touch him, to put her hand on his cheek, to feel him again, not in a venue, but IRL.

"He was *this* close," she whispered.

Like looking in a mirror.

28

The Worldstream Knows

Pairs of faces floated before Chrysalis's eyes. She swiped right if they were definitely the same person, left if they were definitely different, and down if she wasn't sure. None of them were easy calls—they were all images captured by cameras and sensors of the All-Seeing Eye, kicked out by the Worldstream's facial recognition algorithm as being too ambiguous for certain classification. Such uncertainties were among the last, shrinking vestige of problems too difficult for artificial intelligence. Human eyes and human brains still held an edge.

Chrysalis struggled to focus as images popped up, more than one pair per second. *RIGHT...RIGHT...LEFT... RIGHT...DOWN.* With each swipe her credit total ticked up, and her accuracy rating, based on consensus with a thousand other pattern-matching Shade, fluctuated between 85 and 90%. If she could raise her rating above 95%, she'd double her rate, but even at one-twentieth credit per match, her contribution to the Kaleidoscope treasury would be meager, a fraction of what a coding gig might pay. But the high-paying jobs went to the sponsored crews, or to the best freelance coders, of which there were many.

One face bled into another, all of them looking the same. Her eyelids drooped. With the last five matches, her rating dipped to 84%. She slowed down, but her rating continued to slide. Her credit total plateaued. She heaved a thick sigh, dropping her hands to her lap as the last pair of faces lingered, two images of what could be the same woman—or maybe not.

"Chrysalis, you have an alert," Daystar's voice said in her headset. A scroll appeared in her field of view: *Dylan is in the dance venue.*

"Daystar, end the sequence." The disembodied heads faded out. She pushed her visor to her forehead and peeked over the cubicle wall. The tops of the Shade at the other workstations bobbed above the partitions, some in hoods, most in their masks. She scanned the Engine Room for a gold mask with black trim, but couldn't find it.

Chrysalis repositioned her gear. "Daystar, where's…"

"Yes, Chrysalis? Are you trying to locate someone?"

She inhaled and held it, then blew it out. "No, Daystar. Initiate the persona."

"Yes, Chrysalis. Which venue?"

"Dance venue. With Dylan."

"Yes, Chrysalis. Interactions are limited to visual-only by default."

"Daystar."

"Yes, Chrysalis?"

"Disengage the limits. Full interaction."

"Disengaging the interaction limits is not advised."

"Understood, Daystar. Proceed."

The reticle converged; the staging venue dissolved to the dance floor. Chrysalis stepped out of the staging vestibule, next to a gaming booth, the title *ARMY MARKSMAN* scrolling overhead. She stayed by the wall, making herself as easy to spot as possible without wearing an animated glow-in-the-dark costume.

She looked over the crowd, trying to pick out Dylan's face from the mob of color and light, but few of the faces were even visible. She looked for someone of Dylan's size and build, finding no one. She took a step, then stopped. A boy and a girl, both in dark, nondescript costumes, stood at the edge of the crowd, just a few meters away. They were centimeters apart. The boy took the girl's hand and placed it on his chest. He put his hand on her chest, and she covered it with her own. The music grew painfully loud; the boy and girl drew closer.

Suddenly the boy glanced up. Chrysalis caught Dylan's eye.

"Dylan," she whispered. "Don't."

Dylan pushed the girl aside and strode to Chrysalis, so fast that she put up her hands, expecting him to collide with her.

"Who are you?" he demanded, shouting over the band, his face aggressive, but not angry and threatening the way he was the last time she saw him.

"Dylan, are you well?"

"Am I what? Who *are* you?"

Dylan was a lot taller than the Indian man. Chrysalis looked up at him, wondering if he would seem as tall if they were facing each other IRL, or if he would look as old.

"I just want to know if you're doing well," she replied. "I want to know if you're happy." She felt her mouth go dry and her throat catch, but the Indian man's voice sounded calm and composed.

The girl appeared out of the darkness. "Oh, *this* guy again," she said. She took Dylan's arm, grabbing him as if she were snatching a child from a rabid dog. She glared, as if to say *Hands off, he's mine.*

Dylan ignored her. "Tell me who you are, because I think I know."

The girl clutched Dylan's arm with both hands, pulling herself to him, turning her body as if to shield him from the stranger. She had a look Grace knew well, the look of a mark in a con game who's already bought the con, the look of a prospect who *wants* to be seduced.

"Girl, for your own good, please leave."

She tugged harder on Dylan's arm. "No, *you* leave. C'mon, Dylan."

Dylan turned toward the girl, looking annoyed. "Mia, later," he said. "I need to talk to my..." He tilted his head. "To this guy."

The girl pushed Dylan away, getting in Chrysalis's face, spitting spite, before stalking away.

"Are you..." Dylan began.

Chrysalis interrupted. "Don't ask, Dylan. I'm only here to see if you're doing well."

"What's that to you?"

Chrysalis had seen Dylan's face, VR and IRL, a thousand times, but she couldn't read him, not at that moment. Was he angry, accusing, confused? All of these? She didn't know.

She ached to tell him. Though she'd exceeded all safe limits of interaction, revealing herself in the presence of the All-Seeing Eye might be a step too far. But it wasn't necessary. She was certain he knew.

"I want to tell you not to repeat the mistakes of others."

"Others? What others? What mistakes? *Who are you?*"

"I can't tell you. But I know someone who's made a lot of mistakes. Her whole life was a mistake, except for one thing —just one." She moved her hand to reach for him, to touch his face, then stopped, her hand hovering between them. "*You*, Dylan. You're the only thing she did right. And she wants to know that you won't go the same way she did."

Dylan softened his voice, his eyes searching hers. "What way is that?"

"She used people. She preyed on people, for her own pleasure."

Dylan turned away, clenching his teeth. "I'm not doing that."

"Good." His denial was as familiar as his face, the same denial that Grace had mouthed so often without meaning it. "That's good, Dylan. And Mia, she would back you up on that?"

"She's nothing to me."

"And yet, you went after her."

He squeezed his eyes shut. "I don't know why I did that."

"An addict never knows why."

His eyes snapped wide open. "An *addict?* Addicted to *what?*"

"That feeling of power—power over another person. It's like a drug."

Dylan lunged, grabbing Chrysalis by the shoulders. She flinched and pulled back. "That's not me!" he said. "That's *not me!"*

Dylan's face pixelated and the venue shivered. "Wait!" Dylan shouted. "Raúl wants to meet with you."

"Raúl? Where? When?"

Dylan's voice sounded remote and hollow, as if he were at the far end of an empty auditorium. "The Cloakroom. Soon, tomorrow…nine o'clock. At night."

The dance venue faded; the pounding racket of Cadaver Dog trailed off, leaving her ears ringing. She pulled off her gear and turned toward the screen on the table next to her, and reacted with a start.

There was another Shade in the cubicle with her, dressed in his cloak but no hood, wearing instead a gold mask with black trim.

"Nemesio?"

Nemesio said nothing. He sat at the table, perusing the list of status messages scrolling past the screen.

"He was in the venue again," Chrysalis explained. "I tried to find you, but…"

Nemesio held up a hand. "You disengaged the interaction limits."

"I wanted to talk to him," she murmured. "I wanted to *warn* him."

"So you went in on your own."

"I tried to find you."

"And you didn't engage any of the *fucking* limits!"

"Why are you getting angry?"

Nemesio turned in his chair and gestured toward the screen, still scrolling status.

Chrysalis stared without understanding, until the meaning of the messages became clear.

"The Worldstream knows."

"Yep. Jahbulon's onto us. And he probably knows *exactly* where we are."

29

DEATH TO JAHBULON

The sign on the door hadn't changed in the two years since Chrysalis last saw it:

CLOAKROOM
IN VITA OCCULTA LIBERTAS EST

In the hidden life, there freedom lies. Grace felt as though she was in bondage then, the viral lifestream woven from her drug-and-alcohol-fed binges filling her thoughts every waking hour, daring her to surrender to the addiction. Two years later, living the *hidden life* as Shade Chrysalis, she was certain she'd traded one set of chains for another.

The Cloakroom attendant verified that Chrysalis was disconnected before admitting her. The crowd was typical for a late night, between three and four dozen black figures, either Cloak or Shade—there was no way of knowing by sight—and scattered civilians, identifiable by their white robes, the only garment they were allowed to wear after removing every connected item on their persons. Most were seated; some stood in groups of two or three, their monotone voices blending into a non-stop hum. One Cloak wandered alone, approaching first one, then another cloaked figure, looking for an anonymous encounter. All of them had one thing in common: they were completely disconnected from the Worldstream, inside the copper-lined, electromagnetically opaque walls of the Cloakroom.

One was different however—a tall, thin man, dressed in a gray jacket over a black tee, his long, silver hair pulled back from his bronzed face. He sat alone at a table, a half-smile on his face as he watched the others. He turned to Chrysalis as she approached.

She stood silently by his table, reacquainting herself with his face. He raised his eyebrows.

"Chair's taken," he said. "I'm waiting for someone."

Chrysalis smiled behind her hood.

"I'm called Chrysalis."

Raúl stood and pulled a chair away from the table. "You have arrived."

"Hello, Raúl," Chrysalis replied as she sat.

"Hiya, Chrys. You're looking well."

"Still as funny as I remember."

Raúl's eyes wandered over the room. "That guy's looking for some action," he stated, pointing to the lone Cloak. The individual went up to another Cloak, leaning close as if whispering in the other's ear. A head shake *no* and the Cloak was off to try again. Raúl laughed. "That never fails to amuse."

"Have you been well, Raúl?" Chrysalis asked.

Raúl tilted his chair back, hands in his pockets, staring at Chrysalis as if he could see through her hood. "I've thought about you from time to time, wondering how you were getting on. You must have done okay for yourself. Paid me back your debt, and then some."

"I owed you."

"And I had a feeling—a completely unfounded feeling—that you'd make good." He nodded, a u-shaped smile under his hawk-like nose. "Making it in the Land of Shade—not for sissies. I figured you for a tough lady."

"Was that the reason for the 50,000 credit stake? Your unfounded faith in me?"

"*Unfounded faith*," he laughed. "That's redundant." He leaned forward. "The 50,000 was an investment. It paid off."

"You're welcome." Chrysalis tugged at the hem of her hood, adjusting the position of her voice synthesizer. "You contacted Dylan. He told me to come here."

"Yeah. Dylan and I are buddies. We get together a couple times a month."

Chrysalis leaned closer, turning an ear toward Raúl. "Tell me about him."

"He's a smart kid, and stubborn, like his mom. He gets a notion and nothing stops him. No patience, either. If he'd only learn to take things step by step, he'd go far. Maybe as far as his old lady."

Chrysalis sucked in a deep breath. "I only learned patience a little while ago myself."

Raúl turned his head, looking at her with a half-wink. "You ain't learned it yet."

"What do you mean?"

He pointed his finger. "This thing you're doing, putting yourself in the Worldstream—that's dangerous stuff."

"We're being careful."

"*Careful* might not cut it, not the way things are these days."

"What?"

"You Shade might not be up to date on the political situation."

"The Kliegls. Dax."

Raúl raised his eyebrows. "I'm impressed."

"We used Dax rallies for our early tests."

Raúl nodded. "Makes sense. Big crowd, lots of distractions, venue server close to capacity. So you know what's going on."

"But the Kliegls aren't in power."

"They don't have to be. There's a crime wave underway. Nobody knows why, so people are scared, and Dax is using it. Sentiment's running high against the Shade. The coalition government's caved. They're on alert for crime of all kinds, but especially cyber-crime." Raúl rested his chin on the back of his hand, looking at Chrysalis with raised eyes. "Bad news for my bud Dylan."

Chrysalis put her gloved hands together over her chest. "What do you mean?"

"You're not the only one who's been tinkering where they shouldn't. Your boy's been trolling the Worldstream for signs of his shredded mother."

"Oh, *Jah.*"

"Yeah, Jah. He tripped a circuit breaker and brought Jahbulon down on him. He's confined to quarters, in the iron grip of Aunt Donna."

"Is he in trouble?"

"Well, *yeah.* Blockchain data breach, a level six transgression. It's what got my attention in the first place. He's definitely on probation. Another slip-up and he'll be in confinement."

Chrysalis rose from her chair. "*No.* That can't happen. *You* can't let that happen."

"Hey, Chrys, I warned him already."

Chrysalis sat down. "You said that you visit Dylan. IRL?"

"Ha. I don't visit *nobody* IRL unless they're off the Worldstream and wearing a cloak."

"VR then."

"Only in venues *I* control, safe from Jahbulon's and Aunt Donna's prying eyes."

"What do you do together?"

"Geek stuff." Raúl sat back and crossed his legs. He looked down, tugging at the lapel of his jacket.

"You're teaching him, aren't you?"

Raúl adjusted his other lapel. "I'm trying to keep him out of trouble."

"I don't want him…"

"What? To grow up like Raúl?"

"That's not what I meant. I just…I don't want him to get hurt."

"By dicking around in the Worldstream's gears? That'll hurt him, all right, if he doesn't know what he's doing. And he's *going* to do it. Like I said, he's got the notion."

"Can't you stop him?"

"Could I stop *you?* You wanted to shred your life and you were going to shred it or know why. I stepped up to make sure it got done right." He turned away. "Dylan? Same thing."

Chrysalis put both hands to her mouth.

"Chrys," Raúl said, showing the palm of his hand as if taking a pledge, "I won't let him do any permanent damage."

"Please," she pleaded, her fingers muffling her synthetic voice.

Raúl lowered his hand. "All right, then. Now let's talk about *your* extra-curricular activities."

"My what?"

"Showing up in Dylan's venue, dressed like a little Indian guy."

Chrysalis lowered her head. "I wanted to see Dylan. Jah, I miss him."

"You're asking for a raft of crap."

"I can't see him IRL. Ever since I shredded, he's been tagged."

"It's a risk, I know, but what you're doing is riskier."

Chrysalis raised her head, hands flat on the table, leaning forward. "But it's *my* risk. If something goes wrong, Jahbulon comes for *me*, not Dylan."

"For you and your whole Shade crew."

Chrysalis closed her hands into fists. "Do you think so?"

"Folks are in a Shade fever, thanks to Dax. If they find you, they'll come for you."

She turned away. Raúl pressed a knuckle against his lip. He peered at Chrysalis through narrow eyes. "I can help."

"You can…what? *How?*"

Raúl leaned close, lowering his voice to a whisper. "I want to know."

"What?"

"How you're doing it. You're not stealing a key, are you? You're *forging* one."

Chrysalis nodded.

"And you're synthesizing the avatar from disconnected data?"

She nodded again. "And some data we're creating."

Raúl sat back in his chair, one hand over his mouth, the other slapping the side of this thigh. "*Jahbulon on a platter!* Do you know what that means?"

Another nod. "I can go back into the Worldstream. I can be with Dylan."

"Go back? No, no, no. It means a *lot* more. You'll break the Worldstream—death to Jahbulon."

30

Identity at Risk

Chrysalis rushed to the Engine Room, pulling on her VR gear as she went, as soon as the alert came through: *Dylan is in the dance venue.*

"Daystar, initiate the persona."

"Yes, Chrysalis. Interactions are limited to visual-only, by default."

"Disengage the limits."

"Nemesio has locked the limits on the persona."

Chrysalis pressed a gloved fist against her mouth.

"Daystar, override the lock."

"I'm sorry, Chrysalis. I'm afraid I can't do that."

Chrysalis looked out over the Engine Room. She saw no sign of Nemesio, but it didn't matter. She didn't want to ask him to disengage the limits; he would never agree to it, and besides, she had other options.

"Daystar, open the back door."

"Yes, Chrysalis. Passphrase, please."

"My head is bloodied but unbowed."

After a pause, Daystar replied, "Confirmed. You have root access."

Within seconds, Chrysalis had rastered into the dance venue. She spotted Dylan before she'd even stepped out of the vestibule. As he rushed toward her, she held up her hands.

"I saw Raúl. He told me what you're up to."

"Mom, I…"

"Don't talk, just listen," she spoke in a rush. Every word she said, every second spent in the venue, every interaction with Dylan added to her exposure. "Do *not* try to find me. I'll find you. Do you understand?"

Chrysalis waited for an answer, but Dylan stood still, eyes down, as if transfixed.

He looked up. "Connor, *Transformed…*" He paused.

"Dylan?"

The boy looked exasperated. He stared directly at Chrysalis.

"*Transformed…Alert…Cherubs.*"

"Dylan, listen to me!" Chrysalis pleaded, reaching toward him.

A glowing yellow message floated in her field of view: *UNAUTHORIZED ACCESS…IDENTITY AT RISK… EXIT THE VENUE IMMEDIATELY.*

"What's that?" Chrysalis asked. "What's happening?"

The venue vanished in a blinding flash of light. Chrysalis squeezed her eyes shut, then opened them to slits. The venue reemerged from the light. Dylan's avatar flattened and rastered out. She looked around, but he was gone.

❖ ❖ ❖

Chrysalis sat alone in her dorm in full Shade costume, her elbows on her knees, when another Shade entered.

"I'm called Nemesio."

Chrysalis pulled off her hood and cloak. Nemesio did the same, then they peeled off their masks.

"Celeste said you're looking for me?"

Grace nodded. Adrian stood by while she mustered her courage.

"I used the persona again."

Adrian rolled his eyes, sighed, and sat. "Dylan, I assume."

Grace nodded.

"And what happened?"

"Nothing out of the ordinary, according to the log."

"That's good, then."

"Except…"

Adrian held his breath.

"There was one message I've never seen before. *UNAUTHORIZED ACCESS…IDENTITY AT RISK.* I don't know what that means."

Adrian turned his head slightly. "Was it only in the log?"

"I saw it in the venue, too."

"What were you doing at the time?"

"Talking to Dylan."

Adrian furrowed his brow. "About?"

Grace kept her eyes down as she stood and faced the door. "I told you what he was up to, right? Accessing the blockchain. Remember?"

"Uh-huh."

"Adrian, I was only going to tell him stop doing it. I don't want him to get into any more trouble."

"And that's when you saw the warning?"

She shook her head. "Dylan said something really weird —*'Transformed…Alert…Cherubs'* I think. That's when I saw it." She turned to Adrian. "What is that? A passphrase?"

The color drained from Adrian's face. "Oh, *Jah.*"

"What? What is it?"

"After he said that, did the venue go blank?"

"Yes. What's it mean?"

"I'm not sure, but your son might have stolen our key."

The discussion between Adrian and Grace escalated into an argument, and then to a fight. Adrian accused Grace of recklessness. She pleaded for understanding. He committed to analyzing the log to see how much damage she had done, and she promised never again to use the persona to contact Dylan.

Keeping her promise was easier than Grace had expected. She received no more alerts that Dylan was in the dance venue—or in any other venue.

31

Slipshod Operation

THE BAST LIVED away from the Summerland. To find them, Elisha had to go outside the walls, walking more than five kilometers to a neighborhood where the gentry once lived, before the Worldstream had democratized all luxury. A big house with multiple floors and separate rooms for cooking, dining, sleeping, and entertainment was an economic burden most people had jettisoned decades ago.

Elisha went at night, when the Cloak came out, wearing the same black costumes as the Shade, scurrying in shadows to their RL encounters after a day working VR jobs. The Shade ventured out of their enclaves *only* at night, when they could be credibly mistaken for the connected, ostensibly law-abiding Cloak.

Few Cloak roamed the street that night. Those who did kept close to the buildings, away from the glare of streetlights. Elisha saw for the first time the roving bands of Kliegls, three, four, or five to a group, distinctive in their white uniforms, a wide red sash across their chests, wearing red caps bearing the Kliegl symbol: two stylized searchlights with crossed beams.

On the other side of the street, three Kliegls blocked the way of a passing Cloak. Elisha slowed to listen:

Shade vermin!

No, I'm Cloak! I'm called Denton.

Show us. Show your face to us and to Jahbulon.

The Cloak tried sidestepping the Kliegls. The three white-shirts blocked his way, until he pushed past them, breaking into a run.

Elisha picked up his pace, leaving the Kliegls' laughter fading in the distance.

❖ ❖ ❖

Forty minutes later, Elisha found the street, lined with abandoned shells without glass in their windows or paint on their doors. One house stood out from the rest; it resembled its younger self, when its owners kept it up. The location of the place was its most valuable asset—nobody came to the neighborhood, shielding the Bast from accidental discovery.

Elisha mounted the steps. He stood in front of a door not much taller than he was, peering through a tiny glass portal. The interior was dark, the view obscured by a sheer curtain. He pressed the doorbell, but there was no sound. He knocked.

"Stand back," a voice commanded through a hidden speaker. Elisha took a step backward. "Identify yourself."

"I'm called Elisha of the Kaleidoscope."

"Wait there."

Elisha looked around the neighborhood as he waited—no signs of life, not even a stray cat. The walkway he followed to the house was cracked and buckled; the street was filled with potholes. There wasn't even an auto-bus kiosk on the street.

The door opened with a creak. A cloaked figure motioned Elisha forward. He passed a small metal rectangle over Elisha from head to foot and shoulder to shoulder. The device flashed green.

"He's disconnected," the Shade said, turning toward the door.

A second Shade appeared from the shadows.

"Elisha, I'm called Leon. Why are you here?"

Elisha stood thirty centimeters taller than Leon, and half again as wide. He stepped forward, causing Leon to take a step back.

"You're behind in your payments," Elisha replied, his synthesizer set to render his voice in a lower, more menacing tone. "I need a transfer of 100,000 credits immediately. I can wait while you do it."

Leon crossed his arms. "We're current."

"You've already made the transfer?"

"The transfer isn't due until next week."

"It's *past* due."

Leon dropped his arms to his sides and tilted his head back, as if to look down his nose at the taller man. "Do you guys talk to each other?"

"What do you mean?"

"Your man, Nemesio, gave us a deferral."

Elisha paused. "Why would he do that?"

Leon turned to his Bast colleague. "Do you believe this?" He turned back to Elisha, his nose as high as before. "We lent him two of our gen four Belts. And he still has them."

"You're lying," Elisha accused, taking another step. Leon stood his ground.

"Don't try to intimidate me," Leon's voice synthesizer crackled on overload. "Check your facts. The Kaleidoscope has our valuable property. We have a four-week deferral. And we're not due until *next week*."

Elisha looked from Leon to the other Shade, who was even shorter, and raised a fist. "I'll be back tomorrow. If you're lying, there *will* be consequences."

Leon's synthesizer emitted a scratchy sound in response, recognizable as a laugh. "The Kaleidoscope used to run a tight operation. Tell Chrysalis he's slipping."

Elisha grabbed Leon by the arm. "What I'll tell Chrysalis is that the Bast can't be trusted to pay their debts."

Leon twisted, trying to break Elisha's grip, but Elisha held firm.

"I'm *not* lying. Go talk to Nemesio. And when you come back tomorrow, I'll expect an apology."

Elisha gave Leon one last, brutal squeeze before letting him go.

❖ ❖ ❖

"Did you know about this?"

Thomas and Celeste were alone and unmasked in the Kaleidoscope dormitory. Thomas leaned in a corner, wedged between the wall and a desk. Celeste sat in a chair, pulled back from the table, slumped down, her arms crossed.

"No, of course not," she replied. "Adrian never told me a thing. If I'd known, I'd have updated the collection schedule, you wouldn't've looked like a jerk, and the rest of us wouldn't've looked like a bunch of fuck-ups."

"Uh-huh. Do you think Grace knew?"

She snorted. "I'm guessing *yeah*."

"What's that mean?"

Celeste blinked, a look of pity on her face. "Haven't you been paying attention, Thomas? Adrian is fucking our fearless leader."

Thomas's mouth dropped open as the light of understanding left his eyes. *"Huh?"*

"A-yup. Banging her right here in the bunkhouse."

He winced. "Is that what 'canoodling' means?"

"I know a few more synonyms."

"Are you sure?"

"When we had to make room for Armengol, why do you think they volunteered to find other quarters? We get the barracks, they get the love nest."

Thomas glanced at the bed where Grace once slept, and at the bunk above it—Adrian's bed. He wrinkled his nose.

"I want to hear it from Grace."

"Sure. Why should you take it from me?"

He dropped his chin to his chest. "That's not what I mean. I just…it's not like Grace, you know?"

"Love makes ya crazy." She slipped on her hood. "C'mon, Big Guy. Let's go find her."

❖ ❖ ❖

Bjorg and Elisha found Chrysalis in the Engine Room, seated in a cubicle with her hood off, recognizable only by her violet mask. She was in VR gear, gesturing as if turning the pages of a book. Bjorg tapped her shoulder.

"Daystar, pause the venue." Chrysalis pushed the headgear back far enough to see who had interrupted her.

"I'm called Bjorg. What're you up to?"

Chrysalis removed her gear and donned her hood.

"Pattern matching. A quick gig to bring in a few credits."

Bjorg shook her head. "Pattern matching. That doesn't pay."

"It *pays*."

"It pays *mouse nuts*."

Chrysalis stood. "I had some time and it came up. What do you need?"

"Elisha has a question for you."

Chrysalis looked up. "Yes, Elisha?"

"I went to collect from the Bast. They're overdue." He took a breath, rendered as a sizzling sound, like static. "They said Nemesio told them they didn't have to pay until next week."

"Oh." Chrysalis tugged at her cloak. "I should have told you. We borrowed some peripherals from them."

"Thanks for keeping us abreast of developments, Chief," Bjorg snapped. "Ol' Elisha here will get over his humiliation, I'm sure."

Chrysalis stared at Bjorg before jerking her head toward Elisha. "What did they say?"

"They said they got a month deferral for the loan. And that Nemesio still has the Belts."

"Anything else?"

Elisha shifted his weight to the other foot. "They said you're getting sloppy."

Chrysalis looked at the floor as she crossed her arms. "Meet me in the dorm..."

"*Our* dorm," Bjorg sneered, "or *yours?*"

"Yours. I'll have the Belts. Elisha, you can take them to the Bast tomorrow."

"Okay," Elisha replied. "Thanks."

Bjorg grabbed Elisha's arm as he turned to leave. "Is this sort of thing going to keep happening?" she challenged. "Because Elisha and I aren't sure we want to be associated with such a slipshod operation."

"I didn't say..." Elisha began.

"Elisha," Chrysalis interrupted. "We're not sloppy. When you take the Belts back, get the payment."

"They said it wasn't due…"

"I know." Chrysalis sat down and reached for the VR gear. "Get it anyway."

❖ ❖ ❖

Elisha waited for Leon in the foyer of the brownstone. He held the two Belts in his left hand, inside the folds of his cloak. His right hand clenched and unclenched for the five minutes it took for Leon to arrive.

"Elisha, no doubt," Leon said as he emerged from the darkness, followed by another Shade. "What did Nemesio tell you?"

Elisha held out the Belts. "Here they are."

Leon took the Belts and inspected them, checking for snags in the fabric or breaks in the electrodes. He nodded as he handed them to the other Shade.

"Thanks for bringing these by," Leon replied. "I hope you liked 'em."

"I wouldn't know."

"You didn't try one out? Really?"

"Really, I didn't."

Leon and his companion looked at each other, sharing a synthesized laugh. "Man, this is a *gen four*. You *need* to try it."

"Some other time. For now, you can make the transfer—100,000 credits."

"No. Next week. That was the deal."

"You have your Belts back."

Leon leaned closer. "*Next week.*"

Elisha grabbed his arm. "*The deal's changed.* Do the transfer today and we'll forget the late penalty."

Leon didn't move. Six more Shade appeared from the shadows, one of them even larger than Elisha. They closed in on Elisha and Leon.

"That's starting to hurt," Leon commented. "Can ya let up a bit?"

Elisha looked over at the featureless hooded figures. He loosened his grip, then dropped his hand to his side.

Leon massaged his bicep. "What's *wrong* with you guys? You used to be a top-tier crew, really hi-res. Now you pull this shit in *my* dorm?" He pressed a finger against Elisha's chest. "Go back to Chrysalis. Tell him his reputation among the Bast is *tarnished.*"

Elisha turned to the door, facing two Bast Shade. "Let me by."

"They'll let you go after you pay what *you* owe *me,*" Leon said.

Elisha looked back at Leon. "What do *I* owe *you?*"

"Remember? That apology?"

Elisha pushed aside the two Shade standing in his way. The biggest Bast filled the gap, blocking him.

"Sorry," Elisha mumbled.

"Say again?" Leon prompted. "I didn't hear. Do you need to recharge your voice box?"

"I said, I'm *sorry*, Leon, for doubting your word."

Leon nodded. "Apology accepted."

"I'll be here next week if we don't see that transfer on time."

Leon smoothed his hood against his chin and neck. "You know, I've been worried about our cash flow lately. We're going to start stretching out our payables. You can expect to see that transfer in *three* weeks."

Elisha took a step toward Leon. The Bast Shade tightened their circle. He took one last look around before elbowing two Bast aside and bolting out the door.

32

CASH FLOW

"YOU HAVE ONE *job*."

Thomas sat at the table, hands folded and head bowed. Grace, wearing trousers and a tunic, paced in front of him.

"We count on you," Grace went on. "You're the one who keeps accounts current. Without you, we're defenseless."

"I know that, Grace."

"You need to get back to the Bast *tonight* and collect."

Thomas raised his head, shoulders hunched. "Can't it wait until next week?"

"They *challenged* us, Thomas. We *cannot* let that go unanswered."

He dropped his head again. "Can I take someone with me? You, maybe?"

She cleared her throat and studied the floor. "I *could* go, but you need to handle this yourself."

"I was just thinking, if *you* came along, you know, the leader…"

"Thomas, it's your *job*."

The big man dropped his head another centimeter. "Okay," he muttered.

Grace nodded. Thomas stood, anxious to leave the dorm. Halfway to the door, the latch snapped open and a Shade burst in. Celeste pulled off her hood, looking first at Thomas, then glaring at Grace.

"A little *ex parte* meeting?"

"Thomas and I were having a *discussion*," Grace replied.

"It's over."

"What discussion?"

"It's *over*."

Thomas put up a hand. "It's nothing, Celeste. I'm just behind in my collections is all. We straightened it out."

Celeste tossed her hood on the table. She pulled her cloak over her head, draping it over the back of a chair. Her shirt and pants, unlike Grace's, were tight-fitting, revealing the curves that most female Shade took pains to conceal. "You're talking about the Bast, aren't you?"

Thomas nodded, lowering his eyes. "Uh-huh."

"Yeah." She turned to Grace. "What were you doing? Dressing him down for missing the collection?"

Grace glared. "It's between me and Thomas."

Celeste's eyes widened. "You *were!* You were giving *Thomas* grief for *your* fuckup!"

"I'm seeing that he does his *job*."

Celeste put the back of a hand to her forehead. "You're *unbelievable!* First, you and your…your…*man* go behind *our* backs, and make some deal with the Bast, and now you have the *gall* to blame Thomas when Leon and the rest of the Bast tell him to pound sand?"

"Our cash flow…"

"Don't tell *me* about *cash flow*. I keep the books, *remember?*"

"We're falling behind."

"And that's *Thomas's* fault?" Celeste leaned stiff-armed against the bunk, head hanging. "I want a meeting. *All* of us. You, me, Thomas, Adrian, and the new guy."

Grace shoved her hands in her pockets. "Tomorrow."

"Ha!" Celeste laughed, shaking her head. "*Now*."

"We're occupied. Tomorrow."

"No, *now!*"

Grace's clenched fists bulged under the fabric of her pants. "Four hours."

"Two."

"*Four*."

Celeste narrowed her eyes. She pulled on her cloak and hood, and left the room. Thomas glanced up for a moment before pulling on his own hood and following Bjorg out the door.

❖ ❖ ❖

Five bodies crowded into a room barely big enough for four: the three founding members of the Kaleidoscope and Adrian seated at the table, and the newcomer, Billy—known by his Shade name Armengol—a thin Asian man with a grim mouth and intense eyes, standing by the door.

"All right, Celeste," Grace said, calmer than she had been four hours ago during their confrontation. "You have the floor."

Celeste sat turned in her chair, an arm resting on the back. She looked first at Billy, then at each of those seated in turn.

"Thanks for calling the meeting, Grace," she began. "I want to make sure everyone is aware of our situation."

"We're aware," Grace replied.

Celeste gave her a flinty look. Grace raised her hands. "Go on," she prompted.

"This morning, Grace told Thomas and me that our cash flow is slipping. That's why Grace is putting pressure on Thomas…"

"I'm just making sure…"

Celeste lofted another stern look.

"…why Grace is putting Thomas under the taser to accelerate collections. Now, I don't want to talk about this incident with the Bast…"

"Celeste, I apologize for that—Adrian, too. Thomas, I was unfair to you."

"It's okay," Thomas replied.

"Glad that's behind us," Celeste continued. "Can we get on with the agenda?"

"Go on," Grace replied.

"The cash flow—it's a big issue, and it affects *all* of us." Celeste looked around the room as she spoke. "Team, we're bleeding credits."

"It's not that bad," Grace objected.

"We can let the *team* decide how bad it is."

Thomas looked up from the table, his eyes drooping

above fleshy cheeks. "How bad?"

Celeste pulled a slip of paper from her pocket. "I only jotted down a few figures. If you want to dig into the details, we can go to the Engine Room."

"Just…" Grace began, then paused. She sighed. "Tell us."

Celeste held up the paper. "Every week we're spending almost fifteen thousand credits more than we're taking in. At this rate…"

"We have adequate reserves," Grace interrupted. "More than four million."

"Is that your plan? Burn down our reserves?" Celeste looked at Thomas. "Is that okay with you?" She twisted in her chair to face Billy. "How about you, newbie? Sure it is. Why wouldn't it be? You just got here. *You* didn't bust *your* ass to build up our *reserves*."

"I thought…" Billy looked at Grace. "I'm only entitled to a share of new revenue."

"That's right," Celeste confirmed. "That's the deal. But we don't have *new revenue*. What we have are *new losses*."

"It's temporary," Grace said.

"Oh, well then, show me the business plan. How are we turning this around, Chief?"

"The persona…"

"*Again* with the persona." Celeste turned in her chair, leaning on the table. "The persona's the reason we're in the red."

"It's our key program," Adrian replied.

"So, that's why you brought back your freelancers," Celeste waved her arm, "without telling the rest of us."

"One. I brought back *one* freelancer."

"That's seven thousand credits a week for the freelancer, plus fees for Billy Boy." Celeste turned around. "How much are you bringing in these days, Billy? You have a big backlog?"

Billy turned away. "I'm working on the persona."

"Yeah. Zero, in other words." She turned back. "Like Adrian. And Grace."

"I'm *working*," Grace protested in a strained voice.

"Oh. Oh, yeah. The pattern-matching. How much does that net?"

Grace clenched her teeth.

"That's okay," Celeste said, "I know already. One thousand three hundred credits last week. That doesn't even cover your fees."

No one spoke. Celeste and Grace locked eyes; everyone else's gaze wandered.

"Here's what we'll do," Grace said. "We can't sustain our operation just on banking and freelance gigs…"

"We *could*," Celeste interjected, "if *you* all got to work."

"We're not cutting back on the persona."

"That's so unfair!"

"*Celeste.*" Grace sat and felt herself shaking, a barely perceptible trembling. She took a deep breath. "Celeste, we *need* you in the Kaleidoscope. You're the heart of the banking operation, and you bring in more freelance revenue than any of us…"

"Than *all* of you."

Grace took another breath, holding it for a second before going on. "Yes. Than all of us. And I know you're not a fan of the persona…"

Celeste raised up, resting her fists on the table. "*Don't do that.*"

"Do what?"

"Don't label me just because I question your decisions."

Grace got in her face. "Are you with the program or not?"

"We're *losing credits!*"

"*Are you with us?*"

Celeste dropped into her chair. "You know I am."

"All right, then." Grace sat back down, putting her hands together in her lap to hide their trembling. "Celeste, you're right. We need more revenue. But as long as we're independent, we can't bid on the big jobs like the affiliated crews. I'm going to look for a sponsor."

Celeste rolled her eyes as her hands fell to the table. "Then what's the point of the persona?"

"It's just until the persona is ready."

"You think you can hook up with a sponsor and then just kiss them goodbye?"

"Do you have a better idea?"

Celeste stared at her; Grace stared back, game-faced, fearing Celeste would call her bluff. Celeste's gaze broke first.

"Keep Billy on the persona," Celeste murmured, "but get rid of your freelancer." She sat up. "And you two, start bringing home a paycheck."

"The freelancer is gone. Adrian and I will go to work."

"*You?* More pattern-matching?" Celeste mocked.

Grace gripped the edge of the table. "I'm getting to be a pretty good coder, Celeste."

"Yeah. Right."

Grace bristled. "Don't forget our stringers. Thomas brought on a new one just this week."

"Hmmph," Celeste grumbled.

"We'll review the books again in two weeks. If the cash flow situation hasn't turned around, we'll take action." Grace looked from one face to the next. "Anything else? No? Meeting over."

Everyone stood and put on their hoods. Chrysalis tugged on Elisha's arm. Nemesio hung back, but Chrysalis tilted her head toward the door and he left, leaving Chrysalis and Elisha alone.

"Elisha," Chrysalis began, "I know I put you in a bind."

"It's okay. I told you it was okay."

"Good," Chrysalis replied, then she squeezed his arm. She leaned closer, speaking in a monotone.

"I want the Bast paid up by tomorrow."

33

BIG DOG BITE

"I'M CALLED ELISHA, of the Kaleidoscope."

The Bast Shade stood silently, staring up at Elisha for a moment before sighing. He passed the detector over Elisha, verifying that he was disconnected.

"Leon isn't expecting you."

"Tell him I'm here."

"Didn't he say *three weeks?* Come back then."

Elisha put his hand on the Shade's shoulder, bunching the man's cloak and whatever clothing he wore underneath in his fist. He lifted him until his toes barely touched the floor. "Take me to him, or bring him to me."

The Shade wrapped his fingers around Elisha's arm and pulled, but Elisha's grip stayed tight. "All right, all *right*," he relented. "Follow me."

The Shade led Elisha through a narrow hallway, down a staircase, to the underground dormitory of the Bast. It was an open space, more than thirty meters square, with bunks along one wall, and racks of hardware along another, behind a glass barrier which did little to muffle the sound of cooling fans. Tables were scattered in the center of the space, where Shade operators hunched over workstations, some in VR gear, their gestures offering vague clues as to what took place in their venues. The Shade led Elisha to one operator in a shining golden mask, staring with intense concentration at a desk screen.

"Leon, look who's back," the Shade said. "Elisha. Of the

Kaleidoscope."

Leon looked up. He closed his eyes and shook his head, sighing, then reached for his hood and pulled it over his head.

"You're early," Leon said. "About *three weeks* early."

"Make the transfer," Elisha replied sternly. "One hundred thousand. And another twenty thousand for my trouble."

Leon's synthesized laugh sounded like a rusty hinge. "Go away. And come back in *four* weeks."

Elisha took Leon by the arm and lifted him out of his chair. Leon struggled, unable to break free.

"Armand, go get Graf," Leon ordered.

The Shade Armand hurried away. The other Shade operators in the room stopped what they were doing and stood to watch, some leaving their workstations to gather in a circle around Elisha and Leon.

The tall Shade who had menaced Elisha the day before ducked through the door; two more Shade followed in his wake. They lined up facing Elisha, the middle one towering over the other two.

"Graf," Leon said, "do you remember what I told Elisha here yesterday? Well, he didn't retain it. See if you can reinforce the message."

Elisha dropped Leon. Graf took a step. The other two Shade closed in.

"Is this how it's going to be?" Elisha asked. "Three against one?"

Leon waved off the other two Shade. They joined the circle, which now formed an impromptu arena around Elisha and Graf as would-be gladiators.

Graf removed the hood and cloak, facing Elisha in his black mask, a stylized third eye in blood-red staring from the center of his forehead. He wore a close-fitting shirt of black synthetic fabric, with a sheen that reflected light from overhead, highlighting the definition of his muscled arms and chest. His black pants were loose, the kind a martial arts master might wear, of sheer fabric flowing like water as he moved. He kicked off his shoes and bounced on the balls of his feet, shaking his arms and twisting his neck; then he crouched, one foot forward, in a fighting stance.

Elisha pulled off his own hood. His mask was sky blue, its edges and eye holes trimmed with a narrow strip of white. He removed his cloak. The loose tunic he wore hid a thick waist; his pants seemed a little too small. He kept his shoes on. He turned a shoulder toward Graf, keeping his arms close and fists high. The crowd, now numbering more than twenty, remained silent as the two circled each other.

"Elisha, why put yourself through this?" Leon asked. "Go tell Chrysalis that the Bast are too much for you. He'll understand. Come back again in a month and we'll settle accounts."

Graf grinned, emitting a low, breathy laugh. Elisha shook off the taunt, keeping his eyes on the big Bast as he lunged, stopping short of Elisha. Elisha jumped back, stumbling a few steps before recovering. Graf turned in a full circle, arms raised. The ring of spectators murmured, their synthesized voices blending in a din, rising and falling like chirping cicadas.

Elisha felt his heart beating so hard and fast that he saw it in his vision, a sparkling aura surrounding Graf's smirking face, flaring in time with his pulse. He reacted to another Graf feint, flinching, raising his fists higher. The buzzing from the crowd surged, then subsided.

Elisha matched Graf's movements, retreating as he advanced, pursuing him when he backed off, always maintaining more than an arm's length distance. After about sixty seconds, Elisha judged that he could hit Graf with a left and follow with a right before the man could react. Elisha dropped his left shoulder and turned, preparing to jab.

Graf pivoted, turning his back, his right leg curling under him, then uncoiling, a taut spring releasing with all the momentum of his body. Before Elisha could even move his fist five centimeters, he saw a black streak—Graf's leg raised in a kick aimed at his head. Elisha lifted his elbow in a reflex reaction, deflecting Graf's foot into his forehead instead of his jaw. Elisha saw a flash as his head snapped back. The blow sent him sprawling into the ring of spectators, knocking two of them to the floor.

"Elisha, give it up!" Leon shouted from across the ring. "Is Chrysalis going to kick your ass worse than Graf? I don't think so."

Elisha got to his hands and knees, then stood, barely righting himself before Graf took a step, crouching low, then launching himself in an arc as he extended his leg. Elisha turned away, expecting the kick to land on his back. It landed instead on the back of his knee, collapsing his leg. Elisha went down, rolling forward, letting out an agonized scream.

Leon crossed the circle and bent over Elisha. He pointed at Graf. "He'll break something if you let him. Seriously. Kill you as soon as talk to you. He's got a body count IRL, not just outside the Worldstream. *We're* scared of him, that's the kind of badass he is."

Elisha rolled over onto one knee, holding the injured leg to his chest. He stood, supporting himself on his good leg.

Leon turned to Graf. "Restrain yourself. Ditching a dead body isn't on my to-do list today."

Elisha hobbled along the edge of the circle opposite Graf, less than a meter from the ring of spectators. Graf came to the center, turning in one spot as Elisha limped around him. The crowd hummed.

Graf took three quick steps in a spiral path, then lifted off, right leg extended, aiming directly at Elisha's face.

Elisha went back on his good leg, raising his arms. Graf's foot missed his head, his trailing knee just grazing Elisha's shoulder as Graf went into the crowd. In the tangle of bodies, Elisha saw an opening. He dropped elbow-first with all of his weight on Graf's leg, dislocating his knee with a sickening *pop*. Graf bellowed like a wounded bull.

Elisha retreated to the center of the circle, putting as much weight on his injured leg as he was able. Graf struggled to stand, his bad leg incapable of holding any weight at all.

Elisha made a move toward him now that Graf was unable to stay ahead of him. Elisha threw a roundhouse punch, landing behind Graf's ear. Graf stumbled to his knees, and swung his arm, throwing himself off-balance. Elisha trapped the arm, then delivered one brutal punch after another to Graf's face. Blood poured from open cuts as Elisha kept punching. The droning of the crowd was drowned out by Elisha's enraged screams as he continued until exhaustion set in and he finally dropped an unconscious Graf to the floor.

Elisha stood panting over Graf's hulking form. A few Shade stepped forward but retreated when Elisha menaced them, his eyes showing fiercely through the holes of a blood-spattered mask.

Leon stepped into the circle. "So, now what?"

Elisha gathered a handful of his cloak in a bloody hand. "The transfer," he growled, not bothering to don his voice synthesizer.

"A hundred thousand. I'll take care of it today."

"One hundred twenty. *Now.*"

"Let's be reasonable, Elisha. We owe you a hundred."

Elisha put his hand under Leon's chin and lifted him off the floor.

"Okay, all right, let me down," Leon croaked. Elisha dropped him.

Leon smoothed his cloak. "You can all get back to work," he said to the Bast Shade standing around. "The show's over." The Shade returned to their workstations. "Elisha," he said, leaning close, "everyone Graf has ever faced backed down without a fight. Not you. I never figured you for such a tough mother."

"Do you have a point?"

"I can cut a transfer of fifty thousand today—to you, personally—if we forget the debt and you come work for the Bast. Chrysalis will never find another collector like you. Once you're with the Bast, he'll write off our debt."

Elisha studied Leon, trying to imagine what he looked like under the hood. He wondered if the Bast followed the same custom as the Kaleidoscope, showing themselves to each other when alone, with nothing to disguise their faces or voices, a sign of trust, loyalty, and commitment. He wondered if the Bast opened up to each other, sharing their RL past, forming a personal bond among the Shade that they had never known IRL.

Elisha limped to where he'd dropped his cloak and hood, put them on, and walked back to Leon.

"I'll wait here while you make the transfer. One-hundred-twenty thousand, to the Kaleidoscope."

❖ ❖ ❖

It was a 45-minute walk back to the Summerland on healthy legs. Elisha had walked for nearly an hour with still a kilometer to go, when he leaned against a rusty lamppost, its light having stopped working years ago. He steadied himself, focusing his thoughts, trying to crowd out the pain in his leg and the memory of the bloodied face at the end of his arm. His stomach churned. He lifted his hood and vomited on the sidewalk.

❖ ❖ ❖

Celeste touched the swollen joint gingerly. Thomas groaned.

"How bad?" he asked.

Celeste tilted her head, looking at the knee from all directions. It was twice normal size and turning purple.

"Hell if I know. I'm not a doctor." She looked up at him with watery eyes. His head sported a large lump, and his eye was black. "How bad does it hurt?"

"A lot." Thomas tried to stand, grimaced, then sat down again. "Walking five klicks on it didn't help."

"I'll go to the commissary, see if they have ice." She leaned forward, testing the lump with the tip of her finger. He winced. "I'll get some painkillers, too." She stood. "You stay in bed."

Celeste was reaching for her cloak when the latch clicked and the door swung open. Chrysalis pulled off her hood and mask. "Armengol...*Billy* told me. Thomas, are you okay?"

"He got your credits for you, Boss Lady," Celeste snapped. "Isn't that what counts?"

Grace knelt next to Thomas's knee, ignoring her. "Oh, Jah. We need some ice."

"I'm on it," Celeste replied. "And painkillers." She pulled on her cloak. "Try not to send him out on any more collections right away."

Grace turned to face Celeste from where she knelt. Her face was flushed, and she was blinking tears from her eyes. Celeste looked down, then pulled on her hood. "Ten minutes, tops," she said.

"Thanks," Grace replied. She turned back to Thomas. The big man smiled.

"The other guy got worse," he offered.

Grace laughed, then covered her mouth and squeezed her eyes shut. Her body shuddered with each muffled sob. She composed herself as she stood, wiping her face with both hands.

"I see the account is current," Grace said. "A 20,000 credit surplus, in fact."

"If I was going to make a special trip, I wanted something to show for it."

Grace smiled. "You did *good*, Thomas, for yourself and for the Kaleidoscope." She sat next to him and stroked his face, avoiding the bump on his head. "One thing is for sure: everyone now knows that our big dog can *bite*."

34

UNCANNY VALLEY

ARMENGOL ENTERED THE dorm and pulled off his hood. Thomas sat with his back to the desk, his leg propped on a chair. He was reading a magazine, a printed copy more than fifty years old.

"What's that?" Billy asked.

"Printed paper. Look." Thomas held up the magazine. It featured text in two columns, and color photos. The edges were tattered and most of the corners missing.

Billy held out his hand. Thomas gave him the magazine.

"I've never seen one IRL," he said, turning the fragile pages carefully. "Where did you get it?"

"It's Celeste's. She keeps it in her desk."

The magazine was open to an article about multi-player online games, the kind kids used to play before life moved to the Worldstream. There were pictures of rendered scenes from popular games—venues set in fantastic worlds, or in different eras, all realistically rendered, but still noticeably artificial—especially the people. *Uncanny Valley*, the article called it—facial rendering almost, but not quite perfectly human-like, somewhere between obvious animation and modern avatars, indistinguishable from Real Life. According to the article, such near-perfect avatars caused users to feel uneasy. Billy knew the history—VR was all gaming and entertainment, as long as avatars were less than perfectly human. For VR to become the medium of commerce and social interaction, realistically rendered avatars were necessary, but its adoption hit a plateau when avatars fell into Uncanny Valley. Users of VR during this period reported dissatisfaction with the experience—some hated it—but often could not say why. They just felt *icky*, despite the high quality of the rendered avatars. Once Uncanny Valley was crossed, and avatars looked as human as RL, the adoption of VR—with its advantages of convenience, cost, and flexibility —exploded.

"Where did she get it?"

Thomas took the magazine back. "When Celeste was in the world, she collected old printed books and things, mostly about computing and coding. It was a hobby." He turned the pages idly. "When she shredded, she only took a few with her." He leaned over to Celeste's desk and opened the drawer. It contained a stack of magazines and a few books. Billy bent closer. The smell of old paper, an earthy smell with a sharpness to it, was utterly foreign to him.

"Wow. Books, too. That's amazing." Billy sat down on his bunk. "How're you holding up?"

"Fine." Thomas flipped a page. "No. Terrible."

"I'll bet. Holed up here, no entertainment."

Thomas held up the magazine. "I've got entertainment."

Billy nodded. "Uh-huh." He scrutinized Thomas's face: soft features, with round cheeks and fleshy lips. His small eyes scanned the magazine, dull and uninterested. He looked quite undeserving of the fierce reputation he'd gained since his fight with the Bast.

After another page, Thomas glanced up at Billy, lowering his eyebrows. "What?"

"You look bored out of your mind."

Thomas tossed the magazine on the desk. "Yeah. I've heard that people used to read for fun. Do you believe that?"

"Hard to swallow."

Thomas stared into space, dropping his hands in his lap, and sighed.

"How's the leg?" Billy asked.

"It's better. Celeste got me some meds."

"Can you walk on it?"

Thomas tilted his head and wrinkled his nose. "Don't know. Let's see." He stood, putting some weight on the bad leg with a groan. "Still hurts. I suppose I could walk on it if I had to."

"Do you think you could make it to the Engine Room?"

"Oh, sure." Thomas tested his knee again, wincing. "No problem."

"Great. I have a lifestream I want you to try."

"Beats reading. What is it?"

"Adrian and I made some changes to the persona. We've been testing it in venues, but now we're trying it out in lifestreams. We found some good ones."

Thomas wrinkled his brow. "I don't get it. If it works in a venue, why wouldn't it work in a lifestream? The validation would be a lot less strict, wouldn't it?"

Billy nodded. "Oh, yeah, sure. The rendering engine isn't rendering the stream rider's avatar, but the Worldstream still validates the persona's key. We're checking to see if there's any significant difference."

"Why would it be different?"

"Well, it *shouldn't* be different, but if we don't test it, how will we know?"

"I guess." Thomas sat back down and massaged his knee. "I'll take your word on that. You're the master."

"Anyway, that's not important. It's the lifestream. It's a good one."

Thomas shrugged. "Now?"

"Hey, brother Kaleidoscope, I'm just trying to get you out of the dorm and away from these old ragged magazines. Remind you what life's like."

Thomas pulled up his pant leg. The swelling had gone down, and the bruises had lightened from blue-black to a rainbow of colors ranging from violet to yellow. "What's the lifestream?"

"Parasailing."

"I don't know what that is."

"It's hi-res for sure. You're behind a boat with a big engine, and you've got a parachute on, and the boat pulls you off the beach and up into the air. You're going about a hundred klicks an hour, a hundred meters above the ocean."

"Sounds insane."

"It's massive fun."

Thomas looked at the magazine, lying limp on the desk. The cover was torn and faded. The letters, though legible, were almost as unfamiliar as hieroglyphics, taking time and effort to decipher. The articles read like ancient scrolls, myths of ages past.

"Massive," Thomas said. "Okay, lead on."

Elisha sat in a cubicle of the Engine Room while Armengol queued the lifestream.

"Here," Aremngol said, handing him a limp fabric sash.

"What's this?"

"You'll need it for this lifestream." Armengol lifted one edge of the fabric. The label read:

Dermal Contact Neural Interface
Generation 4
Stimulus Rex
Eau Claire, Menominee District

Elisha recognized the label; it was the same label as the ones on the two Belts from the Bast. "A gen four Belt. Where'd you get this?"

"A guy I know, unaffiliated. I have to get it back to him today."

"Never used a gen four."

"Never…what?" Armengol grabbed the Belt, holding it in both hands. "Oh, brother, if all you've tried is gen three, you don't know." He handed it to Elisha. "Strap on. This thing's ready to launch."

Elisha remained seated as he worked the Belt into position under his cloak. "Wear it just the same as older gens?"

"The closures are a little different, but otherwise just the same," Armengol answered. "Cinched up? Ready to rock?"

Elisha made final adjustments to the Belt, then put on the

VR headgear. The reticles converged. The headphones chimed. Elisha gave a thumbs-up.

Elisha heard the sound of water lapping against a pier, and an engine idling on a boat at the end of a hundred-meter cable. He squinted against the sun in the burning blue sky, as it rose up from the green ocean. Palm-tree-lined beaches stretched in both directions. He felt the heat of the sun, the hot sand under his feet, the coolness of sweat evaporating in the sea breeze, the harness pressing against his chest and shoulders, and the lines of his parasail tugging.

"How's that?" Armengol asked through Elisha's headphones.

Elisha nodded. "No way! Incredible! Just—*wow.*"

Armengol chuckled. "Get ready."

Elisha felt a hand on his shoulder. The avatar he inhabited looked to his side. A skinny black man in dreadlocks stood next to him, his hand steadying the rig, teeth and eyes shining against ebony skin.

"The boatman gon' take you up," the black man said. "Fifteen minutes 'roun' the bay an' he bring ya down. Ya ready go, mon?"

"Ready," the voice sounded in Elisha's head. He gripped the handhold on the rig.

The black man waved and shouted, "Let it hap'n, cap'n!"

The boat revved its engine. The cable went taut, pulling Elisha forward. He took one step before he was airborne, rising at a steep angle, the beach falling away as the boat headed out to sea.

The wind rushing past his ears muffled the sound of the engine, now more than fifty meters below. The water was a vista of mottled green, sprinkled with whitecaps. The lifestream avatar scanned the horizon, then turned to look at the beach, dotted with cabanas, sunbathers, and swimmers shrinking in the distance, frozen in time.

"You're up!" Armengol said. "Hi-res, right? Did I lie?"

Elisha was too overcome to answer. He nodded, not knowing if Armengol saw his response.

For five minutes the boat sped away from the beach.

Elisha hovered over open water, with only the boat as a reference point. If not for the wind, he could have imagined himself hovering motionless in an infinite space of green and blue.

The boat began its long, looping turn back inland. Elisha banked left; the beach swung into view, canted at a steep angle, as though he were stationary and the whole world was turning around him.

The image blurred, the sky, sea, and beach running together like a watercolor in the rain, the colors blending until the entire view was a dull, uniform tan, then brown, then black. As the visual blanked, Elisha's thoughts ran together, then stopped.

An image flashed, strobe-like: Graf in a fighting crouch, wearing his black mask with its red cyclopian eye; then another, Leon in his Shade cloak, Elisha lifting him by the shoulder; and another, Grace kneeling beside his swollen knee. Yet another series flashed, images he hadn't seen in years—since before became Shade Elisha, when he was still just Thomas, a coder by day and a hacker by night, from before Jahbulon detected his ham-handed meddling in data streams to the blockchain, before he'd been sentenced to twenty years of RL confinement for being curious. He was transported to the time before he'd shredded his life: a girl he knew IRL and thought he might want to marry; his sister, ten years younger, to whom he'd never had the chance to say goodbye; an RL café in the city, where hackers gathered.

A series of images from the café flashed: posters on the walls, promotions for *movies*, two-dimensional entertainment popular two generations ago—*Snow Crash*, *Ready Player One*, *Neuromancer*; benches lining the walls behind grimy tables and chairs in bad repair; faces he knew but hadn't seen since before he shredded, comrade hackers, their names now forgotten. It was a silent slide show, except for the final image, a cloaked figure standing over him, as if he were lying on the ground and the figure silhouetted against the sky. It spoke in a hollow voice: *Are you affiliated?*

The after-image from the last strobe faded. The vague

outlines of the sky, beach, and sea formed in Elisha's visor, then sharpened to clarity. He blinked and shook his head to relieve what seemed to him like a momentary lapse, a brain freeze brought on by the intense parasailing experience.

The boat headed straight for the beach, then slowed. Elisha swayed from his parasail, the wind rushing in his ears quieting to a murmur as the breeze carried him toward the beach. The skinny dreadlocked man watched him, judged his trajectory, then loped toward Elisha's landing spot. Dreadlocks reached up to grab Elisha's leg, then his arm, then the lines of the sail as it fluttered to the sand.

"Wha' ya think, mon?" Dreadlocks asked.

"Ya mon," Armengol added through the headphones. "What was the res?"

The lifestream froze. Elisha pulled off his headgear and gloves, his face hidden behind the blue and white-trimmed mask. "Whoo," he said. He put a finger to his neck; his pulse was racing. "Yeah, that was nice."

Armengol slapped Elisha on the back. "Glad I could get you out of the dorm. And the test was a success—not a peep from the Worldstream."

Elisha stood, took a halting step toward the cubicle desk, picked up his hood and put it on.

"Thanks," he said. He dug under his cloak and pulled out the Belt, dropping it on the desk. "I think I'll go see what Chrysalis is doing. Maybe I can make myself useful."

"Go get 'em, brother."

Armengol watched Elisha limp out of the Engine Room. He turned to the desk screen, and scrutinized the status messages from his Worldstream monitor. The lifestream had gone off without the slightest reaction from the Worldstream. He swiped the screen, reviewing a series of images: Graf, Leon, Grace, Thomas's girlfriend and sister, multiple pictures of a hacker café in the city, and a cloaked figure, almost solid black against a clear sky.

Yes, indeed—the test had been a success.

35

ARE YOU AFFILIATED?

ELISHA WISHED HE had a cane. Every step was a jolt as his weight shifted to his injured knee. He had hoped it might loosen up after a kilometer or two, but it just got worse. He'd walk until the pain was too much, then he'd rest a few minutes, leaning against a wall. His rest stops became more frequent the closer he got to his destination.

Flash Drive Café—he hadn't seen that retro neon sign in more than four years. The café was a gathering spot in a neighborhood of hackers. They regularly escaped to the Worldstream from their squalid flats, of course, but preferred the Flash Drive for RL camaraderie. The café's Faraday screen and fat stealth pipe made it the ideal spot for hacking.

Thomas could spend ten hours a day for weeks at a time in the Flash Drive, trading tips, sharing hacks, or just jawing with fellow cyber bums. On workdays, Thomas dropped by for breakfast, then jacked into his workspace for the morning huddle. He'd do just enough coding to convince his supervisor that he was making progress. Sometime before lunch, he'd patch a spoof into his workspace, making it appear that he was on the job, and not in some clandestine venue trying out Worldstream hacks or bargaining for contraband. He wasn't very good at it—certainly not up to the level of those who made a living stealing and fencing keys and assets—but he didn't do it for credits. He did it because he *liked* it.

The place hadn't changed—the same tables and chairs,

same wall decorations, even the same waitstaff.

"Get you something?"

Elisha looked down at the waiter, a short, balding man in the unconnected tunic and trousers commonly worn by civilians in such places.

"You want a connection?" the waiter continued.

"Just something to drink. Iced coffee. Do you still serve that?"

"Huh? Sure, we serve it. With a straw?"

Elisha put a hand to his face. It was the first time he'd been cloaked in the Flash Drive. "Yeah."

"There's an open table by the wall. I'll bring it to you."

Elisha went to the table. He was one of four cloaked patrons, the rest being civilians, about twenty in all. They might have been the same people he knew from his past, only older. The man at the table in the center—was that Todd from his building? The one who claimed to have traversed the blockchain back to block zero? Elisha had heard that Todd went to confinement for a fifteen-year term. Yet, the man looked exactly like Todd, down to the mannerisms and the black cowlick on the back of his head.

Elisha hobbled over to the other table and tapped the man's shoulder. The man looked up, furrowing his brow.

"Yeah?" he asked.

He wasn't Todd. His face was too round, and his lips too thin.

"Sorry," Elisha intoned, "I thought you were someone else."

The waiter appeared with the iced coffee. "You want it here, or there?"

Elisha went back to his spot by the wall. "Twenty credits," the waiter said. Elisha held out a coded card to scan.

He sipped his coffee, letting the memories flash through his mind, like photos in an album. There was a girl near the counter, a brown-haired civilian, talking with friends, laughing, tossing her head in a familiar way. Elisha sat up, trying to get a closer look.

Angel? he thought. *Is it…can it…?*

He set down his coffee and limped across the floor. The girl saw him coming and looked at him, smiling, until his hulking figure got within two meters with no sign of slowing down. She leaned back, crossing an arm over her chest.

"What?" she asked.

Her features seemed to morph in front of Elisha's eyes, from the girl Angel—to whom he'd considered proposing marriage—to a stranger who looked not the least bit familiar.

"Nothing," Elisha said.

The waiter came around the counter. "Look, is there a problem?"

"No," Elisha mumbled. He went back to his seat.

Elisha continued drinking his coffee. He'd just set it down when two Cloak approached, one standing at a corner of the table.

"Are you affiliated?" one of them asked in a monotone.

He looked from one to the other. "I'm called Elisha."

"Are you affiliated?" the Cloak repeated.

"I won't answer that. I'm called Elisha."

"You'll need to come with us."

"Why? Because I won't tell you my affiliation?"

"Then you *are* affiliated?"

He paused. "I'm called Elisha."

"You're coming with us, Elisha."

He stood up, towering over the two Cloak. They stepped back.

"Elisha," one of them said, "are you affiliated?"

Elisha's vision darkened. Images flashed before his eyes— of Grace, Celeste, and Adrian...of the fight at the Bast.

His vision returned. "I'm called Elisha, of the Kaleidoscope."

"Come with us."

Elisha followed the two Cloak outside the café. A noisy, smelly vehicle, long and low, with fat black tires rolled up to the curb. One of them opened the door.

"Get in."

Elisha peered into the dim interior, his thoughts a confused jumble. He stood immobile, until one of the Cloak took his right arm and tried to force him inside.

Suddenly his mind cleared. He broke the grip of the Cloak on his right, turning away from the car, when the Cloak on his left grabbed his arm with both hands. Elisha struggled to break his grip. He pulled off the Cloak's hood, revealing a forest green mask, trimmed in yellow.

"Fidelio, do it now!" the hoodless Cloak shouted.

Elisha felt a hand under his hood, then a cold liquid sensation on his neck. His vision narrowed, then went dark as he collapsed on the sidewalk.

"Jah, what a beast," the hoodless one said.

The two Cloak muscled Elisha into the vehicle, squeezing in after him and slamming the door shut.

"What happened?" the driver asked.

"Something broke the spell, I guess," the Cloak in the green mask replied.

"That can't happen," the driver protested.

"You're the expert, Jayla," the hooded Cloak said. "But it looks to me like your calculations are flawed."

"It can't happen."

"Hey, we said the magic words 'Are you affiliated?' and they bounced off him twice before they took. Then he came out of his trance just as he was about to get on board. You say it can't happen? I'd say it *happened*."

"Fidelio, Jayla," the green-masked Cloak said, "let's talk about this while we're *moving*. The Eye of Providence is expecting us."

36

DAMN BABYSITTER

CHRYSALIS WAS IN the Engine Room working her first gig as a coder. The task wasn't complicated—adding physics to semi-rigid inanimate assets—and it didn't pay much, but it was something.

Her job was to make a new line of body-conforming furniture look and feel real in VR. She had taken the job promising that she had experience programming asset physics. She'd lied of course, but the programming got easier once she had finished two chairs and a sofa, and the client accepted them with only minor revisions. It was a welcome distraction—Daystar hadn't notified her that Dylan was in a venue in almost a month.

Chrysalis met her quota after six hours. She spent another hour getting a jump on the next item in the queue before clocking out.

She dragged herself to the dorm room she shared with Nemesio, now also occupied by two Kaleidoscope stringers. Chrysalis had offered to share dorm space as a cost-saving measure. It put a crimp in her love life, but she was committed to making every credit count. It wasn't the stringers' presence that was hardest on her, but the fact that she and Nemesio had to remain cloaked whenever one of their boarders was in the room. And they seemed to *always* be in the room.

The loss of intimacy, the disconnect with Dylan, the pressure to earn—they all took a toll on Chrysalis, and it showed.

❖ ❖ ❖

Chrysalis carried her tray to a vacant table in the commissary. She dropped into a chair, pulled off her hood, leaving only her mask, and bent over her midday meal: a casserole of some kind, creamed corn, and a roll. She had to talk herself into eating, her appetite having flagged over the past week.

"Are you called Chrysalis?"

Chrysalis looked up at a tall Shade standing by the table. She put on her hood.

"Who's asking?"

"I have a message for Chrysalis. Are you called Chrysalis?"

She picked up her roll and tore it in two. "I'm called Chrysalis. What's the message?"

"Raúl will answer your questions."

Chrysalis's head snapped up. "What are you called?"

"I'm called Red, of the Quill. Will you meet Raúl?"

"How do you know him?"

The Shade slumped. "Look, I don't know any Raúl. I was at the Cloakroom and there was this guy. He was asking around about the Summerland. Said he had an errand and he needed someone from the Summerland. Said his name was Raúl. What the hell? I thought. Do you want to meet him or not?"

"What does he want to talk about?"

"Hey, guy, I *gave* you the message. You gots questions, he gots answers. Interested? You want time and place?"

Chrysalis nodded.

❖ ❖ ❖

The Cloakroom was nearly deserted. Chrysalis chose a table by the wall. She was one of three cloaked patrons—the other two sat huddled in a corner, their synthesizers adjusted to the lowest volume. Raúl showed up fifteen minutes later. She stood and Raúl made a beeline for her.

"I'm called Chrysalis."

"Yeah, yeah, I figured. What's the res, Chrys? Isn't that what the kids say?"

"I've heard."

Raúl sat down and leaned back. He ran his fingers through his hair, pulling it back, then letting it fall.

Chrysalis leaned forward. "Well?"

"Huh? Oh, yeah. *My meeting.* Sure." He tugged on his sleeves.

"Raúl!"

He nodded, his chin dropping further with every nod, until it rested on his chest.

"It's Dylan."

Chrysalis inhaled, her synthesizer rendering the sound like crinkling paper.

"He had another run-in."

"Jah, *no.*"

"Jah, *yeah.*"

"What did he do?"

"He stole a key. He used some hacker app, from what I could glean from the records. I warned him about hacker code. Chrys, I *warned* him. I *thought* he'd be careful."

Her synthesizer made a sound like steel pipes banging together.

He reached across the table. "Chrys…"

She came off her chair and slapped his hand away. "You were going to *watch* him," her synthesizer over-modulated. "You were going to *make sure.*"

Raúl held a hand to his chest. "I never said that."

"You *said* it," Chrysalis growled. "'*No permanent damage,*' you said."

"I said that under duress."

"Jah, what does that even mean?" Chrysalis buried her face in her hands. Her elbow slipped and she splayed across the table, shuddering. Raúl watched, laying his hands first on the table, then in his lap, then back on the table.

She lifted her head. "You could have watched him— monitored him."

Raúl's breath quickened. "Chrys, I'm not a damn *babysitter.* I'm not! And Dylan's almost a man. He understands consequences. He can make decisions for himself."

"You *promised.*"

"No, Chrys, I *did not*." He stood. "Look, I did you a courtesy by telling you. I didn't have to do that."

She turned away, twisting in the chair, wrapping her arms around herself. "Where is he?"

"Confinement. I don't know where. I'm still looking."

"How long?"

"Is he in for?"

"Yes, how long?"

Raúl paced, brushing the hair out of his face. "Five years."

"*Oh. Oh, Jah.*" Chrysalis slid further down in her chair.

"It could have been worse."

"*Dylan.*"

"If I could get him out, I would."

Chrysalis sat up. "Would you?"

"I said *if* I could."

"Could you try?"

Raúl sat down. "There's one way."

She reached out and took his hand.

"If I can find a buyer," Raúl said, "I could get him out."

"A buyer?" she asked.

"The only way to spring Dylan is if he goes to work in a Shade crew."

"But that means…"

"I'll have to shred him."

She dropped his hand. "No. Absolutely not."

"Then there's nothing I can do."

Her head fell, and she laced her fingers over the top of her head.

Raúl fiddled with his hair, looking everywhere except at Chrysalis.

"Chrys."

She didn't answer.

"*Chrys*, I'll check into it."

She took his hand and pressed it first to her forehead, then to her hooded cheek.

"Meet me back here in one week, same time," Raúl said. He slowly drew his hand away from her, then went for the door.

He'd taken a few steps when Chrysalis called after him.

"You said…"

He turned back.

"What?" he answered.

"You said he stole a key."

"That's right."

She stood and walked to him.

"What key?" she asked.

"Chrys, I don't know. Do you want me to find out? 'Cause that'd take some time."

Nemesio's word's echoed in her head: *I'm not sure, but your son might have stolen our key.* She grabbed Raúl's arm to steady herself.

"No," she croaked. "I already know." She reached up to embrace him. "Raúl, I'm sorry. I'm *so* sorry. It's not your fault. It's *mine.*"

❖ ❖ ❖

Chrysalis walked back to the Summerland in a daze. A Kliegl gang began following her, taunting her until they were distracted by two Cloak on the opposite side of the street. She ducked into an alley, waiting long enough to be sure they had moved on before coming out.

She descended the steps to the Summerland's only entrance, a single door below street level. She passed the common area, then the commissary, and went down four flights, through narrow hallways, past the Engine Room to the dorms. She found the room she shared with Nemesio and two stringers, hoping for a few minutes of sleep before heading back to the Engine Room to work down her queue. She opened the door to find two Shade, hoodless, one in a gold mask, the other in saffron, standing in the middle of the room.

Chrysalis bolted the door and took off her hood. "What?"

"Do you know where Elisha is?" Bjorg asked.

Even in their masks, Chrysalis could tell how upset Bjorg and Nemesio were.

"No. You haven't seen him?"

"No," Bjorg replied. "He had a gig scheduled, and he

didn't clock in. He's pretty easy to spot, and *nobody's* spotted him."

37

Six Layers Deep

"Haven't seen him in two days," Billy said, wide-eyed.

Grace, Celeste, Adrian, and Billy crowded into the Kaleidoscope dorm. None of them had seen or heard from Thomas in the last thirty-six hours.

"Where did you see him last?" Grace asked.

"Um, here. In the dorm. He had his foot up. He was reading a magazine."

"A what?" Grace questioned.

"Was it one of mine?" Celeste asked. She went to her desk and opened a drawer, pulling out a ragged copy of *Metaverse* magazine. "This one?"

"I think so, yeah. He was reading an article about the old days of VR, about Uncanny Valley."

"That's in this issue." Celeste carefully laid the magazine back in its drawer. "Did you and Thomas talk about the article?"

Billy looked at each face in turn. "What is this? An interrogation?"

"We're trying to find our *friend*," Celeste snapped. "*Your* friend, right? Don't *you* want to find Thomas?"

"Yeah, yeah, sure I do. I just…I don't know where he is."

"But you were the last one to see him."

"I suppose. That's not my fault."

"Maybe he went to the Bast," Adrian offered. "There's a rumor that Leon's trying to recruit him."

Celeste snapped her head toward him. "Thomas would

228

never do that."

"No, he wouldn't," Grace agreed. "Thomas is one of our founders. He couldn't betray the Kaleidoscope. It's not in him."

"But *you*," Celeste said, pointing first at Adrian, then at Billy. "And *you*. You're not founders. Where's *your* loyalty?"

"Where's *that* coming from?" Adrian shot back. "We're just as loyal as Thomas, or Grace, or you, for that matter."

"That's enough," Grace said. "I'll go talk to Leon."

"He didn't do it," Celeste repeated.

Grace looked down, avoiding Celeste's eyes. "I don't believe it, but I still have to check it out."

❖ ❖ ❖

"The famous Chrysalis! We meet at last."

Chrysalis stood in the entryway of the Bast dormitory, facing Leon and three other Bast, including the hulking Graf.

"To what do we owe this extreme honor?"

"Do you know where Elisha is?"

"Don't *you?*"

"We haven't heard from him in almost two days."

"And you thought he might have joined up with the Bast." Leon's synthesizer let out a scratchy rendition of a laugh. "What's happening over there in the Kaleidoscope? Discontent in the ranks? You guys are losing your edge."

"Hardly. But I know you've been trying to recruit Elisha."

"We'd love to have him, but no. When he laid out Graf…"

"He got lucky," Graf protested.

"You let down your guard, Graf," Leon retorted, the irritation evident in his synthesized voice. "Like I was saying, when Elisha *kicked Graf's ass*, I made a play, but he wouldn't bite. Seems he's got some weird attachment to you and the rest of your crew. That's loyalty—I admire that. How do you do it?"

Chrysalis closed the gap between Leon and herself. "When they talk, I listen," she replied. "And I *never* let them down."

❖ ❖ ❖

"Find anything?" Celeste asked. She and Grace were alone in the dorm.

"Nothing. You?"

"Nothing on Thomas."

"But…?"

"I did hear some dirt about Armengol."

Grace looked down, waiting for the rest.

"Seems Billy Boy was angling for a spot in the Kaleidoscope *long* before Nemesio met him."

"We know that. Adrian told us. Armengol wanted to work on the persona."

"Sure, that's what Nemesio told us. But how did Armengol know about the persona *before* Nemesio blabbed it?"

"You're saying…"

"I'm saying Nemesio told us that Armengol liked freelancing, but he wanted to work on the persona. But if he didn't know about the persona, why was he asking around about the Kaleidoscope?"

Grace furrowed her brow before opening her eyes wide. *"Go get Armengol."*

❖   ❖   ❖

Billy was alone in the dorm room when Nemesio walked in on him. He pulled off his hood.

"Where is everyone?" Adrian asked.

Billy shook his head. "Celeste told me to be here ten minutes ago."

"Me, too. I'm late. Grace almost never is, and Celeste is usually early."

"Do you know what this is about?"

"Celeste said it was about Thomas."

"They must have learned something."

The latch opened. Two Shade entered and took off their hoods. They wore no masks.

"Thanks for coming," Grace said. She remained standing as Celeste sat.

"What have you heard?" Billy asked.

"Nothing definitive. Adrian?"

Adrian's head snapped up. "Yep?"

"When did you tell Billy about the persona?"

"Oh, Jah, I don't remember. A couple months ago?"

"I mean how long before we brought Billy into the Kaleidoscope? How long before that?"

"Three weeks, maybe four. Why?"

"Yeah, why?" Billy asked.

"I'm trying to work out a timeline."

"Thomas went missing two days ago," Adrian said. "Why does it matter when Billy found out about the persona?"

"We heard that Armengol was asking around about the Kaleidoscope," Grace replied.

"A *long* time before you found us," Celeste added, staring at Billy.

"How'd you two meet?" Grace asked. "You and Adrian?"

"I don't remember."

"I remember," Adrian offered. "Armengol found me in the commissary. He asked if we had any piece work for hire."

"*He* found *you?*"

"Yeah. Came up to me in line and asked if I was Nemesio."

"Sure, that's right," Billy agreed. "I heard that the Kaleidoscope had a great rep, and that Nemesio was their best coder."

"*Ha!*" Celeste said, her eyes still fixed on Billy.

"Why's she looking at me like that?"

"Billy," Grace continued, "we heard that you were asking about the Kaleidoscope as soon as you showed up in the Summerland, on the very first day."

Billy looked back and forth between Grace and Celeste. "What's so mysterious about that? Crews outside the Summerland know the Kaleidoscope. Like I said, you have a great rep."

"Adrian, what else did Billy say in the commissary?"

Adrian narrowed his eyes at Billy. "He said he had experience with blockchain and security."

"In other words," Grace said, "the *exact* skills you were looking for."

"Damned convenient," Celeste muttered.

Billy stood up. "What are you getting at?"

"You said the last time you saw Thomas was three days ago," Celeste replied.

"Yeah, about that."

"And all you did was talk? About the magazine article?"

"Yeah."

"Nothing else?"

"Jah, no. How many times do I have to say it?"

"You're lying."

"I don't have to listen to this." Billy reached for his cloak and hood. Grace and Celeste blocked the door.

"What can you tell us about the parasailing lifestream?" Grace asked.

"Parasailing? I don't even know what that is."

"A big parachute pulled by a motorboat. Thomas rode that lifestream the day before he disappeared."

"So he rode a lifestream. What's that got to do with me?"

"You're good, Billy," Celeste replied. "You edited the logs. Then you covered your tracks. It took me some time to find it, six layers deep."

Billy got in her face and tapped his chest. "What's that got to do with *me?*"

"Why would Thomas go to so much trouble to hide his lifestream?"

"You'll have to ask him when he shows up."

"Thomas didn't do it—he's not that good. Someone else doctored those logs, someone with some chops."

Billy put on his cloak and hood. "It wasn't me. Let me out of here."

Grace and Celeste exchanged glances before pulling on their hoods. Chrysalis handed Adrian his hood, then she and Bjorg stepped aside. Armengol opened the door.

A cloaked figure blocked the doorway. He ducked low to enter, then pulled off his hood. He wore a black mask with a blood-red third eye staring from his forehead. He pulled his cloak over his head, and his muscles bulged under a tight-fitting shirt as he pressed a fist into his other hand.

"Graf," Chrysalis said, "Armengol has something he wants to tell you."

38

Badass Cred

The car idled roughly, transmitting its vibrations through the seat directly to the passengers' spines.

"We should turn off the engine, shouldn't we?" Chrysalis suggested.

"I don't think so," Leon answered. He tapped the accelerator, revving the engine. Chrysalis and Bjorg cringed.

"You're going to attract attention," Chrysalis said in a hoarse whisper.

"From *who?* The whole district is deserted." Leon revved it again. "Nice spot. The Aletheia chose well."

"Chrysalis."

She turned around from the shotgun seat to face Bjorg in the back.

"You worried?" Bjorg asked.

"About Elisha?"

"About the Eye of Providence."

Chrysalis faced forward. "Maybe she's not in there."

"What in hell did this lady *do* to you?" Leon asked.

"She was my therapist." Chrysalis stared out the window. The street was dark, the only light coming from a streetlamp at the corner fifty meters away, just visible from their location in an alley. "I trusted her."

"And she fucked ya."

Chrysalis snorted. "Yeah. That's what it felt like."

Leon turned off the engine. "Here they come."

Twin beams of light appeared at the end of the street,

sweeping an arc on the pavement as a car turned the corner, approaching their position at a steady speed. The windows were tinted, almost opaque. The streetlight glinted off the patches of clean paint, not rough with dirt or primer.

"Is this the right one?" Leon asked.

"They're right on time, according to Armengol," Bjorg replied.

"It's the right one," Chrysalis concurred. "I've seen it before. I've been in it."

Leon waited until the car passed, then started the engine again and pulled onto the street, following at a distance, headlights off. The car ahead continued without speeding up.

"We're invisible," Leon stated. "This is going to be good."

The car's taillights disappeared as it made a leisurely left turn. Leon made the turn a few seconds later. The street was deserted.

"Jah, we lost them!" Leon cursed.

"No," Chrysalis replied. "I remember. The alley, twenty meters ahead, on the left. That's it."

Leon followed her directions. The alley was completely dark. He turned on the headlights. It was a blind alley, ending in a solid brick wall.

"I guess we'll find out if your guy Armengol is on the level, 'cause if he's not, we're going to end up splattered all over those bricks."

Bjorg held up a small device, the size of a pocket screen. "I double checked the code, but it's anybody's guess if it's the right one."

"Armengol knows the consequences if he double-crosses us," Chrysalis said. "We won't be the only ones splattered on the wall."

"All the same," Leon cautioned, "fasten your seatbelts."

He gunned the engine, accelerating down the alley. Chrysalis braced herself against the dash. Bjorg held the device high. At twenty meters, she pushed the button.

An opening not much larger than the car appeared as the wall slid away, a reddish-orange light streaming from inside. The car cleared the entrance; Leon stood on the brake, fishtailing to the left as the car skidded to a halt. The sliding door slammed shut behind them.

Six cloaked figures surrounded the car, five of them aiming taser rifles.

"*Shit!*" Leon said.

The unarmed figure stepped forward, putting her hand on her hood and removing it. She wore a crimson mask, decorated in gold filigree.

"That's her," Chrysalis said.

"Madeleine?" Bjorg asked.

"Yes—Madeleine. The Eye of Providence."

The red-masked Eye of Providence handed her hood to one of the others. She went to the car and motioned for Leon to lower the window.

"Chrysalis?" she asked.

The passenger-side door opened, and Chrysalis stepped out. Six taser rifles pivoted to the spot.

"I'm called Chrysalis."

The Eye of Providence rounded the car until she stood facing Chrysalis. "I hope you've been well."

Chrysalis removed her hood. Her cheeks sagged a bit more than they had the last time the two had met, and there were additional lines at the corners of her mouth, but her brown eyes showed the same grim determination through the holes in her violet mask.

"We've come for Elisha," Chrysalis whispered.

"He's here, safe and comfortable." She turned to the Shade on her right. "Speranza."

The Shade lowered his rifle and stepped forward.

"Go get Elisha. Tell him his friends are here to take him back to the Summerland."

Speranza left and returned, trailing another Shade.

"Elisha?" Chrysalis asked.

The big man took off his hood, uncovering his blue and white mask. "I'm sorry, Chrysalis."

"It's all right. Are you hurt?"

"No. I'm fine."

Chrysalis took a step toward him. Five rifles took aim at

her. She turned to the Eye. "Can we go now?"

"Elisha is free to go," the Eye replied. She pointed to the person in the back seat. "Which one are you? Nemesio or Bjorg?"

"I'm called Bjorg."

She bent low and looked at Leon in the driver's seat. "Then you're Nemesio."

"I'm called Leon."

The Eye looked back at Chrysalis. "Where's Nemesio?"

"That sniveling coward refused to come," Bjorg replied.

Chrysalis held out a hand as if to quiet Bjorg. "What do you want with Nemesio?"

The Eye straightened up. "We knew this might happen. No matter."

"You said we're free to go," Chrysalis said.

"*Elisha* is free to go, is what I actually said. You and I, Chrysalis…we have things to talk about."

"I don't know what that could be."

"A merger."

"*Ha!* A *merger?* Between *me* and *you?*"

"Or a technology exchange. We have some powerful technology based on our lifestream research."

"Madeleine…"

"Eye of Providence."

"You're *stealing* lives. You're making credits from other people's *misery.*"

"Can we talk in private?"

"We're not going to *talk.* There's nothing I want from you, and there's nothing I have that you could possibly want."

"Actually, we're very interested in your persona."

"Whatever Armengol told you, it's wrong. That technology's not practical."

"Not yet, but we think it holds promise."

"Are you going to let us out of here or not?"

The Eye motioned to Speranza. He led Elisha to the car.

"Leon, Bjorg, Elisha, you're all free to go. Chrysalis, I'd hoped we could come to an agreement, but you've made this more difficult than it needs to be."

"You have no idea."

All heads turned toward the entrance as it slid open at high speed. A black car sped in, screeching to a halt, just inches from Leon's car. Four Bast sprang out of the car with military precision and trained taser rifles on the Eye's crew. The front passenger door opened. An immense Shade emerged.

The Eye's crew pointed their tasers at the newcomers.

"Let's stay calm," Chrysalis said, her arm extended, a pistol in her hand pointed directly at the Eye's head.

"That's not a taser," Speranza muttered.

"Damn right," Leon confirmed. "That's an old-school firearm that shoots *real bullets*. From the Bast armory. Makes your tasers seem kind of tame."

"The Bast were good enough to lend it to me," Chrysalis said, "after a shooting lesson."

"Speranza," the Eye scolded, "you were supposed to change the code after they got in."

"I changed it."

The big Bast by the car opened the back door and pulled out a cloaked person, his arm looking spindly in the grip of Graf's enormous hand.

"Graf," Leon said. "Your timing is *perfect*."

Graf let out a scratchy synthesized laugh as the scrawny Shade struggled in his grip.

"We weren't certain that Armengol wasn't holding something back," Chrysalis explained. "He was a little *too* eager to give up the temporary code. Graf convinced him to give us your universal passcode as well."

"Chrysalis," the Eye said, leaning closer. Chrysalis pressed the barrel of the gun against her temple.

"She's bluffing, Chief," Speranza said.

The Eye of Providence remained motionless. "No, Speranza. She's *not* bluffing." She turned her head a tiny bit toward Chrysalis. "What now, Grace?" she whispered.

"You take Armengol, we take Elisha."

"Okay." She stood straight. Chrysalis kept the barrel of the gun pressed against her head. "It doesn't have to be like this, Grace. We could have done a lot of good—*together.*"

"I don't agree."

"So be it. But you may think differently when you get back to the Summerland."

"I doubt it."

"In any case, I'm willing to talk, if circumstances change. Speranza."

Speranza pushed Elisha forward. He walked slowly toward the Bast's car. Graf let Armengol go. The two Shade passed each other as they went to their camps.

Graf got in his car; Leon got in his. Elisha joined Bjorg in the back seat. Chrysalis backed away from the Eye, keeping her pistol aimed at the blood-red mask until she was in the car.

Graf pressed a button. The door slid open. Leon followed Graf out the door, speeding down the alley as the door slid shut behind them. The two cars parted ways as one headed for the Bast dorm and the other for the Summerland.

"Grace?" Leon questioned.

"Yes," Chrysalis answered. "That's my name."

"You're a *woman.*"

"Surprise, surprise."

"No, seriously, I had *no* idea. You have such badass cred, I just assumed…"

"Keep driving, Leon. I want to go home."

39

THOSE RIDICULOUS OUTFITS

LEON TURNED THE corner onto the Summerland's street, in a district far from the densest populations. Pedestrians were a rare sight around the Summerland; for the most part, residents kept to themselves.

This night was different.

"Look," Leon said, pointing. Cloaked figures crowded the street, holding their cloaks at their waists, coming at them in a dead run.

"Stop the car," Chrysalis said. She rolled down the window. *"I'm called Chrysalis!"* she shouted. "What's happening?"

One Shade stopped. Two others nearly collided with him.

"They're raiding the Summerland!" the Shade cried.

"Who? Civils?"

"Civils and Kliegls," the Shade yelled. He looked behind himself, then ran. Five drones hovered in formation thirty meters back and ten meters high, rotors thrumming. In quick succession, the drones fired taser rounds at the Shade, some striking the pavement with an electric burst, others hitting their targets, bringing down a Shade, then two, then two more, their pained cries sounding like bleating sheep through their synthesizers. Running Shade sidestepped the convulsing bodies, slowing them down long enough for drones to lock on. The street was littered with quivering forms, a living obstacle course for the fleeing mob.

A line of more than twenty men advanced, all in the black

uniform of civil agents. They fired tasers at the Shade that the drones had missed, bound the hands of those shuddering on the pavement, and hauled the Shade who'd recovered into mass transports.

"Shit, this looks nasty," Leon growled. "Better head for the Bast dorm, assuming *we're* not overrun."

"We have to find Nemesio!" Chrysalis shouted.

Bjorg grabbed Chrysalis's shoulder. "We can't go in there."

"I'm not leaving him!"

"They either have him already or he's on the street. He'll find us."

"*No.* He's still in there. Leon, keep moving."

Bjorg pointed. "Jah, what's that?"

From the center of the line a stream of men broke through and fanned out. They wore similar uniforms to the agents', but white instead of black, with a vivid red sash across their chests. Instead of tasers, they carried long, narrow sticks, which they used to beat the stricken Shade into submission.

"Who the *hell…?*" Bjorg gasped.

"Kliegls," Leon answered. "Let's get out of here."

"Nemesio!" Chrysalis cried. "We have to get him."

The drones approached, panning their cameras over the panicked crowd, firing rounds in a spread pattern. When a drone exhausted its magazine, it peeled off and headed back to base, replaced by a fresh drone, fully loaded. Beyond the drones the ranks of civils and Kliegls advanced, tasing and beating every cloaked figure within reach.

Leon backed the car in a turn, then went back the way they came.

"Leon!"

"Sorry, Grace," Leon shouted, "you're going to have to let him down this one time."

Chrysalis yanked the handle on the door, pushing it open. She pulled away from Bjorg, leaning out over the pavement. The car lurched to the right as Leon reached for her. She was halfway out the door when Elisha came over the seat and grabbed her arm.

"Let me go!" Chrysalis tried to break free, but Elisha's grip was firm. He pulled her back inside and held her with both hands. Leon accelerated down the street.

◈ ◈ ◈

"Why didn't Adrian come?" Thomas asked.

Grace, Celeste, and Thomas sat in a makeshift dorm room in the Bast dormitory, accommodations compliments of Leon. The door was bolted shut, and the three founding members of the Kaleidoscope were uncloaked and unmasked.

"I told him to stay behind," Grace replied.

"That's not the *whole* story," Celeste challenged.

Grace crossed her arms and looked at the wall.

"When we decided to bust you out of the Aletheia, your comrade Adrian was…how would you put it, Grace?"

Grace glared at Celeste.

"Not enthusiastic," Celeste continued. "I'd say that's fair. He was *not enthusiastic.*"

"What's that mean?" Thomas asked.

"It means *his* ass means more to him than *yours* does."

"That's enough," Grace snapped. "We still have to find him."

"Why?" Celeste asked. "What do we need him for? We've got the Kaleidoscope right here. Our funds are still on account, minus the money we paid the Bast."

"How much?" Thomas asked.

"About half our reserves," Celeste answered.

"Jah. That'd be…"

"Two million, to be precise."

Thomas shook his head. "You shouldn't have done that."

"I'd have given it all," Celeste said, laying her hand on Thomas's arm. "Every last credit. Grace, wouldn't you?"

Grace leaned against the wall, her arms still crossed. She looked at Thomas with shining eyes and bit her lip as she nodded.

"Of course you would. But not Adrian."

"Be fair, Celeste," Grace pleaded. "He wants to finish the persona. He was worried about funding."

Celeste stood up and faced Grace. "*He* didn't bust his hump like *we* did to build up our crew. *He* didn't earn, he only spent. He was a *leech* who…who…"

Grace's mouth turned down. Tears streaked her cheeks. She closed her eyes and turned her face to the wall.

Celeste opened her arms and pulled Grace to her in a hug. Thomas stared awkwardly at the floor.

❖ ❖ ❖

Leon sat at a table in the Bast dining hall, a cramped space just big enough for half the Bast crew. They ate in shifts; both shifts had already eaten. Leon lingered as Chrysalis, Bjorg, and Elisha spooned cereal and soy milk from their bowls, their hoods lying folded beside them, their faces hidden by masks.

"What's next for the Kaleidoscope?" Leon asked.

"We're still talking about that," Chrysalis whispered.

"Split up the funds," Bjorg suggested. "Everyone for herself."

"We haven't decided."

"Throw in with the Bast," Leon offered. "I like your style. I'll give you a top position."

"I want to finish the persona."

"*Chrysalis*," Bjorg rasped, "*drop* it. No, seriously. I've been thinking—why did the civils come for the Summerland and not for the Bast? Or the Aletheia? Or any of the other Shade dorms?"

"We don't know that they didn't," Chrysalis replied.

"Yeah, we do," Leon countered. "I've checked around. They targeted the Summerland—nowhere else."

"See?" Bjorg said. "Why do you think that is?"

"I don't know."

"*I* know. It's the persona. We broke security protocol. Jahbulon homed in on it. And Nemesio's probably in confinement."

"Tell me more about this persona," Leon prompted.

"It's this thing that Nemesio…" Bjorg began.

"Bjorg," Chrysalis interrupted, shaking her head.

"What's the big deal? The program is *dead*. And it was a

failure, judging from the results. Why keep it a secret?"

"*It's not dead*," Chrysalis croaked, standing. "It's not. I was there, in the venue with Dylan. I was there. We were together."

"Whoa, wait, you jacked into the Worldstream from the Summerland?" Leon said. "No stealth?"

"We had safeguards in place," Chrysalis muttered. "We could go into a venue indefinitely as long as we didn't interact."

"But you disabled the safeguards, didn't you?" Bjorg asked.

Chrysalis sat down. "Yes."

Leon stood and stepped back from the table. "Jah, that's messed up. You put a lot of Shade at risk. Put a lot in confinement."

"I didn't mean to. I just wanted…"

"Doesn't matter!" Leon paced in a random pattern, hands on his head. "Holy shit. You busted protocol. You busted the fucking protocol. That's the unpardonable sin." He went to the corner. "You can't stay here. Out by noon."

Then he left the room.

"Now what?" Elisha asked.

"The Eye of Providence is looking better by the minute," Bjorg replied.

"No," Chrysalis countered. "We have other options."

Chrysalis walked up stairs she hadn't climbed in more than two years, in a run-down building on a street full of more run-down buildings. She walked the sixth-floor hallway, her footsteps echoing, until she reached apartment 6F. She pushed the button.

"Announce yourself, Cloak," said a voice from a hidden speaker.

"I'm called Chrysalis."

"What the hell? Are you alone?"

"Yes."

The bolt slid aside instantly and the door flew open. Raúl stood in the doorway in shorts and a hoodie.

"Jah, get in here."

He pulled the door shut. Chrysalis took off her hood and mask.

"That was a bad scene last night," Raúl said. "You caused a stink."

"I know."

"Did you get your crew out?"

"Two of them," Grace replied.

"Where're they?"

"The Cloakroom."

"Well, they can't stay *there* forever," Raúl muttered.

"That's why I'm here."

"I'm not following, Grace."

"We need a home."

"Yeah, you do. What's that got to do with me?" Raúl sat at his console, his screens showing scenes from virtual worlds or walls of code.

"We need a sponsor," Grace replied.

"You need *something*."

"Can you help us?"

"I don't run an employment agency."

Grace looked for a place to sit. The only other chair in the room was covered with a tangle of cables and VR gear. She sat down on the floor.

"The Eye of Providence offered to take us on."

"Oh, the *Eye?* I'd pass on that, if I were you."

"We did. Now we're homeless."

Raúl pressed fingers to his eyes, then ran his hands through his hair, letting it fall in a silver cascade.

"I'll see what I can do. No promises."

"Any idea when? We're out of options."

"Jah, you've gotten demanding."

"I'm looking out for my crew."

"Like you did when you brought Jahbulon down on the whole Summerland?"

Grace scowled, then her expression softened. "I made a mistake." She turned away, toward the window. The light filtered through the dirty glass as sunlight crept over the roof and into the air shaft. "I had to see Dylan."

"Oh, yeah—on that topic."

Grace turned back from the window. *What?*

"Your boy's in some serious trouble."

Grace got to her knees. "You told me."

Raúl pulled at the strings of his hoodie and shook his head. "I told you he was in confinement."

"Raúl, what happened?"

"He's been a bad boy."

"Raúl!"

"He tried to escape. They upped his term."

"Oh, Jah." Grace fell back to the floor, steadying herself with one hand. Her throat went dry. "How…how long?"

"Fifteen years."

Grace put a hand to her face, closing her eyes. She fell flat as her arm collapsed underneath her.

❖ ❖ ❖

"Quite the accomplishment," Raúl said. "You're outcasts in a world of outcasts."

The Cloakroom seemed even more secretive than usual. It was nearly deserted; the few Cloak who were there spoke quietly, glancing often at the door, as if they expected civils or Kliegl thugs to break in at any moment. Chrysalis, Bjorg, and Elisha sat with Raúl at a table by a corner, huddled near its center.

"Word's spread. Not a single Shade crew will take you. Forget about sponsors—you're *pariahs*."

"We can sneak in," Bjorg suggested. "Change our names."

"You can try. You'd have to split up. Every crew is on the lookout for two smalls and a big traveling together. And you'll be starting from scratch—no cred. You really wanna go back to square one?"

"Not especially," Bjorg muttered.

"Raúl has another suggestion," Chrysalis said.

Bjorg and Elisha leaned in.

"It's kind of radical," Raúl added.

"We're ass-deep in radical *already*," Bjorg replied.

"All right. I can hook you up with room and board—I have a client who owes me. Strictly limited time period. *No* access to the Worldstream, stealth or otherwise. And it won't be cheap."

"Naturally. What does *limited time period* mean?"

"Two weeks, tops. Maybe less, depending on how things break."

"What're you getting us into?" Bjorg demanded.

Raúl raised his hands, as if to calm her down. "You'll be comfortable. You'll be safe. You'll be outside the Worldstream—*way* outside." He rested his hands on the table, speaking softly. "You *will* have to work for a living. But you won't have to wear those ridiculous outfits anymore."

40

THE PERIMETER

THE SUMMERLAND WAS a resort by comparison. The Kaleidoscope were accustomed to a shared, but *clean* bathroom, not a mildew-infested toilet with a bucket for flushing, filled from the hose which served as the shower, zip-tied to an overhead pipe. The sink emptied into a hole in the corner of the floor, its faucet impossible to shut off completely, its basin cracked from the rim to the drain.

The sleeping arrangements were commensurate with the lavatory. Grace and Celeste shared a single bed, while Thomas rolled himself in a blanket on the floor. They'd managed to log two or three hours of fitful sleep the first two nights, until exhaustion set in and they slept from twilight until dawn. Not even the roaches and water bugs kept them awake.

Their host, Jamal, insisted that his three guests wear their cloaks and hoods at all times.

"Ya don't know when Jahbulon's lookin' at ya," he explained. "Y'all raise a tag an' my ass is fried."

Access to the Worldstream was forbidden. Daytime activity consisted of conversation and cleaning the bathroom. For almost two weeks, the world of the Kaleidoscope was limited to the basement walls of a condemned tenement.

Near the end of the second week of their confinement, they propped a chair against the door and risked uncloaking.

"Was it worth it?"

Celeste sat on the bed next to Grace. Thomas crouched in the corner.

"No," Grace answered.

Celeste leaned forward, hands between her knees. "Was it all about seeing your son?"

Grace leaned against the wall. She threw a fleeting glance at Celeste, then stared at the floor. "That was part of it. I really do miss him. But it was more than that."

"You hate it when you're not in control."

Grace laughed. "I hate that I have to choose between being with my son in the world and not having my every move watched and recorded."

"And hacked."

"Yeah. There's that." She rubbed her eyes. "Jah, how'd it come to this? I wanted to see Dylan. I wanted to be there for him."

"But not just that."

Grace turned to Celeste. Her eyes flashed defiance for an instant before lapsing back into surrender. "What you said— I wanted control."

"Of what?"

"Me. *Just me*. No one else. The All-seeing Eye can watch whatever it wants, as long as it's not watching me."

"It's not just you, is it?" Thomas challenged.

"What?"

"You didn't have to ruin the Summerland to make *that* happen," Thomas replied. "You're already outside the Worldstream. You're Shade."

"I think the big guy's on to something," Celeste agreed. "I get that you want to be Mom to your boy, but you don't have to *kill* Jahbulon to hide from him. We were *all* hiding."

"And now the Summerland's gone and they're all in confinement," Thomas continued. "They'll get reinserted into the Worldstream, and they'll all be tagged. No more hiding from the All-Seeing Eye."

"I know, *I know!*" Grace said. She put her head in her hands. "But I think you're wrong. I *do* have to kill Jahbulon."

"I don't get it."

Grace dropped her hands between her knees. She faced Thomas, looking haggard. "Jahbulon will keep pushing us into the shadows as long as he's able. If he hadn't found the Summerland this time, he would the next time."

"You don't know that," Celeste challenged.

"Celeste, I *saw* those Kliegl rallies. I was there. They mean to find the Shade and take them out. They found us first because I made us easy to find, but they'd have found us eventually. We don't call it the All-Seeing Eye for nothing."

The door opened a crack, jammed against the chair. The three surviving members of the Kaleidoscope scrambled to put on their cloaks and hoods.

"Wha' ya doin'? *Open up!*" Jamal shouted. Elisha unblocked the door. Jamal poked his head in. "Your ride is here."

"Right now?" Bjorg asked.

"Taxi's waitin', he's blowin' his horn. Get packed."

Jamal closed the door. Chrysalis pulled off her hood. She looked first at Bjorg with wide eyes, then Elisha. "It's not too late. You can still stay with the Shade, change your names. You don't have to come with me."

Bjorg pulled off her own hood. "We can go now. I got nothing to pack."

"Me, neither," Elisha agreed.

❖ ❖ ❖

The vehicle was massive, a black, boxy machine as large as Jamal's guest room, with windows tinted to opacity. Even its wheels were enormous, as high as Chrysalis's chest, and the bottom of the doors were almost a meter above the street. The vehicle emitted a menacing rumble as it idled by the curb.

The passenger door flew open, kicked out by the driver.

"*Jah*, get your butts in here," Raúl ordered. "It's a long drive, and I want to cross the perimeter as quick as we can."

The three Shade climbed into the vehicle, Elisha helping Chrysalis and Bjorg, then stepping up himself.

"Buckle up, kids," Raúl said. "Once we get outside the city, it's going to get rough."

❖ ❖ ❖

Chrysalis woke up bouncing on her seat.

"You can take off your hood now, Grace," Raúl said.

She pulled off her hood, then slid the cloak over her head. She peeled off her mask. The vehicle was on open ground, no roads in sight.

"We crossed the perimeter an hour ago," Raúl explained. "You all were crashed, so I let you sleep."

"What's the 'perimeter?'"

"The limit of Jahbulon, where the All-Seeing Eye is blind."

"That's right. You mentioned that. How far are we from the city?"

"Three hundred klicks from city center. A hundred and fifty from the periphery. Seventy-five from the perimeter."

"Then we're almost there?"

Raúl laughed. "Another four hundred." A wheel hit a hollow and bounced Grace off her seat. "And it's all like this."

❖ ❖ ❖

By the time the sun set they still had another hour to go. As the last vestiges of light faded, a waning moon rose huge on the horizon, as if to light their way. Raúl found a gravel road, still rough, but passable compared with open country. They drove on in near blackness, the only light coming from the moon and the SUV's headlights, the only sound the engine's steady growl.

"Does he know we're coming?" Grace asked.

"I didn't tell him," Raúl replied. "I told Jackson what I had in mind, but not Dylan. I doubt Jackson told him."

"Don't you think you *should* have told him?"

"No. Too many things could have gone wrong. I didn't want to get his hopes up until I was sure. And there's no way to send a message to Orwell. They're completely off-stream."

"He's going to be surprised."

"Does he like surprises?"

Grace laughed, then fell silent. "I don't know," she whispered. "I don't know if my son likes surprises."

Raúl looked at her. The moonlight erased the lines in her

face, making her appear—for a moment—like a young girl.

"You'll have plenty of time to find out," he said.

❖ ❖ ❖

Grace was awakened with a nudge to her shoulder. Celeste pushed forward between her and Raúl.

"There," Celeste said, pointing at a glow in the distance.

"Is that it?" Grace asked.

"Orwell," Raúl answered. "Land of the free."

"I hope so," Celeste said. "At least they have electricity."

"Compared to the Summerland, it's a vacation spot," Raúl replied.

"No VR," Thomas grumbled.

Raúl looked at Thomas in the rear-view mirror. "Where's VR gotten you up to now?"

"At least we made a living at it."

"Yeah, speaking of which," Celeste interjected, "how's one go about making a credit in Orwell?"

"They don't use credits, not in the town. Every few weeks one of their contacts in the city makes a supply run, and they'll use credits for that, but it's just too damned inconvenient when you're off the Worldstream."

"How do they keep track?" Celeste asked.

"Of buying and selling? A lot of barter. Everyone knows what they owe and what they have coming to them."

"Does *anyone* own credits?" she pressed.

"Like I said, they have a town account for business with the outside world. That's run by Jackson and the town council. But day-to-day?" Raúl shrugged. "I don't know. Ask Jackson when we get there."

Celeste tapped Grace on the shoulder. "How much do we have left?"

"I transferred the cost of our room and board," Grace replied. "And Raúl's fee."

"My *reasonable* fee, considering the risk I'm taking," Raúl added.

"About a half-million," Grace explained.

"Jah, that's nothing," Celeste said dismissively.

"It's not *nothing*," Grace corrected. "Not a lot, but

definitely not nothing."

The glow on the horizon resolved into a grid of lights mounted on high poles. Raúl came to a fork in the road and turned toward the lights. He crested a low hill and stopped. Below them lay a scene such as they'd never seen before: a field of grass, surrounded by lights, a high fence at one end, rows of benches on tiers, and lines laid out like a diamond. Grace saw a few dozen people scattered in small groups near the fence.

"What's that?" Celeste asked. "It looks like…is that a *baseball field?*"

"Close," Raúl replied. "Softball. It's like baseball for sissies." He pointed at a group near the benches on the far side. "Grace," he whispered. "Look there."

Grace craned her neck. A group of three men stood talking. One of them held what looked like a club. Another was a tall, skinny kid with dark skin and black hair. The third was a young man with red hair and a big, toothy grin.

"Oh, Jah," Grace whispered, putting a hand to her mouth. "That's him."

"Let's go say hi." Raúl drove down the hill to a path leading behind the fence, where the lights didn't shine. Raúl and his three passengers got out and walked toward the field, Raúl in the lead, followed by Grace, with Thomas and Celeste bringing up the rear. As they approached, the group of three men turned and walked off the field toward them.

"Wait," Raúl said. "Hang back a little."

Raúl stepped into the light. Raúl and Dylan spoke like old friends, just out of earshot. Grace felt a palpitation when Dylan looked her way. She walked forward, leaving Thomas and Celeste in the dark.

As Grace stepped into the light, Dylan's face went blank, then his eyes widened. He took a step, but one foot got in front of the other, and he stumbled. Grace rushed forward and touched her son for the first time since she shredded her life.

PART THREE

MADELEINE

41

A WALK IN THE PARK

CUTTING THROUGH THE park was the last in Ava's string of bad choices.

She could barely see the path, lit by a half-moon rising behind thin clouds. Even in daylight the path was obscure—a few islands of asphalt in a river of rocks and dirt, buried under sticks and branches from trees pruned by the wind. The trees themselves were monuments to neglect—most dead or dying, naked snags so decrepit that neither birds nor squirrels would nest in them. At night, they lined the path like black ghosts with kindling arms and knothole eyes.

Ava was still six blocks away from her building, in a park where not even the scattering of people on the streets wandered after midnight. Hardly anyone went out at night, or in the day for that matter. Holed up in a one-room flat, jacked into the Worldstream, food and other necessities delivered by drone—that pretty much described the twenty-four hours in a day for all save the rebellious, the resistant, or the curious few who preferred Real Life to Virtual Reality.

Ava had met Stanley in a venue for singles, a gathering place for VR sex, or, for the adventurous, a place to arrange a hook IRL. Ava was feeling adventurous that night. Stanley's avatar was promising, even allowing for the limited alterations that the Worldstream tolerated, the VR equivalent of makeup or minor cosmetic surgery. When they'd met IRL, in an all-night bodega, Stanley's looks were only a bit disappointing—a little older, pudgier, and somewhat grungier than his avatar. Ava bought wine; Stanley bought condoms and a bar of soap before taking her to his apartment, a twenty-minute walk from the bodega, in the opposite direction from Ava's building.

Stanley's flat was typical—a single room with a corner kitchenette, a bed no bigger than a cot, a chair amid VR gear scattered on the floor, and a medium-sized screen hung on an otherwise bare wall—essentially a prison cell without bars, from which Stanley could escape to any location on earth or any time in history, simply by strapping on his VR gear and jacking into a venue.

The sex was satisfying, if uninspired. Forty-five minutes later, Ava dressed in the dark next to the bed as Stanley snored. Eager to return to her apartment for an hour or two of sleep before strapping in for the workday, she took a shortcut through the park.

She could hear whispered conversation—she was certain there was more than one person following her. She tip-toed, holding her breath…nothing…not even rustling leaves in the damp, airless night. Then…a few unintelligible words, and more silence. Ava turned her head as far as possible, straining to see behind her from the corner of her eye. She saw only shadows. She walked faster, pulling her jacket closed and hunching her shoulders as if to make herself smaller.

Her arms and legs tensed involuntarily, thoughts jumbled and unfocused. Her head jerked toward a movement in the ragged bushes a few meters from the path—a feral cat, besides the ubiquitous pigeons, the only significant wildlife population left in the city. She picked up her pace to a slow jog.

This is nuts, she thought.

If anything should happen, one call to Jahbulon and his agents would arrive in seconds, as surely as a dropped rock falls to the ground. She snickered at her own silly fear as she slowed her pace, walking only a little faster than normal.

The whispered voices ceased. Ava breathed more easily, realizing her followers had taken a side path and she was alone again. *Three more blocks.*

Suddenly she heard a thin *snap*, like a twig breaking. She stopped and turned without thinking. A hand shot toward her like a viper strike, aiming for her neck. She ducked but a thumb struck her in the eye, blinding her and sending her toppling backward.

"Sophia, pause the venue," Dominick said.

The action froze; Ava hung suspended in mid-fall, the attacker's hands motionless, centimeters from her neck. Dominick peered out through Ava's eyes. One man's face was hidden in shadow; the other's savage grin glinted in the moonlight. Though all movement had ceased, Ava's feelings continued, induced with agonizing fidelity by the dermal contact neural interface strapped to Dominick's waist: tightness in his chest, nausea, paralysis—the involuntary reactions of a woman in terror. Her physical stress and mental trauma were stuck, unchanging, intensified by their persistence, like a recording halted at peak volume playing a piercing note boring into his brain. Dominick wanted it to stop like nothing else he could remember.

"Sophia, second person, first male."

Dominick's field of view narrowed, receding into the distance as if through a camera lens zooming out, shrinking to a black speck in a field of white. Ava's anxiety winked out, leaving a residual angst, like queasiness following a bout of seasickness. It lasted less than a second. The speck expanded, a blurred rush streaking toward him, pulling him forward into the head of Ava's attacker. Dominick saw through the man's eyes, the action still frozen, his hand poised to grab Ava by the throat.

He felt new sensations—dry mouth, heat behind his eyes, tension in his groin, the feelings persistent but wavering, as if balanced on a knife's edge. His breathing deepened as he let the moment linger.

"Sophia, resume the venue."

Ava fell back, just out of the man's reach, rolling and scrambling away, hands and knees losing traction in the litter of twigs and dry leaves. He lunged, falling on top of her, grabbing her arm and twisting it until it gave with a noise like a breaking branch. Ava screamed and kept screaming. The man covered her mouth with his hand; Dominick could feel her face, hot and wet, until a pain shot into his hand and up his arm, so intense it blurred his vision, as Ava's teeth sank into the man's flesh.

He cried out, jerking his hand away and pressing it against his chest. Dominick mimicked the movements of the man whose body he inhabited, over which he had no control, yet whose every sensation Dominick felt as if he were living in that moment. Dominick's breath came in spasms; his eyes watered; the image in his visor shuddered.

Jah, he thought, *this is intense.*

He went to his knees. Ava lifted herself up, but fell to the ground groaning, her injured arm crumpling under her.

"*Jah,* she fucking bit me!" the first man said. The second man took a step as if he were approaching a soccer ball, landing a kick to the side of Ava's head. Her neck snapped; her body went limp, arms and legs forming a crude swastika, skirt hiked up.

Dominick felt the man's hand throbbing; the other sensations continued, a mixture of lust and fear and ferocity, and a new emotion—animal rage—welling up in his chest. He grabbed Ava's leg and threw it to one side. He fumbled with his buckle, the bitten hand now too painful to be of much use, managing with one hand to loosen his belt and undo his pants.

"Sophia…"

The action froze as Dominick's voice responder waited for the rest of the command.

"Yes, Dominick?" a female voice asked through his headphones.

The toxic mix of emotions persisted, clouding Dominick's mind and freezing his movements. He kept his eyes on Ava's motionless form, legs spread, head twisted on her neck, eyes half-closed, jaw slack.

Is she dead? he wondered, almost as if the thought of her being dead hadn't come to him, but had been placed there. He *wanted* her to be dead, and he regretted that it had not been *his* kick that had killed her. The thoughts kept coming, almost audibly, layered on top of the anger and lust. He tried to shake them off, realizing a moment of detachment, a flash of grim fascination that he could be capable of thinking such things.

Then his thoughts slowed and stopped, as if he were falling into a dream state.

The image softened, the field of view fading to black. The woman's terrified face appeared for an instant, lit up by a flash, like a strobe light, then disappeared. Another flash, another image: a hand in Ava's mouth, blood flowing as her teeth broke the skin; and another, a foot landing a brutal blow to Ava's head. And another. And another. After the last flash, the memory of the images left Dominick's conscious mind.

The scene in his visor returned. Ava still lay helpless. The man's pants hung at mid-thigh.

"Sophia, suspend the venue."

Ava, the second man, and the surroundings all faded, replaced in Dominick's headgear with a white staging venue. A glowing blue caption floated in front of him: *A Walk in the Park—Venue Suspended, Time 1:35:05. Command* Resume Venue *to continue.*

Dominick tore off his headgear and tactile gloves, damp with sweat, mopping his forehead with a sleeve. He felt the veins in his neck distend with every heartbeat, his hand throbbing in time with his pulse. The worst of the pain had passed. He examined his hand, half-expecting to find a deep bite wound. It was unmarked.

As he recovered, he felt heat around his midsection, overlaying a tingling, like a leg that had gone to sleep waking up again. He stood and pulled up his shirt, exposing his dermal contact neural interface—*the Belt*. It was the latest model, gen four, which he'd bought for a little more than two weeks' pay, and just experienced for the first time. He ran his fingers over the smooth, black fabric.

"Jah," he whispered. "*Jahbulon almighty*. Worth every damn credit, including the tax."

❖ ❖ ❖

Frannie trudged home, one hand in her coat pocket clutching a bottle of multi-symptom cold remedy. Her husband Danny was miserable, having come down with a cold the previous day, a rarity in a world where most human contact was limited to Virtual Reality. But Danny and Frannie didn't live in VR. The elderly couple, making do on basic guaranteed income and a modest pension, were *real school*. Exotic venues, titillating lifestreams, big virtual events simply didn't register with them. Those things weren't *real*; therefore, Danny and Frannie weren't interested. Frannie read books, indoors in bad weather, or on the pavement in front of their building when it was nice, looking up from her book to greet the very rare passers-by. Danny spent his days at a Real Life café with friends his age, drinking tea and playing chess. Shaking hands —the customary end to a chess match—is how colds spread.

It was almost midnight. Frannie didn't like going out after dark, but Danny's coughing and nose blowing were too much to bear. Danny told her he'd be okay and not to bother getting anything for his cold, but Frannie put on her coat, saying, "You're lying, old man." She walked the four floors down from their flat and five blocks to the drugstore, choosing a generic brand of cold medicine, submitting to a face scan, and paying with her monthly voucher. She walked back home, retracing her route through the park. Carefully, she tread on loose gravel, stepping over the larger stones and walking around fallen branches.

A little more than halfway through the park, the path curved into shadows, shielded from distant streetlights. The crunch of gravel under her shoes was the only sound. She felt the bottle in her hand, squeezing it, thinking about Danny and how terrible he sounded, and how he seemed to get a lot of colds.

The blow struck Frannie on the right shoulder, spinning her around, her foot catching on the broken asphalt. She stumbled forward, unable to pull her hand out of her pocket in time to break the fall, coming down with all her weight on one shoulder and dislocating it. A searing pain shot through her body.

Her assailant brought his knee down on her hip, then pulled at her coat, ripping it open. He grabbed at her dress, trying to pull it up to her waist. Frannie flailed with one good arm but the man was stronger and pinned her to the ground.

She cried out in a thin voice, hardly louder than polite conversation, *"Jahbulon, help me!"*

Within seconds the air was filled with the high-pitched buzz of four police drones converging on the scene, directing their spotlights at the perpetrator, who raised an arm to shield his eyes from the light. Four rounds issued from miniature cannons mounted to the undercarriages of the drones. The projectiles embedded themselves in his torso, each taser round injecting an electric current at a potential of 50,000 volts. The assailant collapsed in convulsions.

Two agents arrived on the scene, dressed in black from shoes to helmets to gloves. A visor hid their eyes and covered their faces from cheekbones to foreheads in a smooth silvered surface, with retinal-resolution cameras on either side.

The first agent restrained the downed man with zip-ties.

"He's zipped," Agent One said. "Zipped and zapped."

The second agent turned Frannie's face toward him. Her identity and vital signs scrolled across his visor.

"Jahbulon, we need medical evac. Huxley, Frances, female, age 72. Multiple trauma. Onset of shock," Agent Two said, and knelt next to Frannie, stroking her hair. "Help's on the way, citizen."

The sound of the evac drone grew louder, a buzz like a police drone, but deeper and more powerful. A drone the size of a two-person transport settled to the ground, its six massive propellers raising a cloud of leaves and dirt. The gleaming white composite enclosure opened to reveal a stretcher, surrounded by instrumentation. The agents secured Frannie to the stretcher, attached electrodes to her head and chest, immobilized her arm, and fixed a respirator mask to her face. A voice from the interior boomed: *"Patient secure and stable. Please stand back."* The blades revved up; the enclosure drew shut as the drone lifted off.

Agent Two turned to his partner. "Do you have an ID on this prick?"

Agent One turned the man over. A photo, name, and address popped up in his visor. "Trigg, Dominick. Male, 29. He lives nearby."

Agent Two toed Dominick in the thigh. "Well, he's not going home tonight."

42

Auntie Em

Dominick didn't know the place or how he had gotten there. He lay on a firm mattress, under a thick comforter, head resting on a pillow with just the right loft. He wore soft, warm pajamas—red flannel with blue fish swimming across them. He stared at the ceiling, oblivious to the flowers on the sturdy nightstand, or the artwork bolted to the walls, confused but comfortable, despite the Kevlar restraints chafing his wrists and ankles.

Dominick saw the lifestream replaying in vivid detail, as if his eyes were projecting it on the ceiling: a woman walking through the park before dawn, feeling pleasantly weak after sex, turning fearful as she heard voices behind her; a rapist and his accomplice assaulting her; the woman fighting back; and then—the young, strong, defiant woman morphed into a weak old lady. He remembered the lifestream—he did *not* remember the metamorphosis.

What he *did* remember were blinding lights, noises like exploding tires, blows to the thorax, convulsions, paralysis, blackness. Then—a comfy bed, the scent of flowers, and a rape scene playing before his eyes in an endless loop.

He heard a tap on the door before it opened.

"Hello, Dominick? Are you up?" a short, plump lady asked. She was perhaps 50 or 55, graying brown hair pulled back, wearing a black dress with white polka-dots and a frilled apron.

Auntie Em, Dominick thought. *I must still be in Kansas.*

"How are you feeling, dear?"

"I don't know," he mumbled. He tried to lift himself, but the restraints on his wrists kept him from rising more than a few centimeters.

"Oh, let me get those for you, Dominick." She undid one hand. "Do you like to be called Dominick?" she asked, rounding the bed to undo the other hand.

He sat up, massaging his wrists. "Yeah, Dominick."

"Hello, Dominick. I'm Felicity, your therapist."

He blinked slowly as feeling returned to his wrists. He touched a welt over his lower rib cage: two swollen bumps topped by twin lacerations.

"Oof."

"Oh my, let me see that," Felicity said, reaching to undo the buttons on his pajamas. He twisted away, blocking her hand with his elbow.

She knitted her brow, opened the drawer in the nightstand and took out a foil packet, holding it up for Dominick to see: *Pain Relieving Antibacterial.* He unbuttoned his pajamas to expose the impact points of four taser rounds. Felicity tore open the packet.

"What therapy?" he asked.

"This is a public intervention facility," she replied, dabbing at the wounds. "We help people return to society."

"*Return to society?* What does that mean?"

"When people violate Jahbulon's laws, we bring them here," she replied between dabs. "We help them to understand the nature of their transgressions, why they were wrong, and why Jahbulon can't allow them to continue." She tilted her head, examining the four pairs of welts, now glistening with antiseptic gel. "Once we've had time to understand your case, we'll make a decision."

"What decision?"

Felicity reached to redo his buttons, but he pulled away and rebuttoned the pajamas himself. She sat back with her hands in her lap. "We'll decide how long to continue your therapy."

"You don't know how long I'll be here?" Dominick asked.

"No more than a week."

"A week?"

She tugged his covers higher. "Then we'll transfer you to another facility for the remainder of your therapy."

"To confinement?"

"Yes."

"Oh, *Jah*."

Felicity put her hand over Dominick's. He pulled away.

"You're here because you violated another citizen. Do you remember that?"

He lifted his eyes toward the blank ceiling—the rape scene had vanished.

"I was riding a lifestream. *That's* what I remember."

"Civil agents apprehended you in a park. You hit a lady and knocked her down." She pulled a pocket screen from her apron, holding it so he could see the photo of his victim. "Frances Huxley. Do you remember her?"

The image of the young woman Ava flashed before his eyes, looking surprised and fearful as the rapist's hand reached for her, the entire scene suspended in time. She was *not* the woman in the photo.

"That woman wasn't in the lifestream."

She returned the pocket screen to her apron. "Dominick, this is where we'll begin, okay? When you were taken, you weren't wearing any VR gear. You *weren't* riding a lifestream. Do you understand that?"

Dominick touched a welt on his waist. It was still tender, but the painkiller had done its job. He closed his eyes, trying to replay the sequence of events: the young woman—the attackers—a kick to the head—the woman dying—the repeated rapes—the hurried disposal of the body in a public reclamation bin—the escape—and an intense, toxic mix of lust, rage, gratification, panic, and relief induced by the gen four Belt. Then another scene, also in a park, a different woman, a different outcome, but with the same emotions at the same intensity.

"I think I was wrong. I think the old lady *was* in the lifestream."

Felicity spoke very softly. "Dominick, I can tell you, she was *not*. When you attacked Mrs. Huxley, you were IRL."

His eyes began to water. "The lady…"

"She was hurt—a fractured hip, a dislocated shoulder. We have her in a full-time recovery venue. It's serious, but she'll be okay."

Dominick's throat tightened. He sucked air with a snort. His eyes shut, tears running down his cheeks as he let out a breath in a shuddering sob.

"It'll be all right, Dominick. We'll make you better." She touched his shoulder, encouraging him to lie down. "Yes. We'll make you all better."

"Did you also get the other guy?" he asked as he lay back, recovering his breath.

"There wasn't another man—you were alone," she replied, patting his hand before refastening his wrist straps.

❖ ❖ ❖

It was the third time that day that Dominick had relived the events. Felicity decided three times was enough—his psychometrics indicated desensitization. A night's sleep, and additional medication, would help to reinforce the therapeutic effect of revisiting the scene of his transgression.

"No more today, Dominick," Felicity said through his headphones. She removed his headgear and gloves, undoing the Belt from his waist. His head fell forward, eyes closed, jaw slack, a line of drool hanging from his lip. She dabbed the spit from his mouth with a tissue. "Poor dear. You've had a rough day." She checked the Kevlar restraints on his wrists. "I'll be back soon with your dinner."

❖ ❖ ❖

"Report, please."

Felicity sat across from Madeleine in her office venue, all of its furnishings—potted plants, prints on the walls, a homey throw rug—designed for therapeutic effect. Felicity's back was stiff and chin raised, hands folded in the lap of her polka-dot dress.

"You jacked into the first and final sessions, Doctor. You have all the psychometrics. I don't think there's anything I can tell you that you don't already know."

Madeleine folded her hands under her chin, resting both elbows on her knees. "Well, Felicity, factually that's true. But your experience in these cases is valuable. I would like to know *your* perspective on Dominick's therapy."

Felicity crossed her arms. "Well, since you ask, I'm uncomfortable with his progress."

"Mm-hmm. And why is that?"

"He continues to cling to his delusion."

"You mean his delusion that this transgression was part of a lifestream?"

Felicity loosened her arms, hands dropping into her lap. "Yes. Until he accepts the reality of the events, and takes responsibility, his therapy is…"

"At a standstill. Yes, I agree."

Felicity narrowed her eyes. "I'm glad."

"What do you think is at the root of this delusion?" Madeleine asked.

"*You're* the doctor."

"Felicity, please."

"I don't know," Felicity sighed. "I'm beginning to think that he really *was* in a lifestream."

"I don't understand. He *did* assault that woman."

"Of *course* he did. What I mean is, maybe he was in a lifestream sometime *before* the assault, a lifestream similar to the RL events. And he got them confused."

"Interesting." Madeleine tapped her chin. "Why do you think so?"

Felicity leaned forward. "I've facilitated delusional subjects before. They can't be reasoned with. Whatever contrary evidence I show them, no matter how convincing, they *won't* be shaken." She sat back. "It's the nature of delusion."

Madeleine smiled. "Well, it's a *little* more complicated than that. But you *did* say he continues to cling to his delusion. Isn't that consistent with the pathology?"

"Dominick is different. It's not like he's *stuck* in a fantasy; he's *questioning* himself. He's being reasonable, as though he's entertaining the *possibility* that these are real events, but his memory is conflicting. He really *does* believe he was in a lifestream, but he also really wants to know the truth."

"Then he *is* making progress."

Felicity sighed loudly. "He was like that from the *start*. And yes, he's made a *little* progress, but he's still confused. And I don't know why."

Madeleine reached out to pat Felicity's knee. "I'll work on figuring that out, dear."

Felicity turned in her chair. "*Don't* call me 'dear.'"

Madeleine took her hand back and crossed her arms. "Continue therapy tomorrow. From now on, I'll be attending every session."

❖ ❖ ❖

Felicity rastered out of Madeleine's venue.

"The arrogant…" she whispered, before catching herself. Alone in her staging venue, she slipped her fingers under the visor and rubbed her eyes.

"Dorothy—ambience," she commanded.

"Yes, Felicity," her voice responder answered.

Soft music of acoustic instruments dubbed with the soothing nature sounds of bird calls, a burbling stream, and distant thunder filled her headphones. The staging venue became a pasture, sloping away toward a creek meandering through a stand of trees, the grass so green it seemed artificial, dotted with pink and blue cornflowers. The sun shone overhead as storm clouds crowded the horizon.

"Dorothy, sunglasses."

A pair of dark glasses materialized on Felicity's nose. She sat in the grass to think for more than half an hour.

As she meditated, claps of thunder sounded nearer and more often. A cloud passed over the sun, and a few drops of rain fell. Felicity removed her sunglasses and looked up, expecting to feel raindrops on her face, then remembered that she wasn't wearing the Belt—the venue could induce no sensations other than those from her tactile gloves.

"Dorothy, suspend the venue."

Felicity was instantly transported to her staging venue.

"Dorothy, search for lifestreams, theme: violence or rape."

"Yes, Felicity. Search complete. I've located more than fourteen thousand results."

A window appeared, scrolling through the search results: *Defending Your Home…Mass Mayhem…Twenty-Car Pileup.*

"Dorothy, refine search: rape only."

"Yes, Felicity. Search complete. I've located more than three thousand results."

"Dorothy, refine search: rape and park."

"Felicity, disambiguate *park*, please."

"Park, as in an outdoor area, you know, like a public park."

"Yes, Felicity, I understand. Search complete. I've located one hundred four results."

She scrolled through the list. Nothing in the titles suggested that one was more like Dominick's imagined lifestream than another.

"Dorothy?"

"Yes, Felicity?"

"Can you do a correlation between a transgression record and a lifestream? Rank these results by similarity?"

"Yes, Felicity. Which record did you have in mind?"

"Transgression: assault. Offender: Trigg, Dominick."

"Yes, Felicity. I have the record. Please stand by."

The list's contents jumped up and down as the items reordered. A few seconds later they stopped.

"Ranking complete."

A new column appeared: a score indicating the degree of similarity between the crime record and the lifestream, on a scale of one to one thousand. Number one on the list had a score of 880.

"Felicity, open item one, *A Walk in the Park.*"

"Yes, Felicity. This lifestream has graphic content—nudity and violence. Do you acknowledge?"

"Yes, Dorothy."

"This lifestream includes peripheral-specific content."

"Which peripheral?"

"Stimulus Rex Dermal Contact Neural Interface, gen four recommended."

"Override, please."

"Peripheral content overridden. Note that your lifestream experience will lack full-fidelity sensations. Do you acknowledge?"

"Yes, Dorothy. Please begin the venue."

43

PHYSICAL TRANSGRESSIONS

"GOOD MORNING, FELICITY. Please bring in the subject."

Felicity and Madeleine were in the therapy venue. Standard procedure called for the therapist to review the status of the therapy with the patient and to establish the protocol for the session. The doctor, if attending, rarely interfered.

"I'd like a minute with you before we bring in Dominick, if that's okay," Felicity said.

Madeleine sat up. "Ah…of course. Certainly."

"I have an idea of what might have happened."

Madeleine turned her head slightly. "Go on."

"It might be easier to show you than to explain."

Madeleine nodded.

"Dorothy, *A Walk in the Park.*"

Felicity and Madeleine dropped into a venue occupied by young adults in their twenties and early thirties. Some avatars stood alone; others talked in groups of three or more, but most had paired off. New attendees, always single, rastered in from time to time. Occasionally, couples rastered out, presumably for an RL rendezvous.

"What is this?" Madeleine asked.

"Dorothy, please take us to time stamp 1:25:00."

"Yes, Felicity."

The venue dissolved from the party venue to a public park. From their third-person vantage point, Felicity and Madeleine saw a young woman walking alone, in what appeared to be late night or early morning. Two men followed her at a distance of twenty meters.

"Dorothy," Felicity ordered, "pause the venue."

Action in the venue ceased, the two men walking on tip-toes, the girl in mid-step, craning her neck to see behind her.

"I found this lifestream after searching for scenarios that matched the circumstances of the assault. This morning I asked Dominick the name of the lifestream he rode. This is it —*A Walk in the Park*. I should have asked him that question before. I just assumed he was deluded."

Madeleine crossed her arms and put a finger to her lips. "I don't see what this has to do with the therapy."

"Really? You don't see it? He was telling us the truth from the start—he *was* riding a lifestream. Do you remember him asking if they got the other man? This lifestream has *two* assailants."

"I still don't see the relevance."

"When he attacked that woman in the park, he thought he was still in the lifestream, or something like that."

Madeleine pursed her lips and cleared her throat. "That seems like a leap to me, Felicity."

"I don't think so. I rode this lifestream, and..."

"*You* rode the lifestream?"

"Yes, of course I did. The circumstances..."

"Do you think that was wise?"

Felicity furrowed her brow. "Wise? I'm trying to *help* this subject."

Madeleine put a finger back to her lip. "Did you...I mean, were there any, ah, special requirements?"

"Special requirements? For what? The lifestream?"

"Yes. That's what I meant."

"Well, it had some Belt content."

"And did you..."

"Use the Belt? No, I don't *own* a Belt." Felicity lowered her chin. "Not on what *you* pay me," she muttered.

Madeleine glared, then softened. "Felicity, I think you may be on to something. Yes. This may be a breakthrough."

Felicity smiled for the first time. "I think so too."

Madeleine leaned back in her chair. "Felicity, I wasn't going to say anything to you until after the session, but with this new development, I think that now would be a good time. I'm promoting you to section supervisor."

Felicity jerked her head back. "You're *what?*"

"Section supervisor. You've earned it. I want you to manage the entire physical transgression section for the district. I think you'll do an awesome job."

Felicity shrugged with her palms up. "We already have a supervisor—Chastity. What happens to her?"

"I've been concerned about Chastity's performance for some time."

"Well, *I* haven't. Chastity is doing a great job."

Madeleine shook her head. "There are aspects of her performance which aren't visible to you. Trust me, Chastity will be better suited to other responsibilities."

Felicity looked aside, then smiled. "Okay. All right—I'll do it!"

"Excellent."

Felicity beamed. "Thank you, Doctor." She smoothed her dress and adjusted her hair. "I'll get Dominick ready for the session."

"No need for that, Felicity. I'm cancelling the session."

"What? *No!* Interrupting the therapy at this juncture will be counterproductive."

"Oh, I don't think it'll be a problem. Your breakthrough will more than compensate for the interruption. But if you're concerned, don't be. I'll take over the therapy myself. I'll conduct the next session this afternoon."

Felicity's smile faded. "Are you credentialed for restorative therapy?"

"Felicity," Madeleine answered, blinking slowly, "I *developed* the restorative protocol."

Felicity lowered her eyes, then shrugged as her smile returned. "Very well. I suppose I should transfer my caseload."

"Wait on that, dear—*Felicity.* The promotion is still in process. And we haven't informed Chastity yet."

"Oh, I see. Of course. You'll let me know?"

"Certainly. Thank you, Felicity, and congratulations."

Felicity folded her hands over her chest, smiling widely. She gave a little shiver of excitement. "Dorothy, exit the venue." She rastered out, leaving Madeleine alone in her office venue.

"Elsa, suspend the venue." The surroundings faded to the staging venue. Madeleine pulled off her VR gear. Her RL office, a separate room in a spacious apartment, was all business—tile floor and bare walls except for a single wall screen—unlike the inviting surroundings of her therapy venue, with throw rugs and potted plants.

"Elsa, v-gram, division supervisor Perez. Begin message. Anthony, I've decided to make some personnel changes to the physical transgression section. I'm moving Chastity out as supervisor. I know it's not a good time, with the sharp spike in incidents, but when is it ever? In any case, I'm shifting Felicity into that spot and we need to find another role for Chastity. Let me know what's available. End message.

"V-gram, facility head Gill. Begin message. Paula, I have some sad news. I'm filing my report today on Dominick Trigg. Unfortunately, I've concluded that additional therapy will be ineffective. It's so tragic when we fail to reach one of our subjects, but in this case, I feel we have no choice. I'm recommending permanent confinement."

44

Wakey Wakey

THE BALL OF the Earth rotated in a field of stars. As each continent crossed the terminus of night, scattered dots of light appeared in primary colors, tight clusters marking population centers. China lit up in a sparkling array, a random scattering of megalopolises separated by wide swaths of blackness. Europe crossed into night, the dots so close together they blended into ragged blotches of white, marking the major cities. The Atlantic Ocean passed by, then a beacon flashed on the edge of the globe—North America, the east coast shining solidly, then the Midwest and West, looking more like China, with concentrations of stream riders in the metro areas scattered in a black expanse.

Speranza's avatar floated in space above the spinning globe. Separated from the Worldstream, behind the firewall of the Shade alliance Aletheia, with no compliance engine to validate his avatar, Speranza appeared in his usual form: a tall, thin man, black hair and mustache, meticulously groomed, in an elegant suit—the resurrected image of Nikola Tesla.

"It's ticking up," he said.

The Eye of Providence hovered nearby, seated upon a simple bench, her avatar taking the form of Ma'at, a goddess of Egypt, arms adorned with feathers, a white plume waving from a crimson headband. She tapped her chin. "How does it break down by theme?"

"Sex and violence—still the most popular combo. More than 90% riding assault, rape, or plain old consensual sex in all its forms. *A Walk in the Park* still tops the chart at 43%, more than three-quarters with the gen four Belt." Speranza gestured and a list appeared, a menu with a 3D icon next to each item. He tapped one. Most of the glowing dots flashed and disappeared, leaving a scattering of lights in a spectrum of colors. "Here—double the number of riders with the gen four Belt, more than six thousand in the last week, and more than a hundred online right now. One out of eight riders getting the total Belt experience, a full-on head trip mainlined to the solar plexus. That's great penetration."

"Congratulations, Jayla," the Eye said to the avatar on her right, a blue plush teddy bear on a playground swing. "That's three straight weeks in the top spot. And give my thanks to your team."

"They live to serve, Boss," the teddy bear replied.

"Speranza, run down the other themes," the Eye ordered.

"Sure." A 3D graph appeared, like a landscape with mountains and valleys, each feature representing a lifestream and its ridership. As Speranza counted down the list, lights on the globe flashed on and off, showing each theme's popularity by region, mountain peaks lighting up, representing penetration by demographics.

"At the bottom of the list, three empathy streams— mother and child, helping the downtrodden, like that, two percent." Lights flickered out across the globe, leaving specks scattered at random. "A little more popular, three life crisis streams—loss of a loved one, for example, three percent. Next, two personal danger streams—failed parachute seems to be a favorite—five percent. Climbing the charts, two violence streams, one brawl and one mass killing—if you haven't seen that one, I can tell you, it's nasty—ten percent. Getting into the top draws: four sex only, including two group sex and one homosexual encounter, thirty percent. And at the top, with fifty percent of all the rides, are our two sex and violence streams, with *A Walk in the Park* making up the lion's share." The lights flashed on again, lighting up the population centers of North America. Speranza waved a hand; the visuals disappeared; the star field brightened, leaving Tesla, Ma'at, and the teddy bear in an empty venue, surrounded by pink light.

The Eye folded her hands under her chin. "The empathy streams disappoint me."

"Our riders are a damn twisted bunch," Speranza observed. "They'd rather fight and fuck than care for a sick child. Go figure. I gotta wonder if our data set isn't skewed toward sickos and pervs."

"It can't be helped," the goddess explained. "All these lifestreams are based on case studies. For every patient I've taken with a family issue, I've treated fifty criminals, addicts, and sociopaths."

"So what does that get you? We're just your little crew of Shade coders. Don't know nothin' 'bout psychology. But these stream riders don't seem representative."

The Eye smiled wryly. "I've been doing this for years. Sad to say, they're more representative than you think."

"If you say so," Speranza replied doubtfully. "You're the doctor."

"I can have the weavers tweak those tender lifestreams if you want," Jayla the teddy bear suggested. "See if we can't get a few more riders."

"Do that," the Eye agreed, "but don't take anyone off the deviant themes. They should be your priority."

"We're on it, Boss." Jayla pulled at the chains and swung higher. "I've got rushes, if you want to see them."

"Which?"

"*Subterranean Blues.*"

"Roll it."

The pink surroundings turned black. A light appeared—a shaft of sun through a tiny window, just above eye level.

"What are we seeing?" Speranza asked.

"Wait for it," Jayla answered.

The scene panned from right to left, away from the window: an old-style gas-burning furnace; stacks of boxes, the bottom ones crushed under the weight, the top ones open, flaps torn, hanging by a shred of cardboard, coils of cables and castoff electronic gear sprouting from them; a shelf stocked with home-canned fruit and vegetables; magazines, relics of the long past era of print media, slid to the floor in a heap of curled covers and mouse-eaten edges.

"A storage facility?" Speranza guessed.

"Wait for it," Jayla repeated.

The scene continued to pan: in the corner, a bench made of steel; on the bench, lying on her back, a woman, no more than twenty years old, wearing only panties, her arms and legs bound by nylon cords to eye bolts embedded in the concrete floor.

"Whoa," Speranza said.

Jayla snickered.

The scene closed in on the woman's face. She was unconscious, head lolling to her right, mouth open, the tip of her tongue hanging from the corner of her lips. A hand appeared in the field of view, slapping the woman's face, bringing her around.

"Wakey, wakey," said a man's oily voice. The woman came to, opening her eyes, then shutting them. She cried weakly before starting to heave, a thin stream of yellow liquid dribbling from her mouth.

"Oh, Jah," Speranza groaned. "This is fucked up."

"It gets better," Jayla promised, pulling her swing higher.

Two hands wrapped a leather belt across the woman's mouth and around the bench. The hands tightened the belt, until the leather cut into her skin. The woman gagged.

"*Enough!*" Speranza protested. "I get the picture."

"Let it run," the Eye of Providence commanded.

The left hand threaded the end of the belt through the buckle, pulling it tighter, until the woman passed out from the pain. The unseen person loosened it, patted her on the cheek, and revived her with another "Wakey, wakey." His left hand went to her breast, kneading it roughly; she moaned as he stretched her nipple. His right hand came forward, holding a shiny object: a large pair of sewing scissors.

"*Isis! Pause the venue!*" Speranza shouted. The action froze, the hand brandishing the scissors centimeters from the woman's breast.

"You sissy, it was just getting to the *good* part," Jayla taunted, swinging in a wide arc, the swing nearly horizontal at its peak.

"Isis, staging venue," the Eye ordered. The basement dissolved into pink surroundings.

"What's the verdict, Boss?" Jayla asked, dragging her feet, bringing the swing to a rest.

"Where are you with it?"

"First rendering; second rendering is about a quarter done."

"And the emotional responses?"

"Storyboard. It's pretty intense."

The Eye scratched behind her ear. "That was a very troubling case. I wasn't able to help that man. He's in permanent confinement, IRL."

Speranza tugged at his lapels. "Well, I *hope so*. Jah, that was fucking *pathological*. Who likes this garbage?"

"*Subterranean Blues* will be as popular as *A Walk in the Park*," the Eye predicted. "Maybe more so."

Speranza rubbed his eyes, as if trying to wipe away the memory. "Eye, if you want insight into the human psyche, doesn't it make sense to tap into *all* areas of the mental model, not just the perv centers? Aren't we narrowing the limits of applicability?"

The goddess's eyes closed halfway. "Not at all. These cases are all deviants, that's true, but that's hardly limiting. To a greater or lesser degree, *everyone* is a deviant."

45

MACKENZIE

THE LATE-NIGHT walk from the Aletheia to Madeleine's building took the Eye of Providence from the decaying inner city, past streets of crowded tenements, to the upscale sector, closest to the distribution centers. Here, food and other RL amenities were just minutes away by drone, and residents accessed the most realistic venues through the fattest pipes. She came in through a side entrance rarely used by the residents, taking the elevator to the 20th floor. Peeking around the edge of the door, she made sure the hall was deserted (which it always was this time of night, when all the tenants were jacked into their favorite venues). A Cloak in the hallways of her building was a rarity, and the Eye had no desire to draw attention. She hurried to her apartment, ungloved her hand, and pressed it against the biometric panel. The latch slid aside, and the door opened.

The Eye pulled off her hood and cloak, then slid the scarlet mask back from her face, tossing it on the sofa. Madeleine collapsed into a chair, eyes closed and head back, taking deep breaths. After a minute, she took her VR gear from a side table and put it on. The image converged, transforming into the staging venue.

"Elsa—Mackenzie."

"Yes, Madeleine."

She was transported to a fanciful landscape of watercolor skies and tempera trees, their leaves a riot of color, gradations of hues shimmering in the light of a crimson sun.

The tree trunks were rendered as metallic sculptures; Madeleine touched them as she passed, fingertips catching on layers of texture like burlap. Sheep-sized rabbits the colors of Easter-eggs bounded by, then stopped to nibble on cobalt-blue grass.

Madeleine followed a meandering path to a clearing, where she found a short, stocky man with an impressive nose on a jowly face, large, liquid eyes under generous eyebrows and mad-scientist hair. His arms waved wildly, the billowing sleeves of his maroon shirt laying waves in the air, hands flitting from floating palettes of colors and racks of tools—brushes, spray guns, and trowels—to his subjects: the fantastic fauna and flora of his make-believe world.

"Hello, Mack," Madeleine said.

The man turned with a start, face blank; then he lit up. He waved an arm and the palettes and tools vanished.

"Maddie, Maddie, Maddie!" he chanted, rubbing his hands together as he trotted to her, hugging her and kissing her cheek.

"It's more lovely than ever," she marveled, gazing at the technicolor forest.

"The rabbits! Did you see the rabbits?"

"They're big."

Mack threw his head back, holding his sides, laughing up at the red-orange sky. "They're big indeed!" His expression turned serious. "Are they too big? Not big enough?"

"They're as big as they need to be, no bigger, no smaller."

Mack beamed. He plopped down in the grass, cross-legged, leaning back, propped on his outstretched arms, pink dandelions curling around him. "You had a good day, Maddie? You had many accomplishments?"

"Yes, Mack." She reclined on the ground next to him, plucking a dandelion and pulling its petals, before stopping and holding it out. "Okay to pick?"

"Pick all you want. I'll make more."

Madeleine smiled, turning her attention back to the flower. "We're making great progress—with our project."

Mack grimaced. "I don't want to hear about *that*. You

know I don't like it."

She placed a hand on his knee. "I wanted you to know—because you're my inspiration."

He stood, crossing his arms tightly over his chest. "It's *wrong.*"

"I know how you feel. But the lifestreams are only a means to an end. It's not forever."

"Not just the lifestreams."

"What, then?" she asked.

"People are being hurt," he replied.

"What do you mean?"

"*Hurt.* Some in the hospital."

"Who told you that?"

Mack bent at the waist, dropping his hands to his sides. "I don't spend *all* my time here in Wonderland, Maddie. I do get out. I meet people and they tell me things. They tell me people are hurting other people, way more than usual—*way* more." He turned sideways, looking away from Madeleine. "And I know why."

She rose up on her knees. "What do you know?"

He turned and pointed. "It's *you.* Your project. It's making people do things they wouldn't do if it wasn't for you."

"Do you really believe that?"

He pointed to his head. "I'm *smart*, Maddie, you *know* I *am.* I figured it out. It's *you.*"

She tilted her head, an imploring look on her face. "Mack."

"It's true, isn't it?"

She closed her eyes, nodding. "I can't lie to you." She stood up. "But it's *not forever.* And when we're done, worlds will open up, not just for you and me, but for *everyone.*"

Mack crossed his arms again and hung his head. "I want to go back to my painting now." He waved an arm. His array of tools and colors reappeared. He chose a thick brush, filling it with colors from his palette, then drew it through the air, leaving a gnarled tree trunk in its wake.

"*Mack*," Madeleine pleaded.

"We'll see each other tomorrow, Maddie." He let go of the

brush, leaving it hanging in mid-air. He gave her a hug. "And when we do, can we talk about something else?"

46

Delegate from Tidewater

"The delegate from Tidewater is out of order!"

The Kliegls in the council venue shouted in protest, joined by thousands of spectators who were jacked in from across the continent. Although the Kliegls controlled fewer than fifty of the 500 council seats, the spectators were overwhelmingly sympathetic, and loyal to their leader Dax—the delegate whom the council parliamentarian had just reprimanded.

The council speaker banged a gavel.

"There will be *order* in this venue!" he shouted as the commotion continued. He pressed a button on a virtual console, muting the crowd noise.

The crowd's avatars, however, packed shoulder to shoulder as far as the speaker could see, continued shaking their fists and waving placards scrolling pro-Kliegl slogans.

Dax was undeterred; he stood in the dock, chin raised, hands on the railing. He was a short man, neither handsome, nor ugly; neither slim, nor fat. Yet he did have one memorable feature—a thick mane of raven hair which brushed his shoulders and appeared to move of its own volition.

Now that the crowd was finally silent, the Kliegls' shouting continued in the venue, with the other factions responding in kind.

Dax raised his hand from the rail. The Kliegls ceased shouting instantly; the other delegates quieted gradually, not so much out of decorum as out of curiosity for what the man in the dock would say next.

"You say that I have violated the rules of debate," Dax began softly, "because I have revealed the ties between the delegate from Yerba Buena and the corporate interests in that district…"

"You accused me of corruption!" another delegate shouted, rising from his seat.

"The delegate will remain seated and silent," the speaker warned, pointing his gavel. "There is a delegate in the dock." The speaker pointed at Dax. "Continue, but know that this chair will *not* tolerate further violations of council rules."

Dax raised both hands in conciliation before lowering one hand to the rail again and placing the other over his heart.

"Is it now against the rules to tell the truth? The delegate from Yerba Buena, a former executive of the largest corporation in the world—who still owns shares in the amount of seven hundred billion credits in that corporation, which owns and administers the very *brain* and *spine* and *nerves* of the Worldstream—claims that he has no sympathy for the Shade, outlaws in a hidden world, whom this corporation nevertheless employs in violation of the law…"

"That's a lie!"

The speaker pounded his gavel. "The delegate will remain silent. And *you*," he pointed to Dax, "you're close to crossing a line."

"Then I will let this body, and these citizens watching, come to their own conclusions as to why the delegate from Yerba Buena opposes this appropriation, this *desperately needed* appropriation, to apprehend and confine these criminals known as Shade. He says it's a matter of priorities, but *whose* priorities? The people's, or his corporate master's?"

"Citizen speaker, this is *outrageous!*" the Yerba Buena delegate shouted, leaping to his feet. "Will you allow this slander to go unchallenged?"

"No, I will not," the speaker responded. "The delegate from Tidewater will exit the dock."

Dax placed both hands on the rail, now leaning forward.

"Crimes of violence at a level we have not seen…"

"The delegate is out of order!"

"…in the memory of most of us living…"

"I will *not* warn you again!"

"…spiraling out of control…"

The Kliegls rose, screaming. The crowd waved their placards and shouted, their shouts still muted from the speaker's podium.

"…but those who lived before the advent of Jahbulon remember the horrors of that time, when the people lived in fear, and the law meant *nothing!*"

The speaker pressed another button. Dax's avatar vanished from the dock, reappearing in his seat among the delegates, still standing, fists raised, his body near convulsions, hair morphing from one fantastic shape to another, as if it had been separately rendered for its spellbinding effect.

"And yet we allow this *subterranean mob*, this *invisible horde of outlaws*, not only to exist, but to *thrive*, for the enrichment of global corporations and their servants in this council!" Dax thundered.

The venue descended into chaos, all semblance of order now gone. The speaker pounded his gavel to no effect. He pressed another button on his virtual console. The crowd vanished, each of the thousands of spectators finding themselves alone in their staging venues. Another button pressed, and the shouting of the delegates went silent. Each delegate heard only his own voice, and the speaker's.

"This session is *suspended!*" the speaker cried.

The council venue vanished, each delegate teleported to his private chamber.

❖ ❖ ❖

The speaker removed his VR gear and rubbed his eyes. The wall screen in his chamber chimed the arrival of a v-gram from First Minister Eugenia Sato, the head of government and leader of the Citizens Independence Party. The image of a woman in her late sixties with tired eyes appeared next to scrolling text, narrated by the first minister's synthesized voice.

"That spectacle was witnessed by nearly twelve thousand citizens. I just received the demos on that crowd—84% support the Kliegls. Dax's popularity is now ten points higher than ours. They believe Dax is Jahbulon in the flesh. How that charlatan got to a position of prominence I still don't understand, but there he is, and he's a threat, not only to our coalition, but to the *nation*. We *must* take action in the council. Please advise."

The speaker sighed. He reached for the bottle and glass he kept on the table next to his chair and poured a shot of amber liquor. He sipped it slowly, staring at the image of the first minister, until the glass was empty.

"Reply," he instructed. "Minister, I agree. I recommend a meeting of the coalition leaders to plan for the upcoming campaign. We'll get some idea of how strong our position is by how many accept your invitation, but I already know what we can expect. You won't want to hear this, but the signs are unmistakable. The Kliegls *will* force a vote of no confidence —and it *will* pass the council."

❖ ❖ ❖

Dax remained in his staging venue from his home in Tidewater, not an apartment, but a free-standing dwelling with four rooms, lavish by the standards of most council delegates.

"Ismo," he said, "call the chief of staff and counsel, the usual venue."

"Yes, Dax," the soft male voice replied. "What is the topic?"

"The exploding crime rate and the growing fear of the Shade," Dax answered, "and how to make the most of them."

47

THE BOTTOMLESS POOL

THE WORLDSTREAM CONSORTIUM agreed to meet on Dax's turf, an entirely black venue, as if surrounded by a curtain of obsidian. Dax's avatar rastered into view on an elevated platform, like those at his rallies, arms at his sides, hands clenched, standing at an angle to his audience, as if he were about to raise his fists to fight. He wasn't replicated on a hundred other stages, nor was he surrounded by a quarter-million followers. Alone, he faced the seven stone-faced leaders of the world's most powerful corporations.

A stately woman rose, with soft features, coffee-colored skin, and ink-black hair, her avatar dressed in the elaborate style popular in India, a western jacket and blouse with exaggerated cuffs and lapels, in the brilliant colors and patterns of a traditional *sari*.

"Do you know who I am?" she asked in a mild Indian accent.

"Vimala Mallick," Dax answered, "chief executive of Kanpur Virset Corporation. Welcome."

Mallick nodded. "Thank you for receiving us, Dax. My colleagues have asked me to speak for them. We have concerns."

Dax remained in his stance, eyes fixed on Mallick, fists clenching harder. She stared back, unblinking. After a few seconds Dax relaxed his hands and faced Mallick, shoulders back, arms crossed over his chest. "You're masters of the Worldstream, and you're unable to deal with your concerns with all the resources at *your* disposal? Your concerns are that great? Then why bring them to Dax? Who am I?"

"At present," Mallick replied, "you are merely the delegate from Tidewater, who speaks to his followers about threats, who plays on their fears…"

"Their fears are real," Dax retorted, "and no one listens to them."

"Their fears *may* be real," interrupted a young woman with short pink hair, dressed in retro jeans and an iridescent blue t-shirt. "But the threats are *not*."

"I know who *you* are, too, Eva Serrano. Your company, Stimulus Rex, made a profit of 180 billion credits last year. Surely there are no concerns of *yours* that *Dax* can address."

Serrano rose from her chair. Mallick held up a hand to silence her.

"As I was saying," Mallick continued, "at present, you are a delegate. But after the election, when the Kliegls win a majority, you will be first minister."

Dax looked at Mallick sideways, uncrossing his arms and placing his hands on his chest. "*Me? First minister?*"

Mallick paced, hands folded. "After the vote of no confidence, the council speaker and First Minister Sato were not even able to call the heads of their coalition to caucus. Some of them have already pledged to align with the Kliegls, even if you don't win a majority."

"Perhaps they've decided that the ruling party no longer serves the needs of the people."

"Perhaps," Serrano assented, "but I think they're just afraid of an unreasoning mob."

Dax spread his arms. "Are you *all* this arrogant? You have a monopoly on the Worldstream—does that give you magical insight into the minds of our citizens? To know what is and isn't reasonable?"

He raised his arms like a bird taking flight, then swept them in wide arcs, spreading his fingers wide. The black curtain lifted, immersing the seven corporate leaders in mayhem: a well-groomed young man in simple but stylish clothes assaulting a woman from behind, taking a handful of hair and putting her in a choke hold, close enough to Mallick that she jumped back, toppling her chair; two men who might have been brothers, circling each other with knives drawn, thrusting, parrying, lunging, Serrano trapped between them, crouched in her seat, blades clashing overhead; a woman and a man stripped to their underwear, mid-seduction, the woman teasing, pulling away, until the man, enraged, struck her, sending her sprawling into the lap of the CEO of a network infrastructure supplier. Each vignette continued until it was interrupted by police drones and agents, then vanished, to be replaced by another scene of violence. The seven heads of the Consortium raised their arms reflexively to shield themselves as avatars moved around them, over them, and through them. Dax watched the melee from his platform.

"These are not inventions!" he shouted. "These are not phony Virset assets, Mallick. These are *real crimes*, with *real victims*." He pointed at the head of Stimulus Rex. "Seranno, you said the threats weren't real, that there's nothing to fear. Then why are you cowering from the images in your visor?"

Dax raised both fists over his head, then threw his hands down. The criminals and their victims winked out. The black curtain fell, and the ear-splitting racket reverberated into silence.

The Consortium composed themselves: Serrano sat up; Mallick straightened her scarlet and indigo jacket.

Dax ran his fingers through his hair, the black mane bouncing to his shoulders. He closed his eyes and drew a breath.

"Consortium—tell me your *concerns*."

Mallick glanced at her colleagues, still recovering from Dax's scenarios. They nodded.

"We understand the rationale for that demonstration. Our citizens *do* have reason to fear the recent uptick in crime..."

"*Explosion* of crime!" Dax interrupted.

Mallick continued. "We support any actions by civil authorities to stop the violence. But that's not the concern we want to share."

Dax nodded. "Go on."

"The Shade."

"Outlaws—criminals."

"They are not responsible for these crimes."

"You tell your story; I'll tell mine."

"You know we cannot."

"Because the Shade are your workforce." Dax stepped to the edge of the platform. "Mallick—they design your VR assets and venues. Serrano—they test your visors and haptics and neural interfaces. To the rest of you—*all* of you—the Shade are a bottomless pool of workers. They do the rendering, the coding, the pattern-matching, the maintenance and support your *legitimate* workers *could* do, if you were willing to pay. The Shade earn subsistence wages, which they share with their Cloak sponsors, who grow wealthy from their labor." He smiled. "But you *can't* speak for them, because they're criminals. So, again, what is your *concern?*"

Mallick stepped forward. "You said we have vast resources. When you are first minister, you will also have vast resources. But we will still have the advantage."

"And that would be?"

"We have a choke-hold on the Worldstream."

"A threat?"

"A fact."

Dax's smile straightened, then returned. "Whether the Shade stay or go isn't important. They're a means to an end. That should address your concern."

"Not entirely," Mallick replied.

Dax turned away, so that Mallick and the others could not see the anger in his face. He composed himself before turning back. "Once in power, the Kliegls will do nothing to jeopardize your labor pool. But we'll have to make an example."

"We understand," Mallick answered, bowing slightly. "Most of our contracts are with the *Vita Occulta* cartel. Perhaps you could limit your demonstrations to the *unaffiliated* Shade?"

"So be it." Dax turned his back, waving dismissively.

"You'll have your slave labor, Consortium. Jahbulon will prevail."

"You have our gratitude, Dax. *And* Jahbulon's."

Dax rastered out. Mallick turned to her colleagues with a wry smile.

"After all," she muttered, "*we* are Jahbulon."

48

ZAP

"It's all been random up to now," the Eye explained to Jayla. "I want to implant a command in a targeted subject. Can you do it?"

The two women met in a cubicle in the Aletheia's Engine Room, the Eye in her crimson mask and Jayla in blue. Jayla's team labored in brightly-lit cubicles beyond a glass partition, bent over state-of-the-art displays, or outfitted in latest-gen VR gear. A wall of equipment—the ultimate in high-speed computing machinery—blinked at the far end of the expanse, its liquid cooling virtually silent.

"Duh, *yeah*," Jayla answered. "In case you haven't noticed, this is a crack squad. They *live* for this kind of challenge. Just one little detail, though."

"What's that?"

"We need someone in the venue—an avatar in the clear."

"Why?"

Jayla hopped up on the edge of the table. "You want us to go into a live venue, outside the firewall, right?"

"That's where the rally will be."

"Right. None of *us* can go in. We're all Shade. The Worldstream will puke."

"So…who?"

"Well, *you*. You're Cloak. You're the only one of us who hasn't bailed out of the Worldstream. You're the natural choice."

"I can't risk it—not for a test."

"Hey, would I put you in danger? Have some faith."

"I don't understand how that would work, anyway. It's *your* people who have the know-how. What would I do once I'm there?"

"You're just our eyes and ears. We'll tunnel into the venue server through your connection, totally stealth—tell you everything you need to know. Jahbulon won't suspect a thing."

"I don't know…"

Jayla threw up her arms. "No other way, Boss."

The Eye shifted in her chair. She pressed the back of her hand to her chin. "Tell me how you'll identify the target."

Jayla grinned. "That's the res. We're jacked into the server, right? We can hack it without anyone knowing."

"The Worldstream won't know?"

"That's the beauty of it—we're not *touching* the Worldstream. The venue servers *talk* to the Worldstream, but security is up to the venue servers—and they are *loose*. The Worldstream validates identities, but if the server never hears back, it assumes everything is copacetic. If everyone in the venue's legit, they figure, why lock it down?"

"I'd be lying if I said I understood that."

"Bottom line: the venue servers rely on Jahbulon for a *whole* lot more than Jahbulon can actually do."

"It doesn't sound all that secure."

Jayla shrugged. "It's not, and that's a *good* thing—that gap is our bread and butter."

"Okay, fine, but answer my question."

Jayla's jaw went slack. "I forgot the question."

"*How will you identify the target?*"

"Oh! Oh, yeah. No problem. We just look for the avatars running gen four Belts. When the avatars jack in, the server queries them for the peripherals they're using, so they can serve up the hi-res content. We'll hack that info, then shine a light on the gen four users. You point out the ones you want to go after."

"And you can apply the stimulus right away?"

"Yeah, Boss. You pick 'em; we pop 'em."

"No Shade—Light! No Shade—Light!"

The chant rolled through the crowd, a tsunami of sound on an ocean of avatars, the largest of the campaign. Dax claimed it was the largest in history.

Madeleine jacked in at the arranged time. Avatars stretched as far as she could see, surrounding a regular array of identical stages. Many in the crowd held signs aloft, scrolling slogans or displaying video images—closeups of Dax in mid-oration, gesturing wildly; menacing scenes of cloaked figures; lurid images of crimes in progress. Madeleine appeared in her personal avatar: a tall woman in her late forties, long, black hair with strands of gray tied in a ponytail hanging to the middle of her back.

"Can you hear me?" she mumbled, head down.

"Five by five," Jayla's voice sounded in her head. "Copy me?"

"I hear you."

Madeleine looked over the crowd, some milling around at random; others gathered in small groups, most with their eyes fixed on the man on the stage: Dax, surrounded by his retinue.

"Jah, what a mob," Jayla remarked. "Why'd you pick this thing?"

"There are a lot of people, a lot of distractions. No one will remember seeing me here."

"Plenty of big venues out there, Boss. What makes this one special?"

Madeleine centered Dax in her field of view. "See that man?"

"Yeah," Jayla answered. "Who is he?"

"His name's Dax. He's going to be the next first minister."

"No *way*. And *he's* the one you want to zap?"

Madeleine held a hand over her mouth. "*No*. Not *now*. This is a *test*, remember?"

"Right. Gotcha."

"Is everything ready?"

"A-OK. I'm flipping the switch."

Glowing halos appeared above the heads of scattered avatars, all nearby.

"A halo? Was that your idea?"

"Yeah," Jayla snickered. "Do you like it?"

"I only count a few, not even ten."

"A little detail I should have shared with you. I can only mark the folks in your local deconfliction group."

"My *what?*"

"Your local group. I'm reading more than 600,000 avatars in the venue. If you could interact with all of them at once, that'd be 180 billion connections."

"Spare me the tech briefing, Jayla."

"Sure, Boss. The server only keeps up connections between your avatar and others close by. Keeps the server load way down."

"Jayla!"

"Sorry. Just keep moving. All systems go here. Any gen four within ten meters of you will light up. Let me know when you want to pull the trigger."

Madeleine moved toward the nearest stage, squeezing between avatars. Dax's voice remained steady, piped simultaneously into every head in the crowd. At the end of each crescendo the crowd went mad, shouting and jumping, jostling Madeleine on her way to the front. As she moved, golden halos vanished behind her and reappeared ahead.

"I'm the only one who can see these halos, right?" Madeleine asked.

"I'm pretty sure," Jayla answered.

"Pretty sure?"

"Yes! Yes! Just kidding, Boss. The halos are just for you."

A short man ahead of Madeleine turned around. His glasses displayed tiny videos of Dax on the stage, like two miniature screens. A halo hung at Madeleine's eye level, just over the man's hairless scalp.

"Who are you talking to, sister citizen?" he demanded.

"No one. Myself. It's not your business who."

"Are you hearing voices, sister?" the man asked, grinning, eyes hidden behind the images in his glasses. Madeleine realized they were images of the live speech in real time.

"Your glasses…" Madeleine blurted.

"They're great, aren't they? You can add them to your avatar for a contribution of a thousand credits. You can make a donation right now." The man pointed to his chest. An outline of a handprint appeared on his shirt. "Just put your hand here, and Dax will do the rest."

Madeleine studied the little man with animated glasses, a handprint on his chest, and a golden halo. "Do you work for Dax?"

"I'm a volunteer. Do *you* want to be a volunteer?"

"Do you *know* Dax? I mean, do you ever talk to him personally?"

The man laughed. "I wish! No, I'm just a loyal trooper in Dax's righteous army."

"Why not test it out on that little creep?" Jayla suggested.

"Not my first choice," Madeleine replied.

The man took hold of Madeleine's arm. "I understand. You don't *have* to give a thousand credits. Anything will help."

"You want me to zap him, Boss?" Jayla asked.

"With what?" Madeleine replied.

"With anything you have, sister," the man answered.

"Just a push out of the venue," Jayla offered. "He's well under the threshold for something like that."

"Do it," Madeleine ordered.

The man's grin grew, taking up half his face. He pushed his chest forward. "Just put your hand in the outline."

"Here goes," Jayla said.

The man's avatar froze. The images in his glasses flickered. A thin silver outline surrounded him, like an aura, pulsing with a steady beat. Although Madeleine couldn't see what he saw, Jayla had described it to her: his field of view went black, followed by a series of bright images, each appearing for a split-second. A few moments later, the aura faded and the video show in the man's glasses resumed.

"Are you all right?" Madeleine asked.

The man's mouth hung open. "Can't stay, sister citizen," he replied. "Buster, exit the venue." His avatar flattened and rastered out.

"I'd say that was a successful test," Madeleine murmured.

"Jah, that is *so* hi-res," Jayla gushed like a schoolgirl. "One: push button; Two: agitate neurons; Three: our wish is his command."

49

TRIBES

MADELEINE KEPT MOVING, squeezing past a large man at least thirty centimeters taller than she was, his tight-fitting shirt hiding none of his bulk. The man's shirt displayed a full-length portrait of Dax in a white robe, eyes raised in a beatific expression quite unlike that of the raging demagogue on the stage, radiance surrounding his head, one hand raised as if conferring a blessing, the other pointing to an image on his chest: a flaming heart, girdled in thorns—the Sacred Heart of Jesus. The image transitioned to a second, darker image: rows of cloaked Shade in front of a menacing red sky, then to another—Dax as a winged archangel in heavenly armor, wielding a righteous sword. The man peered down at Madeleine with a scowl, his fat eyebrows pinched together and mouth a straight line between two ample jowls.

"Hey!" he growled, pushing her away with a meaty forearm. She backed up, bumping into two other avatars, one an elderly woman dressed as an Amazon warrior with a flashing tiara, holding the arm of a middle-aged man in full Roman imperial regalia. The couple grimaced before turning back toward the platform.

"What an eclectic bunch," Jayla remarked through her headphones.

"The theme is unmistakable," Madeleine murmured, continuing to move through the crowd. "Heroic iconography —Dax as Christ."

"I don't see it. He's just a little runt with good hair."

"One response to a threat is authoritarianism—submission to a strong figure."

"What threat?"

Madeleine circled the stage. "It doesn't have to be real. The authoritarian figure will *invent* a threat if he has to."

The chant of *No Shade—Light!* trailed off as Dax began his speech.

"We have no *justice*," Dax said softly, "as long as criminals hide in the shadows, out of the sight of Jahbulon. We have no *security*, as long as the Shade commit crimes with impunity, unaccountable to the law. We have no *liberty*, when the Consortium governs our lives, governs even the fabric of our existence, with the help of Shade criminals. We have no *prosperity*, when the Shade, working for less than basic income, steal *your* livelihood from you." Dax's voice built to a new crescendo. "The curse of the Shade, and of this decades-long slide into moral decay ends, here and now, with *you* and with *me!*"

The crowd broke out in a new chant: *Jahbulon! Kliegl! Dax! Jahbulon! Kliegl! Dax!* Madeleine had circled halfway around the platform, a hundred meters from her staging point. Avatars jostled her from all directions, shouting with raised fists. One exuberant avatar collided with her, pushing her into a large man. She turned to look up at him.

"You, again?" the man said irritably, his jowls shaking. His shirt transitioned through a series of images: Dax as savior— the Shade horde—Dax the angelic warrior. She backed away, bumping into two other avatars, an old Amazon woman and a Roman emperor.

Madeleine turned away, hiding her face. "Are you seeing this?" she asked.

"Yeah," Jayla replied. "Didn't you leave those guys on the other side of the stage?"

"I *thought* I did. Can you tell me what's going on?"

"Hang on, Boss. There's something hinky here. I'm running it down now."

Madeleine continued her circuit around the stage, wandering in random directions. Regardless of how far she went from her staging point, she encountered the same people: the jowly man with the Dax t-shirt, the old Amazon, the Roman, and others she recognized.

"They're exaggerating the crowd size, aren't they?" Madeleine asked. "Replicating people, the same way they're replicating the stages?"

"Good guess," Jayla replied, "but wrong."

The crowd roared a coda to another Dax rant. Madeleine stopped wandering. "What, then?"

"There're over a half-million in that crowd. I can verify it from the venue server log. That crowd's just as big as it looks."

Madeleine hunched her shoulders, turning away from nearby avatars, holding her hand across her mouth. "I keep seeing the same characters."

"I get that, Boss. I can see the same things you're seeing."

"Jayla, *what's going on?*"

"Oh. Yeah. Okay, I'm not a hundred percent sure, but it looks like the server is relocating you."

"What's that mean?"

"You *think* you're wandering around, but every so often the server puts you back where you started, near the staging point."

Madeleine straightened up, craning her neck. The stages, stretching in a regular array to infinity, were identical. She could be anywhere, and the scenery would look the same.

"Why would they do that?"

"I have a theory."

Madeleine crouched again, speaking into her hand in a coarse whisper. "Would you care to *share* your theory with me?"

"Yeah. It's pretty hi-res, if they're doing what I think they're doing."

"*Jayla.*"

"Oh. Well, it seems they're trying to keep like-minded folks together, you know, birds of a feather flock together."

"Keep going."

"All those folks you keep running into, I think they've got

some AI going that puts you all in the same category. If any of you wanders off, the venue grabs you and puts you back among your tribe."

Madeleine's eyes widened. *"Peer reinforcement!"*

"Huh?"

"They're keeping people in the same peer group co-located, so they can feed off each other's reactions. The positive reinforcement validates their own beliefs and deepens their commitment."

"If you say so, Boss."

"But why am *I* here, in *this* group? I don't have anything in common with them."

"Hate to break this to you, but you're more alike than you think."

"Why do you say that?"

"You remember me saying that when you jack into a venue, the server checks your peripherals? Well, you and Mr. Jowls and Wonder Woman and Julius Caesar are all using the Belt, gen three or later."

"Everyone uses the Belt. Why's that significant?"

"Because they read you, you and all your authoritarian peeps."

"*Read* me?"

"I'm looking at the log.

"The *log?*"

"Yes'm. Everyone in that crowd with a gen three or four Belt has a bunch of custom metadata tags in the log. The server reads 'em when you all jack in and the AI scores 'em and tags 'em. And avatars with the same tags are in the same vicinity."

"So Dax is using the Belt to read emotional responses."

"Correct."

"I thought only *we* could do that."

"They must've figured it out."

Madeleine looked around. She saw the big man a few meters away, Dax the avenging angel on his shirt; the old lady in the Amazon costume, now swinging a sword and twirling a golden lasso, next to the Roman in a toga and triumphant crown. She saw others she'd encountered many times as she wandered the venue, some in costume—Hercules, Genghis Khan, the one-eyed Norse god Odin—also in wearable displays, flashing images of Dax as hero.

"And these people in costume, they're tagged the same as I am?"

"Right again."

"They read us as sympathetic to god-like figures?"

"Not quite, Boss."

"What, then?"

Madeleine heard Jayla chuckling. "You and them crazies—you all think you *are* the god-like figures."

50

JAHBULON ALWAYS ANSWERS

"ARE YOU SURE about this, Perry?" Camille asked timidly, afraid of triggering a reaction from her husband.

Perry buttoned his white shirt up to its straight collar. He checked his profile in the mirror, turning side-to-side, as Camille stood just outside the bathroom, peeking around the doorframe.

"Don't do this, Camille." He pulled the red sash over his head and across his chest, adjusting the drape. "Don't wimp out on me."

She stepped into the door opening, wearing white shoes, white pants, and a bra. Her shirt hung limply from her hand. "What if there's trouble?"

He combed his hair and put on a red brimless cap bearing the Kliegl symbol of two searchlights with crossed beams.

"Then there's trouble," he answered, tipping the cap slightly to one side, admiring the look in the mirror.

She covered herself, pulling the shirt to her neck.

"Camille, it'll be okay," Perry said softly, putting a hand on her arm. "It's like Reid said, we're establishing a presence, that's all. Just showing these Shade and Cloak that someone knows they're out there. Make them think twice."

Camille looked down. "We don't even know Reid."

"We know him."

"But we've never met him IRL."

"Don't be difficult," Perry sighed, pushing past her. "We've spent hours together in VR," he shouted from the main room. "It's the same thing."

"I suppose," she muttered. She pulled on her shirt and buttoned it without looking in the mirror, tucking it in and fastening her belt. She put on a sash and cap. Perry was buckling his belt when she went into the main room. On the chair lay two black rods, each 20 centimeters long and a couple of centimeters in diameter. He picked one up and slipped it into a holster hanging from his belt, then picked up the other rod.

"Here, take this," he offered.

"I don't want that," she replied with a shake of her head.

"You'd better take it."

"Why do I need the ASP? You said there won't be any trouble."

"It's a precaution."

"Against what?"

"If any Shade attack us."

"Why would they do that?"

"Just *take* it," Perry snorted.

Camille shook her head again.

Perry dropped his hands to his sides. "Okay, how about this? There's a crime wave out there—have you heard? What if you get attacked, and Jahbulon can't get there in time?"

"Jahbulon *always* answers."

"But not always in *time*. People are in the hospital."

"Then *you'll* protect me. With *your* ASP."

"Jah, *Camille*. Who protects *me*?"

She stared at the black baton for a minute before taking it. "I don't know how it works."

"Yes, you do. Reid showed us, remember?" In one motion of his wrist, Perry unholstered the ASP and flicked the baton toward the floor. The telescoping sections slid to full length, more than 50 centimeters, with a metallic, rapid-fire *hiss, click, click*, sounding almost as menacing as it looked.

❖ ❖ ❖

Six white-shirted, red-sashed volunteers stood shoulder-to-shoulder in Reid's tiny apartment. Reid addressed them from the kitchen.

305

"We have some new faces tonight," Reid began, "so just a little longer with the orientation. First rule: you can't tell a Cloak from a Shade when they're cloaked up, so don't assume. Shade are crooks; Cloak, *technically*, aren't. No law says you can't walk around in a cloak—*yet*." He pursed his lips. "Cloak, Shade, same difference in my mind—if you're hiding from Jahbulon, you're doing it for a reason."

"Then what's the point?" Camille muttered.

"Did you say something?" Reid asked, looking straight at her. "What's your name? Camilla?"

"Camille," she answered, eyes down.

"Right. You're with Perry. This is your first patrol, isn't it?"

"Uh-huh."

"Good. Good deal. What's the point, you asked? I'll tell you: the criminal Shade not only hide behind *a* cloak, they hide behind *the* Cloak. We want Shade *and* Cloak to know that we're on to them. If they're afraid of the light of day, we want to shine a light on 'em." He pointed to the symbol on his cap. "That's what we're doing—shining the light of day where the shadows live. Let 'em know there's no hiding from *Dax*."

Camille nodded wordlessly.

"All right. Any other questions?" Reid asked. "Good. Get with your buddies and let's get on the streets. And that's rule two: Stick together if at all possible but never, *never*, leave your buddy." He hooked his thumb in his belt, next to a holstered ASP. "And rule three: no violence—if at all possible."

❖ ❖ ❖

To the civilians on the street the patrol was an odd sight, all dressed in white, visible from blocks away. Over the few weeks that Kliegls had roamed the streets at night, the number of Cloak and Shade had plummeted. As they wandered their route, they passed two other Kliegl patrols of four or five, in the same unmistakable uniform, but had encountered only three cloaked people in almost four hours, and all of them had turned and bolted at the sight of the Kliegls—to Camille's great relief.

"How much longer?" she asked Perry.

"The next patrols come on at midnight," Reid answered before Perry could speak. "That's when the vermin come out in numbers."

"Twenty minutes," Perry added, "and we can go home."

"Thank Jah," Camille whispered.

The patrol turned a corner to face a group of four people in cloaks; they halted at the sight of the Kliegls, but didn't run.

"Ho-*ho!*" Reid shouted. "Look what's here. Two, three, *four* buzzing robots, all in black."

"We're legal citizens," the lead Cloak droned. "We're within our rights."

The patrol surrounded the group, with Camille hanging back. Reid stepped inside the ring.

"How do I know?" he challenged. "You could be Shade criminals."

"We're not." The Cloak bunched more tightly, facing outward toward their tormentors.

"You're hiding," Reid challenged. "Criminals hide; decent citizens don't."

"Do you understand the concept of privacy?" the Cloak countered.

Reid unholstered his ASP and deployed it with lightning speed. The Cloak bunched closer, raising their hands—all except their leader.

"You don't scare us," he droned. "We're law-abiding and we're within our rights. Step aside."

The Kliegls closed ranks. Reid stepped nearer, just centimeters from the Cloak's face, his ASP poised to strike

"When we win the council and Dax is first minister, there'll be a reckoning. And you Shade vermin will be wiped out."

"We're not Shade!"

Reid swung the ASP in a practiced move, striking the Cloak leader on the side of his head. He staggered, falling to one knee. The other three broke away, pushing the Kliegls aside and running in all directions.

"Go after them!" Reid ordered.

The patrol scattered. Perry tore down the street, the only Kliegl chasing one lone Cloak.

"Perry!" Camille shouted, then hurried after him. She was losing ground until the Cloak stumbled. Perry was standing over the dark form when Camille caught up, panting.

"Why are you doing this?" the Cloak's mechanical voice pleaded.

Perry deployed his ASP, pressing it alongside the Cloak's head. "It's a warning," he growled, "to those who hide from Jahbulon. You may think Jahbulon can't find you in that costume, but Dax and the Kliegls will go where Jahbulon can't."

Perry pushed the ASP against the man's cheek until he twisted his head.

"The day is coming," Perry snarled. He slipped the tip of the ASP under the man's hood and started to lift it. The man grabbed the ASP with both hands, pulling the baton from Perry's grip. The Cloak swung wildly, striking Perry in the knee, sending him to the pavement with a howl of pain. The cloaked man kept swinging, landing blow after blow as Perry curled himself into a ball.

"Perry!" Camille cried, kneeling beside him, lifting an arm to shield herself from the baton. *"Stop it!* You're *hurting* him!"

The Cloak rolled to his knees, then got one foot under himself, still flailing away.

Camille gripped her ASP in its holster, pulled it free, and deployed it with a *hiss—click—click,* landing a brutal blow against the man's hood. His synthesizer squealed as if stuck in a demonic feedback loop as he went down, hands to his head.

Camille got to her feet, striking the writhing Cloak again and again, swinging the baton first from the right, then the left, each blow landing with a sickening *thunk.*

She felt someone restraining her. Perry embraced her from behind, trapping her arms against her body. She struggled, then went limp.

The Cloak lay motionless, like a pile of discarded rags. A

thin stream of blood crept out from under his hood.

"Let's go," Perry said.

"We can't leave him."

Perry took her hand and pulled her after him. "We can't stay."

She looked back once more, then ran ahead of Perry as he limped to keep up. They kept going until they reached their building.

"We're in trouble," Camille panted.

Perry massaged his knee as he gulped air. "Maybe not," he wheezed. "It's not like the Shade can call on Jahbulon."

51

Blue Morpho

Mackenzie scurried through dense growth, climbing over sinuous roots taller than he was, buttressing trees so high they disappeared into the clouds. Madeleine hurried to keep up, but Mack's childlike enthusiasm was like rocket fuel. The gap between them grew, Mackenzie becoming dim in the mist, until he vanished in a gray veil of fog.

"Mack!" she cried. There was no answer. "Mack?"

She stepped gingerly through the undergrowth, stopping beside a tree and resting her hand on its trunk.

"Mack?"

She felt a tickle. She jerked her hand away; a fifteen-centimeter millipede clung to her stubbornly.

"Mack!" she screamed, shaking her hand until the creature fell to the floor and inched away.

"What are you hollering about?"

Mackenzie emerged from the fog. He was dressed in a bush jacket and hat, his unruly hair peeking out from under the brim.

"Nothing," Madeleine replied. "Some giant, venomous serpent, I think. It's gone."

Mackenzie came to her, hands cupped together. He held them high, a mischievous smile on his face.

"Look what I've got."

He opened his hands, offering a cluster of brilliant orange flowers, with exquisitely frilled petals.

"They're beautiful, Mack. What are they?"

"Orchids," he answered. "They grow wild here."

"Is it okay to pick them?"

He grinned. "Funny! Whoever comes to this venue will find them exactly where I did." He turned the flowers in his hand, studying them from all sides. "Look at the color—have you ever seen it? That color? Like a sunset in the fall, when smoke from burning fields rises up and colors the sky. Or brighter, not a dull, dirty red sunset, but like the Sun when it's low, still too bright to stare at. Don't you think so? That orange color of the Sun in the evening, before it goes down behind the purple clouds?"

"I think so," Madeleine agreed, smiling. "Your eye's better than mine. But it's beautiful in any case."

"Freebird," he said, "save this for me."

"Yes, Mackenzie," the baritone voice responder answered. "What do you want to call it?"

"Call it 'Orange Monteverde Orchid.'"

"Of course," Freebird answered as the orchid vanished. "Done."

"So, this is where you get your inspiration," Madeleine said.

Mackenzie headed off, pushing aside tangled vines. "One place," he shouted. "Not the only place." He pointed. "Look!"

On a tree trunk, twenty meters high, Madeleine saw an irregular patch of blue—not an ordinary blue like the sky, but an iridescent indigo, mottled in subtle hues. It fluttered.

She squinted. "What is that?"

"Morphos," Mackenzie replied. "Butterflies. Jah, *look* at them—the way their wings catch the sun and throw it down all blue, like the far end of a rainbow."

Madeleine grinned. "'*The far end of a rainbow*.' How did you come up with that?"

He stared rapt at the cluster of butterflies. "Don't you think so? Like the colors of a prism, right at the very end, just before the light goes violet?"

She stared at him, arms wrapped around himself, mouth agape, eyes fixed on the cluster of butterflies.

"I think you're right," she agreed.

"Freebird, save that one, too. Call it 'Blue Morpho.'"

"Yes, Mackenzie."

"Come on, Maddie," he said, "there are toucans here. Fantastic colors."

He headed into the mist with Madeleine close behind.

❖ ❖ ❖

Madeleine and Mackenzie rested in a clearing after saving dozens of colors into his collection. He sat on the ground, winding a blade of grass around his finger.

"We're almost done," Madeleine said.

He looked up.

"I go to a restaurant venue sometimes to meet friends," he told her.

"Do you have a lot of friends?"

"Oh yes."

She smiled. "And they're the ones who tell you things?"

He nodded. "One of my friends, Kristin, stopped coming to the venue. She never missed a Thursday, but I came on Thursday and she was gone."

"What happened to her?"

Mackenzie unwound the blade of grass, flattened it on his thigh, and tossed it aside. "She's in a recovery venue." He looked up again. "I visited her there. *She* told me things."

"What? What happened to her?"

"Her husband Van beat her. Funny thing—seventeen years they're married, and he never hurt her. Hardly even said an angry word. She was always talking about Van, what a sweet man he is. Then one day he lost it. Hauled off and hit her—no reason! She was hurt, bad. Broken arm, broken jaw. Van didn't stop until Jahbulon intervened. Kristin told me that Van liked to ride lifestreams. And he rode one just before he beat her. It was called *Domestic Violence*. Very hi-res, especially with his new gen four Belt. Kristin bought it for him on his birthday."

Madeleine put her hands in her pockets and stared at the ground. "I'm sorry about Kristin."

"Yeah." Mackenzie stood up. He looked her in the eye.

"I'm glad you're almost done, Maddie."

She put her arm around him and rested her head on his shoulder.

"It'll be worth it, Mack. I promise."

52

DECONFLICTION

"C'MON. LET ME show you."

Speranza stood at the center of a circle of screens, surrounded by a mosaic of still and moving images, animated charts, scrolling text windows and crawls. Speranza, as Nikola Tesla, flicked images to and from an overhead ribbon, rearranging data sources, issuing voice commands to alter contents or presentation.

"Not now, Jayla," Speranza said. He repositioned a chart of assaults in each of the fifty North American districts. "I'm working here."

An avatar rastered into view: a purple gorilla with cartoon eyes and a huge grin. "C'mon, c'mon, *c'mon!* This is *ultra* hi-res."

"Get away from me, sicko. I'm not riding any more of your horror shows. I made a pledge to myself."

"*No!* Just ride this one. Just once, for a minute." The ape bounced on her knuckles. "I'll leave you alone after that."

"The incident rate is up sixty percent. The total is over four hundred."

The ape perused the graphs. "How's my new one doing? *Subterranean Blues?*"

"The guy who tortures sex slaves in his basement?"

The ape shook both paws above her head. "They're not *sex slaves*. He never had sex with *any* of them."

"Just filleted them with pruning shears."

"Uh-huh. How's it doing?"

Speranza swiped a graph from the ribbon, expanding it to full size.

"Number two and gaining, right after *A Walk in the Park*."

The purple ape did a backflip. "The Eye said this would happen. She knows her stuff."

"Yeah," Speranza mumbled, "she sure does know her stuff."

The crawl at the bottom of the cylinder began to flash red. Yellow block letters scrolled the circumference of the screen: *ALERT—ALERT—ALERT—UNAFFILIATED AVATAR DETECTED—CHICAGO DISTRICT— ALERT—ALERT—ALERT*

"What's that about?" Jayla the Ape asked.

"Isis," Speranza said, "drill on the alert."

A new window expanded into view. Speranza studied it for more than a minute.

"Pledge or no pledge, I can't ride your slasher flick. My priorities just got reset. Yours too."

❖ ❖ ❖

"All right, I'm here. Why the urgency?"

Speranza (still Tesla) and Jayla (still a purple gorilla) now joined by the Eye of Providence as Ma'at, met in the center of the full-circumference viewscreen. The Eye had jacked in via a stealth pipe from outside the Aletheia firewall. It was a risky way to convene a venue, used only in emergencies. Speranza considered this an emergency.

"One of our sentries threw an alert from the Worldstream," Speranza answered. He flicked an icon from the ribbon. A venue in miniature appeared before them: a political rally, the main stage replicated hundreds of times amid a crowd of tens of thousands.

"A Dax rally," the Eye noted.

"Right," Speranza replied. "Look close."

A tag floated above the crowd, flashing red, with an arrow pointing to an avatar too small to see clearly. Speranza touched two fingers and drew them apart. The venue expanded until they could make out what the tag pointed to: a dark-skinned man, wearing a bag on his shoulder. The woman next to him, in a close-fitting full-body garment displaying videos, had grabbed his arm. The man's flesh deformed, sticking to the woman's hand as she tried to let go. Speranza, Jayla, and the Eye watched as the crowd reacted to the commotion. The two attached avatars began to flicker, flashing colors and winking out, until the man vanished entirely, leaving the woman in a state of near panic.

"What did I just see?" the Eye asked.

"We're working on that," Jayla replied.

"The alarm was *unaffiliated avatar*," Speranza explained.

"A spoof?" the Eye asked.

Jayla jumped in. "Nope. A spoof is a masquerade—a person hiding behind someone else's avatar. The avatar is still affiliated with a real person, just not the person behind it."

"You'd think *that* would raise a flag," the Eye commented.

The purple ape scratched her belly. "Uh-huh. It takes the Worldstream a little while to catch on, but catch on it will. You can't spoof Jahbulon forever. The Worldstream throws a lot of spoof alarms, thousands a day. We've stopped reacting to them—don't even display them anymore."

"Then what? Is this something new?"

"Yeah," Speranza replied. "We didn't even have a detection method for this. The sentry's AI spotted something weird and tipped us off—called it an *unaffiliated avatar*. And that's accurate."

"Okay, explain," the Eye demanded.

"I gotta get into some wonky stuff for that," Jayla said.

The Eye winced. "I'll try to keep up."

"All right, here goes. When someone checks into the Worldstream, they use a key, a personal ID number. The Worldstream patches them through to the venue server right away—nobody wants to wait to get to their venue—but the key still needs to be verified."

"Against the history in the blockchain," the Eye remarked.

The ape nodded. "Uh-huh—yeah, you got it. That key has to exist somewhere, but it takes time for the key to propagate through the network. Once it's found, the Worldstream books the transaction and everyone goes on with their VR good times."

"Sounds foolproof," the Eye said, "unless you can forge a key."

"You're catching on," Speranza interjected. "Spoofers don't forge keys, they steal them. There's a whole black market in stolen keys for celebrities and the like. You want to be famous? Buy some VR player's key and pose."

"You said the Worldstream catches on. How?"

"Two ways. First, if the owner of the key jacks in, the Worldstream will detect a conflict—two guys with the same key. Then the disambiguation algorithms kick in and the poser gets ejected. That can take some time, though."

"And the other way?"

"The guy can change his key. That's messy. He has to pay to redirect his entire history in the blockchain. Most don't bother—they just live with the inconvenience."

"But this thing—not a spoof, you said."

"No," Jayla continued. "This looks like what *you* said—a forged key."

"Okay, I got it. So why is this so urgent?"

"Because keys are generated by the Worldstream. Jahbulon uses a hairy encryption algorithm to do it. Forging a valid key is *impossible*."

The Eye's avatar brushed back her raven hair. "But someone did it."

"They *almost* did it," Jayla said. "You saw what happened. The venue server wised up and kicked him out. The deconfliction algorithm flipped and some weird shit happened as you saw."

"Okay. I still don't see why this is a big deal."

"Because the avatar shouldn't have been able to connect to the venue server in the first place," said Speranza. "If the key's not valid, the Worldstream will chuck it at first sight. This was a valid key; it just didn't belong to anybody."

"Then how did the Worldstream render the avatar?"

"That is a damn fine question," Jayla said. "It looks like it was cobbled together from parts of other avatars, but we don't know how. I have my team working on that."

The Eye's face flashed alarm. "Instead of weaving our new lifestreams? I didn't authorize that!"

Jayla waved a paw at the Eye. "We'll still hit our dates, Boss. This is important."

The Eye shook her head and waved her arms, feathers fluttering in the air. "But why? I still don't get what's so urgent that you'd slow down our lifestream development without clearing it with me first. Explain!"

Speranza held up his hands. "We wouldn't have done it unless we thought there was a payoff. This thing's never been done before—it's brand new technology. And we don't own it."

The Eye tapped her cheek and shrugged. "All right, but what's the payoff?"

Jayla and Speranza looked at each other.

"Well?" the Eye demanded.

Speranza looked down. "Whoever can do this—they can bypass the Worldstream rules engine."

"So?"

"The Shade will be able to enter the Worldstream directly."

The Eye sat silently for a few seconds before a look of understanding crossed her face.

"Without sponsors, you mean."

Jayla and Speranza nodded.

"That'll threaten the *Vita Occulta*," the Eye muttered.

"Yeah," Jayla said. "That'd make the V.O. obsolete—bust up your monopoly."

53
Minimum Threshold

With the election merely two days away, Madeleine jacked into the largest Dax rally to date—a million fanatical followers surrounding a thousand Dax replicas.

She pushed forward, reaching the edge of the stage. Dax was no more than five meters away, flanked by two avatars dressed in white—white shoes, pants, and shirts, with red sashes across their chests and red caps embellished with Kliegl searchlights throwing sharp beams into space—all duplicated a thousand times, the beams weaving a gauzy fabric of light over the crowd.

Neither of Dax's sidemen sported a halo.

"We're out of luck," Madeleine said.

"Hang on," Jayla replied. "Let me work this."

"Am I not close enough?"

"That's not it. This is one of a thousand stages. You can see them, but they can't see you."

"Then…what?"

"Keep your eye on the guys. Wait for it."

Madeleine stood by, shifting her eyes from one attendant to the other, then to Dax. A halo flickered for a moment over the man on the left, then disappeared.

"What was that?" Madeleine asked.

"The venue server cycles through all the stages, nailing up and tearing down local connections. You see them, but Jah only knows what they're seeing from up there. Must look like a blur."

"The guy on the left…that's where I saw the halo."

"Yeah, I caught that. He's in a gen four."

"Zap him."

"Not so fast. I have to wait until it cycles through again."

"How long will that take?"

"Hard to say. Four, maybe five minutes. Keep an eye out."

Madeleine focused on Dax as he stepped back, nodding in each direction in turn as the throng cheered. The crowd hushed when he stepped forward.

"This venue," he began in a barely audible voice, "where you citizens have come to support our movement—our *historic* movement—this venue is a *product,* no different from tissues, or toilet paper, or toothpaste. This world, where we live and work and play, this *universe,* is the creation of a *tiny* number of corporations—the Worldstream Consortium." Dax's voice rose a notch, in volume and pitch. "They package and promote and sell their product—the Worldstream. They are the gods of your world. You do not pray to them, but you sacrifice to them. They demand tribute. They demand loyalty. They demand obedience." Dax raised his fists. "The Worldstream Consortium—remember that name—seven global corporations, who hold *your* world in *their* hands. The Consortium—the makers and keepers of the world." His gestures grew broader, his arms sweeping in wide arcs and voice nearing its peak volume. "Aren't *they* to blame for what happens in *their* world? Aren't theft and fraud in the Worldstream *their* responsibility? Or the crime, which has exploded in recent months—shouldn't the Consortium own *that* as well? We call on Jahbulon for help when we need it, and Jahbulon comes, yet the plague of violence grows. Can we blame Jahbulon, our protector, for this violence? If we do, then we must ultimately lay responsibility on the *Consortium,* for they are the keepers of the Worldstream, and Jahbulon answers to *them!*"

Dax stepped back again. Madeleine felt the crowd surge forward, shoving her from all directions, trapping her against the stages. Their shouts were deafening.

Dax stepped forward once more, and the crowd hushed. It

was like watching a perfectly timed play in a theater venue.

"They will deny blame, of course!" Dax resumed, still shouting. "They will say, 'We only provide a *platform*, an *environment* for your use. We cannot be responsible for what the *users* do in the Worldstream.' But if they are sincere, then why do they employ *criminals* to create their virtual worlds? Why are their *products* designed and coded and maintained by the *outlaw Shade?*"

The audience renewed their cheers for Dax and catcalls for the Consortium and the Shade. The crowd squeezed harder.

"This is getting a little frightening," Madeleine commented uneasily, loud enough to be heard over the commotion.

"Stay with me, Boss," Jayla replied. "Should be…wait… *there it is!*"

The man to the left of Dax froze, a narrow aura of silver flickering around him. When he moved again, his hands came together and stayed there. He looked straight ahead, then at Dax. After a moment, he began clapping slowly, lowering his hands to his sides when Dax signaled that he was ready to speak.

"Who saw that?" Madeleine asked.

"Anyone who was looking, Boss. But they're all so riled up I doubt anyone made anything out of it."

"Did it take?"

"Shoulda. His threshold is *way* below the minimum."

"Get me out."

"Yes, Boss. Isis, exit the venue."

Madeleine's surroundings transitioned from the deafening mob to her spartan office. She removed her headgear and peeled off her gloves, dropping them into a drawer in the desk. She removed her Belt. She sat for a few moments, anticipating next steps.

With any luck, I'll be face-to-face with Dax before the end of the week.

54

SCOOP

MADELEINE SUSPENDED THE therapy venue after her last appointment of the day, an exhausting ninety-minute session with a case of chronic depression. For years she had noted that such cases were surprisingly common; in fact, the incidence of chronic emotional disturbances seemed to increase over time, despite everyone having access to infinitely varied VR venues and advanced medications. She found this epidemic of gloom frustrating—she could treat the symptoms, but the cause persisted.

She leaned back in her chair and took a few cleansing breaths before speaking.

"Elsa—Mackenzie."

"Yes, Madeleine. You have a v-gram, marked urgent. Would you like to receive it before visiting Mackenzie?"

"A v-gram from whom?"

"It's from a stealth site. The sender is unknown."

Madeleine pulled off her VR gear. The wall screen displayed a list of v-grams accumulated over the course of her workday, one flashing red.

"Elsa, open a stealth screen."

The screen flashed and went dark. Elsa narrated the scrolling text: "Madeleine, you have entered stealth mode. Your activities will be secure from monitoring whenever you are using resources compatible with stealth access. Iron Pipe LLC, providers of stealth access technology, assumes no liability for any activities conducted in stealth mode that are not in strict compliance with the law. Do you understand and accept these terms?"

"Yes, Elsa. Access the Aletheia server."

Speranza's Tesla avatar appeared next to the text of the v-gram, narrated by a synthesized Shade voice: *Big break in that deconfliction study. Jack in. Sperz.*

"Elsa, stealth handoff to Isis."

"Yes, Madeleine."

Elsa's breathy alto gave way to the bell-like soprano of Isis, the Aletheia voice responder: "Yes, Eye of Providence. What can I do for you?"

❖ ❖ ❖

Within seconds, Speranza, Jayla, and the Eye were in the meeting venue behind the Aletheia firewall.

"I'm here, Speranza," the Eye announced, her voice betraying mild annoyance.

"Thanks for the quick response," Speranza answered. "I wouldn't have pinged you if it wasn't important."

"Fine, let's go then."

Speranza summoned a miniature rendition of a dance venue for teens, the partiers gyrating to the music of a retro metal band, played at ear-rupturing volume.

"*Jah*, turn it down!" the Eye protested. The music softened to background level.

"Sorry about that." Speranza expanded one section of the floor, where a young man stood toe-to-toe with a slight man of apparent Indian ancestry. The two appeared to be arguing.

"Is that the same avatar we saw at the Dax rally?"

"The very same."

"Isis, let's hear what they're talking about," the Eye said. Their voices sounded clearly above the music:

An addict never knows why.

An addict? Addicted to what?

That feeling of power—power over another person. It's like a drug.

The boy grabbed the man by the shoulders.

That's not me! That's not me!

"Isis, pause," the Eye commanded. She bent low to get a closer look. "Can you identify the boy?"

"Haven't teased that out yet," answered Jayla, this time appearing in the avatar of a fat golden Buddha. "But we heard his name earlier—Dylan."

The Eye snapped upright. *"Dylan?"*

"That's what the little guy called him."

"Can't be," the Eye muttered. "Isis, resume."

The confrontation continued:

Wait! Raúl wants to meet with you.

Raúl? Where? When?

"Isis, *pause!*" the Eye shouted.

"Got something, Boss?" Speranza asked.

"Do you know anything else about this avatar? The man, I mean?"

Jayla grinned, eyes narrow over chubby cheeks, hands on her round belly. "Well, *yeah*. We know where it came from. It's *local*."

"Local? Where?"

"Another Shade hangout…the Summerland."

"Who else knows about this?"

Jayla and Speranza exchanged glances. "The alarm got recorded in the Worldstream, I'm sure," Speranza explained, "but no sign of a reaction. As far as we can tell, we got a scoop."

The Eye stood and circled the dance scene, studying the boy from all angles. He was difficult to see in the low light, but his hair and features looked familiar.

"I want that technology. Let's move on it. We know everything we need. *You* know *where*…" the Eye paused, staring into space, remembering another time, "…and *I* know *who*."

55

ORDER, DISCIPLINE, SECURITY, LIGHT

"MARINA, THE TURNOUT in all districts certainly exceeds *our* projections. Were there *any* outlets that saw this coming?"

The co-anchors, Liam and Silvia, hovered over a gigantic map of North America, each district color-coded by voter turnout. In the middle of the map stood Marina, the field correspondent, a giantess able to move from one district to another in a single step. The continent was solid red, indicating record voter turnout in the council election.

"Liam, Silvia, no news outlet I know of projected turnout at these levels," Marina replied, "more than 80 percent of eligible voters in most districts. Salt Lake, Shasta, and Rainier are over 85 percent. Even the traditionally low turnout districts—Muskogee, Ozark, Shiprock—are in the high 70's. It's unprecedented."

"Silvia," Liam asked his co-anchor, "do we know what's behind this surge?"

"For the answer we'll go to Stefanie in Blue Ridge," Silvia replied.

Marina shrank to doll-size as the map expanded around her, telescoping to a spot in the Appalachian Mountains. The location reporter, Stefanie, stood among a crowd of avatars who had jacked in to vote and who had stayed to watch the election returns.

"Liam, I'm here with these voters in Blue Ridge." Stefanie

325

motioned toward one avatar, a portly lady wearing a metallic pantsuit and close-fitting brimless hat, decorated with stylized animations of Dax in mid-oration. "Citizen, judging from how you're dressed, I can guess who you voted for. Can you tell us why you support the Kliegls?"

The pinch-faced lady looked up, straight-lipped. "We can't keep going on like we've been. Dax will shake things up."

"Yes, citizen, and what needs to change?"

The lady's lips stretched tighter and she squinted more intensely. "Like we've been. The way things are. We can't keep on."

"Yes, and what exactly are the issues?"

"What are you asking?" the lady asked, standing on her toes. "Are you one of *them?*"

Stefanie kept her eyes on the lady, who grew more belligerent by the second. "I'm sorry, I don't know what you mean. One of whom?"

"*Them!* The ones who hide from Jahbulon. The ones who tear down our morals."

Stefanie took a step back. "Thank you, citizen."

"You *are*, aren't you?" the lady shouted as Stefanie retreated. "You're one of *them!*"

"We're moving you," Stefanie's producer said, his voice crashing through her headphones. Her avatar rastered out and teleported to an open spot twenty meters away.

"Liam, Silvia," Stefanie continued, "many of the voters we've talked with said the same thing—they're discontented, but they're not specific. When challenged, they become agitated and bring up this vague threat to our morals from some unnamed *them.*"

"Stefanie," Silvia jumped in, "do you think they're referring to the Shade?"

"Possibly, but obviously I'm not Shade."

"Cloak, maybe?"

"Perhaps, but no one has mentioned either Shade or Cloak —just some nameless *others* who threaten the civil order."

"We're hearing from our correspondents in the other districts," Silvia broke in, "and they all have similar reports."

"I can't say I'm surprised," Stefanie replied. "These citizens may be vague about their concerns, but they *are* consistent. It's almost as if they've been programmed."

"Thank you, Stefanie," Silvia concluded. "We're now joined by Vimala Mallick, CEO of Kanpur Virset, from Hyderabad, India."

Mallick's avatar, in her familiar brightly-colored costume, rastered into view between Silvia and Liam, the three of them suspended over the election map, still updating as vote totals came in.

"Vimala, welcome," Liam began. "How will the Worldstream Consortium react to what appears to be a resounding victory for the Kliegl Party, given that Dax made the Consortium a target during his campaign?"

"Thank you, Liam, thank you, Silvia," Mallick began. "The Consortium is not a political organization. We don't concern ourselves…"

"That's a cop-out," Silvia interjected. "Dax attacked the Shade and the Consortium at every opportunity. Surely you…"

"Excuse me, but the Consortium has *always* cooperated with elected governments across the globe, and will continue to do so."

"You're not concerned about the negative feelings toward you that Dax has stirred up among the citizens?" Silvia asked.

Mallick smiled. "We are not political, but we understand campaign rhetoric. True, Dax has not been kind to the Consortium, but for all his antagonism, he has proposed *no* specific policies that will affect the operation of the Worldstream…"

"Dax has promised that he will eliminate the Shade. Isn't *that* a specific policy?"

Mallick's smile disappeared. "The Shade do *nothing* for us. This lie…"

"But it's common knowledge…"

"It's *nothing of the kind*."

"Will you say once and for all that neither Kanpur Virset, nor *any* of the Consortium corporations, employ the Shade for…"

"I have addressed that question *many times.*"

"Address it again!"

"I won't be interrogated…"

"Then you won't deny that the Worldstream Consortium employ the Shade for jobs that our citizens could do as well?"

"We are *lawful, responsible*…"

"And if Dax attacks the Shade, won't *that* impact the Consortium?"

Mallick paused, pressing her hands together under her chin. "We are a global enterprise. Regardless of what Dax's followers believe, I ask you: How can the leader of any *one* nation challenge the foundations of the Worldstream?"

❖ ❖ ❖

The Kliegl venue looked familiar to Dax's followers, but on a vastly larger scale: two thousand stages laid out in a grid, amid a throng of millions. The arrangement was the same, but the stages were different. Instead of a small stage with a single speaker and an entourage behind him, each stage was a massive circular platform, entirely vacant, illuminated from above by an invisible light. The crowd milled about, murmuring in anticipation, innumerable individual voices together sounding like rolling thunder. Avatars rastered into the venue at a steady rate, a new stage appearing in the grid whenever the headcount passed a threshold. The rumbling of the crowd grew as time ticked toward the closing of the polls in the Western districts, sounding like a monstrous heartbeat as the last few seconds counted down.

The crowd hushed as the overhead lights went black. A moment passed, then they gasped as brilliant shafts of light shot skyward from the center of each stage, an infinitely tall colonnade of blinding white. A cadence of drums sounded, then a fanfare of a thousand horns rose to a crescendo. The rendered voices of a million Kliegl acolytes erupted as Dax stepped from the shaft of light, or rather, seven *duplicates* of Dax came forward on every stage, each avatar with fists raised in a victorious *V*. Dax was rendered as a figure three meters high, dressed in a white floor-length garment resembling the cinctured alb of a priest. Around his head, radiating from his remarkable hair, was a Christ-like halo, an aura of yellow flame.

The cheers continued for five full minutes as thousands of giant Dax replicas gestured in perfect synchrony. The Dax avatars circled the stages, a weird game of follow-the-leader, with a vertical light beam at its center, like a luminous maypole. The uproar showed no signs of flagging when the shafts of light disappeared, and the venue went black. Each Dax avatar reappeared, not from external illumination, but glowing, ghost-like, from an ethereal inner light. The vision stunned the crowd into silence.

On each stage seven colossal glowing Dax avatars bowed their heads, folding their arms over their chests, in blinding white vestments and with hair like fire.

"Citizens, you have chosen!" Dax said, his voice piped directly into each person's head. "You have chosen order over chaos. You have chosen discipline over lawlessness. You have chosen security over fear." Dax's avatars unfolded their arms, raising their fists. "And you have chosen *light over darkness!*"

The crowd exploded. Among the millions of Kliegl devotees stood Stefanie, the location reporter, having exited from the Blue Ridge venue and jacked into the Kliegl victory celebration. Her avatar, and the ecstatic Dax followers nearby, were duplicated in her news outlet's parallel venue, surrounded by viewers.

"Liam, Silvia," she shouted over the noise of the crowd, "Dax, the leader of the Kliegl Party, is speaking to his followers in a spectacle unlike anything I've ever seen." One of the stages appeared in miniature hovering near Stefanie's head, but even shrunken, the sight of seven Dax avatars towering over the audience from each of more than two thousand stages was spectacular. "Now that the Western districts have reported their results, we can declare the Kliegl Party the winner of 390 of the 500 council seats—an overwhelming majority. The Citizens Independence Party has gone down in defeat, and the coalition government of Eugenia Sato is dissolved."

The sound of Dax's voice rose almost to a scream, followed by the roar of the crowd. Stefanie shouted louder. "In less than one month we will have a new majority government, with Dax as our first minister."

❖ ❖ ❖

After rastering out of her interview, Vimala Mallick jacked into a private venue with the other six members of the Consortium.

"What did you think?" she asked her colleagues.

"I'm not as confident as you are that Dax won't complicate our lives," Eva Serrano answered. "I know he promised not to interfere, but I don't trust him."

"I agree with Eva," said Vo Thanh, President of Vietnet. "We hold the keys to the Worldstream, but Dax can still make trouble."

"I share your concerns," Mallick responded, "but Dax is not our most pressing issue."

The Consortium leaders looked at each other, all with furrowed brows except for Mallick and one other.

"Dan," Mallick said, addressing Dan Baltasar, CEO of Chain Corporation, "tell them what you've discovered."

A slim man with dark eyes and a helmet of close-cropped silver hair gestured, conjuring a map of North America, showing vote totals from each district.

"This should look familiar," Baltasar said.

"Of course," said Ekua Ekuban, president of Ahadi Kubwa, an elegant woman with strong features and ebony skin. "We just saw this report. A Kliegl win is inevitable."

Baltasar nodded and gestured again. Another set of numbers appeared.

Serrano stood up. "Those totals are…"

"Yes," Baltasar interrupted. "And they correspond with…"

"The Kliegl vote," Serrano confirmed. She spread her arms, expanding the scale of the map to show individual precincts. "The correlation is unmistakable."

"Correct," Mallick agreed. "The vote—or, more precisely,

the *voters*—were manipulated to favor Dax."

Serrano moved around the periphery of the map, studying it from all angles, before looking up. "I think I know how this could happen."

"I thought you might," Baltasar remarked. "And I'm sure you'll investigate. But there's an even *more* pressing matter."

Baltasar waved away the map. In its place was a miniature venue, a dance scene for teens. Amid the noise and chaos, a red-headed boy stood menacingly close to a small Indian man. A block of text scrolled over the pair—a list of warning messages kicked out by the Worldstream compliance engine.

"We detected this weeks ago," he began, "but it didn't reach the front of our issue queue until recently."

The Consortium members read the scroll with slack expressions, until, one-by-one, a look of understanding and alarm darkened their faces.

"I think we can agree," Mallick said, "that *this* is our most pressing issue."

56

THE CITIZENS HAVE SPOKEN

INSTEAD OF DAX on multiple stages amid a throng of millions, the venue was that of the first minister's cabinet room—a single throne-like chair at one end of a ring of chairs. Dax sat in the throne, flanked by two attendants, listening to the lone guest: a woman seated across from him.

"Congratulations on your party's victory," Madeleine offered. "I'm happy to have been a part of it."

"It was a victory for our citizens," Dax replied. "They *all* played their part. *They* deserve the credit."

"Of course." Madeleine made a sweeping gesture. A relief map of North America appeared in the center of the ring of chairs, the number of voters in each district represented by elevation, the winning margin for the Kliegl Party represented by color. The map resembled an uneven plateau, colored in shades of red, from magenta to crimson. "Record voter volume, record margins for a winning party. The Kliegls are the first outright majority government in nearly twenty-five years."

"Indeed," Dax agreed. "The citizens have spoken. Now we must act."

"That's why I requested this meeting. We're here to work with you in your new government."

Dax narrowed his eyes, lips turning up in a barely perceptible smile.

"All of our citizens will have a role. We thank you for your dedication."

Madeleine gestured again. A list of numbers floated over each district—totals, percentages, probabilities—each list a testament to the Kliegl's domination of the election.

"These numbers tell a story," she said.

"These numbers are our mandate," he answered.

"These numbers didn't happen by accident."

Dax's faint smile disappeared. "What does that mean?"

"We have a certain technology." Madeleine stood, gestured, and the map dissolved; she teleported to the center of the ring. "This technology played a decisive role in your victory."

Dax turned in his chair. "Assuming that's true, why would this concern me?"

"We can use this technology to help you with your agenda."

He leaned forward, putting his hands on his knees. "You cannot be serious. I suppose you want a *ministry post?* Which one?"

His attendants snickered behind their hands, until Dax grinned at them and they laughed out loud.

"We want to help," Madeleine said quietly.

Dax moved his hand in a sweeping arc. A miniature of his election-night rally appeared. Crowds roared in response to his victory speech, delivered by his monumental avatars.

"I have all the help I need." With another gesture, the rally vanished. "Of *course* this doesn't happen by accident. Your technology, whatever it is, is of no interest to me. We have our *own* technology."

She looked sideways at him as he continued.

"Our coalition of citizens is diverse, yet every one of them believes himself to be a part of a monolithic bloc, all committed to the same goals, because *that* is what *we led them* to believe."

"Yes, I know about your technology."

Dax smirked. "Impossible."

"Your people have learned to use the Belt to discern the innermost feelings of its users. You used that ability to reinforce your message within peer groups. Very clever."

Dax's expression went blank, but recovered in a second.

"My compliments." He twisted in his chair. "But that doesn't change anything. Now, if there's nothing else, you'll have to let me go. The transition occupies all of my time lately."

Madeleine waved, and the relief map reappeared. Another wave of her hand and a semi-transparent layer of color overlaid it. "This color key indicates the distribution of gen four Belts among the voters. You'll notice that the densest concentrations of gen fours correspond closely to the areas where your vote totals were highest."

"Of course," Dax replied, sneering. "Our methods are most effective where the Belt is used most often."

"But you can measure responses with *any* generation of the Belt. The gen four distribution is important because *our* technology makes use of the unique features of the *gen four Belt*."

He sighed loudly, rolling his eyes. "Really, I don't have time for this."

The map disappeared with another wave. "Might I suggest a demonstration?" she replied.

"I said, I don't have time."

"I don't mean *now*."

"What *do* you mean?"

"You have a measure before the council, the creation of a special unit to locate and apprehend the Shade."

"It's what we were elected to do."

"The vote is in three days," Madeleine pointed out.

"Is this conversation going somewhere?" Dax asked.

"The measure will be defeated."

Dax laughed out loud, a high-pitched sound like a squeaky hinge. "Every Kliegl in the council will vote for the measure, and many of the delegates from the other parties as well. Support among the citizenry for this measure is too great for them to oppose us."

"The measure will fail by more than fifty votes."

"Your time is up. Ismo, remove this person from the venue."

❖ ❖ ❖

Dax turned to the man on his right, pointing a finger. "Jordan, what do you know about this woman?"

"She contacted me. She asked to meet you."

"Is she who she claims to be?"

Jordan seemed bewildered. "I don't know. I assume she is."

Dax stood, extending his height as best he could over the seated Jordan. "You *assume?* Didn't you verify her credentials?"

"No, Dax, I…"

"You are in charge of my security. I see *no one* whom you haven't vetted in advance. And you've *always* done your job. Yet, not only did you *fail* to check this woman's claims, but you *insisted* that I meet her. How do you explain this?"

Jordan looked at the floor. "Dax, I can't. I only know that it was very important that you speak with her."

Dax massaged his chin as he peered at Jordan through narrowed eyes.

"You have one of those, don't you? One of those Belts?"

"Yes…" Jordan answered.

"I never use it," Dax snorted. "Sending impulses directly into the nervous system—it's indecent! Who knows what that device can do to you?"

"Ah…it's quite the experience."

"I'm sure. And *your* Belt…is it gen four?"

Jordan swallowed hard. "Yes…"

Dax clenched a fist, lip curled.

"You've disappointed me, Jordan. After three years on my staff, this is the first impulsive act of yours that I can recall."

"I promise, it won't be repeated."

Dax nodded slowly. "I expect that it *won't*. But let's make sure."

Jordan's eyes opened wide. He turned slightly, as if cringing. "How?"

"You will not use the Belt in any official venue. In fact, you will not use the Belt *at all*. I forbid it." He turned to the other aide. "And I forbid *you* to use it. Tell my entire staff—

and the delegates. I forbid them *all*."

57

IRRESISTIBLE

EMMA RISKED MUCH, she knew. But the compulsion was irresistible.

Irresistible—Emma didn't get the concept. A rising star in the Kliegl Party, the 27-year-old delegate from Shasta had made self-discipline the core principle of her life. An unshakeable personal code, a rigorous daily routine, a ferocious work ethic—these things, in addition to her oratorical skills, had made her the youngest delegate in the council. Whatever she had set her sights upon in her young life, she achieved. Anything superfluous Emma eliminated by sheer force of will, of which she had a *lot*. She simply did not waste time. That was why her mind couldn't fathom why she was riding the same lifestream every day, hour after unproductive hour. She didn't even *want* to understand, and that frightened her. Scared, nervous, and confused—that was how Emma felt as she pulled the gen four Belt from its hiding place behind a dresser and strapped it on.

Dax had forbidden any Kliegl delegate to use the Belt, gen four or otherwise. It was a ban impossible to enforce, but Emma thought it best to keep her own Belt hidden, if only to fool herself into thinking that if it were out of sight, she could resist strapping on and jacking in. After every session she stuffed it behind the dresser, swearing that she would never take it out again, confident that she could draw on her reservoir of self-control and leave it be, only to pull the dresser away from the wall a day later.

Her obsession wasn't even all that interesting a lifestream. It was compelling—a young mother who resuscitates her baby after he stops breathing—but after forty rides from every possible angle, the novelty was gone. Even the intense emotions—induced by the gen four Belt—had become blasé.

Dax had summoned Emma and the rest of the Kliegl delegates to an emergency meeting. She checked the time— thirty minutes to go. She sat silently in her chair, VR gear in her lap, having her daily internal debate, an argument she always lost.

She walked to the dresser.

❖ ❖ ❖

Dax's red-faced avatar stood in the center of a circular hall. He'd roared non-stop for an hour before summing up in a few words:

"My *first measure!* My *signature issue!* Defeated by *my own party!*"

The 390 members of the Kliegl caucus sat mute in the tiers of the circular venue.

"You! Fausto!" Dax pointed at an avatar in the front row, a short, swarthy man with a face like crumpled paper. "Leader of the majority. Even *you* voted against this measure."

Fausto looked away. "I can't explain," he mumbled.

"What?"

"Dax, my apologies, but I cannot explain my vote."

"You *advocated* for it. You spoke in the council in support of it. You counted votes in the caucus and *assured* me it would pass."

"Yes, Dax. I support the proposal. I believe in the policy. But when the vote was called, I…" Fausto pressed his fingers to his eyes. "I simply…I don't know."

"You *don't know,*" Dax said, his voice saturated with sarcasm. He pointed to a woman in the third tier. "Emma, do *you* know? I campaigned for you myself in more than ten Shasta venues. *This* is how you repay me?"

The buxom woman with long black hair locked eyes with Dax for a second before turning her head. "I support your agenda, Dax. I fully intended to vote for this measure."

"Incredible." Dax spread his arms. His avatar grew until he was tall enough to look down on the tiers of Kliegl loyalists. "My *supporters*. My *faithful flock*. My *acolytes*. Could I be any less heartbroken than Christ was when Judas kissed his cheek?"

Fausto stood, leaning on the railing, looking up at the oversized Dax. "I'm baffled by these defections—by *my* defection. Every one of the Kliegl delegates is committed to your cause."

"Traitors!" Dax rumbled.

"Dax, I've spoken with every Kliegl delegate who voted down the measure. I've contacted delegates from other parties who support us. They all told me the same story—they intended to vote for the measure, but when the vote was called, they felt a compulsion to vote it down. It was as if their minds were made up for them."

Dax looked down, a knuckle pressed to his chin. He raised his head slowly as he shrank to normal size.

"Fausto, do you use the Belt?"

"Dax?" Fausto queried.

"Simple question, majority leader. Do you use the *Belt* when you're in VR?"

Fausto looked in both directions. His face wore a nervous smile. "Dax, you have forbidden…"

"I *know* what I have *forbidden*. Answer my question."

Fausto stared at the floor. "Yes, Dax."

"And you, Emma. Do you use the Belt?"

The black-haired woman nodded.

"Gen four?"

She nodded again.

"And you, Fausto? Gen four?"

"Yes. Why are you…"

"Colin," Dax interrupted, pointing to a tall, thin man in the outermost tier, "you were loyal. What about you? Do you use the Belt?"

"No, Dax," Colin answered.

"All of you who betrayed me with your vote—highlight."

Glowing orbs appeared over two hundred heads.

"You highlighted, go dark if you are *not* using a *gen four*

Belt."

All the orbs remained.

"Jah," Dax cursed. "Ismo, suspend the venue."

❖ ❖ ❖

"I have no objection to putting your agenda into practice," Madeleine said. "Within limits."

"*Limits?*" Dax retorted. He slumped in his throne-like chair, one hand hanging limply over the chair's arm, the other pressed to his temple.

"Your plans to move against the Shade, for example," she continued.

"You've already ruined *that* plan," he grumbled.

"There will be another vote. And *that* vote will succeed."

"You put a defeat on my record. My government—less than a month old, and this humiliation. *Your* doing. I won't forget that."

"The citizens will forget. If necessary, I will *make* them forget."

Dax grabbed both arms of the chair and lifted himself up. "Did you do this simply to demonstrate your power? Or do you have a real objection to our campaign against the Shade?"

"A demonstration, mostly. As for *my* objections, I don't have any that aren't also shared by the Consortium. Or you, for that matter."

"The Shade are criminals."

"Technically, yes. But they're also vital to the economy."

Dax flung his arms wide, then fell back into the chair. "We would only have made *token* apprehensions. Just enough to satisfy the citizenry. We wouldn't have done anything to threaten the interests of the Consortium!"

"I understand. And I won't stand in your way." Madeleine stepped forward, standing less than a meter from his throne. "I do ask one thing, though."

Dax closed his eyes as his chin fell forward. "What is it?"

"*I* will choose which Shade alliances you raid first."

58

THE RATIO

"WHICH ONE IS this?" the Eye of Providence asked.

"He's called Elisha," Jayla answered. "His RL name is Thomas."

"And he knows the technology?"

"Not really. Nemesio is the brains behind the program. Elisha is the debt collector, just a mid-level hacker. He doesn't know anything."

The Eye clenched her fist. Her mouth was grim below the crimson mask. "Then why's he here?"

"Because we could get him to bite."

"*Jayla.*"

Jayla held up her hands. "Look, Boss, once we get 'em in the lifestream with the gen four, we can implant suggestions in *anyone's* mind, but they don't always take."

"What's your point? *This* one took."

Speranza interrupted. "It almost didn't. We gave him the passphrase three times before he cooperated. And then he snapped out of it. I had to dope him just to get him in the car."

"That's unacceptable!" the Eye said brusquely. "Jayla, what in Jah's name happened?"

"This mind-jacking is tricky business," Jayla replied. "A lot of variables."

"I know that!" the Eye snapped. "I *designed* it, remember?"

"Yeah, sure, Boss. I *never* forget that."

"So, what was it? The threshold?"

"Elisha has the lowest threshold of anyone in the Kaleidoscope, by our estimation. That's why we picked him. We also had some intel about his RL history—he and Armengol chummed together in the Summerland. Shade Elisha got chatty about his background. We got some good imagery for the lifestream."

"And it *still* failed?"

Jayla pointed at the door. "It didn't *fail*. I got you your hostage, didn't I? He's in the next room, for Jah's sake."

The Eye looked from one masked face to another, then stood. "All right. Let's go talk to him. Speranza, you're with me."

❖ ❖ ❖

Elisha sat in a room with bare concrete walls, a single luminescent panel on the ceiling, and a steel door, locked from the outside. He couldn't remember how he had gotten there.

Images flipped through his mind like fast-forwarding through a lifestream: the Flash Drive Café—an old roommate—a long-lost girlfriend—two Shade asking for his affiliation—a vehicle—a struggle—darkness. Then here, in a square concrete room, with two chairs and no table. How long? He had no idea.

Suddenly he heard the sound of a bolt sliding. The door opened and two Shade entered, one going to a corner, the other to the second chair.

"Elisha, I'm called the Eye of Providence."

"The Eye," Elisha repeated.

"I'm sure Chrysalis has mentioned me."

Elisha nodded.

"She probably didn't have much nice to say about me."

"She hates you."

"I understand that, after what happened. I had hoped that she'd see the broader picture, that she'd have some perspective. But I did a poor job of explaining," the Eye said.

"Okay..." Elisha replied.

"Elisha—but it's really Thomas, isn't it? Should I call you Thomas?"

Elisha straightened his back. "I'm called Elisha."

"That's the Shade protocol, I know, but among *friends* we use our given names, don't we?" She turned toward the corner. "Speranza, may I have some time alone with Elisha?"

Speranza left. The Eye took off her hood. She wasn't wearing her mask. "I'm Madeleine. But you know that. Grace told you."

"Yes."

"I use my own name with Grace because I consider her a friend. Can we be friends, Thomas?"

"I'm called *Elisha*."

Madeleine sighed as she put the hood back on. "Elisha, we brought you here because we'd like to know more about the persona."

"I don't know what you're talking about."

"You know. You can tell us about it, or not. That's your decision."

"Then I decide not to."

Madeleine stood. "Very well. We won't speak about it again. I'll have Speranza bring you something to eat."

She was almost to the door when he spoke.

"How can you say that you're Grace's *friend*, after what you did?"

The Eye sat down again. She pulled off the hood and laid it neatly across her lap.

"What did Grace tell you?"

"You stole her life. You wove her life data into a lifestream."

"To help people, the way I helped Grace."

Elisha turned away. Madeleine leaned in, trying to catch his eye.

"I was her therapist, Thomas. When Grace came to me, she was desperate. She would certainly have died without help—by accident, by suicide, possibly murder. But Grace would *not* be alive today if I hadn't worked with her to deal with her addiction."

"Grace isn't an addict."

"Oh? Then she never told you her past. She *is* an addict,

and she always will be. She may not indulge her addiction, now, after years of therapy, but she's an addict. And she's alive."

"That's how you rationalize it."

"Not rationalization—*justification*. Some things which we wouldn't do otherwise, we do for the greater good."

"Greater good. You get all this greater good from Grace's lifestream?"

"And others. This is a monumental undertaking."

"How many others?"

Madeleine sat back. "It's a small number compared to the potential millions we can help."

"So, you did the math."

"The what?"

Elisha turned and faced her squarely. "You added up all the good and divided it by all the suffering. And you came up with a ratio. What's the dividing line?"

"The dividing line?"

"Yeah, the ratio where all the good justifies all the suffering. How high is your bar? How did you assign a cost to each person whose life you hijacked? What's the incremental value of helping a person?"

Madeleine shifted in her seat. "You're being facetious."

"I'm totally serious. You can cure all the troubles of all the world, but you're *still* exploiting people like Grace. She didn't agree to this, did she?"

She stood, the hood hanging limply from her hand. "There's no way *you* could *possibly* understand."

"Oh, I understand," Elisha replied. "Whatever the end game, you're hurting people. That's messed up."

Madeleine's hand squeezed tightly around the hood. "This conversation is *over*."

"Good," Elisha replied. "It was making me sick."

Madeleine glared at him, then pulled on her hood and left the room. The door slammed, and the bolt slid into place with a clank.

❖ ❖ ❖

"Any luck?" Jayla asked. She and two other Shade sat at a

table as the Eye of Providence paced.

"You were right," the Eye conceded, "he doesn't know anything. But Nemesio and his other friends at the Summerland do."

"Then send him back," Speranza suggested. "You already put the hook in him. Get him working for us on the inside."

"It doesn't work that way," the Eye explained. "Each command must be implanted separately, from inside a lifestream."

"Plan B?" Jayla asked.

"As we discussed." The Eye looked from Jayla, to Speranza, to the third Shade. "I'm sure Chrysalis and the rest of the Kaleidoscope are missing Elisha by now. If I know Chrysalis, she's doing everything she can to find him and get him back."

"She's that determined?" Speranza asked.

"Oh, yes. I treated her for four years. I know her better than anyone. All she needs is a lead on Elisha's whereabouts."

"That's where I come in," the third Shade said.

"But don't be obvious about it," the Eye cautioned. "Chrysalis will spot a ruse."

"I'll be subtle. She won't suspect a thing."

"I hope not, Armengol. The entire operation depends on it."

<h1 style="text-align:center">59</h1>

WORD ON THE STREET

"MORE THAN A hundred," Speranza said. "That's the word on the street."

"A hundred and fifty, I heard," Jayla added, unusually sullen. "Eight or ten alliances, and sixty independents—the whole Summerland."

"Wow. I wonder where they ended up. Have you heard anything?"

"Some made it out—Chrysalis and her crew, at least the ones we had here. I don't know about the rest."

"The rest have new homes," a familiar voice said from behind.

Jayla and Speranza twisted around to see the Eye of Providence standing in the doorway, light glinting from the gold filigree of her scarlet mask.

"Some are in confinement—the dangerous ones, the low-skilled," she continued. "But most are too valuable to confine and reintegrate."

"What about Dax and the Kliegls?" Speranza asked. "They promised to exterminate us all."

The Eye sat down. "There will be enough Shade sent away to satisfy the citizenry's appetite. A few dozen or so, spread out over time. Dax will claim victory."

"And the rest?" Speranza pressed.

"Split up among the *Vita Occulta* crews—either they are now or soon will be."

"And we're already V.O.," Jayla commented. "Does that

mean we're safe?"

"We're better than safe."

Jayla finally smiled. "Got Dax by the plums?"

"What does that mean?" asked Speranza. "Are the Kliegls in the program?"

"Well, I guess they *are*," Jayla said. "They're like robots— remote controlled."

"The defeat of the Shade proposal was the final proof," the Eye explained. "That, and the daily ridership. More than three hundred Kliegls…"

"Three hundred and six," Jayla corrected.

"Yes, three hundred and six. That's how many of them ride our lifestreams daily or almost daily with the gen four Belt."

"And when they do…" Speranza began.

"…we upload the agenda *du jour*," Jayla replied, grinning, "if there is one. We start with a jolt to the spinal cord just to bring 'em back the next day. Then, if we have commands— votes, public statements, like that—we tack it on at the end."

"And it's working?" he asked.

Jayla's grin grew. "Sperz, this is the *lowest* threshold population we've *ever* attached. Seriously, I don't know if there's *anything* we could tell them that they wouldn't do."

"Is it because they're stupid?" Speranza asked.

"No," the Eye answered. "A subject's susceptibility hasn't much to do with intelligence. In fact, a more intelligent subject often has a lower threshold for suggestion. The Kliegl delegates are all smarter than average."

"Then what?" Speranza pressed.

"Can *I* tell?" Jayla asked.

The Eye sniffed and shook her head. "We measure a *range* of traits to determine if a subject is susceptible. It's not just *one* thing."

"Yeah, but it's *kinda* one thing," Jayla countered.

The Eye curled her lip. "*Please*, Jayla, tell us."

"They like tough guys," Jayla explained.

Speranza looked sideways at her. "Huh?"

"She means they have authoritarian tendencies," the Eye

translated.

"Okay," Speranza said. "Like, what?"

The Eye flashed a rare smile. "An authoritarian personality type gravitates to strong figures—some might say heroic. They demand loyalty; they impose their will through manipulation and repression."

"Like Dax."

"He fits the archetype. He's convinced of the rightness of his own beliefs; he exercises direct control over his subjects."

Speranza ran a hand over his green mask. "Sounds familiar."

The Eye lowered her head, looking at Speranza with raised eyes. "What do you mean?"

"Nothing. You were talking. Keep going."

The Eye stood. "Tell me what you mean."

Speranza looked aside, then at the floor. "You could be describing *yourself*."

The Eye leaned forward, placing both hands on the table. She raised one hand and brought it down with enough force to tip it over.

"Dax is a *fraud* and an *opportunist!* He has *no* motivation other than *power*."

Speranza leaned over and righted the table. "And you?"

The Eye came around the table, standing over him. "I'm curing a *sickness*, the last barrier to the final integration of all humanity into a single, integrated whole in a virtual world."

"I'm sure you believe that with all your heart."

"I believe it because it's true."

"Sure."

The Eye wiped her mouth with the back of one hand and dried it on her cloak. She went back to her chair and sat. "You can't compare me with Dax."

"No, of course not."

Speranza stared at the table. The Eye looked at Jayla, who shrugged and tilted her head slightly at Speranza.

"Speranza..." the Eye said softly.

He looked up.

"What we're doing—it's necessary and good. It could take

generations for the whole population to reconcile itself to virtual reality without suffering the effects of lost intimacy."

"I don't know what that means."

The Eye folded her hands under her chin, resting both elbows on the table. "Do you know about the social upheavals of the technological revolution?"

"No."

"For millennia, families in agrarian cultures had strictly defined roles. Parents raised their children in an intimate unit. Boys watched their fathers plow, plant, and reap. Girls watched their mothers cook, clean, and rear. It's how children learned their roles in life."

"Sounds archaic."

"It was. Thankfully, we're past the time when we imposed gender roles on our children. But the pain that humanity suffered for that accomplishment..."

"What pain?" Speranza asked.

"The alienation of fathers from their families, as they went to their workplaces, away from their children," the Eye explained. "The disorienting effects of centralized education. The social backlash as women demanded the same opportunities as men."

"But it was worth it."

"It was. And that pain was *necessary*, because there was no way to manipulate psychology on a mass scale."

"And now there is."

The Eye leaned back. "Yes. We have the technology."

"And you have Dax and all his delegates, or a majority, anyway."

"We can manage the minds of the masses on an epic scale. Our hands are on the levers of power. We need only one more piece."

"One more piece?" Jayla questioned. "For what?"

"The last piece that will give us control, not only of the citizenry, but of the Worldstream itself."

Jayla and Speranza looked at each other, eyes wide.

"Don't leave us hanging, Boss," Jayla prompted.

A cloaked and hooded Shade came to the door. "Eye," he

said, "he's here."

"Thank you, Fidelio," the Eye replied. "Bring him in."

"Who's here?" Speranza asked.

"The newest member of the Aletheia. I had him assigned from the Summerland raid. He's the key to the last piece."

Fidelio returned with another Shade. "Got him," Fidelio said.

"Good." The Eye stood. "We'll put him in the main dorm. Speranza, Jayla, please show Nemesio to his quarters."

60

WE'LL BE GENTLE

"MACK, IT'S TIME now," Madeleine murmured as she took the brush from Mackenzie's hand.

Mackenzie grabbed it back, shaking his head. "*No.*"

He and Madeleine stood eye-to-eye, both holding the brush, she with a pleading look, he with his jaw clenched grimly. Loren, the third person in the day-glow forest, a tall, dark man, put his hands on theirs, holding them softly.

"It's time, Mackenzie," Loren said. "We'll be gentle."

Mack's lip trembled. "A minute. One more minute."

Loren carefully pried the brush from Mackenzie's hand. "Come now, Mackenzie. The sooner we go, the sooner we'll be back."

Mackenzie looked at Loren with wide eyes, then at Madeleine. He gave her a thin smile, then nodded hesitantly.

"Freebird, suspend the venue," Loren commanded.

The bounding rabbits froze; the rainbow foliage and orange-peel sky melted together into a gray wash, then went white.

Loren and Madeleine removed their gear. The bright staging venue gave way to a gray, dimly-lit room. A door to an adjacent bathroom stood ajar, the light spilling through it illuminating a dresser by the wall, a plush reclining chair, and the man sitting in it, a stocky man with mad-scientist hair, still geared up. His rig was more elaborate than Madeleine's or Loren's—headgear wider, covering nearly his entire face to the back of his head; tactile gloves thicker, engineered with exquisite sensitivity to movement; and lower-body appliances similarly sensitive.

Loren approached the man, who made no movements as Loren reached for his headgear.

"May I?" Madeleine asked.

Loren smiled and stepped back. Madeleine knelt by the chair.

"I'm here, Mack," she whispered. She touched the closures on his headgear, opening them with slow, deliberate movements. "Let's get this off."

Mackenzie pulled away. "Ma-a-a-d," he said in a plaintive moan.

Madeleine peeled the gear off his head. *"Ma-a-a-ad!"* he screamed, twisting away, slapping at her, then flapping his arms on his chest.

She turned to Loren. "Okay, I can use some help."

Loren took a pair of ear protectors from the dresser and put them on Mackenzie. He calmed down, pressing the muffs against his head.

"His legs are twisted under him," Loren said. "Help me get him up."

They stood on either side and each took an arm. As they lifted, Loren straightened Mackenzie's legs and set his feet on the floor. When he was raised to a stoop, he flailed, one arm striking Madeleine in the nose.

"Oh!" she cried, one hand flying to her face, losing her grip on his arm. He kept flailing, then began slapping himself on the head. Loren took Mackenzie's arms one at a time, removing his tactile gloves in two swift moves.

"His mitts," he said, pointing to the dresser. Madeleine fetched the thick mittens and handed them to Loren, who expertly slipped them onto Mackenzie's hands. Mackenzie kept flailing. Madeleine reached for him.

"Don't try to restrain him," Loren instructed.

"I know what I'm doing," Madeleine growled. "I've been doing it for thirty years." She put her arm around Mackenzie and lifted him to full height. "Jah, I'm practically the world's authority on autism."

❖ ❖ ❖

Madeleine and Loren settled Mackenzie into his chair, bathed and fed.

"I'll take it from here, Loren," Madeleine whispered. "Have a good night."

Loren nodded. "Good night, Madeleine; good night, Mackenzie," he said, then left.

Madeleine found the controller on the dresser and pressed a button. The chair reclined with a soft *whir*, until Mackenzie was horizontal. Madeleine sat on the arm of the chair, leaning over him, stroking his face. He fixed his eyes on her. She moved side to side; his eyes followed her, and he smiled.

"Ma-a-ad."

Madeleine laughed. "Time for bed, Mack."

"Ma-a-ad-die."

"I'll be right in the next room. I'll be here for you in the morning. I'll be here for you always. I'll bring you everything you need, Little Brother." She patted his cheek, then his shoulder and chest.

"I'll bring you the whole world."

EPILOGUE

"Look at this, Mom. It's super-real."

Dylan pointed at a floor-to-ceiling screen showing a maze of lines and symbols which meant nothing to Grace. A pulsating circle appeared where he pointed, expanding into a full-screen view of a field of solar panels, the sun glinting from their surfaces, among knee-high prairie grass waving in the wind. Across the bottom a graph scrolled showing power from the array over the past 24 hours. The line rose at sunrise, dipped when clouds passed, and dropped to zero after sunset. An analog dial appeared superimposed on each panel, and a status bar, most of them green, a few yellow, and one red.

"What's the red one?" Grace asked.

Dylan squinted at the screen. "Huh. I don't know. Let's see." He pointed; the pulsating circle appeared, expanded, and zoomed in on the errant panel, overlaid with graphs and columns of data. "The converter is over-temp. Could be any number of things. Silla."

"Yes, Dylan?" a silky voice spoke from the screen.

"Let Jackson know there's a bad converter on panel E-15."

"I've already alerted Jackson and attached a status report."

Dylan grinned. "Of course you have. I should have known. Thanks, Silla."

"Just doing my job."

Grace studied the face of her son, the face she'd been apart from for more than two years, seen only in VR until she saw him again the week before. His round cheeks had hollowed; the freckles had faded; the boyish eyes had lost their inquisitive twinkle and had hardened into those of a man. His shoulders were broader than she remembered, arms sinewed, chest muscled under his tight-fitting shirt. She pondered the transformation with pride, mixed with regret that she hadn't witnessed the changes herself.

"How did you build all this?" she asked.

He kept his eyes on the display, hands on hips. "It took time. Some of the structures they made here or salvaged. The panels and power modules they smuggled out from the world. Jackson and the other founders all made their fortunes before they started *Vitreous Orb. They* bankrolled most of it." He pointed at another panel with a yellow indicator. "Efficiency drop. A dirty panel or maybe something else. I'll check it later."

"So, Orwell is solar powered?"

"The solar panels provide almost half our power." Dylan recalled the maze-like diagram and pointed at another node. The screen displayed an array of windmills, their size apparent from the tiny vehicles and people at their bases. "The wind farm gives us another third. We get the rest from biofuel."

"You're so…" Grace searched for a word. "You *know* all about this, the power and all."

"No," he smiled, shaking his head. "Jackson is the real expert. He designed the grid. He's a genius."

"But *you're* running the power plant."

"I'm just taking a shift. Jackson trained me, but most of it's automated."

"So you do a lot of different jobs?"

"Sure. I started out driving a tractor, harvesting corn. Then I did some repairs, a little construction. I've learned a lot."

"You were always very smart."

He pulled a chair from a console and sat down. "Mom, do you know what it feels like to hold a hammer?"

She pulled in her chin, turning sideways. "A hammer? Like

for pounding things?"

"Yeah," he laughed. "Nails, mostly." He held out his right hand, cradling it in his left, pressing his thumb into his palm. "We built an addition to a house in town. I crumpled a lot of nails before I got it right. My hands got kind of rough after a few days."

Grace looked at his hand; thick calluses covered the palm. She ran her fingers over it. "So rough."

"Like sandpaper."

"Like what?"

"Nothing." He rubbed his palm on his knee. "I'm sure there are VR venues where you can build things, houses and stuff like that, but I never went into them. And if I had, my hands wouldn't look like this, no matter how hi-res, or how many times I did it. And I still wouldn't know how to use a hammer, not really. My mind might understand it, but my muscles wouldn't."

She put her hand on the back of his head. "You're *still* very smart."

A speaker chimed. "Dylan," the voice responder said.

"Yes, Silla?"

"Jackson directs you to replace the converter on E-15. Use one of the refurbished units."

"Right away, Silla."

"Observe all safety protocols. Lockout and zero energy checks are mandatory."

"Yes, Silla. Tell Jackson I won't ruin his day by getting electrocuted."

Dylan opened a locker and pulled out a heavy leather belt, with tools hanging from loops and hooks. He buckled it around his waist. "I gotta get this done. You can come along, if you want, but I have to do the repair myself."

"I'd love to, but I have a training session in an hour," Grace replied.

"Yeah?" he smiled and nodded, hooking his thumbs under his belt. "Which one?"

"Maintenance. It doesn't sound very interesting."

He laughed. "We all have to go through it. Everyone has

to know a lot of jobs, so we can move people where they're needed."

"So, there'll be more interesting ones coming?"

"Yeah, Mom. But you might find out that there's quite a lot of technique to using a broom."

❖ ❖ ❖

Muhammad sat at a table near the wall, while Dylan stood, scanning the room for Grace. He spotted her in the food line as she turned toward him holding a full tray, and waved her over.

"Hello, Muhammad," Grace greeted him as she set down her tray.

"Hi, Grace," he answered. "Did you get your housecleaning certificate?"

"I'm going to frame it!" she laughed. "All checked out on brooms, mops, and dishrags." She sat down. "Dylan showed me the power plant today—so interesting."

"The beating heart of Orwell," Muhammad agreed.

"What do they have *you* doing?" Grace asked.

"Waste and recycling." Muhammad grimaced and rolled his eyes. "Dylan is *Orwell Power and Light*, and I'm the garbage man."

"I have cleanup detail after dinner," Grace laughed. "That can't be much better."

"I've cleaned up before," Muhammad countered. "Trust me, trash is worse."

"You're in power plant training next week, Hammad," Dylan offered. "You'll get your shift."

Grace tilted her head toward a man and woman in the food line. "Thomas and Celeste," she said. "I'm worried about them."

"They're still not adjusting?" Dylan asked.

"Not yet," Grace sighed. "It's easier for me. They were much more into the VR and hacking scene than I was. Even at the Summerland. Celeste spent *all* of her time coding, and so did Thomas, when he wasn't managing accounts. They're not cut out for real life."

Thomas and Celeste left the line in enthusiastic

conversation. Grace tried to get their attention, but they stood in one spot, still talking, juggling their trays as they gestured, diners walking past them on both sides. Thomas chanced to look in Grace's direction.

"What's got into them?" Grace asked as the two approached, both wearing broad smiles, as if they shared a secret too good not to tell.

"Hi, hi, *hi!*" chirped Celeste. She set down her tray and pulled up a chair. "Did you all do your part for the collective today?"

"You bet!" Muhammad replied. "I hauled a mountain of garbage."

"Kept the lights on," Dylan added.

"Why are you two so cheerful?" Grace asked. "Last night you looked like you wanted to die."

"Have you seen their maker space?" Thomas asked, his voice tinged with awe. "Jah, it's *incredible!*"

"Thomas likes making," Celeste explained. "Me, too. All those assets we coded in the world, for virtual venues? Who knew there was technology that can turn them into things, you know, *real things*, that people can use?"

"That's what you're doing?" Grace asked. "You're not cleaning kitchens?"

"They have a month-old backlog of design requests," Celeste explained. She punched Thomas in the arm. "Me and the big guy cleared a whole week's worth in one day."

Thomas nodded. "Yeah, they're printing out now. It's crazy. I think it up, and an hour later, I'm holding it in my hand, IRL."

"We're going to have to slow down or we'll work ourselves out of a job."

"You'll have to sweep floors for a living," Grace warned.

Celeste pulled at the sleeve of her shirt, a loose-fitting garment of hand-woven cloth. "At least I'll be comfortable." She drank from a glass of milk. "That's the best thing about this place—no cloaks. I can be myself."

❖ ❖ ❖

The machine stood spider-like in the center of the room, a

structure of steel tubing and castings, draped with wires, trussed with cables, toothed belts oscillating on cogwheels. It stood half again as tall as Grace; in fact, she could stand on the platform without crossing the build envelope. If Thomas or Celeste had designed a life-sized statue of her, this machine could print it.

The build object wasn't a statue, or even one of the dozens of utensils, repair parts, household objects, or toys requested by the Orwellians. It was a test object, an array of cylinders on a flat base, designed to verify dimensional accuracy, fill quality, and surface finish. Grace started the build, as was standard practice, following the preventive maintenance routine she'd just performed. She'd earned her printer maintenance certificate the day before, and she found the work interesting and challenging. It certainly beat washing dishes.

The machine's three articulated arms traced elaborate figures, depositing one layer upon another. Grace watched intently as the object emerged, micron by micron, as if from nothing. The other technicians in the print shop looked on with amusement at Grace's fascination, which they had once shared, but had lost in the years since their first print.

"Grace."

She turned, still bent over, toward Celeste, who was standing in the doorway, and straightened up.

"You need to hear this," Celeste said. "In the taproom."

Grace followed her out the door and down the street, almost running.

"What?" she asked, more than once.

"Just come," Celeste answered every time.

Grace and Celeste found Jackson in the makeshift tavern with another familiar face.

"Raúl." Grace went to the tall man and hugged him. "You're back."

"Yeah, lady, and for a reason." He drew two beers and handed one to Grace.

"No thanks, Raúl," she replied. "I thought you knew."

Raúl's face reddened. "Sorry, Grace, I forgot," he said,

setting the beer aside.

Celeste grabbed it. "*I* didn't take the pledge," she said, taking a generous swig.

"Raúl," Grace said, "tell me what's going on."

Raúl drank, wiping the foam from his lip. "There've been some developments back in the world. They involve some people you know."

Grace felt her stomach tighten. "My dad?"

Raúl shook his head.

"Donna? My sister?"

"It's not your family. Not directly."

"Not directly?" Grace put her hand on Raúl's. "What is it?"

The door banged open. Dylan came in with Thomas close behind.

Grace looked at her son, then at Raúl. "Did you send for Dylan?"

Raúl nodded. "The Kliegls are making good on their promise to take down the Shade. The Summerland was just the beginning. They've raided four more dorms in the district. They claim they've closed down more than a hundred across the continent."

"Oh, God," Celeste moaned. "You didn't tell me how many."

"It sounds like more than it is, really," Raúl explained. "They're only hitting the independent crews. There are hundreds, maybe thousands of them."

"Like the Kaleidoscope," Thomas added. "Or the Bast."

"Yeah, they busted the Bast about a month after the Summerland. That was a nasty one. They had this big guy…"

"Graf," Thomas said. "I know him."

"Yeah, well, he put up a fight. The civils tased him, but the Kliegls didn't stop at that."

"The Kliegls?" Grace interrupted. "They were there at the Summerland."

"But they're not civils," Thomas said. "Why are *they* involved?"

"They're in on *every* bust. It's a bad scene," Raúl explained.

"The civils show some restraint, but these Kliegls, well, they have some blood lust in 'em. This guy, Graf, they kicked the crap out of him. There he was, laid out by a taser, and they damn near tore him apart."

"Is he okay?" Thomas asked.

"Don't know, not for sure. Kliegls passed a measure to cut off access to the public records. No one knows anything." Raúl drank. "But word in the 'stream is, he didn't make it."

Thomas leaned on the back of a chair before turning it around and dropping into it, falling forward with his hands between his knees. Celeste put her hand on his shoulder.

Dylan spoke up. "This is terrible, but what does it have to do with us?"

"We know a lot of these people," Celeste explained. "The Bast, they helped rescue Thomas. And now they're being persecuted."

"I feel for them," Dylan retorted, "but that's the world we *left*. It's not the world we're *in*."

"Well, then maybe we should go back," Celeste countered.

"I know how you feel," Grace said, "but what can we do?"

"*Something*," Celeste offered.

"I don't know what."

"There's more," Jackson chimed in. "Tell 'em."

Raúl drained the last of his beer and refilled. "Remember I said this is about people you know?"

"Yes, the Bast, and the other Shade," Grace repeated.

"And someone else. Dax has a new minister of public health." Raúl pulled a pocket screen from his shirt. He tapped it with his thumb and showed it to Grace.

The screen showed a news release, announcing the appointment of a new minister, overseeing the physical and mental well-being of the citizenry. The picture showed a woman in early middle age, with straight black hair streaked with gray. Grace leaned closer, then gasped and turned away. She walked to the window and stared out.

Celeste pulled Raúl's hand toward her, so she could read the notice.

"Oh, God. That's her, isn't it?"

"It is," Grace confirmed. "It's Madeleine."

❖ ❖ ❖

The sun shone along the length of the main street of Orwell, shadows lengthening in late afternoon. Grace and Dylan sat on the walkway outside the library on decaying metal chairs, rusting through blistered paint. She held her breath, hand over her mouth, waiting for Dylan's reaction.

He sat with elbows on knees, staring at the concrete through minutes of silence, before raising his head and turning to his mother.

"Maybe," he said. "Maybe I could have dealt with it." He shook his head and looked down again. "I was pretty immature, but maybe…"

Grace wiped a tear from her eye. "You were young, but older than your age. I should have trusted you."

Dylan glanced up for a moment without a word.

"But it wasn't *you* I was protecting," Grace continued, "it was *me*—*I'm* the one who couldn't bear it if you knew what I was."

"What you *were*," Dylan countered. "That's what you *used to be*, not what you *are*. I could have understood that—maybe." He sat up straight. "But I understand it *now* for sure. And it doesn't matter to me."

Grace smiled weakly. "And you understand why I had to find you, and why I had to get between you and that girl."

"Mia."

"Mm-hmm. You were hunting her."

Dylan turned away, squinting his eyes against the sun. "Mom, I wasn't…"

"*Think*, Dylan," she interrupted. "What were you feeling? Did you care for that girl? Was she someone important to you?"

"She was just…" Dylan folded his arms over his chest and stared at the ground. "She was just a girl."

"And all those men I told you about—and the women—they were just *people*. They didn't mean *anything* to me. What does Mia mean to you?"

"Nothing," he mumbled.

"And all the sick things I did with them, because I needed that thrill—did you feel that with Mia? Like you were cornering a wild animal and coaxing it into a trap?"

"She's not an animal!"

Grace touched Dylan's arm. "But how did *you* feel?"

He stood up and paced, arms still tightly folded. "I'm not…I'm *not* an addict."

"I don't know if you're the same as me or not," she answered, "but I *was* an addict, and I *still* am. And you're my son."

He dropped into the chair and buried his face in his hands. "Oh, *God.*"

Grace put her hand on his shoulder. "I'm with you now, Dylan, and I won't leave you again."

He lifted his face from his hands. "And it all started with Madeleine."

She nodded. "She stole my life, and I finally have it back."

"But she could steal it again," Dylan replied, "and all of *our* lives, too."

❖ ❖ ❖

"That's the story," Jackson concluded. "Discuss."

The leaders of Orwell gathered in the community hall, Jackson at the head of the table, Grace to his right. Naia, Benny, and the other functional leaders sat on both sides. Dylan, Celeste, and Thomas sat in chairs by the wall, while Raúl stood by the door.

"I don't know why this concerns us," Naia objected. "We're outside the perimeter. None of this will ever reach Orwell."

"Yeah," Benny agreed. "We're self-sufficient."

"Not entirely," Jackson reminded him. "We still depend on the world for technology."

"Right," Benny conceded, "but that won't change. We'll still be able to get what we need, whether there are Shade or not."

"That's not the point," Grace asserted. "Orwell can continue, and people will still suffer under this regime."

"They're not *our* people," Benny said.

"They're *people*," Jackson retorted. "We should respect that." He turned to Grace. "But I have to agree with Benny. There's not a lot we can do about the Kliegls. Orwell will keep going."

"But I've told you about Madeleine, what she's like," Grace responded. "She'll tell you that she's all about helping people, but that's a lie. People are nothing more than a means to and end for her."

"That doesn't change anything," Benny stated.

"But it does."

All heads turned toward the wall.

"You heard what Mom said," Dylan continued. "What Madeleine wants is for the whole world—*everyone*—to live permanently in VR. When she was just a minor player, she couldn't do too much damage, but even then, she destroyed my mom's life—almost killed her."

"I know this is emotional for you, Dylan," Naia began, "but…"

"*Listen* to me. Listen to *Mom*. Madeleine's not in a minor role anymore. She's got *power*. She won't stop until we're *all* back in the Worldstream, all living fake lives. Orwell's not safe."

"Dylan's right," Celeste agreed. "We have to take her down."

"We have to do *more* than that," Dylan added. "What we have here in Orwell, the *Vitreous Orb*, will always be a threat to whoever's in power."

"But Madeleine, Dax, they're the *real* danger," Celeste pointed out.

"Yes, but when *they're* gone, what then? The Real World is shrinking. We're safe for now because we're out of Jahbulon's reach. But that reach gets longer every day." Dylan stepped forward. "We'll only be safe when the Worldstream is broken…and Jahbulon is *dead*."

The room fell silent. Jackson looked first at Benny, then at Naia. They looked skeptical. Benny shook his head.

Raúl caught Grace's eye, raising his eyebrows as he tilted his head toward Dylan.

Grace felt a palpitation as she looked at her son, seeing a man where an hour ago she'd seen a troubled boy.

Dylan, she thought, *what are you doing?*

If you enjoyed *Shade*, please leave reviews on Amazon and Goodreads.

Also by Charles O'Donnell

The Girlfriend Experience (Matt Bugatti #1)
Moment of Conception (Matt Bugatti #2)
Shredded: A Dystopian Novel (Shredded #1)

About the Author

Charles O'Donnell writes thrillers with high-tech themes in international and futuristic settings. His works include *The Girlfriend Experience,* an espionage thriller and the first book in the Matt Bugatti series; *Moment of Conception (Matt Bugatti #2),* a political and medical thriller; and *Shredded: A Dystopian Novel,* a cautionary tale about the potential for technology to either augment reality or to replace it entirely, and about the erosion of privacy in a world in which everything is shared online, and nobody reads the terms and conditions. His short stories have also appeared in *The Esthetic Apostle, Dreamers Creative Writing, Dark Ink Anthology, The Scriblerus,* and *Lost & Found: An Anthology.*

Charles recently retired from a career of thirty-five years in engineering and manufacturing to write full-time, drawing on his years of experience leading teams in many countries on three continents to create compelling settings in faraway lands.

Charles lives with Helen, his wife and life partner in Westerville, Ohio.

ACKNOWLEDGEMENTS

SO MUCH HAS happened since *Shredded*, it seems like a lifetime. I've taken two writing classes (and one philosophy class), attended a wonderful writing retreat with the *Sun* magazine, took part in the annual Columbus State Writers Conference, exhibited at three (or four?) book shows, read countless works of fiction by writers at every stage of the writing journey, published two short stories in literary journals, published two more in anthologies, been a guest on a podcast and a live cast, founded my own imprint, *Moon Lit Publishing*, and traveled to Ireland to experience the land that inspired James Joyce, Oscar Wilde, and W. B. Yeats.

I sat by my mother's side as she passed away at the age of 94, the end of a life well-lived.

Now, after all that, here's another book.

Every time I do this, the list of people to thank gets longer. I'll start with all the wonderful members of the Columbus writing community.

My new favorite writing aid is MeetUp. I attend seven or so Columbus MeetUp groups regularly, some dedicated to sharing work with colleagues, some to exchanging publishing and marketing tips, and a couple just to get together and put words on the page.

To my fellow Columbus State GEM-C writers, Clay, Kirby, Beth, Rita, Nora, Lynette, and many others, thanks for sharing your work, and helping me with mine, and thanks for letting me add my story to your anthology, *Lost and Found.*

To Jen, the organizer of the Eastside Fiction Writers, you run a tight ship and set a high standard for your MeetUp group—I thank you for that, and I thank Chris, Bill, Rob, Isabel, Janelle, Mallory and the rest of the group for your praise and criticism. You are my go-to crew to workshop my short pieces in their rawest form.

To Jaelyn, organizer of the Columbus Storytellers and Writers, sorry the group petered out; it was one of my favorites. To the members, Max, Gabrielle, Gaberiel (I really *can* keep those straight), Jane, Ian, Ryan, and everyone else, I wish much success with your projects—you're a talented bunch. And Jaelynn, good luck with your new publication!

To Robyn, the faithful leader of Social Wrighting™, you give me two hours out of the week dedicated solely to writing, but you also give me your encouragement and friendship. I'm looking forward to many more Wednesday evenings of productive writing.

Angel, who organizes our weekly Shut Up and Write™ session, gave me the idea to publish each of the three parts of *Shade* as a separate ebook. Thanks, Angel, and thanks for your friendship as well.

To all the members of VR Columbus, my teachers regarding all things Virtual Reality: I'm in awe of you. Thanks especially to the organizer, Chris, and my fans and alpha readers, Joe, Adam, and Nathanael—I could never hope to match your level of expertise and enthusiasm, but I hope I've captured at least some of your knowledge in *Shade*. And Joe: thanks for the *Shredded* plug on your podcast.

To all my alpha readers, of which there were more than a dozen, my unbounded thanks. When I enlisted your help, I gave you instructions in the form of a parable:

A farmer went into the barn one morning to find his son digging furiously in a giant pile of horse manure.

"Son, what's got into you?" the man asked.

"Pa," the young'n replied, breathing heavily, "I just know there's a pony in here somewhere!"

You, my alpha readers, helped me to find the pony in the pile. Some of you were good at pointing out the pony, some focused on the pile. Both were indispensable.

To Mike, who's been an alpha reader since *The Girlfriend Experience*, you get top honors for dedication—you printed out the 400+ page manuscript and schlepped it to China and back so you could give me your handwritten notes.

To my sister Jacki, who grew up in the same tough-love environment as I did, thanks for giving me the raw, unvarnished truth. I know I can count on you to clear away the manure.

To my other alpha readers, Barbara, Sarah, Dave, Lisa, and all the rest, congratulations for making it through the entire first draft, more pile than pony. You deserve a medal—or at least a signed copy!

Jun, my cover designer, came through again, with not one, but *four* covers, including one for each of the three parts, *Dylan*, *Grace*, and *Madeleine*. Thanks again, Jun—you're an artist.

My editor, Rebekah Goodyear, is *amazing*. Her credentials are impressive, with four New York Times bestseller credits to her name, *and* she's a fan of *Shredded!* Working with Rebekah is a pleasure, her contribution to *Shade* is immeasurable, and she's taught me to be a better writer. Thanks, Rebekah, I couldn't have finished without you.

Thanks to my wife, Helen, who always finds something to like in everything I write. There are times when I really need that.

And, of course, thanks, Mom.

Charles O'Donnell
April 16, 2019